THE KNOWLEDGE OF THE IDEN-
TITY OF THE MAN WHO STOOD BE-
TWEEN HIM AND COMPLETE POSSES-
SION OF ANNABET HAD NOT BROUGHT
HIM THE RELIEF HE HAD ANTICI-
PATED.

Haan wanted Annabet, the whole Annabet,
with no reservations and no evasions. He'd
never had that yet. But he must have it. He
would, by the sheer force of his will . . .

He looked at her again. The soft golden light
of the lamp made a halo of her hair as she
bent over her embroidery. Below it, her face
looked shadowy; delicate oval of cheek, sweet,
sensitive mouth, long lashes fluttering over the
downcast eyes—she was lovely.

Mine, mine, Evert shouted to himself greedily.
All mine! It must be, it shall be, entirely
mine. . . .

Silver Nutmeg

by

Norah Lofts

FAWCETT CREST • NEW YORK

SILVER NUTMEG

Published by Fawcett Crest Books, a unit of CBS Publications, the Consumer Publishing Division of CBS Inc., by arrangement with Doubleday and Company, Inc.

ISBN: 0-449-24431-8

Printed in the United States of America

First Fawcett Crest Printing: August 1981

10   9   8   7   6   5   4   3   2   1

There they lie, these romantic exiles, in the shade of the nutmeg trees that were the cause of their exile here, whose fruit built their lordly mansions, paid for the clothes they wore, the food they ate and the hundreds of slaves who toiled for them.

In Javanese Waters H. W. PONDER

I had a little nut tree
Nothing would it bear
But a silver nutmeg . . .

Nursery Rhyme

Apology and Acknowledgment

The irresistible desire to write a book about the nutmeg island of Banda came upon me when I was reading H. W. Ponder's book, *In Javanese Waters*. There, in one short chapter, was outlined a romantic, bloodstained history that called for exploration. But, like all exploration, it presented great difficulties. The Dutch East Indies were in Japanese hands, all contact broken; Banda itself is no more than a speck, the size of a fly dirt on a map; no book that came my way gave any idea of the island's layout. So my geography is the geography of the imagination.

May I beg the tolerance of those who do know upon which side of the harbour the old Fort stood, the names of the flowers which bloomed in Annabet's garden, exactly how, in 1656, a native would address a white man. I admit my ignorance of these and other details.

But there is an island called Banda, and the Dutch did settle there, and they did make fortunes and build mansions of marble. And there were "glove" marriages and "Company's daughters" and nutmeg smuggling and native risings. And there were, of course, as there have been in all places, at all times, men and women who loved and hated, who schemed and lied, who suffered and rejoiced.

To the many people who have helped me out of their greater knowledge, especially to E. A. van Leent of the Netherlands and Netherlands Indies Information Bureau, I offer my most grateful thanks.

N.L.

Book One

BY THE TIME they reached the point of discussing women and marriage, neither Piet Odshoorn nor Evert Haan was really sober enough to tackle any subject seriously. Certainly Piet would never have taken Annabet van Goens's name lightly upon his tongue so long as he was in complete control of his senses. But the occasion was a unique one, and they had celebrated it suitably.

Four hours previously they had met by chance for the first time in thirty years. They had met without recognition, though each, subconciously aware of something resembling himself in the other man, had paid his own vanity the tribute of a covert glance of admiration. Then Kaerko, the agent, had made a formal introduction and the two big handsome men had fallen upon each other with cries of astonishment, recognition, and good will. Kaerko would have found it hard to believe, had anyone troubled to tell him, that thirty years earlier the pair had parted upon the worst of terms, and that in the interval Evert had never given Piet a thought, and that Piet had remembered Evert only with a smouldering hatred. But this sudden meeting on the far side of the globe was dramatic enough to wipe out indifference and ill feeling alike. They had left the office with their arms linked.

Evert had dragged Piet home to his fine new house and given him a dinner fit for a king. They had talked without ceasing and had drunk almost as steadily; and now Piet, whose stomach was to a dangerous extent stronger than his head, was well on the way to noisy drunkenness, and Evert, who carried his liquor better, had blunted the fine edge of his judgement and reached a confidential mood.

Outside the tropical night was full of moonlight which sketched the outlines of Evert's new garden in ivory and ebony. The soft night wind of the islands, heavily laden with spices, blew in from the open verandah. The iron-caged lantern which swung from the nearest pillar swayed and creaked; inside on the littered dining table the wasting candles in their heavy silver sconces bowed their little pointed flames and shed pearl-coloured waxen tears.

11

"Well, that's my story," said Evert with hearty complacency, ending a summary of thirty years experience. "And now all I need is a wife. It's time I settled down. As soon as the house is quite ready I must start looking round. The trouble is that it won't be easy to find the kind of woman I want out here. The local beauties are all too easy to resist."

"Take a holiday and come back with me to Heydberg," suggested Piet jovially. "You could take your pick there. I lose my heart every time I go home. There're the two Van Goens girls, lovely as lilies . . ."

The words were meant as a joke and at the same time as a sly dig at Evert, as one might say to a spoiled, pampered child: "And now would you like the moon to play with?" But even as he spoke them something that was neither jocular nor derisive stirred in Piet's mind. He had a clear sharp vision of the two girls in the Van Goens pew, accompanied by their young sister and old Truitje, and he had to stifle a half-maudlin sigh before he could laugh to show Evert that he had not meant the suggestion seriously.

"Van Goens?" asked Evert, narrowing his eyes. "The old Padroon's family? Why, no, they'd be as old as us, older. D'you mean Adriaan's children? Why do you see them in Heydberg?"

"They live there. Adriaan's widow and three daughters."

"So Adriaan's dead, is he? No loss to the world. By God, how I hated him. D'you remember how he took his crop to me for not doffing my cap quick enough for his liking? Damned puppy."

For a moment time ran backwards, and the two big men, the respectable ship's captain and the wealthy nutmeg planter, were little boys again, little barefoot farm boys in the village of Janshaven: growing up in the shadow of the big house, going in awe of the family of the Padroon who owned everything within sight—the fields which their father hired and tilled so industriously, the forge where the horses were shod, the mill where the corn was ground, everything.

Evert pushed the memory away and with a comfortable, swelling sense of his own success poured generous measures of the best French brandy into the two glasses.

"I used to entertain myself as I worked, planning torments for Adriaan. But what happened? Why isn't his family at Janshaven? Didn't he get a son?"

"Oh yes. There's a son. Egbert. He's in the Army. The Janshaven estate is all sold. If you wished Adriaan bad luck, Evert, you should be satisfied. He ruined his family and then blew his brains out."

"Even that swaggering little sod couldn't get through that much property," said Evert incredulously.

"But I tell you he did." A suggestion of truculence crept into Piet's voice. "Nobody in the world is so rich that they don't want to be richer; haven't you ever noticed that? And Adriaan van Goens was as greedy as the rest of us, I suppose."

"What did he *do?*"

The gift of simple direct narrative was not Piet's to any marked degree at any time, and tonight he was befuddled with liquor.

"Damme if I can remember the name. Maybe you do. Everybody's heard of it. Evert . . . ten—no, more—twelve years ago—what was the name of the new company that started off so grand? Threatened to drive the old company out of business, so all our pay was cut. I know the name as well as I know my own."

"There was the United Eastern Mercantile. But that was nothing to do with Van Goens. That was Herman Heemskerk's job."

"That's the name I was after. The United Eastern Mercantile. Heemskerk lent his name. I suppose Adriaan reckoned that looked better. But it was all his money. They made no secret about that, bless your soul. Every dock hand in Amsterdam knew it. And you think, Evert, what a ship like my *Eastern Venture* costs to build and fit out"—a note of almost fatuous pride sounded in his voice—"and then think that Adriaan laid out the cash for no fewer than seven, bigger than her, not to mention buying the con-con—what-do-you-call-'ems—concessions, and the bribes, and warehouses, and all the people, including soldiers to fight *ours* whenever they came within spitting distance, and great new offices on Hoogenstraat that made ours look like a dog's kennel. It's easy to see where the estate went, and the horses, and even Mevrouw's jewels. That was afterwards, of course, when the U.E.M. was bankrupt within two years and our Company bought up everything for a song. Oh yes, the Van Goens are finished, poor as church mice." He waved his great brown hand in a gesture that indicated the completeness of their fall, and one of Evert's Venetian crystal goblets was shattered on the red-tiled floor.

"My God, Evert, I'm sorry about that," said Piet, embarrassed as a boy by his own clumsiness. But Evert, who loved all his possessions, hardly noticed the disaster.

"So then Adriaan shot himself. Yes, he would do that rather than face poverty. A very fitting end. Quite as good as anything I ever planned for him; in my wildest dreams I never saw him out of Janshaven. And to think that the Eastern that put money in my pocket—and in yours, too, in a way, Piet—should have taken it out of his!" He brooded very happily for a moment. "So then the family moved to Heydberg."

Piet nodded. "That's the place for the poor, it seems," he said incautiously. The few bitter little words reminded Evert that it was to Heydberg that Piet and his mother had gone when Evert's father, who was also Piet's, had belatedly set his muddled house in order. He refrained from speaking for a moment, reached for a fresh glass, poured brandy into it, and pushed it gently towards his half brother. When he did speak his voice was smooth and grave.

"You were as well off in Heydberg as I was in Janshaven after you'd gone, Piet. And that's the sober truth. The Old Man went to the Padroon and asked that I should be counted legitimate when it came to inheriting the tenant rights. But the Van Goens were always on your mother's side, as you know. No tenant rights for little Evert. So then he reckoned he'd buy a farm on some free land. And work! My God, Piet, I've worked in my time, but never like I did then. He fairly starved us, too, and my mother wasn't the help out of doors that yours was. He used to bawl. . . . I should think you could have heard him in Heydberg at times. That's why I ran away. He meant me to have a farm if he killed me to get it, I could see that."

Piet laughed, his momentary bitterness forgotten.

"And there was I, envying you like mad. When I was wet through and frozen, with my hands raw from hauling ropes and my belly full of salt horse, I used to think of you, snug by the fire, guzzling eggs and ham. Things do turn out queer, don't they?"

Evert made a noise of assent. "And the Van Goens girls? What are they like? How old?"

"Oh, Klara's the oldest, seventeen, maybe eighteen now. I only see them across the church when I'm home, you know.

It's a bit hard to keep count of their ages. Annabet's younger by about a year and Maria maybe fourteen. She was just a baby when they left Janshaven."

"I see. And the two grown ones are pretty, eh?"

"Well, you remember Adriaan; and he married his cousin, like all Van Goens do. They looked more like brother and sister. The girls are all that colour." He scowled at his glass for a moment, wondering at the amount of interest Evert was showing, and angry with himself because his description was so halting, so very far short of the vision his memory called up. "Aw, Evert, you can't expect a chap who spends his life at sea to reckon off a girl's points like a farmer does a heifer's. Yellow hair, you know, real golden colour, and curly; and their skin's all white where it isn't pink. And blue eyes."

"Which is the prettiest?"

"I dunno. I tell you, I only see them across the church, or sometimes maybe at the door, coming in or out, or sometimes maybe I just pass them in the street. If you must know, Annabet's the pick of the bunch, to my mind at least. Others mightn't agree."

"Why do you prefer her to what's-her-name, Klara?" Evert asked relentlessly.

Something very nearly approaching misery clouded the candour of Piet's grey eyes. "Damned if I know. But you look at Klara and then at her, and then you don't want to look at Klara again. Maybe her head's put on better, and when she walks . . ." His hands moved on the air in a smooth, undulating movement. "And everything about her makes you—— Look here, Evert, I'm drunk, blathering on about how a girl looks." He lifted his fresh glass and took a drink. "I sound like a fool, I know. But I think about her at times, stuck away in that dull old house, and never a penny of dowry. Who'll she ever find to marry her?" He took a sip from his glass to cover the confusion which the sound of his own voice asking such a question roused in him, and went on in an elaborately careless way, "Not that that's any business of mine. I can't think what put that into my head. In fact, I can't think what we're talking about the Van Goens girls for at all." He blinked at Evert as though he might find enlightenment by staring at his kinsman's face—as indeed a shrewder man might possibly have done.

"If she isn't married by the time you get back I'll make a bid for her," Evert said.

Piet's stare of bewilderment changed to one of utter astonishment. Then he laughed.

"Ha, ha, what a joke that would be."

"Why?"

"Why would it be a joke? Aw, Evert, you must know ——" He laughed again, a little less certainly, and then stopped, struck dumb by the realisation that not only had Evert meant what he said but that he was offended by the amusement with which his words had been received.

"Go on, Piet, tell me. I really want to know. Why should it be a joke?"

"Well, damn me! Surely you don't want anybody to tell you why. Old Jakob Kressle's second bastard and Adriaan van Goens's daughter. Aw, Evert, come on, laugh, or I'll be thinking you meant it. And if it isn't a joke you're crazy."

"But I'm not joking and I'm not crazy, Piet. Why d'you think I'm still single at my age? Why do you think I've waited till now to build myself a house? I've been in Banda for twenty years; the men who settled when I did have had homes of a sort and wives of a sort for almost that long. I lived in a four-room hut very little better than one of my coolie's. Why? Because I intended from the very first to marry a lady. I built this house to be fit for a lady. I'm not a man to be content with the second best. I don't want a planter's daughter or a first merchant's daughter. I want a lady of birth and breeding and I want her to be fit to look at. This Annabet van Goens that you describe so movingly sounds exactly what I've had in mind."

"But she wouldn't marry you. Mind you, I'm not denying that you can aim high, Evert. You're a fine handsome man and you've a fine handsome place. But the Van Goens— why, even if Mevrouw herself didn't remember, one of those old aunts with the parrot noses would remind her——"

"Of what?" asked Evert, leaning back in his chair and enjoying Piet's confusion.

"Of the old days, you fool. About the Old Man and our mothers and us. Why, you now said yourself that Adriaan took his crop to you for not doffing your cap."

"I hope, quite sincerely, that they will remember all those things when they receive my proposal to make a glove marriage with Adriaan's prettiest daughter."

"You hope——"

"Of course. And to make quite certain that there is no mistake you must carry the proposal for me, Piet."

"Me?" Piet made a motion as though he intended to get to his feet and fly from the lunatic's company, but his feet slipped on the tiles and it was only by seizing the edge of the table and sitting down again hastily that he saved himself from falling. "Oh no, Evert," he said, shaking his big head after a glance had shown him that Evert was indeed in deadly earnest. "I couldn't do that, and I wouldn't. Look here, I'll tell you something. Daft as it sounds, I'm still afraid of Mevrouw. Laugh if you like, it's God truth. I know she's poor, I know she always buys the cheapest joints at the butcher's and she hasn't a gown that's a patch on the one I took Mother home for her birthday, but if I meet Mevrouw in the street, though she's always very gracious and smiling—you know how ladies can be when they like—and she asks after my health and about my last voyage, I go dumb, Evert. I twist my hat and shuffle my feet. And I bet you would too." He brought out the last words aggressively.

Evert was not to be goaded. He looked at Piet's glass and added to the liquor that remained in it. Then he said quite amiably, "It is possible that Mevrouw van Goens might have that effect upon me. I have no chance of ever knowing. *But* there is another side to the question. If they are really poor, as you say you know they are, and the girls are stuck away in Heydberg without dowries, seeing nobody likely to marry them, don't you think both Mevrouw and her daughter might be very grateful to the man who brought them an honourable proposal from his kinsman? Think of Annabet for a moment. Where would she be better off?"

Piet fell unsuspectingly into the trap. "Oh, there's no denying that, Evert. The whole of Holland is talking about the nutmeg prices. That's what I'm telling you. There's hardly a family in Holland that wouldn't spare a daughter for Banda—but the Van Goens—that is different. They know your beginnings."

"Isn't that an advantage?" Evert was not offended. "You have to look at these things calmly, Piet. Your Annabet sounds just the person who would, given half a chance, snatch at the opportunity of marrying a man like *me*. Very well. What's she likely to get? We're all alike, more or less. Adventurers, old soldiers, rogues, and vagabonds from five provinces who've made our fortunes either with our fists or our wits. The Van Goens, when they remember Jakob Kressle, will remember that he was industrious and sober even if he was too lusty a man to be satisfied with one

woman. He and his fathers had been in Janshaven for as long
as the Van Goens themselves. They've lost a fortune and I've
made one. I'll bet they'd rather marry their daughter to *this*
nutmeg prince than to one they know nothing about."

"You always could argue," said Piet, scowling as he
concentrated. "Many's the thing you've argued me out of in
the old days. But there's truth in what you say." He stared
around the room again, taking note of the silver-laden
sideboard, the silver and glass and napery upon the table.
The things Evert owned were as good as any there had been
in the Janshaven mansion. And if the things Evert said were
true . . .

"Look here, if I do take a hand in this business you'll have
to make it easy for me. Make it so I don't have to say much. I
know I seem to have talked my head off tonight, but I'm a
dumb dog as a rule and, as I say, Mevrouw frightens me out
of my wits."

"Leave that to me. I'll get everything down on paper. All I
want you to do is to carry the papers and make sure that
Mevrouw understands that I am your kinsman."

"That's odd, you know," said Piet. His voice was
thickening now and his stare was losing its focussing power. "I never— Mind you, I'm not comparing, because
anybody could see with half an eye that I haven't got on in
the world like you have, but I never—kind of thought about
the Old Man as being respectable. What I mean is, if I was
you I'd choose anybody in the world to carry those papers
except *me*."

Evert stared at the simpleton and wondered if it were
worth while, or even possible, to try to make him
understand. The idea which had dropped into his mind,
wholly perfect and utterly delightful, during the few minutes
while Piet tried to describe Annabet van Goens was, perhaps,
too subtle and too completely personal ever to be explained
to anyone. His luck—Evert believed implicitly in his luck
and had every reason to do so—had brought him, by the
merest accident, not only the chance of finding the kind of
wife he had wanted all along, but the chance of the kind of
revenge that came, as a rule, only in dreams. Adriaan van
Goens, the Padroon's pampered only son, on a piebald pony
with flowing hair and mane; Evert Haan, the tenant farmer's
pampered second bastard, bringing home the cows from
milking; that clash of wills; the inevitable endings; the insult
that rankled more with every memory. Indoors I am

everything; out of doors I am like the rest. Why, why? And now to be able to say subtly, without words, to Adriaan's widow: "You see, Mevrouw, I am not ashamed of my family or of my origin; I make no pretences; you see, Mevrouw, one of old Jakob Kressle's bastards brings you a proposal from the other one, and are you not glad to consider it?" Ah, wasn't success sweet?

But Piet, of course, had never understood anything that couldn't be explained in words of three letters.

"Well, after all, this is a family matter and a personal matter. What better messenger could I find, Piet? Damn it, I'm proud of you. The company doesn't trust ships like the *Eastern Venture* to rogues or weaklings. We've made our way in the world unaided. Is that anything to be ashamed of?"

The good-humored smile which Piet remembered slipped across his face. When Evert hadn't been thwarted or scheming he had been a jolly companion. He was that now.

"Come on, drink up and let me fill your glass again. This is a great day."

Piet took his glass from the table and leaned back, obscurely relieved to find that the Van Goens family had dropped out of the conversation. He had been a fool to talk about them as he had done. But most likely Evert was a little flown with drink, too, and would have forgotten his harebrained scheme by morning.

"I c-can't think," he said, his tongue stumbling a little, "why I didn't recognise you at once. You look just like Evert to me now." He ran his hand over his own beautiful brown beard. "There was some excuse for you. I've grown this."

"I had one, just as fine. But I shaved it. Too hot. But even with it, you look just Piet to me now. To tell you the truth, back there in Kaerko's office I just looked at you and thought what a damned handsome fellow you were."

"But that's just wh-what I thought too. Funny, eh? And funny to find you here. D'you know—all these years I never could bring myself to go back to Janshaven, not even for fishing, in case I ran into you. And now here we are."

He looked at Evert with maudlin affection. The slight weight which had lain upon his mind since he had spoken Annabet's name lifted. He emptied his glass and was disproportionately proud of himself for refusing to have it refilled. His last sensible thought was that he must look at the time. Clumsily he drew out the great silver watch which was the terror of the unpunctual aboard the *Eastern Venture* and, squinting at it to focus his eyes, discovered that it was past ten o'clock.

"Damme," he said, stuffing the watch away and preparing to rise from his chair, "I must be off. Got to be up in the morning. Agent comes aboard at daybreak." He rose to his feet, and as he did so Evert's dining room tilted as though a wave had struck it. He sat down hastily.

"I'm worse than I reckoned," he said with another foolish grin.

"Stay the night," Evert suggested. "I can have a room made ready in a few minutes." He reached for the silver hand bell. Piet, exaggeratedly concerned, leaned over and gripped his hand. If once that bell rang, he thought, he would be persuaded into even greater folly.

"No, no," he said. "Don't do that, Evert. I can't stay. I'm damned drunk—and if I go to bed drunk there's only Gijs can wake me in the morning. And to tell you the truth, Evert, I'm in b-bad odour with the Company as it is over my liquor. Fat-arsed directors sitting at their ease at Amsterdam—they've no bowels of compassion for seafaring men that have to take their comfort where they can find it. Sent for me, they did, last time I landed and said, 'One more chance. One more case of derry-derry'—damn the word—'neglect of duty and you're finished, Odshoorn,' they said. And I'll tell you another thing, Evert, old man; that agent, what's his-name —Kaerko, thanks. Kaerko was just going to come aboard and check over when you came in this afternoon. He put it off as a favour to *you*, not to me. I know that. Agents don't favour captains as a rule. So if I'm not there at day-break he'll be mad as a pye-dog. And for all I know he may be a spy. See? It's nice of you, Evert, to ask me to stay; and it was a nice dinner and I'm sorry we haven't been better friends, and, by God, I'm glad to see you so prosperous and all. But please don't ask me to stay now. I gotta get back to Gijs. He'll see I'm all right in the morning."

"I wouldn't think of stopping you," Evert said. "I'll walk down to the quay with you."

"Thanks," Piet said. He took hold of the edge of the table and gingerly levered himself to his feet, as though hoping that if he did it gradually his brain would not notice the change of position. Once upright, he had one of the ideas which, to the drunken man, seem so shrewd and sober. He looked fiercely at Evert. "And don't you go telling anybody I was too drunk to get home by myself. See? Because spies are everywhere. And nobody else has seen me. So if I'm called over the coals and sacked for getting drunk my first night in Banda, I shall know who to blame and, by God, I'll maim you." His mood changed again. "Know what they said to me in that stinking office? 'You'll go to Banda, Odshoorn,' they said; 'there'll be less tem-temptation in a place where you haven't any boon companions.' And then I'm hardly landed, just set foot in the agent's office, and Evert Haan walks in. Good old Evert, after all these years. Boon companions, eh? Funny, isn't it funny?"

"Very funny," Evert agreed. He linked his arm in his kinsman's and steered him out into the hall. There on top of a Chinese lacquered chest lay their two hats—Piet's a formal, heavy, hot, bebadged, shoregoing-uniform one, Evert's a wide light straw of native workmanship. Piet, with his free hand, clapped his on lopsidedly and would not have looked into the gilt-edged mirror on the wall above the chest, but his arm was linked in Evert's and Evert turned with the automatic action of a vain man and looked into the glass. For a moment the two faces, so like and yet so unlike, swam together in the greenish, dimly lighted surface, and the lack of precision in the reflection seemed to exaggerate their salient features: the weakness of Piet's amiable mouth; the hard, thin strength of Evert's; the fan of little wrinkles about Piet's eyes, the result of years of facing wind and weather; the prominent muscles of Evert's jaw.

"By heaven," said Piet with a foolish laugh which on a higher note would have been a giggle, "we do look alike. I never real-realised that I was so like the Old Man." The differences had eluded him; his blurred stare saw only the resemblances, the tough reddish-brown hair which in both men had retained its colour and thickness and would most likely remain the same until extreme old age, the slightly hooked noses with the wide nostrils indicative of physical courage, the gray-green eyes below the thick straight brows.

"I suppose he's dead by now," said Evert, turning towards the door. "Did you ever hear?"

"Not a word. Never wan-wanted to. By God, I'm glad you left him, Evert. Served the old bastard right."

He missed a step just outside the door and stumbled. Evert's grip on his arm saved him.

They walked for a little while in a comfortable silence.

Then a mood of great happiness fell upon Piet. After all these years, he thought, Evert and me walking along together like good friends.

"We didn't always get on so badly, did we?" he asked in a sentimental voice. "We had some good times together. Why, I remember going to the fair with you, and you had money and I had none and you treated me at every booth. And we came home together singing. D'you remember that? D'you remember any of the old songs, Evert?"

"No," said Evert. "And don't you start singing now, Piet. We're nearly into town, and you don't want to make an exhibition of yourself, do you?"

"Aw, come on. There's nobody about." That was true enough, for the town of Banda Neira kept early hours. But, as Evert knew, that very fact would make any unusual noise the more noticeable. And the moon was bright. He didn't want sober citizens brought to their windows to see him, Evert Haan, escorting a drunken sea captain through the streets.

"Come on," Piet said again. "Surely you re-remember 'The Milkmaid's Holiday'—about the young gallant who met the pretty milkmaid and be-begged her to stop and give him a drink from her sweet foaming pail, and she did, but it was slops. It was slops to the ditch she was carrying. 'And good enough for you, fine sir, good enough for you.' You must remember that one, Evert. Come on now, all together.

> "'Twas on a bright fine morning
> The scent of hay perfuming . . .'"

His rich bass voice rang out in the ribald ditty. Along the street Evert heard the creak of an opened shutter. He lengthened his stride.

"How're you going to get back to your ship?" he asked loudly, trying to distract Piet's attention.

"Gijs'll be waiting for me. 'Oh, she was very bonny, and he was very bold——'"

"Will you shut up?" Evert said. "Who is this Gijs?"

"My man."

"Oh. I didn't know the Company allowed their captains a personal servant."

"They don't, blast their meanness! I pay him myself. Damn it, Evert, don't keep disturbing me. 'He said to her, "Oh, maiden, I take it you're a maiden——"'"

"You'll rouse the whole town," said Evert as another shutter opened briskly.

"They want to hear the fruity part," said Piet, singing louder. So, bellowing at the top of his lungs, he emerged upon the quay. And there, alone in the moonlight, Gijs waited. Evert gladly surrendered his charge, said "Good night" abruptly, and strode back towards the streets. Gijs drove a sharp elbow into Piet's diaphragm and said curtly, "Pipe down, will you?" And as Piet hushed at the voice of authority, Gijs asked anxiously, "Who was that? Anybody you know?"

The question struck the drunken man as being exquisitely funny. He broke into great volleys of laughter. "Anybody I know?" he repeated. "Why, I was brought up with that jackalorum. Go to Banda, they say, there won't be anybody there to drink with—and before I've been in the agent's office ten minutes Evert Haan comes walking in."

"Well, that's all right then," Gijs said, a little comforted. "I was afraid it was just somebody you'd picked up in a tavern. And this is a little place. *They'd* soon hear that you was roaring drunk again."

"But I haven't been in a tavern, I tell you. Evert took me back to his house—a fine new place he's building. Like a palace. And what a dinner, Gijs, my lad. Not one thing I could name, but all delishush."

Gijs, bent over the oars, merely grunted. Piet's mood tilted suddenly for no reason. "But I've done a damn silly thing, Gijs. I've made a damn silly promise."

The even rhythm of Gij's labouring arms faltered. For ten years he had been Piet's servant, mentor, father-confessor, and it was largely due to his skill and devotion that that interview in the directors' office had been so long delayed. In the secret places of his heart he believed that, if he had been in Surabaya at the time of the fatal drunken bout instead of in hospital, he would have saved his master the full result of his folly. But since the thing had happened and Piet had been reprimanded and warned—coming out of the office and weeping on Gijs's shoulder and vowing never to drink again except when he was on leave at home—Gijs had been doubly watchful. He had regarded Evert's prosperous well-dressed figure with the greatest suspicion. He did not look like a sea captain's casual drinking acquaintance, more like some well-to-do busybody who would remove a drunken nuisance and then report him. Evert's abrupt leave-taking

had lent colour to the suspicion. Then Piet had claimed
Evert as an old friend and Gijs had felt relieved; and now
Piet was changing his tune and muttering about having
made a promise. Gijs knew those promises made under the
influence of liquor; there had been trouble about them more
than once. Always, everywhere, up and down the route of
the wide-travelling ships of the Company, there were
unscrupulous persons trying to persuade a simple easygoing
seafaring man into some breach of the rules. . . . There was
always a lady whose father was dying in Bandogar and who
hadn't had time to bespeak a passage; there was always the
parcel which contained nothing of any importance but
which could easily be stowed amongst the captain's personal
stuff and for which strange sums—considering its unim-
portance—would be paid for delivery in a certain place
with due discretion. Gijs was wise to them all; and so, in his
sober moments, was Piet. But this was not the first time by a
great many that the captain had returned to his ship saying,
"I've made a damn silly promise. . . ."

The boat drew into the shadow of the *Eastern Venture*.

"Can you manage the ladder, sir?" Gijs asked, shipping
his oars. He realised that Piet was in a garrulous, long-
winded mood and it might take some time to get to the heart
of the matter—what Piet had promised to do, or say, or
carry for the richly dressed red-faced man who had said
"Good night" so abruptly. Whatever it was, if it was against
orders, Gijs would see that it was not done. Praise be to God,
wits were not the prerogative of the well-to-do, and Gijs
knew that his own were needle-sharp naturally, and life had
kept them well polished.

"Damned funny, meeting old Evert," Piet meandered,
dropping onto the side of his bunk. "Thirty years since I last
set eyes on him. Long time. But I remember the day as
though it was yesterday. Pouring with rain, the sort of day
you wouldn't turn a dog out. Not if it had been a good dog;
and, by God's eyes, my mother had served the Old Man
well. Worked in the fields and yard like a horse, she had.
And turned out to starve just like a horse in the end. And all
on Evert's account. Of the two women, the Old Man liked
my mother far the best." He brought his big hand down on
the bunk and emitted a sound of disgust. "And then, blast
me, I'm pleased to see him and go and eat his grub and
promise him things." He looked at Gijs with dazed misery.

At the word "promise" Gijs's slumbering interest revived.

"What did you promise exactly?" he asked, drawing off Piet's boots.

"Something that's going to make me the laughingstock of the village," said Piet bitterly.

"Why?"

Ramblingly, between sips of coffee and what sounded to Gijs's impatient ears like interminable, irrelevant digressions, Piet told him what he had promised to do.

"Is that all?" Gijs asked when the story at last came to an end. His relief was so profound as to be almost tangible. It was a perfectly legitimate errand.

"All? Don't you reckon that's enough?" Piet realised with dismal certainty that for once Gijs' sympathy had failed him. He heaved a gusty sigh and rolled over onto the bunk.

"You'll feel different about things in the morning," said Gijs, who, though puzzled by his master's attitude, had been touched to pity by the sigh. "I'll see you're about in good time. Good night."

"Good night, Gijs. You're a good chap, but you're dead stupid," said Piet. He burrowed into the pillow and was, despite his worries, instantly asleep.

In the morning Gijs was at the bunkside again. The captain was the very devil to wake after a bout of drunkenness; on the occasion which had brought the Company's dissatisfaction to a head he had slept soundly for three nights and two days, lost, anonymous, in some low wharfside tavern. So, thought Gijs, wetting a rough towel in a bucket of sea water, the captain must be up and ready, spruce and bright, by the time the Banda agent came aboard this morning.

He turned to the bunk where Piet lay like the dead, except that the dead do not breathe heavily, and, straining every muscle in his slight frame, took his master by the shoulders and raised the leaden body so that instead of reclining the great form leaned back against the bulkhead. Piet's head fell forward and he slept on, undisturbed. Then Gijs took the wet towel and beat it about the sleeper's head and face. A particularly vicious flip of the towel caught Piet across the cheek, and he turned his head aside with a sound that was half grunt, half groan.

"You little *swine*," said Piet sleepily.

Gijs face cleared. "Come on, sir, wake up," he said, still rousing, but deferential. "Company's agent is coming aboard at daybreak. And you're late as it is. Rouse up, sir. Drink this."

He draped the wet towel round Piet's neck like a scarf, swung his feet over the bunk's edge and pressed them onto the boards, and then set the mug of coffee against his lips. The coffee was still hot and, to Piet, after his drenching with cool water, seemed hotter. He shook his head and opened his eyes. Slowly his great brown hands went to his head.

"I've split my skull," he said mournfully. "You let me fall last night."

"I did not," said Gijs briskly. "But I nearly had to split it to wake you. And you weren't at your worst last night, either. Look at the time. And Mynheer Kaerko is coming at daybreak."

"Mm. I know," said Piet, still fingering his head. "It seems all right, but it feels dreadful. Gimme that coffee."

"Drink it down and you shall have some schnapps," said Gijs, as though bribing a child. He reached for a dry towel and mopped Piet quickly. Then he held out his breeches. "Come on, up now. That's right. We shall be in time after all. Clean shirt, make a good impression. Now here's your schnapps." He whisked away the mug and held out the pewter measure and, as soon as Piet had taken it, snatched up a brush which he plied vigorously over the crisp, curly hair of his master's head and beard. Then, diving into his pocket, he produced a hard ship's biscuit. "There you are, chew that. It'll stay your belly and take away the smell." He stood back with the brush still in his hand and regarded his handiwork with pride. You would never guess, he thought complacently, that fifteen minutes ago the captain was just a drunken hulk who, left to himself, would have slept on and, sure as a gun, been sacked at the end of this voyage. Gijs derived great satisfaction from the thought. Ten years ago he had received from Piet the first really kind, humane treatment he had known in his life, and it pleased him to think that now he was the peg upon which the captain's whole career depended. For although it was acknowledged that the big man was a peerless sailor, cool in an emergency, unruffled in the face of danger, utterly dependable in his sober moments, such virtues hardly compensated for the tendency to babble, to keep low company, and to neglect his duty, which came upon him when he was drunk. Well, Gijs thought, we've foxed *Them* again, and next time he goes ashore, even if it is to the agent's office, I go too.

Kaerko, with his army of clerks, came punctually aboard, and the routine of checking the cargo brought out from Holland for sale or exchange in the islands went smoothly. Piet's head still ached and he talked very little. He noted that the agent's manner had changed subtly since the afternoon of the day before, when it had been the perfectly courteous, formal, slightly condescending manner of a very important official, towards a lesser one. Now there was a show of personal interest, a veiled respect which puzzled Piet until his slow brain—slower than usual this morning—arrived at the conclusion that Kaerko had somehow heard gossip about him and was surprised to find everything aboard the *Eastern Venture* so very shipshape, so spick and span.

But presently Kaerko, ticking off the last item, scribbling his initials at the foot of the last page, and handing all the papers over to the clerk who stood subserviently ready to receive them, said, "I trust you had a pleasant evening, Captain Odshoorn." His voice was that of a man who, finishing a slightly tedious duty, turns to the light social intercourse which attracts him far more. Piet, very conscious of the headache which was the result of that pleasant evening, blinked and managed a wry smile.

"Thank you, yes. Very pleasant. And very obliging of you, sir, to postpone all this business until this morning. Evert whisked me off so quickly I hadn't time to thank you yesterday." He despised himself as he spoke. Sucking up to agents was not in his line at all; he hated and despised the breed, landlubbers with a head for figures and an eye like a hawk's for the slightest mistake. But since that warning interview his confidence in himself had been shaken and he was willing to placate anyone who might, in certain circumstances, turn into an enemy.

"Mynheer Haan is an old friend of yours?" Kaerko asked, his tone pleasantly conversational, his eyes greasy with curiosity.

"Oh, more than that—a relative; though I'm damned if I could put a name to the exact degree." Even to please the agent he was not going to describe the curious tangle which made him and Evert almost brothers.

"Indeed. How strange that you should run into him here! I believe I am right in saying that Mynheer Haan, greeting you, mentioned that it was thirty years since you had met."

"That's right," Piet agreed, thinking, How he must have listened, though he pretended not to.

"Mynheer Haan is a very able man, and very popular," said the agent silkily.

Piet repressed the retort which rose to his lips—"Oh yes, Evert would be popular or die in the attempt"—and said with unusual caution, "That doesn't surprise me. And now, sir, if you are satisfied, I'll get my breakfast and start unloading. The sooner we're empty, the sooner we're full again, you know."

"A true word, Captain Odshoorn," said Kaerko, in whom hunger had been warring with curiosity for some minutes. "You'll have two busy days. Then it would give me pleasure if you would dine with me. That'll be Thursday, at six o'clock. We dine late here; the heat of the day is not conducive to appetite."

"You forget I've been coming East for twenty years," said Piet, who, resenting language he did not understand, had taken umbrage at "conducive," though its meaning was plain enough. Jumped-up little ass, like all agents.

"Have you, indeed? You must tell me about your voyages. I daresay we have mutual acquaintances. Until Thursday then. Good morning, Captain Odshoorn."

"Good morning, sir," said Piet more cheerfully. What with the coffee and the early-morning schnapps, he was longing for his breakfast. Mutual acquaintances, pooh, he thought, spitting into the blue water.

For the next two days, the emptying of the *Eastern Venture's* capacious hold kept him busy, and at night he was too tired to think much, but now and then he spared a thought for Evert, Annabet van Goens, and the promise he had made. The more he thought about the business, the less he liked it. He had made promises before this, when he was in his cups, and had regretted them instantly when he was sober. But always before there was a kind of risk, a challenge to his blood, attached to the performance of the promise; and very often the danger had appealed to the adventurer in him, and more often it had been impossible to retract the promise without the risk of seeming a coward, in his own eyes at least. At any rate, such a job didn't make him feel an ass, and this one did. Some hours before he was due to dine at the agent's house he had made up his mind that next time he saw Evert he would tell him straight that, despite whatever he might have promised—and he was a bit vague as to how far he had committed himself, just as he would have denied having roared the last stanza of "The Milkmaid's Holiday" over and over again—he would have nothing to do with the business. If Evert chose to let his new wealth give him a swollen head and make a fool of himself, he must find somebody else to help him display his swollen-headed folly.

He was surprised and a trifle disconcerted to find that Evert was at the dinner, together with three or four other prosperous-looking gentlemen. "Dining the captains" was well known to be part of the agent's duties all over the wide-flung routes of the Company's trade, a formality, a gesture, and nothing more. Often, as when a cargo was unsatisfactory or the keen, inspectorial eye had discovered some fault, the occasions were very trying, with both host and guest trying to behave like ordinary human beings when both knew that they were merely cogs in a vast machine which at the moment was not working smoothly. And hardly ever was anyone else present at these ceremonial meals.

Piet, who had not yet got into words the exact form of his refusal to oblige, kept away from his kinsman without much difficulty, for everyone seemed anxious to talk to Evert, to laugh at his jokes, and to flatter him either openly or covertly. And Evert, in good company, surrounded by a flattering audience, did seem a very charming person. Piet, looking backwards, could remember how, in the old days, before the breakup of their curious family, he had varied his absolute loathing of his half brother by admiring him prodigiously. Evert took such risks so coolly, enjoyed things so wholeheartedly, and was capable of large good-humored actions which blinded one for a moment to his utter selfishness. There had even been moments when Piet, as a youngster, had wondered whether all the rows in the little farmhouse had been Evert's fault, whether he himself, surly and grudging, had not been sometimes to blame. A similar kind of doubt visited him now as he watched Evert. It was so natural for an exile to want a woman of his own race for a wife; it was natural for a man who had got on in the world to marry a woman who would fit in with his position; it was natural for a man to entrust a delicate errand to his kinsman rather than to a stranger. Aw hell! Piet thought, taking refuge in his more usual frame of mind. He's put me in the wrong again; he always did, he always will. Why the devil was I put on the Banda route, just to run into Evert?

The dinner seemed to stretch out interminably. There was

plenty to eat, but Piet's appetite was less keen than usual; there was plenty to drink, but he was afraid to have his glass refilled; there was plenty of conversation, but he took little part in it. With few and short-lived diversions, it was all on one topic, the nutmeg, its prices, its prospects, its peculiarities. With the exception of Piet, every man in the room depended entirely on the produce of those graceful feathry trees which covered the island so thickly. To the nutmeg they owed the clothes they wore, the food they ate, the wines they drank, the houses in which they lived, and the guilders that jingled in their breeches pockets. And in their conversation, at least, they showed no sign of attempting to escape their sense of obligation to the little shrivelled brown object.

Just before ten o'clock one of the guests rose, saying that he had left his wife alone and had promised to be home early. Men stirred and looked at their watches, but the party might have survived had not Evert risen to his feet and announced that it was time he was moving too. There was then a general movement, and in the hubbub of last greetings and hat findings, Evert, as though sensing that Piet was about to escape, came up and slipped his arm familiarly in his.

"Wait for me. I'm coming your way, Piet. My prahau is at the quay."

As soon as they were alone Evert said, "I want you to come back with me. I've something to show you. The night's young yet and it's only ten minutes by water."

"Well," Piet said reluctantly, "I've something to say to you; might as well get it over."

Evert did not bother to ask what that "something" might be, and the short water journey was passed in trivial conversation, mainly gossip about Kaerko's guests. "Boender's wife is going to have a baby in about eight and a half month's time; that's why he can't leave her alone for long," Evert explained, laughing. "And thanks to her, we got away early. I find Kaerko extremely tedious, poor little man. He's a good agent as they go, but he ought never to leave his office."

Piet stared at his kinsman. He had heard agents called many things, but never had he heard anyone say in that casual, pitying way that an agent was a tedious, poor little thing. More than the new house or the style in which Evert lived, the words revealed how very far Evert had got on in the world. No wonder, he thought, that Evert always got his own way with the Old Man. And then, hard on the heels of that admiring thought, came a stubborn one: But he's not going to get his own way with *me*.

"We'll go to my office," Evert said. "It's quite comfortable."

It was a fair-sized square room with bare walls washed white and a floor of red tiles set in inch-wide borders of mortar. There were four articles of furniture, a big heavy desk with a flat top, two comfortable cushioned chairs with high backs, and a wooden bench along one wall. In the wall behind the desk there were several cupboards, one of them with an iron door. An oil lamp burned clearly upon one corner of the desk. Evert pulled it across as soon as he entered so that its most direct light shone on the wall with the cupboards.

"Sit down," he said, "and I'll give you something to drink. Kaerko knows about as much about liquor as I do about knitting." He unlocked a cupboard and brought out a tall lopsided bottle of greenish glass and a couple of horn glasses with wide silver rims.

"Not for me, thanks," Piet said in what he intended to be a definite voice, only it came out a little wistfully.

"But it's genuine Everett," Evert said, the bottle tilted and poised in his hand. "You won't get that every day in Banda, let me tell you."

"I know. It must have cost you a pretty penny."

"It did," Evert agreed. He poured out the drinks, took a sip from his glass, and turned back to the wall with the cupboards. He unlocked the iron door, which swung open with a heavy squeak, and reached within. When his hand came out it was gripping some sheets of paper and a parcel wrapped in a bit of muslin. He locked the door again and laid the articles on the desk. Meantime Piet, swallowing hard, had thought, This is the moment. And as Evert turned he said firmly, "I promised you something the other night. And now I'm sober I'm just going to say that I can't keep my promise. I'm sorry, Evert. I knew it was a daft idea from the first. . . . But as I say, I was drunk, and you'll have to forgive me."

"This," said Evert, sitting down in his chair and drawing the parcel towards him with one hand while he pushed the lamp back with the other, "is what I wanted to show you." He gave no sign of having heard Piet's speech. "There's an attorney at the Fort, and I saw him the morning after I

talked to you and he's drawn up everything quite properly.
Here is a letter to Mevrouw van Goens. I did wonder
whether it should be addressed to Egbert, but you say he's in
the Army; he might be anywhere and there's no time to
waste, so I sent it to *her*. It explains everything and makes the
formal proposal. This"—he lifted the second paper—"is a
marriage contract, as made for the best families, he assures
me. And here"—he touched the third paper with his
finger—"is a draft on the Bank of Amsterdam." He pushed
the papers aside and unfolded the muslin. "Now look at
that, Piet. Isn't it lovely? Go on, look at it. See if you can
open it." He handed across the desk a square box of
exquisite workmanship, ivory inlaid with silver and mother-
of-pearl and some pink stone which Piet did not recognise.
There seemed to be no hinge or clasp or spring, and when
Piet had turned it about in his big brown hands for a
moment he handed it back.

"It beats me," he said.

"Turn it so that the big pink flower is uppermost. Now
press the centre and slide the whole top towards you. You
haven't seen anything yet," said Evert, enjoying himself.

Piet obeyed the instructions and the box opened smoothly.
He blinked. Inside, bedded on velvet which exactly matched
the ivory, there lay, jumbled by his turning and twisting of
the casket, a mass of jewels, emeralds and diamonds, some as
large as his thumbnail, some no bigger than a pin's head, but
all of the first quality, all catching the light and flashing it
back in blinding white and rainbow rays. He knew more
about precious stones that one would have imagined, for
he had smuggled them in his time, and the finger with which
he straightened the mass into its components parts was vastly respectful. There was a ring, a great square emerald set
amongst small diamonds; a pair of earrings; each a large
emerald swung from a diamond chain; and a necklet of
emeralds and diamonds set in flexible links of the pale fine
gold of Kabistan.

"But it's priceless," he said a little breathlessly. "I've never
seen such stones, Evert, and I've seen a few. The ring alone is
worth a fortune."

"Look well against a white skin," Evert said. His tone was
deliberately casual, but it was plain, even to Piet, that he was
pleased by the impression he had made.

"Last but not least," he said, lifting the remaining article from the muslin and then dropping it again as though unworthy of Piet's notice, "is the glove." It was the custom for these far-off bridegrooms to send a glove which, solemnly placed upon the hand of the bride, was the final symbol of the marriage being solemnised. This glove was ornate and obviously made for the purpose; it was of white leather with a heavily fringed cuff and coloured embroidery upon its back.

"It beats me," said Piet, whose eyes, after one glance at the glove, had gone back to the jewels. "I know you're rich, Evert, I can see that. But I'm not a fool, and I know there's a limit to what a man can make, even out of nutmegs. I don't see how you can afford things like these."

Evert's thick reddish eyebrows drew together in a frown, and for a second his pale eyes looked dangerous. Then he grinned.

"Perhaps I didn't buy them," he said pleasantly. "Besides, you must remember that I have been here for twenty years, and I lived very simply until I decided to build this house. And I often pick up things cheaply. I have done certain favours and have friends who drop me a word where bargains are to be found. Anyway, you may be sure that I came by these honestly, and you may carry them without any conscience qualms."

"But that's just what I don't want to do," Piet began laboriously. "I know you can't see why and I can't make myself plain. But honestly, Evert, I don't want to have anything to do with it. See? You've got everything all ready, and there'll be another ship in next week or the week after —maybe tomorrow, even—and you can get somebody to do the job for you. Do that and I'll wish you all the luck in the world."

"But I want *you* to carry these for me. Surely that's the obvious thing, Piet. Why not? Are you afraid of Mevrouw?"

"Maybe. I don't mind admitting it. You've lived here for a long time, Evert, and perhaps you've forgotten that there's a caste system at home as hard as that in India. I think maybe I could carry the things if you weren't related to me, if you were a stranger; but your being related to me, and Mevrouw knowing all about it, I *know* she'd think I was an uppity fool who'd put the idea into your head. As I did. But I told you I was drunk. Can't you see, Evert, that for me to go and carry your proposal would look as though the next thing would be my making a bid for one of the girls myself? As though I thought just because they are poor now . . . It's no use, Evert. I just can't do it."

Evert's highly coloured face darkened to crimson and seemed to swell, and once again his eyes looked dangerous. Piet prepared himself for an outburst of rage, the grown-up version of those tantrums with which his half brother had so often shattered the tenuous peace of the old farmhouse. But Evert had learned the value of self-control since those far-off days. Without speaking he reached out and took the casket, closed it with careful fingers, laid it on the glove, and folded the muslin back into place. He shuffled the papers until their edges were meticulously even. Then he said, "Well, if that's how you feel, Piet, I must do as you say—find another messenger. I'm sorry."

"I'm sorry too," Piet hastened to say. "I'm very sorry, Evert, especially as I put the notion into your head and as good as promised to carry the things. But honestly, it'll be better for me not to have a hand in it. For one thing, I'm not very lucky."

Evert had risen and was replacing the parcel and the papers in the iron-doored cupboard. With his back to Piet he said in an easy, conversational tone, "Not? You surprise me. You've done very well. You've got to the top in your job."

"That wasn't luck," Piet said, looking longingly at the lopsided bottle. "Damned hard work all the way along. Damme, Evert, I even went to school again. No—of course not, I don't mean the whip-arse place the Old Man pushed us both into. I'd had enough of *that*. No, when I was about twenty I realised that I'd never hold captain's rank unless I could navigate and reckon. And about that time the ship I was in captured a Portuguee pirvateer. My share of the prize money came to a hundred and fifty guilders. My God, that seemed like a fortune in those days. But I gave it all to an old professor in Amsterdam. He'd taught mathematics at Leyden, but he was such a soak he'd lost his job. Half his time he didn't know whether it was Christmas or Easter, he was so sotted. But he could do sums, and he showed me. And a lot of other things besides. Come to think of it, the one lesson I ought to have learned from him I didn't. To avoid that"—he nodded towards the bottle—"like the plague. That's another way I ain't lucky. There's many a man that drinks more than I do and neglects his duty more often—but I'm the one that's caught. See? And just the other day, meeting you and coming here . . . I tell you, if it hadn't been for Gijs I'd have made a mess of it next morning with Kaerko. I'm in a queer position, Evert, like a dog that has had two of his three bites. One more ill report and I'm done." He saw that Evert was giving his words sharp attention and thought, I'm an ass to let him know all this. There was a moment's pause while Evert seemed lost in thought. "Thank God Gijs is with me again," Piet went on. "You know, it's a queer thing, that poor little man is grateful to me because he thinks I'm kind to him. I took him out of the forecastle where he was having a hell of a life and made him my servant. And, by God, it has paid me a thousand times."

Suddenly Evert interrupted him. "When do you sail?" he asked, tilting the bottle. Piet told him. "Then dine with me again on the Friday night, and I promise that we'll both have two glasses of schnapps and more."

"Thank you. I will, and gladly," Piet said. He had thought that his refusal to do the errand would have alienated Evert, and once again he had the feeling that he had wronged Evert; that he himself was the surly, unfriendly fellow.

The farewell dinner was wholly delightful, and throughout its course Piet was acutely aware that, although to be honest he had always reckoned himself a better man than Evert, he would have found difficulty in entertaining so royally a man, a near kinsman, who had stubbornly refused to do a straightforward errand for him. His feelings on the subject were so sharp and so self-derogatory that had Evert broken his word and provided just one drink more than the stipulated two he would probably have said, "Gimme all that tackle and I'll do the job for you after all." But Evert, although he had provided a feast of delicious food, had kept his promise and there were two glasses of schnapps apiece, one before and one after the meal. And the Van Goens were never mentioned, not even by implication. So Piet salved his conscience with the assurance that Evert would easily find another to do his errand and one who would do it far more worthily.

"Would you rather go afoot or by prahau?" Evert asked when Piet, after consulting his formidable timepiece, said that it was time he was getting aboard.

"I'll walk," Piet said. "I'll have enough of the sea after tomorrow. But there's no need for you to come, Evert. I'm sober and I know my way now."

"I'll come a step or two. I've had little enough exercise today," Evert said. He had suddenly the air of a man whose mind was elsewhere; and Piet, noting it, thought, There, now that's over and Evert's finished with me; he's thinking about something else; he's a man of many affairs, many friends. And he thought humbly that it was very good of Evert, after all this time, and considering everything in the past, to have gone to so much trouble to make his stay in Banda so agreeable.

They came out into the hall. Evert, with a superb disregard for habit or climate, had built his new house in Banda as he would have built one in Holland, and from the hall, which was wide and paved and pillared with marble, a staircase sprang, curving and graceful, to end in a wide gallery from which the bedrooms opened. There were tubs of flowering shrubs and plants between the pillars, at the foot and head of the stairs, and at intervals along the gallery. Piet, who had been too drunk upon his former visit to take much note of his surroundings, wondered again where on earth Evert had found the money for such a building.

He was thinking this when he saw a face peering from behind one of the tubs of flowers in the gallery. It was very pretty, though the expression it wore—a kind of mischievous malignance—was not engaging. The small brown oval face was lighted by a pair of great brown eyes and topped by a head of sleek black hair. Below the face Piet could catch a glimpse of vivid scarlet colour, and then the figure was obliterated by a great bunch of flowers, dead white with dark glossy leaves.

Evert, who had been enjoying the glances of admiration which Piet had directed about him, saw the sudden stiffening of his pose, the fixing of the glance into a stare, and followed the direction of it. Unseen by Piet, a curious expression came over Evert's face, part exasperation, part an almost fatuous doting, part the "caught-out" look which comes upon a man whose secret is discovered; the fluid expressions hardened finally into the one most natural upon Evert's countenance —a complacent possessiveness.

"That's my Isa," he said, pronouncing the name so that Piet, if called upon to spell it, would have done so with a double *e*. Then, raising his voice, he called in exactly the tone one would use to a favourite puppy, "You naughty little thing! What're you doing up there? Come down and show yourself."

She rose from behind the flowery tub so that her head showed above the rail of the gallery, but not very far, for she was no taller than a white child of twelve, and moved reluctantly yet with complete self-possession to the head of the stairs, paused for a moment, and then slowly descended, making each step a gesture, as though aware that merely walking down stairs is one of the most graceful things a pretty woman can do. She wore the traditional Malay female attire, the sarong and little jacket which, even to Western eyes, had proved so attractive that most of the white women in the islands adopted it for indoor wear. The sarong was patterned in gold and scarlet, the jacket of unrelieved scarlet. Heavy gold earrings swung from her ears, and both her slim wrists were loaded with bangles. Her finger tips and her lips were touched with colour which held its own even against the vivid scarlet background of her jacket. The old envy of Evert stirred anew in Piet's heart. "My Isa" was a toy any man might covet.

"So you just *had* to peep at my guest," Evert said in a jocularly scolding way. "Well, I hope you are satisfied. This is Captain Odshoorn, a kinsman of mine."

Piet stared hard at the girl, yet spared attention to notice that Evert avoided the use of the term "half brother" just as he himself had done, and thought, Funny that we should feel the same about that.

Isa acknowledged the introduction with a graceful movement of her head and a smile which just disturbed the sulky curves of her mouth and no more.

"I thought it was a woman," she said, speaking good Dutch with a soft, most attractive lisp to it. "You made such a mystery."

"I told you to keep out, if you call that making a mystery," Evert said curtly. "And I've told you not to go upstairs unless I'm there. What woman were you expecting to see here, pray?"

She said with what appeared to be the most disarming simplicity, "The new woman." She had lowered her lids over her great brown dove's eyes when Evert had started to chide her; now she lifted them and added, with an expression of extreme hatred mingled with sly knowingness, "Wang Fu spoke of jewels." The red-tipped fingers flashed, touching a finger, both ears, sketching a circle about her own throat. She stared straight at Evert; they might have been alone in the wide pillared hall and Piet a thousand miles away.

Evert swore luridly. "Damn Wang Fu," he said, "the talkative, pox-ridden son of a yellow bitch. I'll give him something else to talk about tomorrow. As for you, haven't I told you time and again that as long as you were here you weren't to gossip in the compound? It's the curse of the islands," he said savagely, suddenly remembering Piet and turning towards him. "Yap, yap, yap, that's all they find time to do, the damn rogues. And what they don't know they make up. Wang Fu made up that tale, d'you hear me, trying to stir up mischief; and you were fool enough to listen to him. You deserve a good beating. Spying and gossiping like a slave. Get away. Get out of my sight."

She stood her ground calmly, and it was plain to Piet that, whatever else she might feel for Evert, she was not afraid of him.

"Then it was a lie? There is no new woman?"

"No. But there soon will be if you behave like this."

"Then who were the jewels for?" she asked with the relentless illogic of the Orient.

"I tell you there weren't any," Evert shouted. "Any more than there was a woman here tonight. Look at him. . . . Does he look like a woman? Such a coil about nothing."

She took a step or two forward and said stonily, "Wang Fu said——"

Evert lost patience and with a curse laid one of his big brown hands on her narrow shoulder, spinning her round.

"Will you be quiet and get out? I tell you Wang Fu is a liar, or else you are. There is no woman; there are no jewels. You go back to the compound, and don't come near me till I send for you. I'm ashamed of you." He gave her a push which carried her across several paces of the marble-flagged floor, but she recovered her balance quickly, and with considerable dignity, without a backward glance, she walked towards the door in the shadow of the staircase.

"Come on, Piet," said Evert, slapping his hat onto his head and tearing open the front door as though it had angered him. Slamming it behind him, he said savagely, "That's a sample of native behaviour. By God, I'll give that Chinaman something to remember tomorrow. She's a good little bitch and it'll be the best part of a year before I'm ready to get rid of her."

"Other people run brothels for sailors," Piet said. "It's easier than running your own, I reckon."

"No truer word was ever spoken," Evert agreed, linking

his arm in his half brother's. "But of course there isn't the choice——"

"You're right there. Would you believe that once in Bandogar——"

They enjoyed a man-to-man talk about women and brothels, cheatings, trollops, and doxies until they reached the first houses of the town. Then Evert, withdrawing his arm but laying his hand on Piet's solid shoulder, said, "Well, I've come farther than I intended. I'll say good-bye here, Piet. I'm mighty glad to have seen you; I wish you the best of luck on your voyage and I hope to see you next year." The hand moved in an affectionate squeeze with each phrase.

"I'm mighty glad to have seen you too, Evert. And thank you for your hospitality. I'm sure I wish you the best of luck—in everything." He gave the last words a special emphasis.

"Good-bye, then," said Evert, and with a final squeeze dropped his hand.

"Good-bye," said Piet. He reached for Evert's hand and shook it heartily. As he did so there came to their ears the sound of running feet; and Piet, who found this moment of parting with the man whom he had hated and yet liked, who had treated him kindly and who had borne no grudge at the breaking of an all but promise, rather tense and emotional, lightened it by saying, "Somebody in the devil of a hurry."

"Coming this way, too," Evert said, checked in his turning.

The moon, which on Piet's former return from Evert's house had been embarrassingly bright, had waned, and the street ahead was full of the velvet darkness of the tropic night. The patter of feet on the hard-beaten road was punctuated by audible, hard-drawn breath before the figure of the runner was visible.

"None of our business," Evert said. "Good-bye, Piet." He turned and had taken some steps in the direction of his home when Piet, who had for some reason sensed something ominous in the hurrying feet and the harsh breathing and therefore deferred calling his last farewell until the runner should be visible, said sharply, "It's Gijs!"

At the same instant the runner, tumbling up out of the darkness, gasped, "Is that you, sir?" and drew a breath like a sob.

"It's me all right, boy," said Piet with a sinking of the stomach. "What's the matter? Trouble?"

"Ummm," Gijs said, bending double to ease the stitch in his side and straightening up again, fumbling for Piet's arm. "Kaerko's aboard, sir. My God, I don't know how to tell you, sir. They've found some unlimed nuts among the others."

Converging impressions met like arrows driven from different directions upon Piet's mind. There was the shock of horror—it was nothing less—which Gijs's words conveyed, and at the same time he knew that Evert must have heard his exclamation as he recognised the runner; had, perhaps out of delicacy, hastened his step and was now several yards away. He felt as though the one person who could help him was slipping out of reach. Turning his head, he bellowed in a voice accustomed to giving orders through the roar of tempestuous seas, "Evert! Evert! Come back!"

"D'you want me?" Evert asked through the darkness.

"By God, I do," Piet shouted, and was relieved to hear Evert's feet retracing those steps.

"What's the matter?" Evert asked in an ordinary voice as he drew near.

"They've found some unlimed nuts aboard my ship," Piet said in a wooden voice. "You know what that means?"

Evert knew. It was the strictest rule of the islands, the rule upon which the whole security of the monopoly rested, that no fertile nutmeg should ever be taken away. Every nutmeg ever shipped had been rendered sterile by a stepping in limewater. The most stringent precautions—which included the search of every man returning from shore leave and the final tooth-combing of every ship before sailing—were taken to avoid the possibility of a single fertile nut leaving the islands. And such rules were the more easily kept for the simple reason that the planters, the captains, the merchants, and the agents were sensible enough to know that their jobs depended upon the preservation of the monopoly, while the more ignorant people, like the common sailors, found the dangerous unlimed nut difficult to come by. On every plantation the slaves gathered the ripe nuts avidly, for their food and other perquisites depended upon their results; and the nuts, once credited and handed in, went straight into the lime bath. In the whole of the town of Banda Neira, which was all that the seamen ever saw of the islands, there was not an untreated nut to be found. And so although the English, the French, and the Americans in the young colonies would have been glad enough to pay fabulous sums for the germ of a possible new product, breaches of the Company's rules were rare enough to be phenomenal; and the few there were were punished with deterrent ferocity. Piet, standing in the warm night air, felt the cold sweat crawl upon his body as he thought of the result of Kaerko's find.

"Good God," Evert said, and then was silent. The situation was too serious for words.

After a minute Piet, wetting his dry lips with his tongue and swallowing with difficulty, asked, "Where, Gijs?"

"With the others. But done up together in a white bag tied with blue twine. The agent spotted it in a minute. 'What's this,' he says, 'done up so irregularly?' And pulls it out and opens it. You know the different look, sir. There was nothing I could do."

"What could anyone do?" Evert asked harshly. "You've no idea, Piet? You—haven't—been tempted to—smuggle?"

"Dear loving Christ," Piet exploded, relieved at finding a focus for his fury, "what kind of a fool do you take me for? I've smuggled women; I've smuggled jewels. I've doubled my own trade privileges and packed my passengers. But would I be such an almighty, crass, bloody fool as to ship unlimed nuts in a white bag tied with blue twine? Would anybody? Evert"—his voice dropped from the furious to the pitiable— "is there anything you can do?"

"There might be just one thing," Evert said slowly. "It's a long chance and I can't promise that it'll work." He was silent for a moment, while Piet and Gijs waited breathlessly, like children awaiting an adult's decision, an adult's orders. "You go back to the ship, Piet. There's nothing you can do except say that you know nothing about the things. . . . That is true, isn't it? If Kaerko claps you into gaol at the Fort, don't resist him. I'll do what I can. I can't make any promises. Don't, for God's sake, count on me, Piet. But I'll do the only thing that I can think of."

His hand reached out and touched Piet's shoulder, but whether the gesture was one of reassurance or of pity no one could have told. And Piet was past speculation. Then Evert turned away, and his first few hasty strides took him into the covering darkness, though they could tell by the sound of his footsteps that he had taken a side turning and was not going back to his own place.

"We'd better get back," Piet said. "Thank God I'm sober at least. Though I wish I'd a drink or two inside me. To face them with . . ." His voice trailed off miserably. After a moment he asked, "Have you any ideas, Gijs?"

"They were put there to be found tonight," said the little man with complete conviction. "Probably Kaerko did it."

"But for what possible reason?"

"So he could find them and report. Show what a good watch he keeps. It wasn't anybody of ours, sir. I am certain of that. There's not a more"——he hesitated, for although he had for Piet a feeling almost akin to worship, it was a feeling far more easily put into actions than into words——"more popular captain on the whole ocean. Or again," he hurried on, embarrassed, "it might be an accident. Like that time at Surabaya when the governor's lady's laundry was shipped with the tea."

That had been very funny at the time, but now the only feeling that the memory evoked was one of nostalgia for those old happy days before he had been under a cloud, before he had been sent to Banda with its dangerous, ingrown monopoly.

"I wish to God we were dealing with tea now, Gijs," he said.

"Well, we're not," Gijs said literally. "Look, sir. If they take you to the Fort as *he* said, manage to take me too. I could make things a lot easier for you."

"Fat chance I'd get of arranging that——or anything else," Piet grunted. And he thought, I'd rather something had gone wrong in Holland. There is the law there; out here it's all Company, and I'm a Company's servant who's broken its strictest rule, and I'll be flung into the Company's Fort with the Company's agent out for my blood. I'll be lucky if I ever see Janshaven again.

They had reached the water front and Gijs stepped down into the waiting boat, released its rope, and took up its oars. Following him, Piet was conscious of a hitherto unknown impulse. Why not throw himself overboard? He might as well. He was in bad odour with the Company already and he'd get no second chance. Stolid as he seemed, he was not devoid of imagination and he could see himself wasting away in some dark, rat-infested dungeon, probably starving or thirsting to death; or, after some farce of a trial, being sentenced to a whipping, or having his cheek slit and his tongue pulled through. Better be dead.

"Mynheer Haan," said Gijs's voice, answering his thought out of the darkness, "had something in mind. He walked like someone who knew where he was going."

Piet's body, unconsciously tensed for desperate action,

relaxed. Of course he must give Evert a chance. And of course to drown himself would be not only cowardly but almost an admission of guilt. He could imagine the gossip in the places where seamen gathered. . . . "Poor old Odshoorn! Tried to smuggle unlimed nuts and then couldn't face the music!"

The usual watch was on duty aboard the *Eastern Venture*, but there were also two soldiers, stocky little Indonesians in the Company's uniform, standing on guard by the head of the ladder.

"Your name, please?" one of them asked.

"Captain Odshoorn," said Piet dismally.

"Mynheer Kaerko awaits you in your cabin," the little soldier said.

Kaerko, with an expression of determined distress upon his nondescript little face, was sitting bolt upright in Piet's own chair. There were two other men with him; one, a big sallow-complexioned person, Piet recognised as a fellow diner at Kaerko's table. He lolled, very much at his ease, on the end of Piet's bunk. The other, wrinkled and brown as a nutmeg, sat on the small bench below the open porthole.

As Piet entered, blinking at the light, Kaerko rose.

"Your man volunteered to find you, Captain," he said. "And no doubt he told you why we are here."

"Yes," said Piet. "And I want to say straight away that I had no knowledge of their being aboard. I didn't bring them myself and I didn't"—a word he hardly thought he knew popped into his mouth—"I didn't connive at their being brought aboard."

The three men looked at one another with a what-else-could-he-be-expected-to-say expression. Piet felt trapped and helpless. What use were protests? Anyone, even the guiltiest, would say exactly what he had just said and exactly what he was prepared to say.

"You have no suggestion? No suspicion of anyone?" The big man asked the question with the air of one trying to be scrupulously fair, scrupulously just.

Piet shook his head. The crew were all searched when they returned from shore leave. He had no enemies in Banda that he knew of. He had supervised most of the loading himself.

"We have questioned the crew," Kaerko said. "No one admitted having seen or handled the bag which is distinctive enough to be memorable. In the circumstances, Captain Odshoorn, bearing in mind that the captain is responsible for

everything aboard his ship, we have no choice but to arrest
you. I do that now, in the presence of two members of the
Company's administrative staff." He glanced towards the
bunk and the bench, and the nutmeg-faced man stood up
sharply and spoke for the first time. "You will accompany
me to the Fort. Mynheer Kaerko will continue with his
enquiries, and you are assured of a fair trial." The words
rattled out like little stones. He put to his lips a small silver
whistle like a child's toy and blew upon it. Hard bare feet
rustled on the companionway, and the two little soldiers
stood at attention by the cabin door.

"To the Fort," said the brown-faced man, nodding at Piet,
who stood dumb, like a cornered animal.

The little men stepped forward smartly, closing in on
either side. And the thought went through his head that he
should have drowned himself. There was no way out of this.
How the goddamned nutmegs had got aboard was a mystery,
but it wasn't likely that anyone was going to explain it. Talk
of a fair trial was nonsense. How could there be a trial when
there was no defence? And what could Evert do? What
could anyone do? A captain was responsible for everything
aboard his ship—that was the first thing a seaman learned—
and the most deadly form of contraband had been found
aboard his. He was not even resentful of Kaerko, or Sallow-
face, or Nutmeg. They were simply doing their duty.

He turned in silence, forgetting the one favour he had
been told to ask—that Gijs might accompany him. At the
foot of the companionway one little soldier stepped ahead,
the other waited, and Piet mounted between them. Kaerko
and his two companions brought up the rear. It was the same
at the ladder. Two prahaus, each with a lantern at its prow,
appeared out of the darkness. One soldier descended, Piet
followed, the second soldier completed the load. Kaerko,
Sallow-face, and Nutmeg stepped into the second craft, and
they shot away, one slightly ahead of the other, towards the
quay. Now, Piet thought from the depths of his misery, is the
time to put myself overboard; but as soon as he stirred four
little iron hands gripped him, and one of the soldiers said in a
lisping but ferocious little voice, "You will sit still, please."

They came to the quay which, fifteen minutes earlier, had
been utterly deserted. Now, under the lantern which hung
just above the landing stairs, there was something which
gave the impression of movement and the sound of women
quarrelling. Piet was too sunk in his own misery to take

much notice of what was going on, but he gathered that women were quarrelling because someone was sobbing and someone else was speaking in a high, shrill, reedy voice. Speaking Malay, too, of which Piet had only a smattering; but he recognised a few terms of abuse, which, for some reason, are the most easily and quickly acquired in any language. The shrill voice was accusing somebody of being a rogue and a fool, a careless devil and a maker of trouble. The person who was thus accused made no reply but simply wept noisily.

The foremost prahau in which Piet was travelling drew in to the steps and one soldier alighted. Piet followed and the second soldier stepped up alongside. The trio waited until the second prahau had discharged its load.

Nutmeg immediately joined his men. "All right, Kaerko," he said abruptly, "I'll go along with them and just——" A shrill, almost delirious cry from the left interrupted him.

"Mynheer Kaerko, Mynheer Kaerko," cried the voice so recently raised in invective and now changed to abject pleading. "A moment, please. I have been to your house, and no one knew where you could be found. Mynheer, please—it is of the utmost importance. A great injustice may be done to somebody unless you listen."

The group of moving shadows advanced, splitting up into its component parts, just distinguishable in the dim light, one bulky figure wrapped about in yards and yards of white cotton cloth which reminded Piet of grave-clothes, and two ordinary barelegged natives.

"Shal Ahmi," Kaerko said in a low voice and in the manner of one tried beyond all endurance. Then in a brisk yet not disrespectful tone he said, "Look, Shal Ahmi, I can't stop now. I'm very busy. I have business on hand. If you really want to see me about something of importance, come to my office in the morning."

The bulky, wrapped figure came another step forward and the womanish voice said, "But, Mynheer, this is your business. Company's business." He brought out the significant word in long, separate syllables.

"Damned impostor," said Nutmeg, moving around Piet and the little soldiers like an impatient sheep dog rounding up a flock. "I can't wait, Kaerko. Good night. Good night, Vehmeer. Come along, you, quick march."

As Piet moved forwards between his guards he heard the shrill voice saying, "Mynheer, this fellow came to me because he dared not tell his master. . . . Come forward, misbegotten, and show your face. . . . Mynheer, perhaps you recognise him, Mynheer Hoogenbeet's trusted house slave—*trusted*—and was ever trust more misplaced?"

"I can't interfere between a slave and his master, Shal Ahmi; you know that," Kaerko said. And that was all of the conversation which was audible. Piet, the two soldiers, and their commander marched briskly towards the Fort, the ominous bulk of which showed dark, with slits of light here and there, against the night sky. But they had gone only a few dozen yards when there was a bellowing sound behind them. Nutmeg said, "Halt!" and began to retrace his steps. In a few seconds his whistle sounded, and the two little soldiers, turning Piet between them and maintaining their places on either side, scuttled back. Kaerko, Vehmeer, Shal Ahmi, and the soldiers' master stood in a close knot on the quay under the lantern. The two slaves hovered in the background, and the one who had been weeping was weeping again.

"A most peculiar thing," Kaerko was saying, "and most providential. We must get to the bottom of this. We'll go to my office."

He began to walk with quick, agitated steps towards the gap in the warehouse buildings that gave upon the street. The sallow-visaged Vehmeer fell into step beside him; Nutmeg, pushing the soldiers and Piet ahead of him, followed, and Shal Ahmi with his two attendants, the one still sobbing like a child, completed the procession. Kaerko's house was just behind the warehouses, a flat-faced building flush to the street, with a front door reached by three shallow steps. Before they reached the house Piet's dazed, battered mind had realised that, judging from that sudden recall, Shal Ahmi's errand had some connection with his own business, and just as they reached the steps, he turned his head and asked, "Is it something to do with those nutmegs?"

"How should I know?" the brown-faced man snapped.

Kaerko's office, a big square room lined with shelves and containing three large tables all covered with papers, was just inside the front door. He took up a candlestick which stood on a chest in the hall and led the way in. Piet found himself halted upon almost the very spot where he had been standing on that day when Evert had come into the agent's office and found him there. How long ago that seemed. Kaerko went round lighting candles, and when the room was almost as bright as day he waved Vehmeer and Nutmeg to seats by the largest table and dropped down wearily into his own chair.

"Now, Shal Ahmi, let's have the whole story again. You tell it. That snuffling fool would confuse Solomon."

"Of your kindness give me permission to be seated, Mynheer," Shal Ahmi said. And then without waiting for Kaerko's confirmatory nod he dropped to his haunches, saying as he did so, "I have been far today and was but sitting down to my food when this squawking scourge of humanity arrived. I was half tempted to leave the matter until the morning, but, as you know, the White Lords' business is very near my heart." Very leisurely and with the greatest self-possession he arranged the folds of his spotless white clothing.

Piet looked at him with burning interest. He was a stout man, almost fat, but so smooth and sleek, so symmetrically rounded, that to call him fat would have wronged him. He reminded Piet of a seal. His head and face were entirely hairless, but the state looked so natural to him that he was no more truly described as bald than as fat. In colour he was a darkish olive, but his nose was aquiline, his lips thin, and his eyes entirely devoid of the Mongolian cast which distinguished so many of the mixed inhabitants of the islands. And his face was entirely without expression, smooth and blank as a clean slate.

"Cut the cackle, Shal Ahmi, and tell us everything you know," Kaerko said. He sounded impatient and yet, despite the "Cut the cackle," not disrespectful. And indeed, Piet thought, still staring at Shal Ahmi, there was about him something, some queer dignity and power, very difficult to assess, and yet certainly capable of blunting or even turning the edge of any insult.

"They come to me, you know, when they are uncertain or in difficulty." The roll of the hairless head included the two miserable creatures who had taken up positions behind him and, beyond them, all the coloured people of the islands. "And this misbegotten has done great mischief, as you shall hear. Mynheer Hoogenbeet entrusted him with certain special nutmegs. How were they wrapped? Lift up your head and speak boldly, you gossiper in your master's time, you sleeper in public places———"

"In a white bag tied with blue twine," said the man who had been weeping.

"In a white bag tied with blue twine," Shal Ahmi repeated. "As is known to you all, it is a habit with the perkaniers to plant seeds from trees not their own, for so the stock is strengthened, and Mynheer Hoogenbeet had entrusted this precious seed to this rogue to carry to Mynheer Vanderbosch in Lonthoir—for if it is good to change seed between plantation and plantation, how much better between island and island? And what does this fellow do? First, with the bag in his hand, he meets this one, and upon the wharf they talk for an hour under the midday sun. Then he is weary, much chatter has dulled his brain, so he puts the bag safely, as he thinks, on top of other bales on the quay and goes to sleep. When he wakes the little bag is gone. Where, he does not know. But by questioning he learns that the other bales were carried aboard the ship while he slept. And what does he do then? He goes back to his gossiping fellow and says, 'Great grief will come to me, for my master will beat me. What shall I do?' And his partner in mischief, knowing Mynheer Hoogenbeet's strong arm, bids him come to me for advice. I am weary and my stomach within me is clamourous for food, but I know as perhaps these ignorant ones do not the danger of the seed nutmegs lost between ship and shore. So I say, 'I will go to Mynheer Kaerko and perhaps, in gratitude because the thing has been reported and no time lost, he *may*—but of course I can promise nothing, for who am I to say what the White Lords will do?—be lenient. Perhaps he will get back the bag and I myself will take it to Mynheer Vanderbosch so that no anger may be roused and no beating done.' It is well known that the Honourable Company does not approve of beating. Though, were they in Mynheer Hoogenbeet's place, they, too, would see the value of blows. And I should say that I myself did beat him, not lightly, because I do not like business to disturb me at my supper."

The thin, womanish voice ceased. Piet drew great breaths of relief, feeling as though an iron band, forged around his chest by Gijs's announcement an hour ago, had burst and released his lungs.

"So that's how it happened," Kaerko said. His voice betrayed the greatness of his relief. "It was damned carelessness, which might have had the most unfortunate results. And it has given Mynheer Vehmeer, Mynheer Knol, and me a very unpleasant evening."

"*And me,*" said Piet, with such emphasis that everybody turned and looked at him.

"My dear fellow," Kaerko exclaimed. "Of course. But please be assured that our sufferings were on your account. I shall have a word to say to Hoogenbeet about this."

"Please," Shal Ahmi interrupted. "Mynheer, I know that this is your business, but if I may be allowed one word, to report the matter would be a mistake now. How, then, is this careless, long-tongued fool the better for coming to me? He came to ask my help to save himself. So many do that—all the little foolish ones. Look back, Mynheer, and think how many little quiet words have reached my ear alone. If, now, either Mynheer Hoogenbeet or Mynheer Vanderbosch know how nearly those nutmegs were lost, this foolish one will be beaten. That will not matter; he will be the better for it, I have no doubt. But word will go round that to tell Shal Ahmi is to tell the world, and no more little quiet words will come to my ear. The loss, I think, will be greater than the gain. Mark, I could promise nothing, but I *did* say, 'If you come with me and tell everything it will be better for you.' And how better if he is beaten after all? Is that plain, Mynheer? Would it not be better for me to take the little bag to Mynheer Vanderbosch and say that this one has a pain in his belly and could not finish the errand? You see, he must be back by sunrise, his errand apparently fulfilled. No real harm has been done. You could doubtless find the little bag if you looked carefully aboard the ship."

Kaerko seemed to hesitate. The sallow-faced Vehmeer spoke first.

"He's right, Kaerko. They all trust him and we benefit by their trust. This is an instance. We might drop a general hint about care in sending these sample seeds from place to place. Anything more specific would be a mistake."

Knol, he of the nutmeg face whose name had proved to be "Turnip," a grave misnomer, stood up and said briskly, "You won't want me any more then?"

"No," Kaerko said. "I'm sorry you've had all this bother. You see the force of his argument?" He nodded towards Shal Ahmi. "We won't say anything about this outside. . . ."

"You know what I think of Shal Ahmi and everything to do with him," Knol snapped. "But what I think doesn't count. You gentlemen run the place and only send for me when you get in a mess. Come on, you. Back to barracks."

"They won't talk?" Kaerko said. It was more a question than a statement.

"God bless you, they never listen to anything but orders. And I don't give them time for compound gossip. Good night, Vehmeer. Good night, Kaerko." He turned, most surprisingly, to Piet and said with a smile that wrinkled his face more than ever, "Good night, Captain. I'm glad you've been cleared. Personally, I never thought you looked like a smuggler. But then, as I said before, what I think doesn't count. Good voyage."

Shal Ahmi, who was seated near the door, rose and stood aside. Knol and his two little soldiers stepped out briskly. "We have your leave to go?" Shal Ahmi asked. "These are not supposed to be wandering in darkness, and my supper will now be cold."

"Stop by my kitchen," Kaerko said, "and eat your fill, Shal Ahmi. I am grateful to you for what you have done tonight. Give him the bag, will you, Vehmeer? It won't be needed for evidence now."

"These, also, have missed their supper. And it would be a good thing to reward frankness," said Shal Ahmi, indicating his two companions.

Kaerko laughed. "Get along then. And say that I said you could have one drink of tapi apiece. One, no more, remember."

"The hospitality of gratitude is very sweet. Good night, Mynheer," Shal Ahmi said, hustling his fellows before him much as Knol had done.

"Good night," Kaerko said. And then, turning to Piet and Vehmeer, he spoke in a different, relaxed, cheerful voice. "And now I think we should drink too. I'm sorry the thing happened, Captain Odshoorn, but I'm sure you understand my position. And the outcome proves, doesn't it, that Knol and the rest of them are wrong about Shal Ahmi? He can be very, very useful."

He opened a cupboard as he spoke and took out a bottle of Marsala and three glasses.

"Who is he?" Piet asked curiously.

"Shal Ahmi? It's rather difficult to say. A kind of holy man, I suppose," Kaerko said vaguely. "The natives set a lot of store by him."

Vehmeer, whose voice was soft and rather pleasant, said, "To appreciate him properly you need to have lived here before he came—as I did. You see, Captain Odshoorn, the labour situation here is unique. There are no Bandanese *natives*. Most of them died fighting Coen; a great number more Coen killed in the effort to subdue them and make them work; a few got away to the Kei Islands. I'm told that they've settled in two villages called Banda Elat and Banda Eli, where they still carry on with their pottery and ironwork, which they say is the best in all the East Indies. When I—and Evert Haan and a few other old originals—took up our grants, the nutmeg groves that were still standing were just rotting for lack of labour. The Company imported slaves from all over the place—Java, Siauw, Amboina—anywhere where they could spare a few. And there's nothing—or rather there was nothing—to hold the creatures together."

Vehmeer warmed to his subject, cradling his glass of wine between his hands and leaning forward over it, speaking eagerly. "They weren't of the same religion; some were Hindu, some Mahommedan, some had been turned Catholic by the Portuguese, and some were just wild pagans; they weren't of the same blood or the same language. There was nothing you could get hold of, nobody you could treat with and say, 'Look here, if you'll see the work's done and the rules kept we'll see that you get your pickings.' That's how you can talk to a native chief or a Chinese headman. It makes things a lot easier. We had the devil's own job for a year or two, and then Shal Ahmi arrived. What exactly he is or where he came from nobody really knows, but nobody cares because he has got the measure of the native foot. Even the Chinese fear and respect him. All the coloured people, whatever their private creed, firmly believe that if he curses them they're finished, and it is a remarkable fact that one or two people who have offended him have come to funny ends. I don't think I'd willingly offend him myself. I don't say I'm superstitious, but I should sort of expect things to go wrong if he really got busy against me. What d'you say, Kaerko?"

The agent looked uncomfortable. "It isn't that so much," he said after a little pause. "But he is clever, very shrewd, and a very good friend of the Company's. Look at tonight. But for him we'd have Captain Odshoorn in the Fort and the business of finding a master for the *Eastern Venture* on our hands. Even if Hoogenbeet reported the business—supposing that little yellow fool was found out, which he wouldn't be till Hoogenbeet and Vanderbosch met, and even then

Hoogenbeet mightn't bother to tell me—look at the waste of time. Over and over again I've found Shal Ahmi a very present help. Knol hates the sight of him, and I don't think your cousin, Mynheer Haan, approves of him much, Captain Odshoorn."

"Maybe he'll change his mind after tonight," Piet said. Thus reminded of Evert, he began to wonder what steps his kinsman had taken to help him. Was he busying and worrying himself at this moment? And from Evert his mind flew to Gijs. He must get back and end that poor little devil's anxiety. He stood up.

"Well," he said, "I'll get back. I still feel a bit muddled in my head. But I'm happy to think I'm sailing in the morning after all."

Kaerko, looking at him, thought merely what a good thing it was that a first-rate captain was not out of commission. Vehmeer, of a more fanciful turn of mind, thought that the big man looked like an ox which, after one blow from the poleaxe, has escaped from the slaughter-house. It would be days, he thought, before the captain really realised the narrowness of his escape.

"Good night," Piet said. The two men shook him by the hand and wished him a good voyage. He stumbled out to the water front and found Gijs, half demented, walking up and down on the quay.

"Holy Christ," Gijs exclaimed, gripping Piet's hand in his, which burned and shook as though from a consuming fever, "what happened? They've turned you loose? Did they find who put the things there?"

"Yes. It was an accident. It's all right, Gijs. Everything's all right. Let's get back to the old tub." He was too tired to tell the whole story just then. He wanted to get back to his ship, to walk into his cabin and find it completely his own again, to wipe out the shocking memory of Kaerko, Knol, and Vehmeer occupying his chair, his bench, and his bunk.

But when a few minutes later, followed by Gijs, he descended to his cabin, there was still something strange about it. A woven basket of native workmanship, tied at the top with thongs and bearing the official seal which showed that it had been inspected and passed for lading, stood on the table where so lately the damning bag of nutmegs had lain.

"What's this?" Piet asked.

"Oh, that came just after you'd gone. A Company runner brought it. I'd have brought it with me, but I thought if they'd got you in the Fort they might take it away from me before they let me in."

Piet sat down at the table and drew the basket towards him, while Gijs knelt at his side and began to remove his boots. The thongs of the basket untied easily. In the basket was a bottle of the Everett brandy which had cost Evert a "pretty penny" and a smaller basket containing some choice fruit; and below these were certain papers enclosed in stout wrapping, a muslin-wrapped box, and a glove. At the very bottom of the basket was a single sheet of paper upon which were written the words:

"If you are at liberty to do my errand you will not, I trust, think that I ask too much."

Piet stared at the words, but while his eyes were busy with them his ears were hearing Evert say, "I'll do what I can." What had Evert done? Was it possible that Shal Ahmi and the two natives with their carefully concocted tale had been Evert's tools? Their arrival on the quay so apt and timely, their story so simple and conclusive . . . He remembered suddenly Shal Ahmi's arguments against letting Hoogenbeet and Vanderbosch know of the accident. Of course—because Hoogenbeet had never sent the samples of seed to Vanderbosch. Evert had made up the whole story, selected his actors and got them word-perfect, and staged the whole thing in less than an hour.

"My God," he said aloud.

Gijs looked up inquiringly.

"Ko-bet Haan must have been a mighty clever woman," Piet said, to Gijs's further bewilderment. "It must be her head he inherited. . . . I'm sorry, boy, you must think I'm crazy, and it's a wonder I'm not. Take a look at this. That— half brother of mine I was telling you about is sending them to the lady of his choice. Aren't they wonderful?"

He worked the secret spring of the box and flashed the jewels before Gijs's eyes. The little man looked at them without interest.

"Your feet are like stones," he said solicitously. "That's shock. I'm going to get a bucket of hot water, and you're going to put them in it."

As soon as he was alone Piet returned the glove, the inlaid box, and the papers to the basket and tied the thongs. Then, padding in his stockinged feet, he carried them to a hiding place under his bunk. He was too tired, too much exhausted by the events of the day, to have energy enough to imagine

his feelings when, despite all his protests and doubts, he
would carry them along to the bleak white house and face
Mevrouw and perform Evert's errand. But he knew that he
would do it.

Seven months, two weeks, and three days later, dressed in
his best, his beard brushed glossy and his spirit fortified by
two glasses of schnapps, which was as much as he dared take
for fear of muddling his head and bringing disgrace upon his
family, he set out from the trim little cottage in Heydberg
and walked towards the Van Goens house. In his hand he
carried the basket with its thongs untied; the edges bulged,
for on top of the articles which Evert had committed to his
care was a three-pound packet of tea and as much pepper,
cinnamon, mace, cloves, and nutmegs as could be bought in
the grocer's shop for seventy guilders. For some years, ever
since Piet had attained captain's status and gained the
privilege of carrying a limited amount of merchandise for his
own private disposal, he had, at each home-coming, made a
little offering to Mevrouw van Goens.

Old Truitje, the one servant who remained with Mevrouw and who did almost all the work in the bleak white
house, greeted Piet as usual. She remembered him from the
Janshaven days, and her old eyes always twinkled as she
punctiliously called him "Captain."

"Ha, a basket this time too," she said, stretching out her
hand. "Very pretty, and very useful. Thank you very much,
Captain."

Piet swung the basket out of reach. "You can take this,
and this," he said, handing over the tea and the spices. "And
later on you can have the basket. But just at the moment,
Truitje—I—would it be convenient—could I speak to Mevrouw for a moment?"

"I should think so," said Truitje, looking at him and then
at the basket, curiously. "Come in and I'll ask."

Piet stepped over the threshold and stood in the dark
passage. Through an open door he could see the kitchen,
with a small fire and Truitje's old rocking chair and the cat
curled up on the rug and the pot of almost-open hyacinths
upon the window sill. So homey-looking and with such a
homey smell, too; and he remembered the kitchen quarters
of the big house at Janshaven, with the menservants and the
maidservants tumbling over one another. He wondered if
Truitje found life lonely. He thought his idle thoughts des-

perately, as he had been thinking for quite a long time of any matter, however trivial and silly, which would take his mind off the fact that at last he must look Mevrouw in the face and hand Evert's papers to her and watch her gracious smile wither and the look of furious anger and insulted pride take its place. Even in this last moment he was tempted to turn and slink out of the house before Truitje came back; and then he remembered the moment when Knol and the two little soldiers had turned towards the Fort at Banda Neira, and the voice crying after them in the night, and the sweet feeling of resurrection which had come with the telling of Shal Ahmi's story. So he stood in the dim passage, looking solid and stolid and slightly stupid, when Truitje hobbled back to say that Mevrouw would be very pleased to speak to him.

He followed the old woman the length of the passage and into a square stone-paved hall which, even on this mild spring evening, struck very cold. Truitje opened a door and Piet, with as stomach-shaking a spasm of nervousness as he had ever felt in his life, stepped into the candlelighted room, clapped his hat to his waistline, and bowed above it.

Mevrouw was still some months short of forty, but grief and anxiety and what counted to the once-pampered beauty as privation had aged her. Save at the extreme ends, where a glint of gold still lingered as though in mockery, her plentiful hair was snowy white, and the delicate pink-and-white porcelain surface of her face was scored with myriad lines, many of them graved by discontent and peevishness. But the perfunctory social smile with which she greeted Piet and bade him be seated was dazzlingly sweet, and the big man's stomach quaked again as he thought how quickly and completely the announcement of his mission would remove it.

"Truitje tells me that you have brought me some tea, Captain Odshoorn," Mevrouw said, seating herself upon a small straight-backed chair and folding her slim white hands upon her silken lap. "It is indeed very kind of you."

"Not at all, Mevrouw. A pleasure, I assure you," said Piet, hearing his own voice, stiff and wooden. Did she think he had pushed his way into her drawing room merely to collect a personal word of thanks? Horrible.

"I trust you had a pleasant voyage."

"Thank you, yes, Mevrouw. Less sickness than usual and no accidents." Covertly his eyes, which he averted because he was conscious of a desire to stare at her face, took in the details of the room. To his eyes, accustomed to cabins and cottage rooms, the room seemed large and sparsely furnished. Everything in it was old and worn; and he guessed, correctly, that everything which had been of value had gone the way of the other Van Goens property. He tried to hearten himself by thinking of Evert's beautiful house, so full of comfort, and evidence of its owner's wealth; but the thought made him feel worse, not better. It occurred to him that the only marketable thing left to Mevrouw was the desirability of her daughters; and he had come, like a huckster's errand boy, to make a bid for that. He cleared his throat as quietly as possible and plunged into speech before any further thoughts should come into his head to discourage him.

"Mevrouw, I have come to do an errand which I find little to my taste. Before I begin I want you to understand that it was forced upon me and, except to say the words and hand over the stuff, I have no part in the business at all."

The wary look which comes easily to those whose confidence in life has once been shattered flashed into Mevrouw's still-blue eyes. Had some creditor chosen this method of presenting his case, counting upon the big man's chance of gaining access to the house?

"My last voyage took me to Banda, Mevrouw," Piet plodded on. "Do you remember Evert Haan, my father's other son?"

"Indeed I do. Your father wanted him to take on the tenant rights, but my dear husband's father never approved of that marriage, you know, so he refused to make the arrangement." Then she leaned forward and said quite sweetly, but with great earnestness, "You do realise, don't you, Captain Odshoorn, that even if I wished to do anything for your half brother I am quite powerless now?"

"Oh yes, Mevrouw. That's all forgotten. Evert didn't stay in Janshaven; he didn't want to be a farmer after all. He went to Banda and took up nutmeg planting. The long and the short of it is, Mevrouw, that Evert has made a fortune and he—at least I—I mean——— Look."

Finally bogged down, as he had known he would be, he gave up the effort to explain his position, opened the basket, took out the papers, the box, and the glove, and laid them on the little table which stood between the chairs upon which he and Mevrouw Van Goens were sitting, then stood to attention, ready to bid her "Good evening" and retreat in good order. But Mevrouw, who had opened the wrapping of the papers, was reading the uppermost one with eyes that seemed not to take in the words quickly enough. Without looking up she freed one hand and waved it in a gesture which ordered him to sit down again and not speak until she asked him to. Unwillingly he obeyed her.

She read every word of the letter and of the marriage contract and then absorbed the particulars of the banker's draft in one greedy stare. When she had finished she touched the papers so that their edges were level and leaned back in her chair, her head resting against its high narrow back.

When she did speak she asked the question which he had secretly dreaded all along; the question he had tried to avoid by removing himself before it could be asked.

"Who brought my daughter to Mynheer Haan's attention, Captain Odshoorn?"

"I'm afraid I did, Mevrouw," gasped Piet, sweating coldly. "But I swear no such idea was in my mind. We were—we were talking about Janshaven and the old days, and I said in all innocence—I do beg you to believe me, Mervouw—in all innocence I said it, that Mynheer Adriaan, whom Evert remembered, had three lovely daughers. Mevrouw, you must forgive Evert; he has lived abroad for a long time where things are very different, and in Banda he is reckoned an important man. He is very rich. And Evert always did have big ideas, Mevrouw."

Mevrouw's face remained inscrutable. Suddenly Piet realised that she had seen only the papers. He leaned forward, ripped the muslin wrapping from the box, fumbled with the spring, worked it at last, and then, getting to his feet, laid the open box with its glittering treasure in her lap. He heard her draw her breath sharply. But she stared at the jewels without making any comment, and when she spoke her voice was steady. "Show me, please, how the box opens and closes."

Piet showed her. She opened and closed it several times, as though to make certain that she had mastered the secret, and then stood the casket on the table.

"And that, I take it, is the glove."

Piet nodded. She did not look inside the wrapping. Piet had remained standing, and Mevrouw now rose to her feet. She held out one hand.

"Captain Odshoorn, whatever comes of this, I am deeply

grateful to you. Naturally a decision of such magnitude can not be made in a hurry, nor by me alone. As soon as anything is decided I will let you know. Meanwhile, may I ask you a favour?"

"Certainly, Mevrouw. Anything." He was so grateful that she had let him down thus lightly that there was nothing he would not, at that moment, have done to repay her for her restraint.

"Then don't mention this matter to anyone. In a small place—you know what gossip is—and a young girl's reputation . . ." She left the sentence incomplete, obscure, but Piet felt as though he had been honoured by a confidence.

She gave him another smile, warm, friendly; a smile which struck away the years and the graven marks of anxiety, discontent, and self-pity. "Good night, Captain. I shall see you again."

"Good night, Mevrouw." He made another bow and left. Dusk had fallen during the interval, and outside the dark blue sky was scattered with stars and the air smelled of green things growing. For the first time since he had docked he felt the uprush of joy and well-being which always came to him on shore leave in Holland. He would have said that he loved the sea, but buried deeply in him was the farmer whom Evert had driven forth from his familiar acres, and the scent of a cow byre could still rouse more feeling in him than all the Moluccas in full bloom. He was perfectly happy tonight: his task was fulfilled, his debt to Evert paid; now he could begin to enjoy himself. Mevrouw, being a lady, would probably write Evert a chilly little refusal, and if she should ask him to carry it, together with the rejected jewels and glove, back to Banda on his next trip, well, that would be an errand more to his taste. In a very cheerful frame of mind he rolled into his favourite tavern with the comfortable assurance that if he were unable to walk home plenty of friendly arms and shoulders would be at his disposal, his mother would be neither surprised nor disgusted, and the sacred Company would have no grounds for complaint.

A week passed, and four days of another, and there was no word from Mevrouw. Then, returning home from a happy day's fishing, he received a message that Mevrouw van Goens would be much obliged if he would call on her at any hour between six and nine that evening.

He was afraid as he neared the house that Mevrouw would have assembled a whole family to witness the discomfiture of Evert's messenger. But Elsa van Goens was alone, just as she had been on the evening when he had first entered her house. And her manner was even more affable.

"I hope I'm not making too many demands upon your time and your kindness," she began as soon as he had lowered himself cautiously into a chair. "But in any case, I feel that you, as Mynheer Haan's kinsman, will understand."

"Yes?" Piet said.

"I sent for my son," Mevrouw's sweet low voice continued. "He and other members of the family talked the matter over thoroughly and advised me on the final decision. A reply was despatched to Mynheer Haan by the *Great Holland*, she sailed on Tuesday. That should, normally, have been the end of the business so far as you are concerned, Captain Odshoorn. But my daughter has taken a fancy to see you. Quite understandable, if you come to think about it. You have actually seen, within these last few months, the man she is to marry."

"To marry? You mean"—his eyes blinked at her, blank with astonishment—"that you accepted Evert's proposal?"

Mevrouw's slim white hands moved in a little deprecating gesture.

"Not, I should tell you, without considerable misgiving. Banda is *so* far away. I shall lose my daughter so entirely. But, Captain Odshoorn, my feelings must give way to the question of what is best for Annabet. I will be frank with you and admit that in my place, a widow in very straitened circumstances with three daughters, one of my gravest worries has been the thought of what will happen to them. When I am gone. . . ." She added the last words with a piteous little look, implying that while she lived the girls would lack nothing—her own self-sacrifice would see to that—but that the end was near now. Piet shifted uncomfortably in his chair. Mevrouw sighed. Then she braced herself and said more firmly, "Mynheer Haan's proposal was properly made, acceptable in every sense. My son visited one of the directors of the Company, who gave a very favourable account of his position and character. We did not act rashly. I think"—she put her head on one side and regarded him enquiringly—"I think you feel perhaps that we have been a little rash?"

"No," Piet said. No, he was certain that the family

gathering had decided nothing in a hurry. Everything would be considered. Under all this lacy foam of mother love and anxiety the rock of practical consideration lay firm and rooted.

Why, now that he was close to her, being offered her confidence, treated like a friend, was his feeling for Mevrouw undergoing a change? Why, when she spoke of being a widow in straitened circumstances, had he felt, not the expected pity, but a kind of embarrassed scorn? Why did this whole interview stink of humbug?

"I don't reckon I favour glove marriages much," he said bluntly, answering his own questions aloud.

"I'm not sure that I do either," said Mevrouw in instant agreement. "But after all, this isn't quite an ordinary one. We do know something about the bridegroom. And you are here to tell us more. That is why Annabet is so set on seeing you. She wants to know what he looks like—all the little intimate personal things."

Oh, but this was worse than being chucked out on his ear! He'd been steered into carrying the damned papers and the parcel for Evert; now he was being tacked into giving Evert a character.

"It's little enough I know about him. Till I saw him in Banda I'd not run across him for thirty years, Mevrouw. I can't say what sort of husband he'd make."

He had a vision of Evert's hands gripping the brown girl's little narrow shoulders. But you couldn't hold that against him. Any man, exasperated, would use that much violence. And you couldn't hold the girl's presence against him either. Any man who'd lived in the islands for twenty years would have a mistress of some sort. Or something worse, thought Piet, remembering the insolent, painted, bejewelled little boys he had seen.

"Of course not," Mevrouw agreed again. "You had heard, perhaps, Captain Odshoorn, that my daughter had been ill?"

"No. I'm sorry to hear that."

"Oh, she is better now; well on the way to complete recovery. But being ill, of course, has made her fanciful and low-spirited. I look to you to cheer her up a little. You can tell her about Banda. I believe it is a beautiful place."

"Very beautiful. And Evert has a fine establishment."

"That's the kind of thing, Captain Odshoorn. I want her to realise that really she is a very lucky girl."

Piet's mind, which held a certain shrewdness in its

homespun simplicity, could see through *that* well enough. The family was in favour of the match; the girl was dubious. He was to spin a yarn that would set her doubts at rest. It was disgusting. Mevrouw was a greedy humbug, and Evert was a greedy upstart. And between them the girl stood defenceless. He thought of the sweetness of the face which had beguiled the dull sermon hour for him, and something like real physical pain smote his heart.

Mevrouw rose and pulled the bell rope.

"Annabet's looks have suffered through her illness," she said casually over her shoulder. "But we ignore that. She'll recover them in time."

The bell had evidently been a prearranged signal, for now the door opened quietly and somebody entered. Piet jumped to his feet and then stood struck dumb, staring.

Later on in the interview he realised that the girl was still recognisable, just as some old people are recognisable to others who knew them in youth; but at the first glance, in that first horrified moment, he thought that had he not been expecting Juffrouw Annabet, had he passed this apparition in the village street or seen it in church, he would have thought the poor girl a stranger.

She was, literally, nothing but skin and bones, so skeleton-thin that the very gristle of her nose could be traced by its pressure against the skin. Her dress, new and elaborate, ruffled and padded and much befrilled, hung limp and empty, like a gown suspended from a peg. And all that marvellous wealth of downpouring yellow hair was gone.

True, no effort to make her presentable had been spared. The hollow cheeks had been painted; the pen-sharp nose and bony forehead and stringy neck were powdered pearl colour; her mouth was as red as a rose. And upon her head she wore a little cap of velvet matching her gown, edged with lace and looped with ribbon. But, like the stiff, rich gown, the paint and the powder and the little cape all failed in their purpose; made, in fact, grotesque what was simple tragedy.

Piet, still staring in horror, was recalled to his senses by Mevrouw's voice, even, sweet, ordinary, and realised that he was expected to take his part in this elaborate, horrible harlequinade.

"Annabet, my dear, here is Captain Odshoorn. He has kindly come to tell you everything you want to know about Banda. Come and sit down."

Piet bowed in his clumsy, inexpert fashion. Annabet

inclined her head stiffly and came slowly across to the chair
which her mother pushed forward as though to shorten that
jerky, wooden progress. But she's lame, Piet thought wildly.
She's lame, and her head's a bit on one side; my God, it's as
much as she can do to sit down. He felt sick. He wanted to
get up and shout at Mevrouw; tell her to put the skeleton
child to bed; ask her with curses how she could ever have
been so mad and wicked as to contemplate for one moment
sending this pitiable wreck to Banda or anywhere else as the
wife of Evert or any man alive. It was obscene.

But the *Great Holland* had sailed on Tuesday, carrying
Mevrouw's reply. Nothing could alter that now.

Mevrouw van Goens felt that the silence had lasted long
enough and leaned forward, ready to speak again, when Piet,
also aware of it, said gruffly, "I shall be glad to tell you anything I can, Juffrouw."

"I shall be very grateful," Annabet said, and gave him a
half-smile, a formal, rather plaintive recognition of his desire
to please. Her mouth was still pretty, he thought. Too large,
of course, in that narrow wedge of a face, but pretty. She
leaned back stiffly in her chair and folded her hands—no
more substantial than a bird's claws—in her lap and waited.

Mevrouw leaned forward again. "Captain Odshoorn says
that Banda is a very beautiful place," she said promptingly.

"Indeed? I am glad," Annabet said.

"Oh yes, indeed. One of the prettiest places I've seen. And
I've seen many places."

This interview was not of the girl's seeking, he decided.
And could you wonder? What room could there be in her
mind for anything but the fact that she had been pretty and
was now as ugly as sin and was going to be married off to a
man she'd never seen and who was expecting a beauty?

The girl gave him grave attention as he jerked out the bald
mind for anything but the fact that she had been pretty and
quickly the garden was getting settled. Sounds as though I'm
boasting about Evert's house, he thought suddenly, and
stopped, embarrassed. Her eyes at least were beautiful, he
realised. Such a deep blue between dark lashes, each one just
tipped with gold, the colour her hair had been. Oh, what on
God's earth could have happened to that lovely, lovely girl?
What could have stripped off all the flesh, stiffened every
joint, taken away all that beautiful, beautiful hair?

"And she won't be lonely, will she, Captain Odshoorn?
It's a civilised place, plenty of white women, a social life of

its own. Quite a gay place, I believe I remember hearing."

A gay place. Piet felt sick again. Evert had wanted a pretty, young, well-bred wife to sit at one end of his table. He'd said as much. *She* would have had a gay life.

"Captain Odshoorn says——" said Mevrouw relentlessly, prodding him forward again. "Yes, Truitje, what is it?" The door had opened an inch or two and the old woman's face, wearing an expression of urgency, was poked around its edge. Mevrouw rose and went over swiftly. Piet jumped to his feet and said with finality, "I don't think there's much more to say. I'd best be getting along."

"Sh," said Mevrouw, hushing Truitje. "No, please don't go, Captain Odshoorn. Annabet, offer Captain Odshoorn a glass of wine. I'll be back in a minute. . . ."

She rustled out of the doorway. Piet sat down again, awkward, defeated. He glanced at Annabet and saw that all in a minute she had come to life. That was it. Up to that moment she had not only looked like a death's-head, she had been dead, just a stiff, wooden-jointed, painted thing with Annabet van Goens's eyes and mouth. Now, despite everything, she looked like herself.

"You are disgusted by this whole business, aren't you?" she said. "I'm sorry. I do apologise. Mamma—you see, she has to pretend to herself so often. It gets to be a habit. She's pretending now that everything is all right. Do forgive my speaking to you like this. Really, I get so puzzled that at times I'm almost distraught. And I'm forgetting the wine. . . ." She rose stiffly.

"Juffrouw, please don't bother. I don't——"

"Ah, but please. Look, it's Truitje's very best. Rhubarb. As good as any French wine, I assure you. And Mamma meant it all so well. You were to tell me all the nice things about Banda and about Mynheer Haan—your half brother, isn't he? And then we were all to drink—my health, I suppose. It just happens that you and I aren't very good at pretending, but we must try." She gave him a smile that was quite dazzling upon that ravaged face, and Piet knew another pang. Ah, but she's lovely still, and friendly and real. But will Evert see that? Always supposing that she gets as far as Banda.

She hobbled towards him, a glass of pale yellow liquid in either hand. He accepted his, held it up ceremoniously, and said earnestly, "To your happiness, Juffrouw."

"Thank you. Thank you very much." She was silent for a

moment. Then she said, "You were shocked when you saw me. I have been very ill, you know. Entirely through my own fault, too."

She must hang onto that belief or she would be overwhelmed again by self-pity and come to hate Klara, whom she loved. She must remember that she had gone to the Ice Fair on Whitwater of her own free will. But as she spoke the whole sequence of events flashed before her. Klara seizing upon this chance to meet her secret lover. "Do come, Nab, you'd enjoy it too." And the winters so long and dull, nothing happening. Mamma saying that young ladies could not possibly go unescorted. Her own almost automatic protest, "Surely, Mamma, three of us together. In the daylight. And out of doors." Mamma weakening at that; anxious, really, for them to be happy; seeing in her mind's eye the three girls, aloof, arms linked, skating through the torchlighted hours of the brief afternoon. Klara's wild gratitude: "I'll do something for you one day, Nab." And the brief, pitying thought, what could you do for me, you silly girl? Maria protesting that she would rather spend the afternoon by the fire, too young to be in Klara's confidence, too languid to know Annabet's desire for something, anything, to vary the days. Maria overruled, bribed, Klara saying, "You can have my coral necklace." Herself offering her fur hood. "You *can't* be cold in my fur hood."

So they had gone, and in the first five minutes Klara had snapped a skate strap and retired to the bank of the Whitwater, hidden by all the booths and the people. Annabet and Maria had skated together to keep warm, and all the time Annabet had been thinking, What can she see in him? What is it that attracts her to that uncouth, hot-handed, stammering young man? Maria had worried about Klara, and Annabet had several times declared that she could see her amongst the crowds, now at this booth, now at that. Finally, when the early dusk was falling and the sky reddened behind the barrier of dark snow clouds, Annabet allowed Maria to leave the ice. "I saw Klara a second ago by the roast-chestnut stand," she said untruthfully. That was the place of meeting arranged before the skate strap broke. But Klara was not there when they arrived, and it was Annabet's turn to grow anxious about her. Maria was for combing the crowd, but Annabet said with apparently senseless obstinacy, "No, it is better to stand still in one place." Snow began to fall, a few annunciatory flakes at first, then a veritable storm. Maria began to cry from cold and anxiety, whimpering, "After all, your cloak is fur-lined, Nab. I'm perishing of cold. "Have it," said Annabet violently, and swung the garment from her shoulders onto those of her sister.

Klara appeared, breathless and apologetic. Annabet's rebukes were forced from between chattering teeth. The shoulders and sleeves of her bodice were wet from snow, and her feet were soaked because her shoes needed soling.

By the time they had run home Annabet was shaking and shivering so violently that nobody in the house had time to think of anything but warm blankets, hot possets of blackcurrant tea, and bricks wrapped in flannel. And then there had been the days of fever, the delirium, the copious bleedings, the cutting of the hair, partly to relieve the burning head, partly because it was already falling out so fast, and partly because it was a recognised process in fever cases. And then there had been the awful return to life, the knowledge of beauty vanished, the protruding bones, the cropped head, the pain and stiffness of certain joints which remained after the full tide of pain and stiffness had receded.

But she must say that it was her own fault. Because, besides the danger of self-pity and the danger of hating Klara, there was another reason. Father Vincent had spoken of the way of acceptance, and although like many other things he had said, that had been a little vague and mysterious, she knew that it meant not blaming others for the results of your own folly: it meant lying down, not rebelling, not trying to wriggle out of things.

So now she said, "Entirely through my own fault," and saw the look of pity upon the big weather-beaten face opposite her change to something else.

"The doctors hold out the hope that I may, in time, get really better," she said quickly. "It's a pity that *this* should have happened before we had time to know. I suppose that when you were talking of me—Mamma said you were the person who spoke of me to Mynheer Haan—you said I was—well, you know—all right—like other girls. He'd ask you, surely, what I looked like."

"I said you were beautiful," said Piet thickly.

She pressed her hands against her mouth, and he saw her eyes close, pressing against the tears. Oh God, this was as bad as—no, by Christ's wounds, it was worse than—that moment when the nutmegs were found in the cargo. If he had taken his bad luck then he wouldn't have been in this position now. She was so brave, fighting back tears at this moment, so charming—with a charm Evert wouldn't see—handed over just because of the blasted money, and too late, too late to say anything—except the truth.

"Juffrouw, I said you were beautiful. And you are beautiful. You've been ill and the sickness has wasted your flesh. But your eyes haven't changed. Nor your mouth. And your smile is beautiful still."

"But the stiffness? You mean to be kind, Captain Odshoorn, and I thank you for it. You see, I've seen no one outside my family since it happened—since this awful thing happened to me. And my family is so divided. Egbert, my brother, and my sister Klara are against it—against the marriage, I mean. Everybody else says it is a marvellous chance for me. They talk of the rest I shall have on the voyage, and of the warm climate. And the alternative which Mamma suggested seems worse to me."

"And that, Juffrouw? What was the alternative?"

"Mamma has a cousin; she rules a house of Poor Clares in County Down, in Ireland. She would accept me. But, Captain Odshoorn, I have no vocation. It was, truly, a choice between the two. Cheating God or man. My illness cost a great deal. I'm useless. Naturally Mamma is anxious to settle my future. It was Ireland or Banda. I chose. Was I wrong? Captain Odshoorn, I know this isn't what you expected; you didn't come here to deal with this kind of thing; it isn't fair to ask you—but there is time still. I'm not married yet. I'm so puzzled and bewildered. . . . I don't know what to think or what to do."

Not a convent, not a house of Poor Clares in Ireland. You'd be wasted there. You're skin and bones and stiff in your joints, but, by God, I'd marry you myself tonight. Daft as it sounds, you have something better than prettiness; you make a man your friend. There's something in you that'd be wasted in a convent—something that made me pick you from across the church. . . . That hasn't gone with your pink-and-white flesh and your yellow hair. Stripped of them all, you're still the woman that we dream of when we're hundreds of miles from any woman. The woman who meets us fairly, the friend.

He was amazed by the lucidity and force of his thoughts; and appalled, too, because none of them could be put into words. He must sit like a stuck pig, thinking these true but unutterable things, while the girl's eyes sought his, appealing. Oh, if only he could have said, "I brought you into this position; I'll get you out of it." Oh, if only he could have offered some other alternative. Something that would have been right for her mind and her body. The present choice was too harsh, too wide. The convent would be best for that poor shattered body—there was no denying that—yet everything that was Protestant in him, as well as his own vigorous lust for life, rose up and cried, No, not that. Yet there was Evert, soon to hear that his suit had found favour, soon to be preparing for a young pink and white and golden bride.

"Juffrouw," he said at last, "is there no third way? Must it all be decided in such a hurry? Given time——"

"I might get well. But by that time the chance of making an advantageous marriage will be gone. I do see the force of Mamma's arguments. To one in her position daughters, even when they are sound and well, present a great problem. If only——" She pressed her hand to her mouth again, fought and conquered the weakness of self-pity, and then said quite brightly, "Haven't you noticed that directly you have made a choice the alternative seems more attractive, or at least more sensible? I'm quite sure that if I had decided upon going to Ireland I should be just as certain that I had chosen badly. Please don't look so distressed, Captain Odshoorn. I had no right to talk to you like this. I'm sure you have bothers enough of your own. And it was most kind of you to come to tell me things. Could you describe your half brother for me?"

"Well," said Piet, gathering his scattering senses, "he's much my build. My colouring, too, now I come to think about it. But he's much handsomer. He always was a good-looking fellow and he's kept his looks. From what I could see during my visit, he's very popular, too." What could you say about Evert? If only you could be sure that he would be kind—but then, could you really count on any man being kind in such circumstances?

Mevrouw had opened the door and entered so quietly that when she spoke Piet jumped nervously, wondering how long she had been in the room and how much she had overheard. Only the last sentences, he decided, judging from her pleased and complacent look of approval.

"If what you say is true, Mynheer Haan must be almost *too* handsome, Captain Odshoorn. Well, Annabet, it's time for you to take your last little walk around the garden. We mustn't neglect your exercise. Then Truitje will have your milk ready. We still treat her like an invalid," she explained with a smile for Piet.

He was being dismissed too. He rose.

Annabet moved stiffly towards him and held out her hand.

"Good-bye, Captain Odshoorn, and thank you so much. I do hope that whenever you come to Banda you will look on my house as your home."

His great brown fist closed over the little clawlike hand, and as it did so a pang that was half pain and half pleasure shot through him. And with it came a determination which made his heart hammer at the thought of his own audacity. He said good-bye, wished her a rapid recovery and great happiness in a voice that was suddenly breathless. He watched her heartbreaking progress to the door and then, instead of taking his leave of Mevrouw, as he was plainly expected to do, he closed the door and turned back.

"Mevrouw, you can't do this to her. It isn't right. It isn't decent."

"Why, Captain Odshoorn, what are you talking about?" Her manner, her voice remained unruffled, but the pupils of her blue eyes had narrowed to pin points and she looked like a startled, defensive cat.

"Sending her to Banda like that. Evert's a man set in his ways and masterful; he likes to get what he wants. And what he wants, what he expects, is a lovely young girl I told him about, may God forgive me for it. He'll be so shocked and disappointed, he might—he mightn't even be kind to her." His whole heart cried out the last words.

"What utter nonsense," Mevrouw said quite lightly. "Annabet may be perfectly well by the time she reaches Banda. And even if that is too much to hope, there is surely no reason to suppose that her husband would be unkind to her. I have known men to be devoted to extremely unattractive women. Haven't you?"

"Yes. If they chose them that way, or watched them get that way through years of living together. But, Mevrouw, put yourself in Evert's place for a minute. Wouldn't you feel cheated? And a man who's feeling cheated isn't very good company."

Mevrouw's face hardened.

"You are saying some very strange things, Captain

Odshoorn. Cheated. Why should the man feel cheated? He wished to marry my daughter, my second daughter, Annabet van Goens; there was no stipulation that she should be beautiful, or supple, or even in good health. So why should he feel cheated?"

"I put it to you the wrong way," Piet said humbly. "I always do put things the wrong way. I wasn't thinking about Evert's bargain being a bad one. She's too good for him. That's what I'm trying to tell you, Mevrouw. It's her happiness I'm thinking of."

Mevrouw fenced again. "That is a very strange thing to say, surely. You, Captain Odshoorn, are the person who suggested this marriage in the first place. If Annabet, with her superb looks and good health and high spirits, wasn't too good for your kinsman several months ago, how can she be too good for him now, when her looks are gone and she is moody and difficult? What exactly do you mean?"

"She'd have held her own with him then. That's what I mean. Evert was never a one to be content with second best. He'd never handle a cracked thing or a weak thing carefully just on the account of it being cracked or weak. He said to me, Mevrouw, when I said I didn't favour glove marriages, that all he wanted was a pretty, high-born wife to grace his house and do him credit. Is he going to take kindly to—to your daughter? Will he try to make the best of a bad job? Look beyond the outside? Try to make her happy?"

Mevrouw sprang up lightly.

"I'm sure we both worry unduly, Captain Odshoorn. We all have to make our own happiness. Isn't that true?"

Hard as the nether millstone, he thought despairingly. But what could one do? And then suddenly, to his own amazement, the hasty, embarrassed, audacious words were out, audible in the startled silence of the room.

"Mevrouw, if it's a question of money—I'm not a rich man—but I earn good pay. Sixty guilders a month, Mevrouw. Would that be any help till you saw how she shaped and had time to look round?"

Now he had done it. The cold fury which he had been dreading and expecting ever since Evert had laid bare his plan was coming into action after all.

The voice that came from the hard-lipped mouth was icy with hauteur. "Captain Odshoorn, the kindest thing I can think is that you are intoxicated. Truitje will show you out." She tugged at the bell and swept towards the door.

"This thing you're doing is the cruelest, wickedest, wrongest thing I ever——" But Mevrouw was gone.

As he walked from the gaunt white house he had a curious feeling of physical ill ease, as though he had bruised himself or roughly torn a fingernail.

He turned into his favourite tavern, and the men who were his cronies and sycophants because he was on holiday and was generous and had money to spend crowded about him. But even when he had treated everybody and become very drunk himself, when he was beating time to the songs they sang by smacking his pewter measure against the chimney breast, the feeling of ill ease lingered. It was like a nagging toothache. He shouldn't ever have mentioned the girl to Evert. He was to blame for it all.

Book Two

"THAT," SAID CAPTAIN VEHK, handing Annabet his glass and pointing ahead, "is Banda. See the Fort?" Annabet nodded. "See that little fishing boat?" He indicated a small craft with orange-coloured sails running rapidly before the wind. "She's taking in the news of our arrival. Your husband will be ready to greet you." He looked at the girl beside him with eyes in which curiosity and affection and another emotion, not so easily named, were mingled. By God, he thought, how I laughed to myself when she first came aboard, and here I am, downright sorry to part from her. I wonder what the husband is like. . . . If he isn't good to her his neck should be broken, and I'd like to be the one to do it.

Annabet went on looking through the glass, holding it steady with hands which seemed too frail to support its weight. Taking the glass as Annabet relinquished it and watching her as she went back to her cabin to change her dress, the captain thought about the voyage. About the first time he saw her bareheaded and was surprised to find her hair like a child's—so she wasn't an old women long ago betrothed, or wedded for her money. About the cool, composed, and somehow honest demeanour which she had maintained all the time, uncomplaining, undemanding. About the entertainment which her conversation had afforded him. And how, when he had run a fishhook into his hand and the silly little puncture had festered, she had turned the tables by looking after *him*. He realised with a feeling of surprise that, though his most earnest efforts and floods of special goat milk had failed to put an appreciable amount of flesh on her bones, and the heat of the tropic sun had not loosened those stiffened joints, he no longer pitied or scorned the man who was shortly coming aboard to claim her. He envied him.

Vehk saw the prahaus mustering. There they came, the searchers for plague and for contraband, the men who would

73

carry the mail, and once again he was sorry that the voyage was over.

He recognised Kaerko in the foremost prahau and saw, sitting beside him, a big red-faced man. At the same moment there was a rustle of silk just behind him, and Annabet's voice said, "I suppose my husband will come to meet me. If you *could* arrange it, Captain, I would like to see him alone."

"This may be him," said Vehk, his eyes upon the red-faced man. He knew by this time almost all the circumstances which had brought Mevrouw Haan to Banda and how he himself had felt when he saw Annabet for the first time, and he was moved by a curious combination of envy, anger, and pity. This unknown man, Haan, could not be expected to see at a glance what a prize the lottery of glove marriage had given him. He turned towards Annabet and saw that she was dressed much as she had been on the day when she boarded the *Java* for the first time. The dress was richer, that was all, and the hat was decorated with a plume instead of a bunch of ribbons. And it was significant of the relationship established between the captain and his passenger that he should say with an easy familiarity that was not in the least disrespectful, "I'll arrange that, Mevrouw. And you'd do best to take off that hat."

"It shades my face a bit."

"It hides your hair. Take it off and go wait in your cabin until I send for you. Mynheer Haan will be in my cabin."

A glass or two of wine—to blur the sharpest shock, he thought. He looked at Annabet, who was turning away obediently. Suddenly he recognised the dress. She had worn it on the day when, recovered from his blood poisoning, he had been able to dine at his own table once more. "I'll wear my best dress," she had said, "and you must open a bottle of wine. We'll make it an occasion." A feeling, burning and tender, neither pleasure nor pain, rose in his throat at the memory. He swallowed and shrugged as he turned his lean swarthy face towards the side of the ship where Evert was following Kaerko up the ladder.

The little agent was nervous. His natural awe of Evert had been enhanced by the rumours and gossip he had heard about Evert's wife. He had taken refuge in an uneasy facetiousness which, coming into play at this moment, jarred, could he have known it, upon both his hearers.

"Well, well, Captain Vehk," he began. "I believe you have something very special in the way of cargo today. Plainly addressed to Mynheer Haan, I understand. This is Mynheer Haan—Captain Vehk. Come aboard to collect his consignment in person."

The captain acknowledged the introduction with the grace that was the heritage of his strain of French blood, but his eyes rested upon Evert with speculative detachment. Big, handsome, not too old—but not good enough. Not a gentleman—though how he came to that conclusion he did not know—probably one of Gomarus's jumped-up guttersnips. But not without dignity, the captain conceded a moment later. It was, doubtless, quite a tense moment for Haan, and it would have been easy enough for him to let Kaerko's opening words set the key for his own; but Evert said formally, "I trust you have had a good voyage, Captain. You will excuse me, I know, but I am anxious to greet my wife."

"If you will come below, Mynheer . . ." Vehk said invitingly, and led the two men into his own cabin where, by his orders, a bottle of Rhenish and several glasses stood ready. Evert, with difficulty restraining his impatience, looked around the cabin. "Mevrouw will join you in a moment," Vehk said. "Let us drink her health while we wait."

"I never dared venture upon a glove marriage," Kaerko said tactlessly. "I once knew a man in Surabaya who got a cross-eyed wife that way. But if the captain here delivers the goods as ordered and according to description, who knows? I might be tempted to follow your example!"

The lines in Vehk's leathery face deepened. He drained his glass hastily and set it down. "Come," he said turning to Kaerko, "you'll be wanting your letters. Mynheer Haan, if you will wait here I will send Mevrouw to you."

Left to himself, Evert poured another glass of wine and gulped it impatiently. He appreciated neither the wine nor the delay. Contrary to the captain's surmise, he was not nervous; he was merely filled with impatience. It was forty days since the *Great Holland* had brought him the formal acceptance of his proposal, and Mevrouw's accompanying letter had told him the suggested date of the wedding ceremony, the name of the ship upon which, all things being well, Annabet would sail, and the date—as nearly as these things could be forecast—when he might hope to see her in Banda. In that space of time his impatience had grown steadily, like a rapidly maturing plant. Actually, considering the circumstances, the whole thing had been arranged with phenomenal despatch. Only a little more than fifteen months had passed since the possibility of marrying Annabet van Goens had first occurred to him, but Evert was accustomed to having what he wanted, or at least what he was able to buy, delivered into his hands almost immediately, and at times it seemed that he simply could not wait to see his latest bargain.

Well, now at last the moment had come. He heard first a footstep, then another, and attributed the space between them to a becoming reluctance, a hovering shyness; then there was a whisper of silk, and Annabet stood framed in the open doorway.

After a stab of disappointment that his waiting should be prolonged further he looked at the woman without interest. Some other female passenger wandering about—or had Annabet brought a maid? No, too finely dressed. Vehk's wife, perhaps; he'd looked the sort of dapper little cock who'd be pretty uxorious. Good God, though, what a wife to cart round with you. And anyway, she was in the way; surely Annabet couldn't be long now.

"Mevrouw," he said icily, "if you are looking for the captain, I can tell you he's gone on deck. He has lent me this cabin for a little while."

The creature gave a timid smile and a little knowing nod.

"You are Evert Haan? I am Annabet." She tried to step quickly into the cabin, stumbled stiffly, regained her balance, and came to a standstill close in front of him. There she curtsied—not gracefully, but with the assurance of one who had been reared to fine manners.

As she rose he saw that from the foaming lace of her sleeve a white hand, all skin and bone, was extended. At the very back of his mind lay the knowledge that he should take it, raise it to his lips, murmur some words of welcome; but he was too stunned, too utterly overcome by his feelings, to say or do anything. He stood like a stone and stared with steadily mounting horror. It just wasn't possible. Such a thing couldn't happen to him, Evert Haan. There was a horrible mistake somewhere. Or else someone was playing a trick on him. He knew what his Annabet looked like. Hadn't Piet described her? Hadn't he said that she was a true Van Goens? And couldn't he remember the lovely pink-and-white, plump, golden women of the family who had gone past him so often long ago in Janshaven, riding in carriages which flung clouds of dust or spatters of mud over the envious, dazzled boy? It was one of *them* he had bid for. And what had he got? God in heaven, what had he got? All in that same timeless minute which followed the words, "I am Annabet," his mind ran backwards again, reminding him of the things he had said in those first few intoxicated days after the *Great Holland* had brought him Mevrouw's letter. He had boasted, knowing that he was doing so and enjoying it. Now he felt a scorching shame as he remembered the things he had said, and all the vainglorious words seemed to coagulate into a ball which choked him.

Annabet broke his silence. The timidity which had shown in her first smile had no echo in her voice. The sweet, assured tones rang out so clearly that he thought her loud-voiced into the bargain.

"My appearance has shocked you, Mynheer. I expected that, so please be at no pains to conceal your feelings. Shortly before your letter arrived in Holland I was very ill, and although I have fully recovered in health my looks have suffered. I did beg Mamma to warn you in her letter, but she was certain that I should improve on the voyage. So I have indeed, but not quite quickly enough." She paused for a seconds as though expecting some reply. None came and she went on, "I am very sorry. I assure you that what I lack in looks I will make up in behaviour. My sole aim shall be to make you a good wife, Mynheer."

The stilted, pompous words came out with the clarity and precision of a long-prepared speech. Hundreds of times she had visualised this meeting, and every time she had pictured this Evert Haan as someone to be placated and, if it were possible, charmed into overlooking the all-too-obvious defects in her appearance. Sometimes she had steeled herself for anger, the black, cursing, deadly rage such as her father had indulged when things began to go wrong. She had not anticipated the blank, dumb depths of astonishment which now confronted her. And even as she said the long-prepared speech something furious and rebellious cried out from the depths of her being. *And I was the loveliest of the three; if I could have come eighteen months ago he'd have been on his knees to me.* But she quelled that feeling, remembering those days shortly after her recovery when the destruction of her beauty had almost led to the destruction of her mind.

Father Vincent had shown her how to go on living, had pointed out the way of acceptance and resignation. . . . She

must remember the things he had said. And she must
remember, too, what she had discovered for herself—that it
was possible for men who at first looked upon her with
horror to come to look with kindliness and sometimes more
than that. The big sea captain, Piet Odshoorn, had been
horrified at first, but in less than an hour the horror had gone
and his handclasp as he left had betrayed him. Little Vehk,
too, so different in almost every way, had gone through an
almost identical change. And Egbert, whose favourite sister
she had always been, unable to look at her at first, had been
her slave again long before the letter which gave her a
spurious importance had arrived. And this big handsome
man, this husband of hers, was only man after all. Given
time and a modicum of tolerance to work upon, she would
be able to establish at least a friendly relationship. And that,
she thought, being innocent and gently reared, was basis
enough for a marriage.

Evert had cleared his throat and made a sound which
seemed to presage speech, but no words came. "A good
wife"—he didn't want a good wife! At least he did, of course,
but he could attend to her goodness. He wanted a beautiful,
attractive, enviable wife who would grace his house and his
life as a lovely figurehead would have graced a ship. He had
been prepared to receive a cold and possibly resentful girl
who might even despise his plebeian blood. All his frenzied
preparations since the *Great Holland* anchored had been
aimed at impressing and subduing her. He had not cared
whether she loved him or not; he had not looked to her to
bring him the happiness which ordinary men expected to
find in the marital relationship. He had merely wanted a wife
whom he could show off with pride and who would, through
the mere fact of being his wife, remove his grudge against his
humble beginnings. And he had got a scarecrow, something
not merely plain but positively hideous, and who was
promising, as a sop, to be a good wife. God Almighty, he
could have had a good wife if he had wanted one, and far less
ugly a one than this, any moment in the last twenty-five
years. He had always found women easy game. He thought
of the ones he could, at various times, have married. And he
looked again at the thing whom he had married, this living
scarecrow, this animated skeleton.

From somewhere out of sight he could hear Kaerko's
voice, and the sound seemed to bring him to his senses.
Everybody who could possibly contrive some errand to bring

him aboard would be here in a moment, ready with a joke and a slap on the back, avid to view the bride. The thought jerked him into speech.

"We'd better get ashore," he said. And he thanked the private Deity who, lapsing lamentably in the great matter, had at least arranged that he should come in his own prahau. They could go straight back to the house without going into Banda. His one idea now was to get Annabet to the privacy of the plantation without being seen. After that—he had no plan. He must have time.

"If you will get your hat and anything else that you need for the next hour or so I'll send out for your baggage later."

"Thank you," she said.

As she walked out of the cabin his eyes followed her with hatred. This marriage, he thought, was intended to avenge him upon the Van Goens; but, by God, they had won after all. How they must have laughed as they shipped off that crippled bag of bones. And then he thought of Piet. Had Piet known? Was it possible that that slow, stupid fellow with his long-cherished grudge had planned and executed so exquisite a revenge? "Why do you prefer Annabet to Klara?" He had asked that, hadn't he? Was it within the bounds of reason that Piet, first by avid partisanship and then by pretending not to want to have anything to do with the affair, had played a game simply staggering in its cleverness? Had Annabet been a cripple, an ugly cripple, all along? That, at least, was feasible, for what illness known to man could turn a young, beautiful girl into a stiff old woman? Well, if Piet had deceived him, he would find out, and God help the swine next time he came to Banda. He had nearly landed in the Fort last time on account of his stubbornness. Next time there would be no Shal Ahmi waiting on the quay. Evert Haan had been fooled and somebody was going to pay dearly.

"I am ready now," Annabet said from the doorway. Evert looked at her again and drew a deep breath. In a hat she looked worse. She looked like an old crone of fifty painted and dressed in horrid imitation of youth. He could not—he simply could not—go to the deck by her side and risk seeing any of the men who were likely to be there. He knew what he would do and he was going to do it without any regard for her feelings. She might be merely the instrument of her family's knavery, but after all she had come; willingly or unwillingly, she had dared to face him, and she must bear the result. Pushing past her, he bellowed up the companionway, "Captain Vehk! Captain Vehk! Come down here a moment. I must see you. It's urgent."

"Look here," he said as Vehk clattered lithely down the stairs, "have you made any plans for getting my wife off this ship?" His tone was deliberately aggressive.

"Why, no," Vehk said, taken aback. His eyes flew to Annabet, who was standing by the cabin doorway, a small leather bag at her feet, her hat on her head, her gloved hands clasped at waist level.

"I boarded in the usual way, Evert," she said calmly. "Please don't worry. I'm not nimble on the ladder, but I can manage."

Evert ignored her entirely.

"Mevrouw is far from well," he said in a voice that defied contradiction. "I'm surprised that no one except myself has seen how very unwell she is. The idea of her going ashore in the ordinary way is preposterous. How would you land a sick man, Captain—a man, say, with two broken legs?"

"I'd rig a sling, of course," said the captain, nettled by Evert's manner. Then the full implication of the question struck him and he said falteringly, "But Mevrouw isn't— I mean—Mevrouw is as well as when she came aboard. Or——" He turned his back on Evert and took a step towards Annabet. "Mevrouw," he said, suddenly solicitous, "are you *feeling* unwell? Sometimes—I've noticed it myself—the sudden cessation of movement leads to something like seasickness. It will pass. Of course if you don't feel like facing the ladder I'll fix a sling. It's no trouble, but it takes a little time. Would you like to lie down while I make arrangements?"

"I'm——" Annabet began. She had started to say, "I'm all right," but a glance at Evert's face silenced her. She freed one hand and moved it in a gesture more eloquent than a shrug, a gesture which made Vehk spin round to face Evert again.

"I've no time to waste. We want to get home," Evert said. "Who's above there?"

"Three or four gentlemen unknown to me, the agent, and Mynheer Vehmeer."

"Come to——" He was about to say "gape" but sensed in time the self-betrayal of the word. "Come to be introduced and make silly jokes. My wife is in no state to be bothered with them now. And a sling, you say, takes some time to rig. Very well. Can you send me a good strong fellow, Captain?

And will you then be so very kind as to go up and tell the assembly that Mevrouw Haan is not well? Say I'm anxious to get her home without any delay or excitement."

"I should be grateful," said Annabet clearly. "And, Captain Vehk, before you go I want to thank you for everything you have done to make my voyage so agreeable. I won't say good-bye because you're coming to dine with us, aren't you?"

"It would give me great pleasure, Mevrouw, just as anything I have done for your comfort has given me pleasure." Confused, perplexed, he leaped for the companionway, and in a moment a burly, lithe sailor came tumbling down and pulled himself up short with a salute.

"Good morning, Daan," Annabet said, forestalling whatever order Evert was going to give. "You're going to help me up those stairs, across the deck, and down the ladder. I'm villainously stiff today."

"I could carry you easy," he said quite eagerly. Across his broad shoulder Annabet's eyes sought Evert for instruction.

"No," he said. "I think it would be better if you took one arm. I'll take the other, so. And the bag in your other hand. That's right."

There, now, if they looked—and he knew just how avidly they would look—they could see little save a drooping, sick woman moving along between two stalwart supporters. From most angles even her face was hidden.

Kaerko, Vehmeer, and the four planters stood in a little knot in the place where the captain had unobtrusively herded them. Curiosity, a kind of deflated joviality, and sympathy showed on their faces.

"There goes a damned lucky man," said the captain almost provocatively as Evert, carefully keeping the bulk of his body between Annabet and the spectators, crossed the deck.

"What's she ill of?" Kaerko asked.

"She had a bad bout of fever just before we sailed," Vehk said. "And it's an exhausting voyage."

"She's lame," Vehmeer announced with an air of discovery.

"What about Evert's great dinner tonight?" Van Heem asked.

"Think she'll be well enough to attend? You're right, Vehmeer, she *is* lame. Look what a fuss they're making about getting her down that ladder."

"Good omen for tonight," Hootman, another planter, said with a grin. One or two of the others laughed and capped the remark. Vehk's dark face seemed to blacken. He said irrelevantly and truculently, "Mevrouw Haan is one of the most charming people I have ever had the pleasure of meeting." And then, feeling that he had made a fool of himself, he turned and walked away abruptly.

"Well," said Vehmeer, his vast pale face settling back into lines of gravity, "I suppose, unless we hear that Evert has cancelled the dinner, we shall have the pleasure of meeting her very soon."

"And when you do," said Hootman, who was not invited, "take a good look for me and see if her legs are put on right. Myself, I doubt it."

The prahau moved over water as blue as hyacinth. Glassed in its translucence, a thousand little coloured fish, lovely as butterflies, darted. Annabet studied them for a moment and then, lifting her gaze, looked at the island. They were skirting the water front with its white and pink, cream and ochre buildings and leaving the town to their left. In a moment there were only trees, masses and masses of dense, feathery green, divided from the blue water by the edge of creaming foam. And the scent, the flowery, spicy scent of the islands, of which she had first become aware some hours ago aboard the *Java* was here intensified until one might have imagined that great bowls of potpourri were being stirred and wafted just under one's nose. It did seem to be a very beautiful place. She contemplated saying so, for the silence in the boat was growing heavy and unendurable, and she had been brought up to believe that a fund of rippling, impersonal small talk was one of a lady's indispensable assets. But before she spoke she looked at Evert and caught the expression of cold loathing in his eyes. It was so unmistakable and so virulent that her inside turned cold. Even her breathing seemed to stop, and her lips parted, not in speech, but in a gasp for air.

Easily and rapidly as a waterfowl the prahau turned into an inlet, and now there were trees on either side. Presently, upon the nearer, left-handed side, there was a gap, and here, standing back a little from the water, was a collection of buildings, most of them thatched with reed and all of them washed white. From the clear space in front of them a little wooden landing stage jutted out into the water. The prahau's head swung round towards it, and Annabet looked at the buildings. At first she imagined that one of them would be the house to which she had come, and the thought brought a feeling of relief. If one of these low, humble places were Evert's home, then she had been deceived too. For the space of a fleeting moment she entertained the mad hope that, after all, Evert was going to lead her into a hovel. Then she would make the best of it and he must make the best of her and things might work out all right. The boatman, nimble as a cat, sprang onto the landing stage and held the prahau steady. Evert alighted, turned to face her, seemed to hesitate, and then deliberately stepped backwards, speaking, as he did so, a word or two in some language she did not know. The boatman hastily rubbed his right hand upon the folds of white cloth which girded his loins and then stretched it out to her. Stiffly she climbed out of the prahau and set foot in Banda.

"The house," said Evert in a wooden, reluctant voice, "is a short walk away. The landing stage was made for the convenience of loading nutmegs. On the other hand, I didn't want to live amongst the sheds."

"I'm perfectly able to walk, thank you," Annabet said, trying not to hobble too obviously and accepting his words as though they apologised for the distance. And since the dreadful silence was at last broken, she hurried on before it could form again. "I'm not ill, you know. And not nearly so stiff as I was."

Evert said nothing. With obvious impatience he curbed his stride to her slower pace and they walked along a wide, well-trodden path, thick with dust, until it ended in a thick green hedge. Fifteen months ago, when Piet had first visited Coenpark, the bushy little shrubs had just been planted and reached only to his waist; now they were more than six feet tall, and regular, careful cutting had so thickened and restrained their lavish growth that the hedge presented the appearance of a solid green wall. Two apertures with arched tops pierced the green surface, and Evert, ignoring the nearer one which led to the compound and the kitchen quarters, passed on and entered by the second.

Unconsciously he paused there. Now that the active, extrovertive business of annoyance and shame and of getting Annabet out of sight was over, softer, passive feeling could find a place in his mind; and as he stood for a second inside the green archway and looked upon his house and garden he was nearer tears than he had been since his childhood. He had, as he had told Piet, lived very simply before he built the new house. The little low house stood there still amongst the sheds and drying lofts at which Annabet had looked so speculatively. It had been built in the first year of his ownership, when the native troubles were at their worst and nobody knew whether the young plantations were going to pay or not. And he had never troubled to alter or improve it in any way. It was not in his nature to be content with even second best, and in those early days he had had in his mind already the vision of the house he would one day rear and inhabit. And here it was, as perfect as his taste and his means could make it; and the garden, though only eighteen months old, had, in this place of rapid maturity, already the trim, rich, settled look which he had remembered about the gardens of big houses in Holland. So often since Piet's visit his fancy had dwelt, with reserve at first, and then at last with assurance, upon the moment when he would say to Annabet van Goens, "Well, there is the house. . . ." He had planned to say it casually, concealing his sense of pride and achievement. And now the moment had come. The contrast between the place and the woman who was to live in and share it was too cruel. In place of the pink and white and golden girl whom he had pictured moving gracefully amongst the roses he had this hobbling, stiff-necked skeleton, this painted death's-head. It was not to be borne. It wasn't bearable. And deep within him, in the secret places of his mind where so many schemes had been born and nurtured, something stirred. He wasn't going to try to bear it. He had got out of bad corners before and he'd get out of this. He set his foot in motion again and, still in silence, began to walk towards the house.

"It is the most beautiful house," Annabet said. Her voice was less assured than usual. She remembered her thoughts about the sheds and hovels by the landing stage and her mind took note of the inevitable corollary. Evert had promised her a beautiful home and had, no doubt, expected a wife to match and enhance it. A dreadful feeling of guilt shot through her and she said impulsively, "I shouldn't have let myself be persuaded. I should have gone to the convent."

"So that's what they'd planned to do with you, is it?" Evert asked brutally. The words and the tone implied that a bundle of rubbish destined for the midden had been instead posted out to him in Banda, marked "With Care." The cold feeling shot through Annabet again. She had the sensation which comes to happier people only in dreams—of standing obscenely half clad before a throng of jeering strangers.

They walked up to the house, crossed the verandah, and entered the hall. The whole place blazed with flowers. Uncertain as to the exact moment when the *Java* might anchor, Evert had had the house garnished for several days, each bloom and each plant replaced the moment it passed its prime. One of his houseboys noted for his running was even now kicking his heels upon the quay, for it had been Evert's intention, had Annabet been what he expected, to bring his prahau close to the shore and send the boy running back to the house so that the servants should be warned and on duty, with wine and cakes and fruit ready on the verandah. As it was, the runner having not returned, the house seemed deserted and the flower-embowered hall had the air of a church decorated for a festival and then momentarily abandoned.

Near the foot of the curving staircase Annabet came to a standstill. She had promised Father Vincent in those dark days when her tottering mind had leaned heavily on the support of his mysticism that she would waste no more tears over the loss of her beauty when there were so many real sorrows and evils in the world. But her eyes were brimming as once again she looked into Evert's face.

"It is all so very beautiful," she said. "And you are so disappointed in me. . . . Mynheer, I would give twenty years of my life to appear before you as I was."

"But that is impossible," Evert said coldy. "I will show you your room."

At the time of Piet's visit the room had been unfinished. Later, at first tentatively and then wholeheartedly, Evert had thrown himself into the business of making it, in his own words, "fit for a queen." It was all blue and white: the big bed had curtains and covers of blue-and-white silk, blue dragons on a white ground; a sofa covered in the same silk stood under one of the windows, and the two low chairs were cushioned in the material. Under the other window stood a dressing table bearing a silver-framed mirror fitted with candle sockets. The wood of the table and the chairs was like nothing Annabet had ever seen, white, polished to a satin-like finish. Silver-backed brushes and little silver boxes flanked the mirror. The carpet was of a deep, heavenly blue, and by the bed and before the dressing table lay the great skins of white bears. Wang Fu, the Chinaman, taken into favour again, had made the mirror and the trinket set and had also, through one of his numerous relatives, obtained the bearskins. Together with the bathroom which opened out of the bedroom—an original, highly expensive, and vastly imaginative arrangement—the room had cost more than even Evert could afford. But he had spent the money gladly, in spite of the fact that in his heart he was almost certain that the woman who would eventually sleep in this room would, physically, afford him less pleasure than he had known in Isa's embrace. He had never expected the young beauty of Piet's description and his own imaginings to afford him great sexual satisfaction; her duty was one of another kind—to flourish his prosperity, his taste, his success, like a great glittering banner in the society in which he lived, and eventually to bear him an heir.

And the woman to whom he was showing this beautiful room would, of course, do neither. Publicly she would bring him nothing but pity and derision; privately she was equally unprofitable. He had intended to offer his hand to her at the landing stage and then discovered, with an increase of horror, that he could not bring himself to touch her.

Annabet looked around the room. Lovely, exquisite, so obviously planned and furnished for quite another person. She felt the flood tide of despair setting in and thought desperately of Father Vincent's words. (It had been March when he had spoken them—March in Holland, and the soft wind from the west had just defeated the cold blasts that blew from Russia, and the miserable little garden of the Heydberg house had been pricked all over with the spearheads of the bulbs she and Klara had planted in the autumn when life was still normal and shapely. She had looked at the thick knobby buds of the cherry tree by the gate while he spoke.)

Evert had left the door of the blue-and-white room ajar, for he had meant to call the maid he had engaged for Annabet and escape as soon as he could. Annabet now closed it quietly. And since it was *her* room and manners must be observed, she said, "Please sit down for a moment. I have something to say to you." The tears were still in her eyes, making them larger than ever, and her voice was a little unsteady.

Evert hesitated for a second and then, with a might-as-well-get-it-over-and-done-with air, sat down in one of the low dragon-cushioned chairs. Annabet, exhausted by the walk and the emotions of the last hours, sank gratefully down in the other.

"Mynheer," she began. Then, forcing a smile, "I can't go on calling you that, can I? We shall have to use our given names. Evert. I would like, if you don't mind, to make everything plain to you. I know that I'm hideous, and I know that you are extremely disappointed and shocked at the sight of me. The pain that your distaste gives me is, in a way, no more than I deserve. Many things combined to persuade me to come to Banda. But this I must say—whether I was right or wrong to do so, I did determine when I put on your glove in the church that to the best of my ability, in every way that was in my power, I would try to make up to you for having a woman with an ugly face and stiff limbs. Also—and this had a certain influence upon my decision—it is possible, so the doctors say, that I may get better. I am appreciably less stiff than I was, and I gained two pounds on the voyage. As for my hair—it is growing, you may see for yourself. If you can possibly bring yourself to have patience and look upon me with tolerance, I do assure you——"

Evert seized upon the opportunity given him by the slight halt in her speech. "This is a very distasteful position," he said, getting to his feet. "You have been very ill and are to be be pitied. The blame lies with those who allowed you or persuaded you to come here. For one thing, you are obviously unfit to have made the journey. If you take my advice you will go to bed at once. I have engaged a maid for you. She is native, of course, but she understands Dutch and has been trained in a good household. I will call her."

He went to the door and, opening it with a sharp feeling of relief, clapped his hands loudly three times. From nowhere, it seemed, and in no time a stoutish, almost middle-aged woman with black hair oiled smoothly back from her brown face and beady, very observant dark eyes appeared from the far end of the gallery.

"Your mistress has arrived," Evert said shortly. "Go to her." Leaning back into the bedroom, he remarked, "She is called Katje."

The loud handclaps had informed the household that the master had returned, and Josef, the chief houseboy, a man of some fifty years, was waiting at the foot of the staircase. From the bottom stair Evert could look straight across the hall to the dining room, where the long table glittering with silver and glass and napery was set for twenty guests. The sight made him want to spit. The moment when his bride, young, beautiful, well-bred, should have taken her seat at one end of that table was to have been the crowning moment of his life.

"You can clear all that away," he said sourly. "Mevrouw has arrived in very ill health and must keep to her bed. Now, let me see. Juan is still in town, I suppose. I was so anxious to get Mevrouw home I forgot about him. Send Abbas for him while I write some notes. Then send him round with them. Mevrouw will dine in her room and you can bring mine to the office."

Swinging sharply to the right of the stairs, he strode away to his office. There he poured himself a glass of schnapps and observed with an almost impersonal pang of pity that his hand was unsteady on the bottle. He had never been so thoroughly upset and shaken in his life before. Even his confidence in his own luck—an attribute which had, as much as anything else, made him lucky—was tottering to a fall. It was not only the Van Goens who had foully tricked him; it was life itself. Everything had gone right with him for so long, and then, over this very special and important matter, everything had gone wrong.

It took him some time, and another glass of spirits, to steady himself sufficiently to write out in a legible hand the notes which cancelled the dinner. They were identical and formally worded, but as he folded the one addressed to Cornelis Byskin, his best friend in Banda, he took up his quill again and wrote, "Isn't it bad luck?" under his signature. Juan, recalled from the quay, was waiting outside the door, chewing a lump of nutmeg cheese, long before the notes were finished; and he was the first person upon whom Evert vented his mounting fury.

"I'll teach you not to come into my presence with your ugly mouth full of filth," Evert said, landing him a swinging blow off the ear.

Annabet, left to herself, moved stiffly about the room, looking out of the windows, one of which gave upon the garden, the other upon the dense green fastnesses of the nutmeg grove, touching the pieces of furniture and coming to a halt at last before the silver-framed mirror of the dressing table. She stared resolutely at her reflection. It was horrible, especially in that beautiful frame, with the glimpse

of the beautiful room as a background. Klara and Mamma
had insisted upon the paint and powder, saying with loud
confidence that the colour detracted from the hollowness of
her cheeks and the aging pallor of her lips. But though she
had faithfully adhered to their rules of application she
thought now that they were wrong. It made her look older,
not younger; and it obscured the one thing that the illness
had left her, the fine rose-petal smoothness of her skin.
Suddenly she drew her handkerchief from her sleeve and
rubbed her face vigorously. And as she did so the thought
went through her head: Here I am thinking about my face
again, and I did promise Jean Marie I wouldn't think of him
except as Father Vincent. . . . Oh dear, what a mess I have
made of everything. She eyed her reflection again, and her
face looked back at her with an expression of sorrow none
the less valid because it was tinged with self-deprecatory
humour. If only, she thought, I hadn't gone to that silly
carnival on the ice . . . If only Jean Marie hadn't been a priest
. . . And here I am, a wreck, a hideous wreck in Banda, with a
husband who hates me. I know he hates me, and who could
blame him?

All very well for Jean Marie—Father Vincent—to say
that the flesh was nothing. To young women and the men
who married them it was everything. She had known that all
along. But she had wanted to go on living; and that, at least,
Father Vincent, with his mysticism, had helped her to do. So
she had lived and stayed sane and come to Banda. Father
Vincent had said with a most convincing air that there was
a purpose in everything. Was there a purpose in the
combination of cowardice and avarice and recklessness
which had brought her here?

Evert had often dined in his office on days when he was
busy and not under emotional stress. Josef, accordingly,
served up the usual meal, and Evert was quite surprised to
find that his ordinarily hearty appetite had altogether
deserted him. His attitude towards food was the one
customary to those who have not always been sure of a
bellyful, and he could have counted on his fingers the
number of times when he had voluntarily missed a meal—
certain days when he was seasick, and other certain days
when he had been in a high fever. Even in his soldiering
days the imminence of danger had failed to quell his zest for
food; and anxiety, of which in his time he had known

plenty, had certainly never made him send a dish away
untasted. But what had happened to him today was
something outside his previous experience. Even the food
which, under Josef's eye, actually reached his mouth was
tasteless, and after a few minutes he said surlily, "Bring the
next dish and then take yourself off, Josef. I've some
business to think about and I don't want you fidgeting
around."

As soon as he was alone he gave up the pretence of eating;
he poured another drink and leaned back in his chair. He
had been turning his problem over in his mind and had
reached no solution, but he had come to the conclusion that
his action in smuggling Annabet off the ship and into the
house had been mistaken. Van Heem and Vehmeer, Kaerko
and the others would have had their already lively curiosity
spurred, and there was the captain at hand, only too ready to
satisfy it. Katje, too, had probably spread a description of
her mistress all over the compound, and news like that
spread like the plague. Probably by this time the whole island
was gloating over the rumour that Mevrouw Haan was badly
pocked, a hunchback, and one leg shorter than the
other. That was the curse of the East—not just the gossip,
but the gross exaggeration.

His wretched train of thought was disturbed by a familiar
sound, a scratch at the window. He leaped to his feet, crossed
the room in a few swift strides, and locked the door; then he
strode to the window and opened it.

"You are alone?" asked a thin high voice.

"Shal Ahmi!" Evert exclaimed in a pleased voice. "I've
been thinking about you. I was coming to see you later on.
Come in."

Shal Ahmi stepped with dignity into the room, and Evert,
having carefully adjusted the shutter again, pulled forward
the other chair with a gesture of attentive politeness. Shal
Ahmi watched him, a little quirk of amusement twisting the
corners of his mouth. He sat in the chair, adjusted his white
drapery, and let his eyes rest upon the meal which Evert had
scarcely touched. He looked from the dishes to Evert's face,
and the glance was insolent and amused. His manner was
quite different from that which he had used in Kaerko's
office on the night of Piet's arrest. It lacked at once the
superficial cringing and the underlying dignity. An observant
watcher could have seen at a glance that Shal Ahmi and
Evert were on old established and familiar terms.

Evert looked at his rejected meal uneasily. He had no objection to taking Shal Ahmi into his confidence—indeed, he intended to do so—but he had a constitutional dislike for betraying himself.

"Rizplatzen, too," said Shal Ahmi meditatively. And Evert countered with, "Would you like some? It could be heated in a moment."

"Thank you, I have eaten. But you, my dear Mynheer, have not." A sly, mocking smile crept across his smooth face. "Can it be that the bride did not arrive on the long-awaited ship? Or did you fall in love at first sight? Love, so we are told, is the enemy of appetite."

Evert sat down in his chair.

"Lay off, Shal Ahmi. Tell me the worst. What are they saying in the compound?"

"Frankly, that your bride is a cripple, past the age of childbearing, and remarkable in that she wears a wig of spun gold which is so cunningly fitted that she can wear it in her bath." He brought out the words in a voice of light, impersonal reporting and then added in a changed, kinder tone, "I thought you might as well know the worst. Why did you act as you did? If only I could have advised you!"

"I ask your advice on every matter that I can foresee," said Evert harshly. "But who could have foreseen this?"

"The gossip of the compound is, for once, near the truth, then?"

"No," Evert snapped, "but it might as well be. She's been ill. She's seventeen and she looks fifty. Her knees and her elbows and God knows what else are set stiff. She's half a head shorter than I am, and if she weighs an ounce over seventy pounds I'm surprised. Her hair, so far as I know— but I haven't investigated—is her own." He looked at Shal Ahmi, and his eyes were more abjectly miserable than he realised.

"Once," said Shal Ahmi in a dreamy, ruminative voice, "you gave me a glass of very special brandy with a queer English name. Everett? Yes, that was it. If I remember rightly, under that benign influence, my thoughts were inspired——"

"I'm sorry," said Evert, jumping to his feet. "Very remiss of me. I'm all at sea tonight. Here you are. But is the liquor made that can inspire you to think a way out of this mess? If it is you shall swim in it."

"To swim in any liquid lessens its value," said Shal Ahmi

sagely. "That is why so few people drink water except in necessity." He sipped in silence for a few moments. "Of what nature?" he asked presently.

"Full of hardihood, or she would not have dared to come. Inclined to argument. Loud-voiced. She invited the captain of the ship that brought her to dine with us without consulting me. A lady of family, Shal Ahmi—even now there is no gainsaying that—but ugly beyond words."

"And that matters?" Shal Ahmi asked. "So much?" Evert scorned to reply to what seemed to him an absurd question. "Ugly women have been greatly loved——"

Evert interrupted him with a sound of disgust. Then he said fiercely, "I am not a boy, Shal Ahmi. The question of love does not come into the matter at all. How could it? Does anyone expect love from that sort of marriage? I wanted a woman who would grace my home and my table, uphold my position, and bear me a son. And I've saddled myself with one whose appearance has already made me a laughingstock and who is physically so abhorrent to me that I couldn't bring myself to help her out of the prahau."

"Not even for the sake of the son?" Shal Ahmi asked. The smooth, shining planes of his face did not shift, but his eyes twinkled. Evert shook his head with a grimace of disgust.

"That is very bad," said Shal Ahmi. "What will you do, then? Send her back to her family?"

"I couldn't do that," said Evert, who had thought of the same thing and rejected it. "They are"—how could one describe the Van Goens so that Shal Ahmi would understand?—"lords in their own land. They would make trouble for me. Even the Company would listen if they complained loudly enough. They've cheated me, damn them to hell, every single one of them, but it was a legal cheat. When I asked to marry her I did not stipulate that she should be plump or pretty or sound of wind and limb. I asked for her, by name, in marriage. And I got her."

"I suppose"—Shal Ahmi's reedy voice was thinner still as he put the question—"there could be no question of her virginity?"

Evert gave the question his full consideration and then said slowly, "No. The illness came upon her more than a year ago. Before that she would be only a child—or so counted, in Holland. And the great families are careful of their daughters. Besides"—a note of something that was almost panic crept into his voice, and for a moment the whites of his eyes showed like a startled foal's—"to bring that up I should have to go to bed with her. And I could not do it, Shal Ahmi."

"Yet a son from an ugly woman," said the native, almost as though he were speaking to himself, "is as good as a son from a beautiful one. And the night is kind." The twinkle showed in his eyes again and was immediately quenched. "All this I know from hearsay, for as you know I have no traffic with women. Yet I hear many men's confidences, and I see with my eyes. And out of what little widsom I have stored I say, 'Get you your son.' For whom else is your house reared and your coffer filled? The day will come when you will say, 'Ah, she is ugly, but my sons are many and good'; and by that time your hatred will have changed to respect. I have seen it happen many times."

"It wouldn't happen with me. I tell you that when I would have put out my hand to assist her my arm weakened. When I speak to her my mouth is dry and my tongue is stiff. How then . . . ?" There was no need to finish the sentence. Shal Ahmi, as though convinced, nodded his shining hairless head.

"What then?" he asked. "You can't send her away, you say, having no reason. She stays here like an old, barren wife? And the sons you get elsewhere are by your law illegitimate, looked at a little sideways. Bearing always with them a stigma which neither wealth nor position can remove. Come, Mynheer, you are not the man to give in thus easily."

"What alternative have I!" Evert asked bitterly. But his eyes had lost their look of frenzy and dwelt upon the native with something rather more eager than speculation but less than hope.

"I could think of many things," said Shal Ahmi, avoiding Evert's glance and staring straight ahead of him at the wall. "And I think you have somewhat the same in mind too. When I came in tonight you said you had been thinking of me and would have come to me had I not come to you. Why? Was it to tell me of your ill fortune? To weep, as you say, upon my shoulder? Rather had you got in mind the memory of those few times when I have been of service? Come, open your mind to me. What did you hope of Shal Ahmi?"

"I don't know," said Evert, faced with the blunt question. "But sometimes a fresh mind—— And anyway, Shal Ahmi, your advice is always worth having. . . ."

"You have had my advice upon this matter," Shal Ahmi said smoothly. "It is not my advice you ask. Rather my aid. Am I not right?"

"Your aid then." His control broke suddenly and his voice became pleading and piteous. "Shal Ahmi, if you can think of any way out of this, any way to rid me of her without scandal, without making me more of a laughingstock than I am already, I shall be in your debt forever. Even when all our business is finished, all my promises kept, I shall be forever your debtor." Then slowly the magnitude of what he had asked crystallised in the words "Rid me of her." It seeped into his mind with the realisation—I'm asking him to kill her—and his red face blenched and his heart began to pound heavily.

Shal Ahmi spread his smooth brown hands against the whiteness of his clothing and studied their backs with attention and interest.

"Suppose," he said at last, "your bride liked you as little as you like her; suppose she ran away tonight—to the governor—and told him that she had never wanted to come to Banda and asked his help to get back to Holland. What would he do?"

"But she wouldn't do that."

"Never mind what she would do. What would *he* do?"

"Send her back to me. She is my wife," said Evert confidently.

"So she goes to the governor and tells him a story of being in love with a young man in Holland and being forced by her family to come here. And she is beautiful as the morning and so plainly the well-born girl of whom you have boasted. Thus is your face saved, Mynheer. And he sends her back, perhaps with an escort; maybe, since she is a lady and Mevrouw Haan, he brings her back himself. But in the morning she is gone again and an experienced boatman is gone too. A fishing boat has seen a prahau heading for the Kei Islands where those few of my race remaining have taken refuge. Suppose, after a time, there are rumours of a white woman, living as a native, living with a native in those islands in the villages of Banda Elu and Banda Elat, where the old trades flourish and the old beauty lives untarnished. What then is the position of Mynheer Haan? Can he divorce her and beget his legal issue elsewhere?"

"Of course I could," Evert said. "But she would never ——"

"My friend," said Shal Ahmi, looking him in the face at last, "in less than an hour I could send a white woman, beautiful and young—but unfortunately so far barren—to play that part with the governor. And in another hour I could find a boatman who would carry your ugly bride farther than the Kei Islands at my command. Ah, and he would live with her, too, if it were a matter of a friend of mine wanting a divorce." His voice changed, dropping from the fanciful to the practical. "All that is mere word spinning. I have, as you know, given the matter no thought at all. But in a moment, as you have seen, I have already hatched a plan that would rid you of her. Slow and cumbrous, yes. But I could think of others. There are a hundred ways." He paused and then asked sharply, "Do you trust me?"

"Have I not given you proof of that over and over again?"

"Prove it again," Shal Ahmi said lightly. "First, of course, I must see the woman. And then—is there any business urgent enough to take a newly wedded man away from his sick wife's bedside?"

"Yes. Because—and thanks to you, but they don't know that—I have been successful with my slaves, I have been commissioned to buy for the island. I should, by rights, be in Bandogar at the quarterly market. But as the *Java* was all but due, I decided to wait until the next. I could go tomorrow."

"Your bride being sick and you being a man of public conscience. Good. But not tomorrow. The next day. Tomorrow you will give the dinner which, with me to advise you, you would have given today. You will be a man completely satisfied and charmed with his bride, but unfortunately she is ill. You leave her in good hands, none other than those of Dr. van de Lijn."

"And when I return?"

"Then you act as you must, remembering always that she was dear to you."

Evert's mouth was suddenly dry. He was like a child who has played innocently with some unknown thing and realised, too late, its lethal properties. He said feebly, ridiculously, "I don't want her to be hurt."

"Why should I hurt her? Am I a thug? I have yet no knowledge of what I shall do. Now, will you go and see that the way is clear so that I may see her?"

Evert rose and, moving like a man in his sleep, unlocked the door and went out, leaving the key upon the inside. Shal Ahmi turned the key again and then went and stood by the

desk. Fumbling amongst his drapery, he brought out a small
bag. He untied the string which secured its neck and tipped
out into his hand five stones somewhat resembling dice, but
slightly larger and more rounded at the corners. Upon each
of the six faces of the stones was a cryptic symbol cut into
the stone and then filled in with colour, black, scarlet,
orange, green, and blue. He weighed the stones in his hand
for a second and then flung them haphazardly on the desk
top. Leaning forward, he studied the combination, at first
with impersonal, professional interest, and then with a sharp
intake of breath. His sleek, smooth face wore a look of
intense absorption. Almost reverently he lifted the black
stone and set it a little aside. The others he gathered in his
hand again and flung carelessly as before. He pushed the
green-marked stone to the side of the black and juggled with
the other three. Orange next, then blue, and, last of all, the
scarlet were laid in a line. Then, as though reading a few
words in plain print, he ran his finger along the serrated
stones and followed the finger with his eyes. A curious
smile broke the immobility of his face: it was amused and
yet incredulous, as though someone had just whispered an
unbelievably funny joke, swearing that it was true. The smile
lasted until he heard Evert's hand upon the door. Then with
lightning swiftness he swept the stones back into the bag and
into the fastnesses of his clothing. Expressionless again, he
unlocked the door and joined Evert in the passage.

There were candles everywhere alight now, but in the hall
and up the stairs and along the gallery which Evert had built
to satisfy his pride and yearning for magnificence they did
less to lighten than to point out the size, the hardly banished
darkness of the place. Here a piece of polished furniture
reflected a gleam, there a bowl of flowers basked in the soft
radiance, between stretched an eternity of gloom. The scent
of the flowers and the potted shrubs was heavy on the warm
air, and despite himself Evert thought of the candles and the
flowers which were offered to the dead. He shuddered. But
his feet were firm on the stairs.

Annabet had spent the hours since Evert had left her in a
state of misery that was alternately dazed and clear-sighted.
Katje had come up from the kitchen with the information
that Mynheer had ordered Mevrouw's dinner to be served in
her room; and presently with apparent artlessness, she spoke
at some length of the glories of the dinner which had been

ordered and largely prepared for this day and abruptly canceled. For the sake of her own pride Annabet took refuge in feigned invalidism. Intent upon demonstrating that it was her state of health which had put a stop to the festivities, she put on the nightdress which she had brought ashore with a few other essentials in the leather bag and got into the big bed. She regretted the action as soon as it was performed, for she had experienced nights of sleeplessness immediately after her illness and knew that the energy released by the supine body flew to the brain and encouraged thought. She did not want to think. If she could have had her way she would have dressed again, limped about the house, gone into the garden, probably ventured further into the nutmeg groves, forcing herself all the time to take an impersonal interest in what she saw, following Father Vincent's advice to "look outside yourself," and so would have gained some temporary relief from the misery of spirit which beset her.

Katje pottered about the room for quite a length of time, pretending to be busy, and when that failed at last she squatted down on the floor, apparently prepared to sit there forever. She was perfectly still and quiet because Annabet was pretending to be engrossed in her book; but Katje's presence irked her nerves and after a short time Annabet said that she would sleep until dinnertime and would like to be alone.

As soon as she was alone she turned her face into the big soft pillow and gave way to tears. True, in those days when she had been almost mad with crying and Father Vincent had come and talked her back to sanity, she had promised him that she would never again shed a tear over ruined looks; but strictly they, although the prime cause, of course, were only part of the reason for crying. She cried from remorse because her wilfulness had brought her to Banda, and from self-pity because no palatable alternative had been offered her, and from hurt pride because Evert had taken her so exactly at her face value and not even bothered to feign ordinary courtesy: he had allowed her no time, no margin. Also, she was suffering from the ebb-flow of altruism. All along she had been much borne up by the sense of having greatly helped her family, a feeling not entirely worthy, since vanity and a lust for power were involved in it, but there had been, too, a genuine impulse for self-sacrifice. She was fond of her mother and Klara and Maria, and that draft on the Bank of Amsterdam was going to sweeten their lives. Klara

and Maria could have new gowns, and Mamma could afford
coach hire to take them out to places where they could be
seen. So often Mamma had said, looking at her pretty three
girls, "If only there'd been a *little* more to spend I could
marry you all yet. But girls have to go out. Nobody comes
knocking at a house door asking, 'Does a pretty girl live
here?' " So true, of course, like so many of Mamma's
sayings. And Mamma, coming frankly into the open a few
hours before they parted, had said, "This husband of yours
may be cool at first—that is to be expected—but he is your
husband, bound to honour and cherish you, and if you try to
please him he will soon forget your looks." And that dictum
had dovetailed—though its essence was so divergent—with
Father Vincent's exhortations to forget the mere body and
cultivate the beauties of the spirit. If the spirit were right—
and she had honestly meant well by Evert—then the colour
and shape of the covering flesh did not matter.

But now she realised with a complete and abject realisation that between a wordly woman and an unworldly
man she had been led utterly astray. Little as she had seen of
Evert, few as were the words they had exchanged, she knew
that there was nothing to hope for from him. She would
never forgot the cold loathing in his eyes.

She began to think about Evert and admitted, with a slight
sense of shock, that he was extremely attractive. Her way of
life had encouraged a fundamental innocence combined
with trained technique in sexual matters, but for four years,
between the ages of twelve and sixteen, she had been
extremely pretty and that had made her conscious of men.
She knew that on the rare occastions when she went to the
butcher's she had got far more meat for her money than
Truitje ever received; her new shoes were finished before
Klara's, though Klara's had been ordered first; when the
roof of the hired house leaked and leaked through a wet
winter and Mamma had written and made a personal appeal
in vain, she, Annabet, had met the landlord and half in jest
complained of the drips in her bedroom, and next day the
men arrived with ladders and new tiles. Almost despite
herself she had developed an eye for masculine charms, and
Evert's size and good looks had stirred her even while his bad
manners waked her hurt resentment. He was just the
husband she would have liked fifteen months ago—fifteen
months ago, before this horrible thing happened to her. And

here she was, back at the beginning, with a fresh spurt of tears over her lost loveliness.

She completed the circle several times before Katje peeped in to say softly that dinner was ready whenever Mevrouw liked to have it. Dusk was flooding into the room, and Annabet was glad that her tear-strained face and swollen eyes were hidden.

"I'm only just awake," she said. "Bring it in a quarter of an hour."

"Shall I light the candles, Mevrouw?"

"You can do that when you bring the food."

When Katje had gone again Annabet went barefooted across the room and bathed her face for several minutes in cool water and then in the dusk coloured her cheeks and lips and brushed her hair. She imagined that she had no appetite for food, but she must eat; always, however she felt, she must eat, in the hope of restoring some flesh to her bones. And when the dinner, profuse, exotic, and delicately served, appeared she found that after all she was hungry. Presently, with two dishes already disposed of and a glass of burgundy inside her, her spirits took an upward turn. After all, she thought, I might have been in Ireland now, in a cell, with a pallet bed and only the coarsest, nastiest food. I did it. I chose the world and Banda and Evert Haan; I must make the best of them. . . .

"It is not for lack of eating that her bones break free," Katje reported. Evert had seen her downstairs and locked the outer door, telling her that he would call her when she was wanted again. "And now," she added with a change of voice—envy, memory, and downright astonishment mingled in it—"Mynheer has gone in to her."

A sensuous languor fell upon all her hearers.

But Evert did not even enter the blue-and-white room, did not even bother to explain who the visitor was. He left Shal Ahmi at the door and went on to his own room and took a large drink of brandy from the flask which he kept by his bedside. By this time, what with the shock, the vehemence of his feelings, his hours of thought, his lack of food, and the quantity of liquor he had drunk, he had a feeling of complete unreality. He *knew*, because he had seen it and heard it happen, that his bride had arrived and that she was ugly beyond imagination, that he had smuggled her into the

house, that Shal Ahmi had arrived and promised to rid him
of her and was even now in the blue-and-white room plotting
ways and means. But none of this had any connection with
the normal, ordinary life of a nutmeg planter in Banda
whose name was Evert Haan. The whole thing had the
unreal but none the less dreadful sharpness of a nightmare.
If only he could cry out and awake. But if he cried out he
knew that it would be only with the remembered words,
genuine enough, but fatuous in their conflicting sense. "I
don't want her hurt. I don't want her hurt, but I want to be
rid of her." How could Shal Ahmi, cunning as he was,
pander to both these wants? Nobody could.

He drank again and, going to put the now empty flask
back on the table, caught a glimpse of his face in a mirror
that hung on the wall. I'm a murderer, he thought solemnly.
And then he seemed to lose his holding in the real world and
to pass into the mirror. There—see that big man with the
reddish-brown beard standing in that dimly lighted room—
that's Evert Haan, the poor farm boy who starved and
sweated and nearly died of fever during Gomarus's
campaign of 1638; he got a grant of a nutmeg plantation in
Banda and made a tidy fortune—shush, don't say how—and
built a fine house and married a lady. She was ugly and a
cripple, so he did away with her. No, he didn't; he had her
done away with. Is there any difference? He's a murderer.
Murderer. *Murderer.* What a sound that word has. A filthy
word. It soils the tongue. Murder is the crime for which there
is no redress. For any other wrong, if you are sorry, you can
say so and make amends, but no man can call back the dead
and apologise.

Overcome, he stepped back, feeling for the edge of the
bed. And as he sank down upon it the mirror passed out of
his range of vision. That was me! That is me! This is Evert
Haan, tumbling onto his bed. I've tumbled onto the bed, but
I can still move. I can go to Shal Ahmi and say I've changed
my mind. He'd be glad. This, and all the other things I've
made him do, so many things that I've made him do, are
outside what he wants, really. But there's no need for me to
move. He won't do anything tonight. My door is open and I
shall hear when he comes out of *that* room. I'll ask what he
means to do. I'll . . .

But even in his moment of semidrunkenness and maudlin
sentiment he knew that he would do nothing to stop Shal

Ahmi, provided only that the plot he hatched was feasible
and safe.

When Evert had opened the door and beckoned Katje
away, Annabet's heart had begun to beat rapidly. She judged
that he meant to return, for he had left the door ajar; and
she braced herself to face what would, in any case, she imagined, be an ordeal and, in these circumstances, with a man
who hated her, would be almost certain to be terrible.

Mevrouw had mentally destined her daughters to
marriage from their cradles, and all of them, even the young
Maria, knew the little arts of pleasing men; knew that you
mustn't be argumentative or too silent or too talkative; knew
that men avoided the slightest indication of "boldness" and
abhorred, almost beyond everything else, the idea that you
ever had a thought in your head other than being agreeable
and pleasing. That was before marriage, of course.
Afterwards one settled down and was permitted to show a
degree of intelligence over such matters as running a
household and keeping servants in order; afterwards, too,
one cultivated virtues such as obedience, loyalty, self-
sacrifice, and tolerance of male peculiarities. Even in her
most despairing moments when it seemed unlikely that any
one of her daughters would marry, except to contract a
flagrant *mésalliance*, Mevrouw had never weakened, never
said, "Be yourselves, please yourselves." So she would have
said, if she had ever spoken of so private a matter, that
Klara, Annabet, and in time little Maria were perfectly fitted
for matrimony, and she would have believed what she said.
But of the physiological aspect of the married state she had
said nothing. For one thing, she had no words with which to
describe what happened in the connubial bed; for another,
such information was entirely unnecessary. She herself had
come from Brussels to marry her cousin Adriaan with no
conception of any caress more intimate than a kiss. She had
managed very well, and the girls would do the same.
Innocence was as much an essential of a bride as her veil.

But Annabet's innocence had been partially shattered by
Klara. The undesirable young man who had met Klara in
several furtive rendezvous and whose dalliance was actually
directly responsible for Annabet's rheumatic fever had
carried his love-making, not quite to a conclusion, but very
near it. And before Annabet sailed for Banda, Klara, rather

hot in the face and stammering, but feeling very old and experienced, had said, "There's more in it, Nab, than Mamma has said. And I think you ought to know. . . ." Annabet had listened with the avid attention that she gave to most things and had been shocked and horrified, not by the thing itself so much as by the knowledge that Klara's tutor in the matter had been the red-faced, hard-breathing, and, to Annabet, utterly unattractive young farmer who had sweated so profusely at the skating. It was partly the idea that Evert Haan might also be red-faced and hard-breathing—in fact, just an older version of Klara's lover—which had made her so anxious to ask Piet Odshoorn about him. There was, of course, one man in the world with whom it would have been possible, if slightly disillusioning, but he was a priest, and to think of him in such a connection was to risk eternal damnation—but she would have risked it quite happily. And, failing him, always supposing that this unseen husband were not definitely ugly or repulsive, she supposed she could bear it. Piet had at least put her mind at rest on that score, and she had seen for herself that he had told her the truth. Evert was, indeed, very attractive. But he hated her. Would that have any effect upon this curious relationship about which Klara had whispered so embarrassedly? Well, she would soon know.

She pulled the pillows behind her and sat up straight in bed, glad that for Katje's benefit she had bathed and coloured her face and brushed her hair until every curl shone. She heard Evert's tread along the gallery and no other step, for Shal Ahmi in his sandals moved as silently as any jungle creature; and then the heavy tread passed by, but the open door was pushed wide and a strange, indeed rather terrifying, figure stepped into the candlelight.

"Please," said Shal Ahmi immediately, "do not be frightened. I come as a friend. And your husband is within call."

"He sent you?" She pulled the sheet upwards over her flat chest and wriggled a little lower in the bed.

Shal Ahmi nodded and closed the door.

"Why?"

"Because I am skilled in many arts, medicine amongst them, Mevrouw. But the good Dr. van de Lijn who will come to see you tomorrow does not approve of our Eastern ways. So before I even look at you I want you to promise me that you will never mention to him or anyone else that Shal Ahmi has been to see you."

"Is that your name?"

"I have many names, Mevrouw. In Banda I am known as Shal Ahmi. And if you stay here you will hear that I have many reputations as well."

"*If* I stay here. I must stay here. This is my home now. Why did you say *if?*"

"We will speak of that later, with your permission, Mevrouw. First, like a good doctor, I will ask about your illness."

"But I am not ill. I have already tried to explain that to— to my husband. I *was* ill. I got better and now I—I—perhaps it is difficult for another person to believe it, but I am perfectly well. The flesh went from my bones and in places the stiffness remains, but I am in good health. You say you have knowledge of medicine. Perhaps you would be so good as to tell my husband that what I said to him today is true. I am perfectly well—otherwise I should not have come. I eat, I sleep, I enjoyed my voyage; when Captain Vehk poisoned his hand I looked after him—he was delirious for three days and nights. I gained two pounds in weight on the way. That is not much, but it shows. By the time I'm forty, at that rate, I shall be the right size again. . . ." Her lovely, humourous, self-derisive smile flashed out; and Shal Ahmi, who seldom smiled except when he was alone, smiled back at her.

Yet his answer was unkind. "That will be too late, Mevrouw."

"I know. My husband has been talking to you, hasn't he?"

"I should like to explain something to you," said Shal Ahmi, grave again. "Your husband, like many other gentlemen in the islands, disapproves of Shal Ahmi. As you see, his skin is brown; as you hear, his Dutch is not perfect. When I was young, Mevrouw, brown skin and the Malay tongue were the ordinary colours and speech in the islands. All that is changed now, and it seems that I must walk humbly because of my colour and my speech. Like you, Mevrouw, who was once very beautiful. Oh yes, I have eyes that see beyond the covering. You have the bones of beauty. But that, for the moment, is by the way. I was telling you that your husband, like the others, despises Shal Ahmi. But—and here he is different from the rest—his mind is not closed. So, knowing that in Holland you would have had the best doctors, with all the wisdom of the West at their command, and still you are not restored—I don't say to health, but to the state in which you were—your husband, overcoming the prejudice of the white man for the lore of the brown, has asked me to consider your case. Now will you tell me from the beginning the story of your sickness?"

When she had finished—and the story stretched from the fatal visit to the Ice Fair to the day when the Dutch doctor had said that time and youth were on her side and she might possibly improve in looks—Shal Ahmi nodded his head. Then he moved, uninvited, to one of the blue-and-white chairs and sat down.

Annabet said, "I'm sorry. I should have asked you to take a chair. . . . I just wasn't thinking."

"I know that, Mevrouw. Now I am going to ask you a strange question. Indeed, a number of strange questions. Suppose I said that I could cure you. Suppose that I did it. Would you then regret having come to Banda?"

"That would be base of me, seeing that I had been cured there." The smile flashed again.

"I ask my questions badly, Mevrouw. I meant, would you, restored to health and looks, wish yourself unmarried? I noticed that in your story the affliction came before the proposal. Had it any bearing upon your decision?"

His eyes, which missed nothing, took note of the look of wariness which, visible as a cloud, crossed the shining candour of her gaze. And his ears caught the restraint beneath the formal words of her reply.

"It was my first proposal and acceptable to my family. A year earlier I should have come to Banda with more confidence but with less gratitude." The sentence seemed to need a conclusive word, and "Mynheer" almost fell from her lips. But did one say "Mynheer" to natives? On the other hand, she could not call him Shal Ahmi on so short an acquaintance. So "gratitude," ending the little speech, seemed to hang upon the air with a note of uncertainty in it.

"So you are content to stay here? You like the place and the man to whom fate assigned you? You may answer me frankly, Mevrouw. No word of any conversation we hold together will ever be repeated by me. And I ask these questions, not from impertinence, but from a desire to help. There is no other man with whom, given back the beauty of which you spoke with such becoming modesty, you would rather mate yourself?"

A shade of true colour, deeper and lovelier than the false hue of the paint, showed in her face. She had been violently and precociously in love with Cousin Jean Marie when she was ten, and for two years had derived great comfort and hope from the knowledge that within the Van Goens family marriages between cousins were the rule rather than the exception. But Jean Marie had taken orders when she was twelve. He had gone to Spain, and wounded vanity and a strange kind of repulsion had carried her through a critical year; and then, with the spiritual afflatus which so often accompanies the onset of adolescence, she had resigned herself to hopeless love. She would love him forever, making no sign. But side by side with this feeling there had paced, through the next years, the natural emotions of her development; vanity, because she was pretty; a desire to be married, because an old maid was a pitiable, scorned thing; a desire for children. And she had known for some time before her illness that one day, if by some extreme and improbable good fortune a likely suitor presented himself, she would marry him and make him so good and proper a wife that he would never suspect that she had loved her cousin who had become a priest.

Then had come her illness and, after all its torments, the even deadlier misery of seeing herself in the glass for the first time. She had cried, ceasing only from exhaustion, for a whole week, refusing food, unable to sleep, well on the way to madness. She had been determined to die, and she had wanted to see Jean Marie once more. The wish, whispered to Klara and reported to Mevrouw, had resulted, after further weeks of slow, relentless self-destruction, in Father Vincent's appearance by her bedside. He had changed so much as to be almost unrecognisable. "I wanted to say good-bye to you," she had said hoarsely. And he had said, "Rubbish!" He had sat down by her bed and had taken her limp, fleshless hands and had begun to talk. He had used, for the resuscitation of the life force in this afflicted, vain little cousin of his all the eloquence which was going to sustain and strengthen so many despairing souls before he died of pneumonia in an unheated priest hole in Commonwealth England. He had been, to a degree, responsible for her coming to Banda, for it was he who had said again and again that it was not what happened to you that mattered but what you were; the flesh was nothing, the spirit was all.

Today she had proved him wrong, in one respect at least. She had met Evert in the right spirit, humble and placating, but he had hated the look of her and had never given her spirit a thought. And now this queer brown man, all wrapped about in shrouds, was asking if there were any man she would prefer to Evert. What could it matter? She must deny Jean Marie, who was, anyway, no longer a man in the accepted meaning of the term. She did it firmly.

"There is no one else."

"I ask that, Mevrouw, because with skill and certain arts I have it would be possible, even now, to make this marriage as though it had never been; but afterwards, when with my other arts I have restored you to health and beauty, Mynheer Haan will possess you as he possesses his other treasures. It will be too late then."

"It is too late already. I married Mynheer Haan in good faith. He is displeased with me. But *if* you can make me acceptable to him, all will be as it should be. Can you do that?"

"Of a surety. Mevrouw, you have two evils and two only. You have no flesh upon your bones and there is a stiffness in your neck, your elbows and wrists, your hips and knees and ankles. Within a very short time, if you place yourself fully in my hands, you shall be smooth and supple. I ask only that you shall maintain the secrecy which I shall demand and follow my instructions faithfully. You have eaten today?"

"More than usual." She leaned forward eagerly. "It is not a question of eating. I have eaten everything put before me for fifteen months."

"And digested nothing. Outwardly, Mevrouw, you have maintained a calm spirit; there are no marks of discontent or fretfulness upon your face. I am glad of that; they are hard to remove. You have accepted your affliction because of an influence, very powerful, working in your mind. But there has been war within you. When you would have wept you have withheld the tears; when you would have rebelled you have spoken pleasant words; you have cultivated the spirit at the expense of the flesh, Mevrouw. Thus I have seen holy men whose bones belied the brimming plenty of their begging bowls. I will say now, briefly, what I must say, and then I bid you lie down in your bed and think—know—that soon you will be lovelier than ever. I, Shal Ahmi, who never broke a promise save to those who first betrayed me, vow and swear that the stiffness shall be gone from your bones. Think that, know that, as you lie in your bed. Know more than that. The signs which do not bother with a lie promise that your future shall be very bright, Mevrouw. There is much love in it. But you must have faith, Mevrouw. You see me, a stranger; I promise you great things. I ask in return only that you should trust me. Can you do that? Have I perhaps already shown that I understand something that has escaped the notice of your Western doctors? Will you believe that what I can recognise I can cure?"

She looked at him for a moment in silence. There had been an air of fantasy about the whole interview. But he had been right about what he so fancifully called "war" within her, right about the powerful influence, right about the withheld tears. And although if she wrote a detailed account of this interview to Klara (only of course she would not do that until its results were proved), Klara would think she had come to a very strange place indeed, yet somehow this brown man and his confident promises and his insight into her mind were really all of a piece with the happenings of the day, with the house and the blue-and-white room, with Katje and Evert.

"I *want* to believe it," she said. "And I will do whatever you tell me to."

"That is good," said Shal Ahmi. "Now listen carefully . . ."

For twenty-four hours Annabet van Goens and the wildfire rumours regarding her appearance and her state of health usurped the ubiquitous nutmeg from prior place in the islanders' conversation. But by late afternoon of the second day Evert's few real friends were relieved and his envious acquaintances disappointed to hear, on the authority of no less a person that Dr. van de Lijn, that Mevrouw Haan was suffering from nothing more interesting than exhaustion and cramp due to her long voyage. He had based this opinion upon a view of Annabet's head as she lay in bed with the sheet smoothed under her chin, showing little more than the golden curls on the pillow, and upon what she had told him herself.

At the dinner, which was lavish beyond anything ever imagined in the islands, Evert announced his intention of leaving next morning for Bandogar; and full of his meat and drink, nobody had a thought beyond the obvious one—that Evert Haan was waiting to consummate his marriage for a few weeks until his beautiful bride was recovered from the effects of her voyage, and that he was, as ever, attentive to his business. There was not a man at the table, friend or foe, who did not admire and covertly envy him. For nobody knew that, thanks to Shal Ahmi's machinations, his bride

would not be there when Evert came back from Bandogar.
For that matter, nobody knew that Shal Ahmi had ever
crossed the threshold of the fine house where they sat
carousing; and when at one point the conversation dwelt for
a moment upon that queer person, nobody guessed that for
once, for the first and only time, Evert's sour remarks about
him were at least half genuine. For in this moment of utter
dependence upon Shal Ahmi's help, Evert was angered by
his silence and secrecy. On the previous evening Shal Ahmi,
escorted to the door by Evert, who was far from sober, had
refused to give the slightest inkling of his plan.

"All will be well. When you come back from Bandogar
you will be pleased. Ask me no questions."

Yet Shal Ahmi was shrewd and cunning. Hadn't that been
proved again and again? Hadn't it been proved by the matter
of the unlimed nutmegs? Hadn't Evert gone to him and said,
"There is a man who will not do an errand for me"? And
hadn't that worked out perfectly? At least perfectly so far as
human foresight could see. He wouldn't worry any more. He
would just take Shal Ahmi's word: "All will be well." But of
course all had always been well with Evert Haan; it always
would be, because he was clever and let nothing, not even
sentiment, stand in his way.

"Fill the glasses," he cried. And they filled the glasses and
drained them, wishing their host well even as they envied
him. For there is something cheering and inspiring in the
sight of a really successful man.

Afterwards, looking back upon the weeks which followed
her arrival in Banda, it seemed to Annabet as though they
had been detached from her real life and set apart. Solitude
and a curious quietness, like a globe of fine glass, shut her off
from the world. Outside amongst the nutmeg trees the doves
kept up a perpetual soft grieving, and sometimes she heard
sounds of voices and laughter, but they emphasised rather
than dispelled the quiet of the blue-and-white room. Katje
moved about, soft-footed, and sometimes murmured a bit of
gossip or genuine news, but as the days passed she grew less
talkative and seemed to develop a degree of awe for her
mistress; and since there was little to employ her, Annabet
often sent her away so that she might be alone with her
secrets. Day followed day in a trance of wonder and delight.
And the nights were full of fantastic interest, waking dreams.

Evert had left for Bandogar in the early morning after the

dinner party, and midway through the day Katje had come into the room bearing the smallest and lightest piece of the baggage Annabet had left on board the *Java*, and two of the boys had staggered in with the rest. Tied securely to one of the valises was a flat whitewood box which she had never seen before, and as soon as the boys had put down their burdens and departed she had raised herself in the bed and asked Katje to bring the box to her. It was addressed to Mevrouw Haan, and she opened it with eager curiosity. Immediately under the lid was a slip of paper upon which was written in letters curiously formed, as though they had been made with a brush dipped in some thick black substance, "These are not for you. Your kindness will bestow one on Katje each evening. So may the means to recovery come and go." The box was full of sweetmeats, such things as Annabet had never seen before, brightly coloured, sticky, moulded and cut into curious shapes. A little puzzled, she put the box aside, not without regret that the message forbade her to sample its contents. But in the evening when Katje dragged into the room a mat of woven straw, a small round bolster, and a rug of many colours, she began to understand.

"What are you doing?" she asked.

"It is my bed," Katje said simply. "When the master is away the maid sleeps in the room of her mistress. That is the custom." Her beady eyes looked at Annabet speculatively. In former days the custom—for it was a custom, well established—had once or twice been a source of profit to her. The rings which hung from her ears were of real gold, less ornament than a form of insurance against old age or hard times, and they had been bought with guilders which she had earned by the simple expedient of moving her mat into another room. Here, she thought regretfully, such easy money was unlikely to come her way. Who but a dutiful husband would ever wish to lie with this bag of bones?

Shal Ahmi knew everything and was very clever, Annabet reflected; and presently she reached for the box of sweets and invited Katje to help herself. She made a pretence of selecting one for herself. Katje took the silver pins from her black hair and placed them for safety under the bolster. Then she said, "Good night, Mevrouw. I shall hear you if you call me," and with that—promise or threat?—lay down, pulling the rug over her fully clothed body. In five minutes she was asleep.

Far below in the depths of the house Josef conscientiously went his rounds, bolting the shutters into place, locking the doors. When everything was made fast he went to his wife in the compound.

Annabet, without difficulty, for she had slept during the day, stayed awake. When Katje was sound asleep she got out of bed and put on her gown and slippers. From the single candle which had been left burning by her bed she lighted others, and by their light, for the sixth or seventh time that day, she studied her face in the mirror. It did look less haggard. Shal Ahmi had been right. The war within her which had worn the flesh from her bones was ended; new hope, new assurance had already left their marks upon her. Impatiently she waited the sign.

It came at last, the tapping of a light bamboo cane upon the window; and, though she was waiting for it, it startled her. She turned to the mat where Katje lay sleeping. Profound and peaceful slumber dwelt upon the hard bolster. She called loudly, "Katje! Katje!" There was no response. She took a branched candlestick and held it before the sleeping face. A gout of wax fell upon the brown hand, but Katje did not stir. Of course not. Her visitor of evening before last did not send sweets for fun. Moving jerkily but without restraint, Annabet hobbled down the stairs lighted by her candles, crossed the vast dark hall, and, using both hands to the massive key, opened the door.

Then she was frightened. And for a moment—but a moment so packed with feeling that it seemed an age—she thought what a fool she had been. Indeed, the perfect prey. Misled by baseless promises of cure, she had willingly, eagerly, laid herself open to nameless horrors. She had herself drugged Katje; she had herself opened the door—upon the night; upon Shal Ahmi of whom she knew nothing; upon these formless, faceless things which accompanied him.

The breath went out of her body and she gasped for air; she fumbled with the door as though to close it again, but her hands were weak with terror.

"Do not be alarmed, Mevrouw," said Shal Ahmi. "These are but women. Their eyes are darkened and their ears are deaf—but in your service. As Katje sleeps, in your service."

The fluttering candlelight showed the two figures, slight, a little pathetic in their complete dependence upon the man who held each of them by the arm. He guided them towards the doorstep, and Annabet, stepping back, watched them enter the house.

"They have skill in their hands, Mevrouw. Skill I have had no time to acquire. You are suspicious. They are old and frail. See." He twitched aside their veils one after the other and showed the faces of two old women, bound about the eyes with strips of white linen and with lumps of wool protruding from their ears. He let the veils fall again, and something in his attitude denied to the two old women any identity, any human importance. Comforted but a little appalled, Annabet led the way to her own room, where Katje still slept like the dead.

Shal Ahmi was like a person who had come to demonstrate the efficiency of a machine. He pushed and pulled and guided. Only to Annabet, whose eyes and ears were unmuffled, did he use the ordinary means of communication.

"Now, if Mevrouw will lie in her bed and give herself into these hands, the work may begin. Do not fear, Mevrouw, they have their orders. And I will wait outside the door as soon as I have put them in their places."

He pushed one woman on one side of the bed, towards the foot, and the other upon the other side, towards the head. Then he muttered to himself a few words which Annabet did not understand and walked towards the door. Annabet, still wondering, lay down upon the bed.

Four hands, small hands with firm strong fingers, set to work with confidence and precision. First they pushed her bedgown down from the neck, up from the knees, up from the wrists and elbows. Then they moved the stiffened joints one after another, carefully, testingly. And then, as a sempstress might take to pieces an ill-fashioned garment or a carpenter dismember an ill-made piece of furniture, the four little hands set to work.

Annabet, who had earlier submitted herself hopefully into old Truitje's hands and suffered several violent rubbings with horse liniment, braced herself to endure pain; but there was no pain and no pleasure in the process. The hands neither gently stroked nor roughly wrenched. Through her skin they reached for and found the taut muscles, the stiffened places where bone touched bone, just as a child might feel for and loosen his sticky sweets through the paper bag which held them. Despite their blinded eyes and deafened ears there seemed to be some curious accord between them, for when they wanted her position changed the four hands moved as one, lifting or rolling her body as though it were a lump of dough. And presently, as joint after joint was dealt with and laid, as it were, aside, finished, a doughlike feeling of lassitude and anonymity fell upon Annabet. The busy loosening fingers seemed to unfasten the bonds between mind and body until at last she, Annabet Haan, had no connection with the cage of flesh and bone, muscle and blood, which had housed her so comfortably for sixteen years and then confined her so cruelly for nearly two. There on the bed it lay discarded, while above it, out of it, beyond it, her spirit floated peaceful and free.

She was sorry when Shal Ahmi stepped back into the room, and there was the inevitable fusion of mind and body as she hastily pulled the sheet over her limbs. The four little hands stopped working as soon as she moved, and the old women stepped back from the bed. With almost identical gestures they lifted the edges of their veils and wiped their faces. She saw with a pang of pity that what had seemed so easy and effortless must have been, in reality, hard work. Both the brown faces were wet with sweat, and the four hands which had been so firm and inhuman in their impersonal skill were unsteady now, vibrating, as though blown in an invisible wind.

"Well?" said Shal Ahmi. "How do you feel now, Mevrouw?"

She stretched under the sheet. She had not known such ease of movement since the day when she had scampered off in hilarious high spirits to the Ice Fair.

"It's marvellous," she said with a gasp of wonder. "I can never thank you enough." She looked at him with shining eyes.

"Then we will go." He picked her dressing gown from the foot of the bed and laid it within reach of her hand; then, turning his back towards her, he took each of the old women by the arm and began to propel them towards the door. Annabet slid her feet to the floor and stooped—without difficulty for the first time in many months—to pull her slippers on.

"I could cry with joy," she said, stumbling across the room behind the trio. After the long time of checked and fettered motion, the new freedom seemed greater than it was and she felt so light, so loosely put together, that her steps were uncertain, like a colt's. And she thought, I'm cured, I'm cured, and now I shall grow fat. Everything will be as it was.

"Oh, Shal Ahmi," she cried again, "how can I ever thank you?"

"No need for thanks, Mevrouw," he said. "My skill, like everything else in the world, has its price. Your husband will pay me—happily, I hope. But I am glad to have given you back your youth." The last words were kindly spoken. He halted by the mat where Katje lay and, looking over his shoulder at Annabet, said, "She sleeps well." His eyes twinkled, and Annabet laughed aloud.

"Do not be disappointed if tomorrow the cure does not seem as complete as it does tonight, Mevrouw," he said, moving off again. "Rest well tomorrow and the next day, eating all that you can. On the next night we will come again. You will remember to lock the door when we are gone."

She slept soundly, dreamlessly, and woke to find Katje with her hair smoothly dressed and her clothing so neat that it was hard to believe that she had slept in the same clothes she now wore, standing by her bedside with the breakfast tray. Before she had come to full memory and a realisation of what happened since last she looked into that broad brown face she was aware that Katje was looking at her curiously.

"Mevrouw is better this morning?" Katje asked formally when their eyes had met and engaged one another for a full minute.

"Yes—I believe I am. My neck"—she put her hand to the place where the short curls ended and jerked her head backwards and forwards and then to each side—"my neck is better." It was that which Katje had seen. Ah, and there was so much that she could not see—the ankles and the knees and the hips, the shoulders and elbows. Hadn't she run up the long curving stairway and down again and then up for the sheer pleasure of the movement last night after she had locked the door behind Shal Ahmi?

"Give me the mirror," she said.

Katje handed her the silver-backed, silver-framed toy which Evert had ordered from Wang Fu for his beautiful bride. Yes, there was a difference about her face; probably no one else would notice it, but the bones in her nose were less prominent, and that awful monkeyish look which came from having nothing but skin over her teeth was going. And of course being able to turn her head made her look very different.

She flung the mirror on the bed and turned to inspect her breakfast.

"I want more than that," she said when she had reckoned the bulk of the little new bread rolls, warm and wrapped in a napkin, the slices of imported ham, the dish of native fish, the jar of mango preserve, and the basket of fruit. "I want as much again. You forget, Katje, that for nearly seven months I have *starved*." For that was the story that Shal Ahmi had put into her mouth, the story that she had told Dr. van de Lijn, the story which had been crystallised into a short entry in his book of notes under the heading, "Haan, Mevrouw," above the entry, "Obviously a privileged person, but suffered loss of weight and energy due to monotonous diet devoid of fresh food."

Annabet wrote to Klara after three weeks:

I live like a Strasbourg goose. I lie in my bed and cry for food until I am sure that those of the servants who have not seen me must imagine me a monster. And I am getting fatter, *fatter*. But even more marvellous is the lessening of my stiffness. There are women in Banda skilled in some art for which I have no name, but with their fingers they charm the stiffness from one's bones. You had better not tell Truitje this, just tell her that I am better and so it is on account of the climate, because, dear soul, she did try so hard with her horse medicine. This is quite different and very difficult to describe, but when I say that this morning I touched my toes without bending my knees, you will rejoice with me, I am sure.

Of my husband, Evert [Annabet wrote after some nibbling of her quill] I can tell you little because a business journey took him away before I had recovered from the effects of my voyage, so I hardly saw him at all. The *Java*, by which I hope to send my letter to you, will sail before he returns. He is handsome; tall and broad, with reddish-brown hair and grey-green eyes. He gave a dinner party to celebrate my arrival, and of course I should have been there, but I was too exhausted. Besides, my appetite is not a thing to expose to the public at the moment.

Three of the Banda ladies have "called," Mevrouw van

Heem, Mevrouw Vehmeer, and Mevrouw Byskin. I saw none of them. I mean to *burst* upon them when I look like myself. Do you realise, Klara darling, that I am going to look like myself, and quite soon? It sounds like a miracle, doesn't it? And perhaps you will think that I am exaggerating and telling you a traveller's tale. But it is *true*. And I just can't wait until Evert returns. He will be so surprised and so pleased. All the time, when he met me on the ship and brought me home (I must tell you all about the house, it is *magnificent*) I kept thinking, If only, if only all this had happened before I was ill. And now it is as though I hadn't been ill. There are still many days to go, and when he comes back I shall be *pretty*. . . . Oh, Klara, I do wish you could be with me to rejoice. . . .

She nibbled her quill again and then, plunging it into the ink, sent it racing over the page.

Klara, I can't write to Father Vincent, though he was so kind to me, because *I don't know where he is now*. But when Mamma writes she is sure to mention me. Will you tell her—I'll tell her in the letter I write with this, but you tell her, too, to remind her—I want him to know that I was right to choose as I did because I had *no vocation*. And if I had gone to County Down I shouldn't have been *cured*. Will you see that he knows that I am cured, please, and that I am happy? If I could write to him myself I could tell him a great deal more about the flesh and the spirit. I don't think one is much use without the other, and that must be why God gave us bodies as He did. . . . I mean if the spirit was enough by itself why did we have to have arms and legs and faces? But if he knows that I am well and cured and happy, that will be enough. I put all this in because he was so very kind to me. . . .

The letter ran on with its touches of humour and pathos and nostalgia, and it was not until it was folded and sealed and accompanied by another to Mevrouw, less frank, less voluble, but equally affectionate, that Annabet remembered that the person who would convey the letters all the way over the sea to Holland was Captain Vehk, whom she had, in all good faith, invited to dine with her before he left.

She remembered him just as she was handing the letters over to Katje to give to Abbas to take down to the quay, and her hand flew to her mouth. He had been so very kind and had done so much to restore her shattered self-confidence. He had taken such care of her, too, and been so frankly pleased when she had gained those two poor pounds. His interest in her had even extended to giving her advice about not covering her hair before she met Evert. And he would think that she had forgotten all about him—or had never intended to invite him properly. It would be dreadful if he went back to Holland thinking that.

"Wait a minute," she said to Katje, and drew another sheet of paper towards her and plunged the quill into the ink. "Dear Captain Vehk," she wrote vigorously, "will you give me the pleasure of your company at dinner tomorrow? I will send a——" She hesitated; what was the word they used? And how did one spell it? No matter, he would know what she meant. "——boat for you. The bearer will await an answer, and if tomorrow is inconvenient for you, please suggest another day. Yours sincerely, Annabet Haan."

"Tell Abbas there is an answer," she said, hastily folding the paper and not bothering to seal it.

When Katje slipped into the room again Annabet asked her, "Katje, who is the most important servant here?"

"Josef is head boy."

"Ask him to come and see me."

She was comforted and yet intimidated when Josef presented himself. He looked old and sensible.

"You're Josef? You know all about the house? The stores? You know what food we have?"

"Yes, Mevrouw. Mevrouw desires some special dish?"

"Not for myself. But tomorrow, or another day—I'll let you know in an hour—I shall be having a guest. I want to give him the best we have. And although I have enjoyed everything you have sent up to me, I don't know what to order."

"There are chickens, Mevrouw, in the compound. Chang Koo has a litter of suckling pigs. There is fish. There is rizplatzen; there is marchpane; the cook is skilled in chupatty; there is fruit. Or the pudding, boiled in a cloth. Mevrouw has only to say what she desires."

The names rattled in Annabet's ears like the stones in a fool's bladder.

"No," she said. "I have no idea what I want, but I want it to be the kind of dinner which will honour the guest. And what about wines?"

"They are all locked, Mevrouw. Mynheer took the keys with him. They hang upon his chain."

"Oh, bother!" said Annabet, using the childish expression which dated from the days when the fire wouldn't light, or the carefully contrived renovation of some old garment proved unsatisfactory, or Mevrouw had disapproved of some high-spirited plan. "Where are the wines kept, Josef?"

"Some are in the cupboard in the dining room, Mevrouw."

"I'll look at it," said Annabet, and she rose to her feet more easily than Josef expected. Katje had certainly reported that of late Mevrouw seemed better, but her first reports had been so enthusiastically gloomy that "better" had seemed to leave a good deal to be desired.

She had been in the dining room of Evert's house, her house, before, but always, obeying Shal Ahmi's instructions, secretly and at night. She considered it a magnificent but oddly gloomy room. The walls were white, like all the walls of the house, and the floor was made of red tiles set into wide borders of mortar coloured white. There was a table which could seat twenty, and twenty chairs with leather seats and twisted legs and high backs. On one wall the expanse of the whiteness was broken by a huge mirror, under which stood a sideboard laden with silver, and another contained the cupboard of which Josef had spoken so reverently. Perhaps with many guests, uproarious, merry people at their ease, the room might be habitable, but it would be very gloomy holding just herself and Captain Vehk.

"I don't want my dinner served in here," she said positively, when, followed by Josef, she had entered the room and stood looking meditatively at the cupboard in the wall. "Where is there otherwise?"

"A little table in the drawing room," Josef suggested.

Annabet shuddered. She knew the drawing room, too, and privately deplored it. She had, after all, spent most of her formative years in the small, poorly furnished Heydberg house, and the room which Evert had planned with the idea of some beautiful, graceful lady dispensing tea to the ladies of Banda had struck her as being too large and overfurnished. And there wasn't a chair in it in which Captain Vehk would feel comfortable.

"No," she said positively. And then, without any warning pang of premonition, she went on, "I'll have the dinner served in that little room off the verandah at the end of the passage."

"Mynheer's study?"

"Is that what it is? You can put a small table in there, Josef, and plenty of candles. And as for the meal, you must order the best that there is at the moment. And now will you bring me whatever it is that you would open a stout box with?"

"Mevrouw wishes a box opened?"

"No, thank you, Josef. I want the tool that you would use to open a box."

When it came it was a perfectly ordinary chisel. She took it into the dining room and after fifteen minutes' hard work succeeded in opening the cupboard in which some of Evert's liquor was stored. Faced with the rows of bottles, she felt young and silly again but decided that Captain Vehk could choose his own. Presently Abbas returned from his run into Banda and back, his slim, uncovered torso heaving with every deep, effortless breath, and handed her the captain's acceptance for that evening. Afterwards the simple events of that morning gave her a whole series of "ifs" to ponder over—if she hadn't remembered and honoured that invitation; if she hadn't thought the dining room too large and stiff; if she hadn't opened that cupboard and got at the brandy; if Captain Vehk had chosen another day—how different everything would have been. Or wouldn't it? Would some other chain of little happenings have brought about the same results?

Jean Vehk came to Coenpark in what he imagined to be a mood of detached interest. Nobody had mentioned to him that Evert Haan had left for Bandogar two days after his bride's arrival, and since it was now some time since the pair had made that odd, furtive exit from the *Java*, the captain was anxious to see how, in his own phrase, they "had shaken down." It had taken him only a day or two to realise that the scrawny, ugly woman against whom he was prejudiced from the start was a charming companion; and he hoped, for her sake, that the man she had married had not shown less perspicacity.

Any surprise he felt in finding Annabet alone was engulfed and forgotten in his astonishment at the change in her appearance. The graceful, easy, undulating movement with which she came forward to greet him, the perfect poise of the head which had been so stiffly, awkwardly held, the curves which were replacing the hollows in her cheeks and temples—all were equally incredible.

"But for the dress, Mevrouw, I should hardly have recognised you," he said in all sincerity.

"And even the dress has been let out," said Annabet happily. And then a kind of awkwardness fell between them. Now that the young lady looked like a young lady, Jean Vehk found himself remembering too late that one should not comment upon a lady's appearance so bluntly. And Annabet, realising that she was no longer his cherished passenger, his almost patient, sexless because of her affliction and their relative positions, judged that a lady ought not to refer to such matters as her increasing girth and the consequent letting out of her dress seams. She rushed into the stiff little silence with formal words which did credit to Mevrouw's training.

"I am sorry, Captain Vehk, that my husband is not here to meet you. He had to go away on business, and you will have sailed before he returns. I know he would have enjoyed making your better acquaintance."

"And I his, Mevrouw," Jean Vehk said.

That avenue of communication closed, Annabet thought, If we go on like this it'll be a very tedious dinner and he'll be sorry he came. What's happened to us? He's the same person who used to curse and swear and then apologise, nearly crying, when I put the bread poultice on his hand; and I'm the same person, though, thank God and Shal Ahmi, I look different. And she laughed and said, "Why on earth we're talking to one another like this I can't imagine. I'm so *glad* to see you. I've a hundred things to tell you. When do you sail?"

"The day after tomorrow, Mevrouw."

"You could keep a secret for two days, couldn't you? Then I can tell you everything. All the mavellous things that have happened to me. I haven't had anyone to talk to, you see. And writing to people isn't the same. But first of all I want you to come here."

She led him into the dining room. "You know about wines and things, don't you? Do you remember that day when you got up for the first time? Well, look—there seems to be a lot of things there, and I didn't know what you would like. Will you choose? That's right. And now look at this room. Isn't it horrible? By rights we should be in here tonight, but I just couldn't bear it."

"It is rather large for two people, Mevrouw, but it is a beautiful room. An exceedingly beautiful room."

"Is it? Why?"

"It is nobly proportioned, Mevrouw. The arch of that window, the fall of the curtains, the sheen of polish on the furniture. Your husband must be a man of taste and discernment." He looked at the room as he spoke and then back at his hostess and wondered. This unknown, once-seen, and considerably disliked Mynheer Haan evidently had the eye of an artist. How that first meeting with his bride in the little cabin must have hurt him! How long had he been away? How much of this remarkable transformation had he seen? He put the question into words as, at Annabet's repeated request, he selected bottles from the cupboard.

"Oh, I hardly saw him. I do hope he will have a pleasant surprise when he comes back. He had a nasty one when he met me. You're my friend, aren't you, Captain Vehk? Can I say to you, without being misunderstood, that he made no secret of his feelings? And ask you a question? Is the change in *me* sufficient to justify me in expecting a change in *them?*"

"I should wait and see," he said with his head in the cupboard. She was almost lovely now. At this rate, soon she would be very lovely indeed—lovely, frank, honest, engaging, kind. What luck some men had!

The dinner went smoothly, and after coffee Annabet told about her cure and her oath of secrecy.

"That's why," she said, rounding off her story, "I couldn't ask anyone else to dine with us. Shal Ahmi was most insistent that I should see no one until Evert returned. That should be nine days from now. . . ." She stopped speaking suddenly and seemed to listen. "You aren't breathing queerly, are you? Somebody is. Listen!" He listened obediently and heard nothing. "Open the door sharply," Annabet said in a whisper, and in a normal voice went on, "And that is why Dr. van de Lijn said that you'd starved me. . . . You see, all this time I am supposed to be recovering from——" Jean Vehk had moved softly to the door and flung it open abruptly, expecting to find some startled, cringing native gabbling out some ready-made excuse about changing the candles or thinking he had been called. But outside the door the passage which led inwards to the house was bare and empty. On a bracket halfway along its length a little lamp burned steadily.

"Nobody there," he said, closing the door and returning to his place.

"My imagination," said Annabet, smiling. "It's so quiet here, especially up in my room, that I expect I shall get into the habit of hearing things, just as people who live alone get to talking to themselves. No, it isn't. There it is again."

And that time he heard it, a curious low sound, like a breath drawn in an extremity of pain. He remembered that he was not in Holland, nor aboard his ship where every sound was known and recognisable, and a nervous crepitation of which he was ashamed ran along his spine. This was a place where anything might happen. He looked at the silver bell which stood near Annabet's place at the table and had half a mind to suggest that she ring it and summon servants to make a tour outside the house. But even as the thought went through his mind Annabet, who had been listening with her head turned slightly aside, jumped up and said, "It's on the verandah," and ran to the shutter which closed the window.

He snapped, "Stand aside, Mevrouw," and pushed her hand from the bolt which secured the shutter to the floor, and moved it cautiously, opened the shutter an inch or two and, staring into the blackness, asked sharply, "Who's there?"

An unmistakable sound of distress answered him and he opened the shutter a little wider, and the candlelight, faint in itself but brilliant against the blackness of the moonless night, revealed to his searching eyes the figure of a man who lifted a white face—a *white* face—towards the light and said, "Thank God, Evert," and then seemed to drop, senseless.

Annabet, by this time, was at the captain's elbow. He turned his head.

"You called your husband Evert, didn't you?"

"Yes. That is his name." She pressed closer. "What is it? Who is it?"

"Somebody who seems to know your husband's name. No, wait a minute. Will you stand back?" He reached into his pocket and his pistol met his hand reassuringly; then deliberately he drew the shutter closed behind him and stepped onto the verandah. Nothing stirred. After a few seconds his eyes became accustomed to the darkness and he could see dimly the posts of the verandah, the edge of its roof

against the sky, the first few feet of the garden beyond. When
he was satisfied that no active intruders were lurking behind
the man who lay at his feet, he pushed the shutter open with
his elbow and, bending, seized the fallen man by his clothing
and pulled him into the room where Annabet waited, her
face expressive of anxiety, her hands clasped together high
on her chest.

"What is it? Who is it?" she asked in a whisper.

"I know no more than you do," he said, and dragged the
body into the light. "There. Ever see him before?"

Easy enough to say no; Evert was the only white man in
the whole of Banda whom she could have recognised by
sight. And it was not Evert. It was nobody whom she had
ever seen before. Yet, as she stared down at the upturned
face, so still, so shuttered and defenceless, and as her eyes
and her mind pronounced their verdict of nonrecognition,
she was pierced by a feeling similar to that which might
come to a blind man suddenly restored to sight, a man who
had handled and smelled a rose in the days of his blindness
and was now seeing one for the first time and knowing it for
what it was. A recognition not of touch or sight but of
essence.

For a moment during whch Jean Vehk thought her
shocked into silence he studied the man's face. Why should
it have this singularly moving quality? Why should it give
her a sense of fulfillment, of home-coming? In features it
was ordinary enough. A squarish face, tanned by the sun but
bleached now to a dirty pallor; a short, blunt nose that jutted
arrogantly; straight black brows, and long, rather childishly
curving lashes. But even now, in the complete relaxation of
unconsciousness, the features were of less significance than
the expression. It was, Annabet thought, such a very
bittersweet face. The lines that ran midway down the
slightly hollow cheeks, the lines that ran between nostril and
mouth, the curve of the mouth itself were all so eloquent of
bad luck borne with grim good humour, of disillusionment
accepted with resignation, and of a vast, almost fierce
determination. You could see at a glance that life had gone
hard with him, and that he could be gay, that he was
reckless and stubborn, and that his youth had been brought
to manhood oversoon. And it occurred to her that she was
reading a story that might already have reached its end.

"Is he dead?"

Jean Vehk did not answer immediately. He had dropped

to his knees beside the body and was feeling for the heart-beat of the stranger. The man wore a shirt, once white but now yellowed from the sun and bad washing, but ruffled at its front and cuffs. Vehk pulled it out of the waistband of the buff-coloured breeches and laid his hand on the man's chest.

"No, he is alive, Mevrouw. His heart beats." And as he spoke he saw, in the candlelight, the red pool widening about the man's shoulder. At the same instant Annabet said in a thin frightened voice, "He's bleeding! Can't we do something?"

"Mevrouw," said Vehk, sitting back on his heels, "this is no sight for you. Leave us. I will do what I can." But she gave a kind of wordless gasp of protest and put her hands on either side of the man's head, easing it over as Vehk turned the body.

The back of the white shirt was soaked with blood. Vehk pulled it up and exposed the wound. Just behind the right shoulder was a little gash, not more than an inch in length, narrow as the blade of a knife, but bleeding steadily. Vehk put his hand over it.

"Mevrouw, he has been stabbed in the back. Please—a lady . . . If you wish me to help him, go away yourself and send me one of your servants."

"I shan't faint," said Annabet quickly. "I'll stay and help. You see—he came very secretly, to the window, not to the door. And he asked specially for Evert, by name. It might perhaps be something they oughtn't to know about." As she spoke her mind shot off to Shal Ahmi and his secret comings and goings, and she realised that his visits had prepared her for secrecy. Back in Heydberg, faced with such a situation— if that were imaginable—her first thought would have been to call Truitje. But not here. Not Josef. Not Katje:

"Could we bring him round and ask him first?" she suggested.

Jean Vehk looked at her curiously. She had been in the house for three weeks and might know something which in this crisis made her judgement more valuable than his own. It was true enough, the stranger had come to the window, not to the door, and had said, "Thank God, Evert," and had promptly lost consciousness, as though, thinking that he recognised Haan, he could relax and leave the rest to him.

"As you will, Mevrouw," he said, and bent again over the body, which now lay face downwards. His quick brown fingers pressed the lips of the wound together and the bleeding lessened. Holding it so, he fumbled one-handed for his handkerchief and held it out to Annabet.

"Fold that into a tight hard pad. . . . Thank you. Now, have you anything handy which would be long enough to tie round his chest?" She thought quickly and said, "My stockings. Would they do?"

Vehk nodded and she stripped them off. "Tie the toes," he said. When they were knotted together he placed the knot over the folded handkerchief and, keeping it in position with his hand, turned the man over again. "Pull the ends clear and hold them a moment, will you?" Then, when the stranger's body was on its back again, handkerchief and knot pressed against the wound by its weight, he tied the ends of the stockings securely.

"When I was a boy," he said reminiscently, "my father cut his wrist with a billhook, and my mother stopped him bleeding to death with a piece of yarn and a cooking spoon. It's the quickness that tells. There. Now we'll lift his head— otherwise we'd choke him—did you know that? And now a little brandy in that glass, please." She poured it, surprised to find her hand so steady. "And a small spoon. . . . Thank you." Very gently he spooned drops of the spirit between the pale lips. He took his time now, holding the lolling head against the crook of his arm and dribbling a few drops, and then waiting, with the care and the patience of a woman feeding a sick child. Afterwards Annabet remembered the moment with gratitude.

Presently, of its own accord, the inert body stirred. Jean Vehk tightened his clasp. The man moaned. His eyelids fluttered without opening, and his lips parted on a deep indrawn breath. Jean Vehk spooned in a few more drops of brandy, and this time the man gulped them and opened his mouth again. He swallowed and then said, without opening his eyes and speaking in a clear voice which mangled the Dutch words with curious delicacy, "I thought I'd never get here." And then, perhaps because he expected Evert to answer him and was shot into complete consciousness by the silence with which Annabet and Jean Vehk received the remark, he opened his eyes. For a moment his stare was like a young puppy's, vague and milky; then it hardened and sharpened; consciousness, fright, suspicion, and caution showed in it. He lifted his head clear of the captain's shoulder and looked into his face.

"You're not Evert Haan," he said accusingly.

"I never pretended to be," said Jean briskly. He pulled a chair towards him and propped the stranger against the edge of the seat and stood up. "There, take your time," he said. "Mynheer Haan is away from home. I am the guest of his wife. This is Mevrouw Haan."

"Don't be silly," said the man. "Evert isn't married." He rolled his head against the seat of the chair and then said sharply, "Whoever she is, get her away. I'm going to be sick."

"I don't think you will be," Vehk said, still in that brisk, business-like voice. "You've been knifed in the back and lost a lot of blood. That's what gives you the feeling of nausea. Here, drink this." He mixed a glass of brandy and water and held it towards the man. "Can you manage?. . . . Good. You'll be all right. It's a perfectly clean wound. Replace your leakage and you'll be all right."

The stranger drained the glass and handed it back. Then he let his lids droop over his eyes again; but Annabet, standing slightly to one side, saw that his eyes were not closed, nor were his features relaxed. Upon that lowered face an expression of frank bewilderment gave way to one of extreme craftiness, and that gave way to a smile as he opened his eyes wide and said to Vehk, "I could sit in this chair if you lent a hand. . . . Thanks. Give me a drink, will you? Plain water." She saw his eyes above the glass as he drank thirstily; they were wary, concerned, speculative.

"Thank you," he said, returning the glass. And then, with a deliberate mustering of strength, "I'm sorry to give you so much trouble. But I thought Haan was here. The light shows through that shutter, you know, and I thought nobody else ever used this room. I'll go in just a minute, and I apologise for disturbing you." His voice tailed off weakly, but he made another effort, straightened himself with a grimace of pain that quickly vanished, and smiled. "You're a friend of Haan's?"

"No. As I said before, I'm a guest of Mevrouw Haan. This is Mevrouw."

"Oh, all right. I'm asking no questions. But I thought you might be a friend. Evert has a hundred of them. Understandable too. He's a grand fellow. And if you stick to it we'll pretend it's Mevrouw Haan. Ask me no questions and I'll ask you none. I'll go away in a minute. I had a little argument with a Chinaman, and he knifed me and I thought of Evert; he was nearest. But you're safe with me. If you say nothing, I say nothing and the whole thing's forgotten."

"But you wanted my husband for something. He is away. Is there anything I can do?" Annabet asked.

He looked at her seriously for the first time, frowning in an effort to concentrate, narrowing his grey eyes between their long dark lashes.

"You're Isa. I've heard about Isa. I didn't know she was—white. Don't bother. Not a word shall pass my lips. Just let me go and we'll forget it ever happened. My God, though, you are beautiful. And Evert thinks the world and all of you. You're a very naughty little girl. But if you'll forget me, I'll forget you—him too. Is that a bargain?"

Something snapped in Jean Vehk's brain. His face flushed. The man was hurt and wandering in his mind, doubtless, but Mevrouw was a wife of three weeks' durance and the most charming woman he had ever met.

"Mynheer," he said incisively, "this is Mevrouw Haan whom I had the honour of conveying from Holland to Banda. Mynheer Haan has gone away on business and Mevrouw, having invited me several weeks ago to dine with her, has been obliged to entertain me alone. Mevrouw will perhaps make allowance for the fact that you are not quite yourself, but until you *are* I should advise you to be silent."

Annabet, puzzled and embarrassed, saw the face muscles tighten under the oddly patched white and dirty tan-coloured skin. He, too, was puzzled and embarrassed. He lifted his left hand and brushed it across his brow and said, "I hardly know what I'm saying or where I am." But she knew that he was lying. Across the back of her mind fluttered the query: Who is Isa? But most of her consciousness was pondering the problem of the man himself. Who was he? Where did he come from? Why had he been knifed? What did he want with Evert? Why, thinking that she was somebody else, had he made that a bargain of secrecy? It was all extremely interesting.

Jean Vehk turned back to the table. "With your permission," he said, and poured first a glass of the yellow wine which she had drunk with her dinner, and then a glass of brandy for himself.

"We've had a shock, you know," he said, handing her the glass.

"I do know," the stranger said eagerly. "It was unpardonable of me. But I couldn't know, could I? I thought there'd be old Evert here, brooding over his accounts, and he'd patch me up, give me a drink, and we'd curse all hasty-tempered Chinamen. . . . I'd no idea. I wouldn't have disturbed a dinner party to save my life."

Vehk took up the words. "Be glad you didn't know, then. For we *did* save your life."

"I am infinitely obliged." He dropped his head and looked at the knot of stocking tops tied in a bow upon his chest. His eyes moved to Annabet, who blushed and looked away. "I am *infinitely* obliged," he repeated. His voice, for all its emphasis, was weakening, and as though he was aware of it he said hastily, "When will Evert be back?"

"In nine days' time," Annabet said.

"Then I'll look in and explain things and apologise." Above the grey eyes the bleached brows met as he frowned. "Perhaps you'd better just give him a message from me. Tell him the cock had a black tail. He'll know then why I didn't buy it for him. That was what the argument was about. The Chinaman didn't like what I said about the bird. Just tell him that the bird had a black tail. Then he'll know to look out for another. Evert"—the weak voice became carefully explanatory—"is very particular about his fighting cocks. And the best ones haven't black tails. Well, I think I'll go now."

He rose from his chair, casual and easy, just as though he had come in for a moment to leave a message about a fighting cock's tail. But as soon as his weight was on his feet he swayed, twisted to grip the back of the chair, missed it, and fell to the floor. He had not lost consciousness again, for his hands scrabbled at the table leg, then at its edge, and finally he pulled himself into a kneeling position and so stayed, looking at Annabet and Vehk with an expression at once piteous and defiant. He said three words under his breath which they did not understand, and his knuckles whitened as his hands gripped the smooth wood. Vehk, with something of deliberation in his movements, took a step forward and hooked his arm under the man's and heaved him back into the chair.

"I don't think you'll go very far tonight, Mynheer," he said when the action was performed. "It's no business of mine. In a few minutes I leave for my ship. You say you are a friend of Mynheer Haan. This is his house and here is his wife. Hadn't you better explain your business and tell her who you are and ask her assistance?" He turned to Annabet. "I think, Mevrouw, that you should ring your bell and summon Josef."

"Don't do that," said the stranger sharply. "Do anything but that."

"I won't," said Annabet eagerly. "You hoped to find my husband here. He is away, but I am here in his place. You may trust me, Mynheer. Please behave as though he were here. What would he do?"

"Presumably," said Vehk coldly, "he would know the man's name and business. Such knowledge eases arrangements, Mevrouw. And until you know——"

"Just a minute," said the man. He put his left hand upon the edge of the table and cautiously, experimentally, levered himself into a standing position. He attained it but dropped back almost instantly. "My God," he said furiously, "the spirit is willing, but the flesh is weak. . . . I never realised what that meant until this moment." He looked at Jean Vehk with a beaten, broken look. "You're a strong fellow. Do me a favour. Drag me down to the landing stage. There's a prahau there. Chuck me into it and set it loose. That's all I ask."

Jean Vehk looked at Annabet. The suggestion was quite to his taste. The stranger had disturbed his last interview with Annabet, was mysterious and uncommunicative, and he would have turned him adrift in a prahau without the slightest compunction. But it was Mevrouw's house. It was for her to say.

"It would be better, surely, to ring for Josef and ask him to prepare a bed. Wouldn't that be what my husband would do?"

"Good God, no!" He was silent for a moment after the emphatic statement, and Annabet, watching his face, thought what a pity it was that a person so near physical collapse should be driven to invent lies. "Mevrouw, your husband is an eminently respectable man. I am not. Our lives only meet because he has fallen victim to the charm of cockfighting. The Company does not quite approve of the sport. So I act for Evert; I buy his cocks and place his bets. I myself, Mevrouw, am a notorious character. If it were known that I had spent a night beneath Mynheer Haan's roof, it would ruin his reputation. I would avoid that at all costs. He has been a good patron to me. Do you understand?"

"And what would the good patron do if he were here?"

"Carry me to the prahau and turn it loose, Mevrouw. I do assure you that is the one thing to do."

"Good patrons are more careful of their protégés,

Mynheer. I think that if my husband were here he would solicit Captain Vehk's aid and convey you to his own room, see you into bed, and lock the door. I think, Mynheer, that it was not in order to be dragged to your prahau and set adrift that you came to that window. Or am I mistaken?"

"Excuse me," said the stranger. "I *am* now going to be sick."

He stretched his left hand across to the right-hand pocket of his breeches, pulled out his handkerchief, and held it in front of his face. Jean Vehk took a quick sideways step so that he might interpose his body between Annabet and the regrettable sight. She stood thinking quickly.

"Captain Vehk," she said after a moment, addressing his back, "will you do something for me? I am sorry to give you any more trouble, but there's no one else whom I can ask."

"I am at your service, Mevrouw. But before you decide on any plan of action I feel that it is my duty—if only because I am older than you and more experienced in the world— to point out that you should be very careful what you do in your husband's absence. We have only this fellow's bare word to show that he has even your husband's acquaintance; he has not told us his name; and the story of his business being concerned with a fighting cock sounds very thin to me. I agree that he is in no condition to be moved at the moment and unlikely to be of danger to you personally, but I should be very reluctant to assist you in any plan which involved harbouring him in your house secretly."

"But reluctant or not, you would do it? Please? You see, Captain Vehk, I'm quite certain that, mysterious as he seems, he *did* come to see my husband and intended his visit to be secret. So I must look after him and keep him hidden if it can be managed. With your help I think it can."

"I wish," said the man, and now his exhausted voice touched the syllables of the Dutch words so lightly that it sounded like a child's prattle, "you wouldn't both talk about me as though I were deaf or insane. I've told you what to do. Get me down to the landing stage and chuck me into my prahau."

"But you'd just drift. You couldn't row or steer. You might die." She said the words eagerly, forgetting to shelter behind the captain's body, staring into the man's face, oblivious of his wretched appearance.

"Well, you needn't worry about that, Mevrouw. It's better that I should drift and die than be caught here."

He bit his lip, and something told Annabet that he regretted the implications of the word "caught."

Vehk pounced on it at once. "This business of the fighting cocks must be very serious for you to talk like that."

"Damn you," said the stranger in a voice so faint that there was little venom in the words. "You're in the Company's service too. I suppose you've never done an errand that involved a few lies and a little secrecy. Evert Haan and I have been on the track of something very curious and shady for a long time. Tonight I got proof—and a knife in my back. If I'm connected with Coenpark in any way, Evert'll get a knife in *his* back as like as not. You're suspicious and bullheaded and Mevrouw, bless her heart, is kind and sentimental. Between you you'll ruin the whole business. My God, when I think——"

"Mynheer," Annabet said before Vehk could find any words, "if we could hide you here so that no one knew, and keep you until you could leave, and swear ourselves to complete secrecy, would that help?"

"But we don't know what we're keeping secret," Vehk pointed out logically. "First it's cockfighting; then it's secret business. Why should we trust either story? God knows, Mevrouw, it is only of you that I am thinking. You have to answer to your husband for what goes on in this house in his absence."

"You needn't worry about that. If you could manage it, Evert'd be grateful. I can swear to that," said the stranger.

"Then if Captain Vehk will help me I will manage it," Annabet said.

"Very well. What do you want me to do, Mevrouw?"

"Just to stay here quite quietly in the dark. I'll send Josef to the compound and get rid of Katje. Then I'll come back."

She blew out the candles and locked the door of the office behind her. The passage was dimly lighted, for the little lamp was growing short of oil, but the hall was still bright with candles, long-wicked in their sockets. After a moment's deliberation she rang the bell which stood on the table near the foot of the stairs.

Josef, who had been dozing, came through the door beyond the stairs, looking sleepy and a little sullen. His turban was loosely wound, and one cheek bulged with a fragment of nutmeg cheese which he had been chewing when sleep overtook him. He would not have dared answer Evert's summons, however late, in such a fashion, and somehow Annabet guessed it, and the knowledge gave her words incisiveness.

"You may lock up. The captain has gone. I have locked the office because there is a good deal of liquor left. I will unlock it in the morning. Good night."

He looked at her, thinking, Parsimonious Dutch housewife. Whoever heard of a lady doing such a thing? But he said very meekly; "Good night, Mevrouw," and shot the bolts on the big door and blew out all the candles as Annabet mounted the stairs.

Katje was dozing, too, but she sprang into wakefulness and helped Annabet to undress, accepting, with something of Josef's feeling, the single sweet which her mistress offered her from the whitewood box. She had never known a box of sweets to last so long. Every night one for Mevrouw and one for Katje. Her last mistress had had a fresh supply of sweets every day, and although she was greedy and getting a little fat as a result, there had always been a great many over when Mevrouw had gobbled her fill and Katje had had them. They had been hers, either to eat gluttonously or to share with other servants. This Mevrouw had made a single box last three weeks.

"I shall read for a time, but the light doesn't keep you awake, does it?" Annabet asked, settling into bed.

Katje lay down on her mat and slept instantly.

Annabet timed ten minutes by the French clock which had been Egbert's wedding gift to her and then rose and put on her gown and slippers as she had done every third night since Evert's departure.

In the study the twenty minutes which had passed since she had left Vehk and the stranger alone seemed like an hour. They had kept silence, not so much because she had ordered it, but because the wounded man found it safe and the captain could not find words with which to break it.

Annabet opened the door, and the candle in her hand shed its light upon the room.

"Now," she said, "if you will help me, Captain Vehk . . ."

"Put your good arm across my shoulders," Vehk ordered. And as the man obeyed he slipped his own right arm around his body, carefully avoiding the knot of the stockings. "Now, here we go."

He knew by the feel of his burden that as soon as the man put his weight upon his legs faintness and nausea made themselves felt. But the man was resolute too. He used his right hand to help himself, though the effort must have pained his wound; he clutched at the chair back, at the edge of the table, at the side of the doorway, and at the passage wall. Annabet paused for a moment and locked the door of the little office and then, edging past them, went, with a solicitous look backwards now and then, before them across the hall and up the stairs. The candle which she carried shed a little pool of light in the pervading darkness, and there was a scent of flowers, and her long loose gown made a little whispering sound on the stairs.

Annabet turned left along the gallery at the top and opened the second door.

"This is Evert's room," she said in an ordinary voice. "I can lock it and keep it locked under some pretence or other. I shall say that I'm moving the furniture to surprise him when he returns, or something like that."

She carried the candle into the room and lighted others. The room was large, furnished with dark heavy pieces, rich, sombre. She pulled back the curtains of the bed and turned down the covers.

"If you will help him into it," she said, and turned aside while Vehk removed the man's breeches and boots and eased the long heavy body into the bed.

"There," he said finally. "That's done. What else can I do, Mevrouw?"

A voice from the bed answered him. "Nothing else, thanks. Except hold your tongue. That is most important of all."

"I realised that," Vehk said coldly. "You are now Mevrouw's guest and, as such, no subject for gossip. Mevrouw, I should like to speak to you."

"I shall come back," she said, addressing the man in the bed, and then she lifted the candlestick again and led the way from the room. She went straight down the stairs and set the candle on the table in the hall beside the bell and the bowl of flowers. She turned and faced the captain.

"I don't know how to thank you. I don't know what I should have done if I had been alone. Please promise that you'll never come to the islands without coming to see me."

"I promise that, Mevrouw. And you——" his voice was suddenly, surprisingly, most shamingly husky—"take good care of yourself. You've a beautiful home and your health again. I hope you'll find life very happy." He lifted one hand after the other and kissed her fingers. And a warm, weakening wave of feeling ran over her as she realised that there was more than mere formality in the action. That part of her mind which had noted and analysed the butcher's good measure, the shoemaker's favouritism, the landlord's instant response sprang into action again after a long abeyance. But not, tonight, simple girlish vanity. The pleasure was weighted on one side with sorrow—because now she was going to open the door and say "Good-bye" again and this moment would be over, ended, sterile—and upon the other with anticipation, because now her looks were coming back and in nine days Evert would be returning and, oh, the whole of life spread out before her, offering who knew what of interest and experience.

She set both hands to the great key and the heavy bolts. The door opened on the warm, scented night, upon the velvet sky so thickly sown with stars.

"Good-bye, Captain Vehk. Good luck on the voyage."

"Good-bye, Mevrouw. God bless you."

"Good-bye."

"Good-bye."

She locked the door and bolted it and took up her candle. Halfway up the stairs she paused and clutched the rail. "God bless you . . ." They had been Father Vincent's parting words too. And he had meant that he wished God to give her the strength to bear being ugly, to give the power to look outside herself, to aid her in living the life of the spirit. But the little captain had hoped that she would be happy; he had mentioned her beautiful house and her regained health—by which he meant, but was too polite to say, her looks. And she thought sadly, Jean Marie would call that feeling I now have *sin*. Sin of quite a deadly kind, because it is a trespass of the spirit. I knew that little Jean was feeling amorous, and I could quite easily have kissed him too. I wasn't disgusted; I was pleased! Jean Marie would say that I'm quite as wicked as though I had kissed him. But can one help what one feels and thinks? Thoughts and feelings come so quickly; they don't wait to be invited.

She felt quite dizzy from the working of her puzzled mind. And in the morning there would be a spatter of candle grease where she had stood and asked herself the questions which had no answers.

Then suddenly she remembered the man lying in Evert's bed; and as though running to a refuge, she straightened the drooping candlestick, lifted the skirt of her long gown, and sped into Evert's room.

He lay flat on his back and his eyes were closed, and for a moment she thought, What a pity. She had intended to tell him of her plans. But as she abandoned that idea and thought, I'll just have to lock him in and trust he has sense enough not to make a sound in the morning or whenever he wakes, the black lashes fluttered and lifted.

"Mevrouw," he said, and his voice was stronger, "I should be grateful to you. My body is. No bed has ever been so welcome. But my mind would have been easier in the drifting prahau."

"I'm not going to ask you any questions," she said hurriedly. "If there is anything I can do for you, I'll do it. Then I must lock the door and leave you. Sometime tomorrow, somehow, I'll bring you some food, and since you are the one who mentioned secrecy, you'll know that you mustn't make a sound. As soon as you feel well enough to go you can go and I promise I won't mention that you've been here, or anything about you. Does that put your mind at rest?"

"It should. But it doesn't. No, don't think that I don't trust you. Curiously enough, I *do*. But it's such a *one-sided* bargain. Mevrouw, I told you the truth when I said that Evert and I had business together; but God knows what he'd say if he knew that I'd involved *you* in it. And sheltering me does involve you."

She set the candlestick down and moved to the side of the bed.

"I said I wouldn't ask you any questions, but I will. Just one. You needn't answer it if you don't want to. If Evert had been here, would he have done what I've done?"

"Almost exactly—but I shouldn't be in *his* bed."

"Then that's all right. Evert's business is my business; and in his absence I must act for him."

"How long have you known him?"

"I don't really know him at all. Ours was a glove marriage, you see. I landed in Banda three weeks ago. And two days later he had to go away on business. I expect you know him better than I do."

The full, beautifully shaped lips curved in a smile.

"I've known him for nearly five years. That's a long time, isn't it?" The smile faded completely. The next words came with startling bluntness, almost effrontery. "Why on earth did *you* make a glove marriage?"

"That would take too long to tell. I'll fetch you some water from my room and then I must leave you. Would you like something to make you sleep?"

"Poppy or mandragora? No, thank you. I'm half asleep now. Water, yes."

She went soft-footed past the sleeping Katje and fetched the water jug from beside her own bed. Putting it down on the little table where Evert's empty brandy flask still lay, she said, "I'm afraid I don't seem to be doing much for you. I haven't had much experience in nursing the sick. I have been ill myself too. Truitje used to bathe my head with vinegar and water. Would you like your head bathed?"

There was something quite touching, he thought, about the little childish question. Dimly, for his mind seemed to be slipping down slopes into slumber, he remembered that he had called her Isa, thought she was Evert's kept woman, and tried to bargain for her secrecy. What a shame.

"No, thank you, Mevrouw. I shall sleep now. And in the morning don't worry about coming to me if it proves inconvenient. I will wait quietly. Good night."

"Good night."

She locked the door and went to her own room. From the bathroom she took one of the water jars and the cloth which Katje used for wiping the bath and the floor and went down to the study. The tiled floor was easily cleaned, but the man had bled onto the rug before Vehk had rolled him over, and some mark remained even when she had scoured it. She stared at the stain with despair for a moment and then poured over it the coffee which remained in the little silver jug. The black puddle engulfed the brownish mark and the wider sweep of the water. When she had satisfied herself that nothing suspicious was left inside the room, she opened the shutter and with some nervous qualms which needed all her resolution to ignore stepped onto the verandah. The night was almost menacingly silent, and she could not help thinking as she held the candle low and searched for the bloodstains that if anything happened now there was no one for whom to call. Katje lay in drugged slumber, and the stranger was not only weak as a kitten, but locked in. Still, it must be done. The verandah was floored with wood, dark in colour, boldly grained, and here and there between the top

of the steps which led to the garden and the study window
there were marks, just discernible to one who expected them
and was searching for them, but the blood had soaked in
beyond the reach of her wet cloth and on that dark surface
did not look distinctive enough to be dangerous. With a little
sigh of relief she emptied the water jug over the rail into the
garden, scuttled indoors, and bolted down the shutters. But
fear went with her. Overstrained nerves suggested that
someone, something, might have crept through the open
window while she was bent over the trail of marks and might
now be hiding—in the shadowy study, in the more than
shadowy hall, around the curve of the stairs, even in her
own room. She could visualise a disembodied smile of sly
triumph greeting her from the shadow of her bed curtains—
Aha, I have you at last. Her skin crawled with cold when at
last she gained the blue-and-white room and found Katje
sleeping on her mat and everything as she had left it. She
tumbled into bed with some muddled reflections upon the
rightness of Father Vincent's arguments. Nothing had
threatened her, yet she had been frightened, had experienced
the physical symptoms of fear because she had conjured
danger from her own mind. The mind was important; it had
great power. She pursued the thought until she was dizzy
again, and then she slept, dreaming wildly.

Katje always brought up enough breakfast for two
nowadays, and without much self-denial Annabet was able
to save a good deal of it, laying slices of ham, rolls, and fruit
in a clean handkerchief hidden in one corner of the bed.
When Katje removed the tray Annabet had her plan ready.
Ordinarily the woman would carry the tray to the kitchen
and then begin to bring up the bath water. Then she would
make the bed, and after her bath Annabet would either
return to her bed for a time, while Katje tidied the room, or
dress and go down to the garden, leaving the room to Katje.

"I'm tired this morning. I shall go to sleep again. I don't
want to be disturbed until eleven. But first I must see Josef."

She put on her gown and slippers, and took the office key
in her hand. Going through the hall, she rang the bell and
then hurried along the passage and unlocked the office door.
In the morning light, when she had thrown open the shutters,
the bare little room and table with fruit and wineglasses and
coffee cups upon it made an incongruous sight.

"I'm afraid you'll have to wash that rug, Josef," she said

pleasantly. "I spilled a whole cup of coffee." She moved to the table as Josef studied the marks on the rug. She couldn't leave him to remove the bottles, since she had made that feeble excuse for locking the door last night, and she didn't want him to know that the dining-room cupboard had had its lock forced. When the door was closed it looked as usual. She said casually, "There's less left than I thought. This can go out, and this. The brandy I'll take to my room."

Going back to her room, she took the bundle of food and the bottle of brandy and the key of Evert's room and stepped out into the gallery.

The man lay just as she had left him last night: his eyes were closed, and in the shadow of Evert's plum-coloured bed curtains his face was waxen and yellow. He looked so ill that for a moment she had a feeling of panic. Suppose he died—she hadn't thought of that. Suppose she found herself with a corpse on her hands. And eight days to go before Evert—the only person who could possibly be told—returned. She locked the door behind her after a first hasty glance and then, almost running to the bed, shook the man quite roughly by the shoulder. He stirred and moaned. She could have shed tears of relief. He opened his eyes and looked at her, blankly at first and then with recognition which merged into a smile.

"You did frighten me," she said. "I thought you'd be awake, waiting for me. I hope I didn't hurt you, but I couldn't call because I didn't know what to call you."

"What a predicament," he said, still smiling.

"How are you this morning?"

"I've hardly had time to decide." He moved his body cautiously. "Ugh! Stiff and sore. But I slept well. I shall be all right. Don't worry about me."

"I've brought you some food. I'm afraid you'll have to drink brandy or water. I couldn't hide any coffee. And this looks horribly rough and ready, doesn't it? But it is a little awkward. Katje almost lives in my room, you see." She laid the food on the table beside the bed. "Can you reach it there?"

"Quite well, thanks." He turned his head and looked at it, hiding the feeling of nausea which the very idea of food aroused in him. "I'll eat and drink, too, presently. I'm still half asleep."

"I ought to do something about the wound, too, oughtn't I? It ought to be bathed and have a clean bandage." She spoke uncertainly, aware of her ignorance in such matters.

"It'll be better left alone, thanks. If we touch it we might
open it again. It's all right now and we'll leave it."

She saw that he was more than half asleep again and too
weak to talk. Dissatisfied with herself, she stole away quietly
and locked the door.

At eleven o'clock Katje called Annabet and prepared her
bath. At midday she carried up the tray of light refreshments
which served to bridge the gap between the substantial
breakfast and the evening meal which was the custom in
Banda. When she had eaten part of the meal and hidden the
rest, Annabet took out the box of sweets and held it to Katje,
saying as she did so, "I may not rest today. I slept all the
morning and shall probably go into the garden. But I shan't
want you, Katje."

Katje selected a pale purple sweet, put it into her mouth,
and lifted the tray. I ought to have noticed how long they
take to work, her mistress thought, watching her through the
door. She might fall asleep on the stairs! She listened; there
was no sound of breaking crockery and no sign of Katje's
return. She timed twenty minutes by the French clock, and
then, feeling like a hunted animal, slipped into Evert's room.
As she unlocked it she remembered that she had made no
excuse for having locked the door. How often did they dust it
in their master's absence? Had the door been tried already?
Would it be safe (as it was desirable) to say nothing for a day
or two? The man had spoken of leaving this evening, but he
hadn't looked fit to move. Oh, what a tangle, she thought,
pushing the door open and turning to lock it again; and what
a worry, just when I was feeling so happy, too.

The bedclothes were all tossed about now, and the waxen
face had a curious dull flush upon its cheeks. The man's eyes
were open, but they did not turn towards the door or towards
her; they stared at the ceiling, and their expression was at
once vacant and wild.

"You don't know me, do you?" she asked, going near the
bed and leaning over him. One lean brown hand moved
across the covers with the gesture of someone brushing a fly
away. Apart from this movement, he lay as before. She could
have wept from consternation and worry. Suppose he cried
out as people did in delirium!

Some part of her mind produced the thought that her
concern should, by rights, be for the man, not for herself;

and at the same time she noticed that his lips were cracked and dry. She looked at the bedside table and saw that he had touched neither the food nor the water which she had placed there. And he had spoken so bravely about leaving at nightfall. He must have been feeling so ill. Everything else gave way to a flood of pity. She remembered how often Truitje or Klara had given her water when she was too weak to reach for it. She poured some from the jug into the glass and then awkwardly slipped her arm behind the man's head, raising it, while with the other hand she held the glass to his lips. He drank thirstily, but his wild vacant stare did not change. She could feel the heat of his neck through the thin stuff of her sleeve. And then the heat seemed to be in her eyes and throat as tears of pity rushed upwards. He must have been feeling so very ill this morning, but he had sent her away fooled by his brave words about leaving this evening. And he was young. She had never thought about his age before; had, indeed, hardly realised him as a person at all. Now, with the brown and bleached hair tumbling against her shoulder and the heat of his fever scorching her arm, she suddenly became acutely aware of him, not as a stranger, not as embarrassing responsibility, but as a man, young, sick, utterly dependent. With a gesture she had never used to anyone in her life before, she pushed back the tumbling hair from his forehead. He muttered something, but in such a low, slurred voice that even had the words been in Dutch she would hardly have caught them. Then he turned his face so that it rested against the still almost imperceptible curve of her breast. His hand moved again in that restless, fluttering way, as though he was reaching for something. Careful not to move her body, she set the glass back on the bed table and then, with the hand thus freed, took his and held it. He gave a sigh. She saw the black lashes drop over the blind wildness of his eyes. He seemed to sleep.

She sat for what seemed a long time, uncomfortably perched on the edge of the bed, looking down upon his closed, secret face and wondering about him. Her speculations had become entirely personal; she no longer wondered what might his business be with Evert or the reason for his secrecy. Instead she wondered what his name might be; how old he was; where he came from, with his delicate limping Dutch and his lapses into another tongue; most of all she wondered what any woman in her position would have wondered—whose place was she filling at this moment? To what remembered breast had he turned as though from habit, seeking a refuge from pain and weakness? To whose handclasp had his own responded unconsciously, instinctively? Was some unknown woman in some unguessed-of place worrying herself sick because he had not come home?

The wonder opened strange vistas in her mind. She found herself imagining what he looked like when he was hale and well. Would he lie like this relaxed from loving, not from weakness; and how would it feel to hold him like this, not with a wondering pity but with delight? Her young, untried senses strained at the leash of reason. How vile, she thought weakly, to brood like this over a sick, senseless man. But the little mental protest was swept away like a paper boat on a flooded gutter. The breath from his parted, cracked lips was warm on her breast, melting her very heart; and all the tiny experience of the mystery of sex which had ever been hers rushed, like parted molecules of quicksilver, into one shining whole. Glances of admiration in the street or in church, little instances of favouritism, the long, abortive worship of Cousin Jean Marie, Klara's whispered warnings and the feeling they had roused, the despair, the emptiness of hope occasioned by Evert's hatred, the sheer joy of living restored by Shal Ahmi's magic, the moment last night when Captain Vehk had kissed her hands. They were not separate things. Widely as they differed in shape and texture, they had all been steps leading to this moment, this final revelation of what it was all about.

She looked down quite wildly at the face, pinched, shadowed, and flushed, which rested between her arm and her body and thought, I love him. . . . I've fallen in love *again*, but how? Why? When I came in at that door I was half regretful, thinking him a nuisance. . . . He's done nothing, said nothing, to change my mind.

It wasn't possible. It wasn't reasonable. It was something which had happened, apparently, simply because she had allowed herself, because of his sickness, to pass the bou..ds which convention imposed, very rightly, between men and women. Mamma had been right in her orders that one must never, never allow liberties. Because obviously the female body was not to be trusted. For the first time Annabet understood how Klara had fallen a victim to the red-faced, hard-breathing young man. Probably he'd just kissed her. And if holding a sick, senseless man out of kindness could work such havoc in a girl, what would a kiss from a whole, sensible one do? God, suppose she had given way to that impulse to kiss Captain Vehk in the hall last night!

I must get out of this, she thought. And very gently she loosed first the hand which held the stranger's and then, little by little, the arm which held him. He stirred and muttered as she laid him back upon the pillow, and something in her, too, cried out at the breaking of the bond. But at last she stood, free and separate, with pins and needles shooting through her arm, beside the bed. And even then she was not out of thrall. Moving jerkily, as though an imperative hand had propelled her, she stooped and kissed the place where the brown hair grew in a little V on the pale brow. Then, like a hunted creature again, she stepped out to the gallery, looked right and left, looked down the stairs, locked the door, and shot into her own room.

Resolutely she turned her mind to practical matters. The man in the next room was very ill and there was, in the circumstances very little that she could do for him if at the same time she preserved the secret of his presence. But—and everything, feeling, reason, even her physical being, seemed to halt and listen as she made the decision—Shal Ahmi would come tonight; Shal Ahmi was a great dealer in secrets; he had knowledge and power. To save the life of the stranger she would confide in Shal Ahmi.

Shal Ahmi and the muffled women arrived as usual, and tonight, as soon as they were safely in the room and he had freed his hands from the women's arms, he took from amongst his garments a little jar of red pottery, wide at the base, narrow-necked, and stoppered.

"Tonight, Mevrouw, they work to nourish, not to loosen. Here are the Five Oils of Guru Sanjitji. It has been known to keep flesh on the bones and life in the bodies of men who could swallow no food because of sickness or because of spear wounds in the face. It is of all things most rare and precious." He drew out the stopper and placed the jar in the hands of one of the women and turned to leave, as was his custom.

"Wait," Annabet said. "Something has happened since you were here, Shal Ahmi. And there is no one whom I can ask for help except you."

She realised anew his utter strangeness, but she beckoned him out of the room and then continued:

"Evert trusts you, or he wouldn't have asked you to help

me. And in this affair I've only tried to do what he would have done if he had been at home. Last night a man arrived, very secretly, asking for my husband. He didn't tell me his business, and though he's hurt so that he couldn't leave, he wouldn't let me call the servants. So I put him in here and did what I could for him. But now he's out of his mind and in a high fever. Will you see what you can do for him? Please, Shal Ahmi."

"Mevrouw, one of my trades is the cure of sickness. Open the door."

The man lay in an uneasy attitude amid the tumbled bedclothes. The flush on his face had darkened, the bleached brown hair was damp and lank with perspiration, and there was a faint, sickly scent in the room. Annabet walked straight to the bedside table and lighted the candles. Shal Ahmi stopped for a moment at the foot of the bed and then, pushing the plum-coloured curtain far back on the other side, bent and took a close look at the patient. As he did so he shot a quick glance at Annabet on the far side of the bed, and she saw the expression on his face change, not to pity or to professional interest or even to curiosity, but to sharp, immediate concern.

"Do you know his name, Mevrouw?"

"No. Nor anything about him."

"But he spoke to you?"

"Yes. He told us some lies—at least that is a harsh word. He tried to make us believe that his business was secret because it was to do with cockfighting—not quite respectable."

"*Us*, Mevrouw? Who was with you?"

"Captain Vehk of the *Java*. We dined in the little office and just as we had finished *he* came to the window. He told us a Chinaman had knifed him in a quarrel about a cock's tail. He thought he could leave and left me a funny message for Evert, something about the cock having a black tail. But he *is* knifed. I saw the wound. He said he'd be able to leave tonight—and now I don't know what to do. I can't look after him *properly*."

"If you worry yourself, Mevrouw, you will undo the good which we have done in the past days." Shal Ahmi's voice was smooth and kind again. And he did seem interested. She was relieved until she looked down at the bed again and saw that the man's eyes were opened, set in a glassy, senseless stare. And her heart knew a pang of pain and she said urgently:

"*Do* help him."

"You may leave him to me, Mevrouw. Will you go now? Empty your mind of all concern; lie on your bed and let the old women ply their trade. Then I will return them to their place and at the same time fetch the things I need. The night is yet young. I can go and come again and still do much before daylight."

The women stood where they had been left. She touched one and then the other and lay down on her bed, loosening her clothing as she had done after the first visit. The Five Oils had a fragrant, musty scent, like that of dying roses; it made their hands slippery and soft. Tonight they stroked her gently, and she thought that, if last night had never been, as soon as they were gone she would fall asleep, more blissfully and soundly than she had done since the unremembered days of very early childhood. But she must keep awake. Shal Ahmi was coming back again; she must open the door for him and probably help him with what he had to do.

The blind hands ceased their ministrations and she rose from the bed; with the perfect timing which he had always shown, Shal Ahmi appeared as soon as she was gowned and slippered. A usual she carried the candle down the stairs and unlocked the heavy door.

"I may be an hour, Mevrouw," he said as with a draped, anonymous, sightless, earless figure on either arm he stepped into the darkness.

"I shall wait," she assured him.

She went straight to Evert's room. And there she stared with astonishment at Shal Ahmi's handiwork. The bed had been stripped to the lower sheet, and halfway down its length the pillow and the bolster had been laid on top of one another. The sick man lay face downwards across this mound, his head hanging unsupported towards the bed's upper end. His shirt had been removed, so had the handkerchief and the bandage of stockings. His back, with the dark gash in its whiteness, was curved over the bolster and pillow. Below the wound, covering him almost to the knees and holding him firmly in position like a vise, was the upper sheet folded lengthwise. It touched the floor on either side and was held down upon the one side by a chest which had been pulled forward, and upon the other by a chair, turned on its back and weighted by the rest of the bedclothes, two pairs of boots, a basin, and ewer. The man's hands, which were free, scrabbled at the mattress, and he was moaning.

It was a cruel way to treat a sick man, she thought, and hurried forward; and then halted, remembering that she had asked Shal Ahmi's help, that he was wise where she was ignorant, and that he had cured her. She dared not touch the curious cage, but she went and sat on the bed, just above the mound of pillow, and edged inwards until her thigh was below that turning head which had no place to rest, and with her hands she lifted it into her lap and gently stroked it. And the man moaned and then sighed, and one of his hands wandered about again until she took it in her own. And then, as before, he grew quiet.

She tried to keep her eyes from the uncovered wound in his back, puffed and purple, so that it seemed twice the size it had been last night; and all around it, for perhaps three inches in every direction, was a dark crimson patch, like a great bruise. It should have been bathed and bandaged, she thought disconsolately; and she knew that she had accepted his refusal of her ministrations largely because of the difficulties in the way of making them.

"Darling," she said aloud, using the word which sometimes, rarely, she had used to comfort Klara, "you must get better. If you don't I shall blame myself forever." And her fingers tightened on the hot limp hand as though pressure and tension might convey some healing virture.

She was so busy with her conflicting thoughts and feelings that time slipped away quickly and she was suprised to hear Shal Ahmi's cane tapping the lighted window. She loosened her hand gently and edged her way off the bed, regretting the uncomfortable position into which the man's head fell as soon as it was unsupported.

Shal Ahmi had a great basket on his arm and a bundle in his hand. He did not wait for her to lock the door but marched straight up the stairs and into Evert's room. He had been hurrying and was breathing in short sharp gasps, but his feet on the stairs were rapid and silent. When she had closed the door again and reached the bedroom he was on his knees in the middle of the floor, a heterogeneous collection of articles spread about him. There were leaves, green and glossy, laid out on a square of white cloth, two more of the small red earthenware jars, a little pestle and mortar of grey stone, a tiny black pot with a long handle, a bundle of stuff which looked like very fine white tow, a knife with a short pointed blade, and, most startling of all, a miniature brazier, shaped like a flowerpot, set on three little legs. Through its pierced sides she could see the dull red glow of charcoal.

As she entered Shal Ahmi finished his hasty unpacking and, bending his head, breathed upon the brazier until the glow brightened. She watched him with renewed admiration for his resource and forethought. And at the same time there was a chill upon her. Such a dearth of any feeling lay at the root of his efficiency. She knew without being told that he had not wasted a single glance upon the patient and that he would not look his way until all the preparations were completed.

As soon as the charcoal glowed he set the long-handled pot over the top of it and straightened himself, still kneeling. He placed the glossy green leaves in the mortar, laid the pestle upon them, and handed the whole thing to her.

"Pound them into a paste. The odour will be unpleasant, but it will do you no harm." His smooth brown hands busied themselves with the black pot and the jars.

There had been truth in his words. As soon as the pestle had fallen upon the leaves, bruising them, a strange, bitter scent filled the room. Annabet's eyes stung and pricked; her nostrils felt as though they were full of acrid dust; she opened her mouth in order to breath more easily, and instantly her mouth was dry. In a few minutes it hurt her to blink her eyelids over her prickling eyes, and her dry tongue moved like a dead leaf against her parched lips. But she pounded away, and the big shiny leaves collapsed and shrank until at last they were only a spoonful of soft moist paste at the bottom of the pestle. By that time a faint steam was rising from the black pot. Shal Ahmi took the knife and held it for a moment inside the pot, and then, rising to his feet, he said:

"Keep your distance, Mevrouw, and take no notice of what you may hear."

Then he advanced towards the bed.

She told herself fiercely that Shal Ahmi knew what he was doing. He had cured her; he would cure the stranger. But the low, infinitely desolate moaning which came presently from the direction of the bed struck at her heart. She wanted to cry, "Oh, don't, please don't hurt him any more." The man was beyond words; she wanted to cry out for him. But she stayed silent and in a few moments Shal Ahmi came quietly to her side, took the mortar from her hand, looked at its contents critically, and went away again. Then he put the mortar, now empty, on the floor and took up a handful of the towy substance, and then he came back for a roll of white linen which lay near the brazier.

"Now, if you wish, you can help me, Mevrouw."

She moved to the bedside and her eyes went straight to the wound. It was bleeding again, but slowly, almost indecisively; and plunged into it was the mass of green paste which she had pounded, and even as she looked the bleeding stopped. Shal Ahmi, with the careless ease of perfect proficiency, placed the handful of tow over the green paste and with his other hand gave the roll of linen a twist so that it uncurled like a white snake.

"Draw the end under, Mevrouw, and return it to me. Ah, that is right. Your fingers are nimble. And again, and again. I think the man told you the truth, Mevrouw. The knife which stabbed him was poisoned. A Chinese trick. But Shal Ahmi is skilled in such matters. I have cut away the rotten flesh, and the leaves will do the rest. Now I will fix this, so." He caught the end of the bandage and twisted it firmly under its own folds. "The wound is now finished, forgotten." He lifted away the weighted chair upon his side of the bed and loosed the sheet. "Shake the pillow, Mevrouw, and place it in position while I turn him." He lifted the man as easily as a child lifts a doll and laid him flat again. "For the fever and weakness I have other cures, but those I can apply alone. Go to your bed now, Mevrouw, and sleep without a care. I shall stay here until nightfall tomorrow. I have all I need. And your uninvited guest will be safe with me. When Katje sleeps tomorrow come to us. Perhaps we may leave together."

"I can never thank you, Shal Ahmi. But please believe that I am *extremely* grateful."

"Thanks, Mevrouw, should be kept for favours. I merely ply my trade. In your service—in his—it is all one. Sleep soundly, Mevrouw."

He turned to his pots and jars. Across his bent head Annabet looked towards the bed and the sick man. He lay quiet and still as the dead. But he was going to live now and perhaps leave with Shal Ahmi tomorrow night. She might never see him again.

She had breakfasted and was in her bath the next morning when knuckles beat loudly upon the bedroom. Katje ran and a moment after returned, her manner excited.

"Mevrouw, that was Josef. There is someone to see you who will not be turned away. Mynheer's orders were that you were not to be disturbed until his return, but this is Mynheer Kaerko, the agent, and he will not leave until he has seen you."

There was an imperativeness about the message which, in the present circumstances, sounded ominous. Horribly conscious of the inmates of the next room, Annabet, aided by Katje, whose fingers fumbled from haste, put on her best dress, coloured her face, and brushed her hair.

Josef was hovering in the hall, and as soon as she stepped from the bottom stair he threw open the drawing-room door, and from quite a distance Annabet could see Kaerko, arrested in an uneasy pacing to and fro, his hat clasped to his chest, his face drawn from sleeplessness and worry. She was not relieved to see his expression change to sharp curiosity as she entered the room. Across the surface of his anxious mind drifted the thought, Van de Lijn was right then; it was just a temporary indisposition; and she walks as well as I do, so I can tell Hootman he was wrong about her legs. But at the moment he could not take comfort in the trivial, gossipy thought. Bowing low, he said quickly, "Mevrouw, I do indeed regret this intrusion, but my errand is serious, as you shall hear."

He waited until she had seated herself in one of the graceful little chairs and then, still standing, hurried on, "I am given to understand, Mevrouw, that Captain Vehk of the *Java* dined with you on the day before yesterday."

"He did," Annabet said with dry lips. Surely, surely little Vehk hadn't talked about the stranger. She remembered that she had not specially begged his silence—she had taken it for granted—but he hadn't seemed to like the man very much and had opposed her plan for hiding him.

"You must excuse this question, Mevrouw, but you will understand that in a case like this it is my duty to make every enquiry which might throw light on the case. I have my report to write for the Company."

"Do sit down, Mynheer, and tell me what it is you want to know." She heard the breathy, frightened sound in her own voice. If she swore that the man had gone, would he search the house? Would he break down the door of Evert's room?

"What did he eat, Mevrouw? Could you tell me that? It sounds an impertinent question, I know. But this is not

Holland—and you being new to the country—and Mynheer Haan away—it is possible that the servants——" He ended in complete incoherence.

"That the servants *what*, Mynheer?" she asked gently, taking courage from his confusion. Not thus were deadly accusations made.

"That they served something which should have been thrown out, Mevrouw. The carelessness of native servants passes the bounds of imagination."

"Is Captain Vehk ill?"

"He is dead."

"Oh no!" she cried foolishly. "Oh, poor man." She thought for an instant of their parting—of the way he had kissed her hands. He couldn't be *dead*. "He was perfectly well when he left here."

"And when he arrived on board. I grant you that, Mevrouw. Whether during the hours of yesterday he felt indisposed or not, of course no one can say. He complained to no one. But shortly after midnight last night he was found almost dead in his cabin, and he died at one o'clock this morning. Dr. van de Lijn, who was called at midnight and who stayed until he died, says that he showed all the symptoms of food poisoning. Was there a dish of shellfish served at your table, Mevrouw?"

"No. Josef served the meal. And I ate dish for dish with my guest, Mynheer. Little cutlets of white fish—steamed, I think." She gulped, realising that little Jean Vehk would never eat anything anywhere again—and he had kissed her hands and she had been aware of a desire to embrace him and had afterwards chided herself.

Kaerko, watching her with the observant eyes which had served the Company so well, thought his mean thoughts. Good God, she was in love with the fellow, a perfectly ordinary ship's captain. . . .

"Mevrouw," he said, rising to his feet, "please do not distress yourself. I am sorry that you have been drawn into the matter at all, but you will understand that it was my duty to pursue every possible path of enquiry."

"Mynheer, I am as interested as you are in bringing home the blame. Perhaps you will be so good as to let me know the result of your enquiries."

She had her hand on the knob of the door handle before he could leap ahead and open it. And then, turning, she said graciously, "Good morning, Mynheer," and left Kaerko wondering.

She stood for a moment near the tub of plants at the stairhead, conscious of feelings more sharply divided than she had often known. She was distressed about Jean Vehk and could have very easily shed tears over his death, but half shamedly she realised that actually Kaerko's statement about the cause of his errand had brought a feeling of relief, almost of triumph. Her secret was still safe. And overlaid upon the sorrow and the relief was a feeling of irritation. Had the upper floor of the house been safely deserted, she knew that she would have opened the white door and said abruptly to Shal Ahmi, "Captain Vehk is dead." And why she should desire to tell the news to that strange brown-faced man she could not understand. It was rather—she delved deeply into her own mind—as though he *ought* to know.

The long day ended at last; the short twilight gave way to darkness, and the little scented wind came coolly over the land. With surging impatience which at times palsied her hands Annabet waited while Katje served the long-drawn-out evening meal. When the meal was over she made Katje brush her hair for half an hour and then said that she would take a bath and go to bed early. The preparation, the bath itself, and the clearing away consumed the greater part of another slow hour. She climbed into bed and tried to fasten her attention upon her book. Katje moved slowly about the room, yawning more from boredom than from sleepiness.

Annabet counted the yawns and presently produced the box of sweets. "I think you are tired, too, Katje. I shall read for a little, but you can go to bed. I'll put the candle out."

Katje thankfully lay down on her mat.

Annabet could hardly wait until the woman's breathing changed to the rhythm of sleep. As soon as it did so she got out of bed and, with the key of Evert's room swinging from one finger, the candlestick in one hand and a parcel of food in the other, slipped along the gallery. As she fitted the key into the door she listened. There was no sound. There had been no sound from the room all day, and the silence had added to the mystery.

The shutters had been closed, and the last inch of candle was guttering in its socket. The room smelled close and airless, full of warring scents, amongst which she recognised only the sharp acrid odour of the pounded leaves and the fragrant mustiness of the Five Oils. She looked round eagerly, her first glance towards the bed. It was empty. And from the big chair which stood between the windows the stranger, fully dressed—how had he found the clothes?— rose shakily to his feet. At the same time Shal Ahmi, with the air of one emerging from a trance or deep sleep, unfolded his limbs and his draperies from the place on the floor where he had been crouching.

"All is well, Mevrouw, as you see," he said in his thin high voice. "I trust your day has gone smoothly."

She nodded, her eyes upon the other man. "Do please sit down. You must be so weak. Should you be up?"

"Thanks to you, Mevrouw, I am well again," he said. He made a stiff, painful little bow and, straightening himself, came forward a step as though to take either the food or the candle from her hand. The light, falling upon his face, showed its haggard pallor, the fevered brilliance of his eyes, and her heart contracted sharply. "Do please sit down," she said again, and set the candle and the parcel on the bedside table. Then she turned to Shal Ahmi. "Ought he to be up already?"

Shal Ahmi moved silently towards the food, and with his hands upon it said smoothly, "Do not concern yourself, Mevrouw. I am his physician, and without my consent he would not have left his bed. Food will be welcome to us both."

His brown hands opened the napkin and hovered about the bits of food which looked so unpalatable all huddled together. He selected a roll of bread and pushed the rest towards the other man. As she watched him break the bread between his long slim fingers Annabet remembered what the sight of the sick man, up and dressed, had driven from the forefront of her mind. She said abruptly, "Captain Vehk is dead. He died last night. Dr. van de Lijn says he was poisoned."

Over the crust which he was lifting to his mouth Shal Ahmi's eyes looked at her so blankly that she felt foolish. It was as though she had burst out with some information about someone of whom he had never heard, Truitje or Klara or Mamma. She said hurriedly in an effort to justify herself, "I told you about him. He helped us——" Her glance included the stranger, and then her heart jolted. The sick man was looking at Shal Ahmi with a kind of startled malevolence. He opened his mouth to speak and closed it again. Baffled, she looked back at Shal Ahmi. The crust of bread had reached his mouth, and he bit off a piece and chewed it once or twice before he said, "Ah yes, I remember the name. He was a friend of yours, Mevrouw. I am sorry if his demise has caused you pain."

Two emotions raced through her mind side by side: one a memory of that farewell moment in the dark hall, the other a sense of wonder that all through this interminable day she should have felt an impulse to convey the news to Shal Ahmi. He was not even interested; she had never heard words so perfunctory.

"I was," she said, "very sorry. And the most dreadful thing was that when Mynheer Kaerko told me the news I could think of nothing except how glad I was he hadn't come about *you*." She turned to the stranger again and met his eyes and felt a tremendous melting in her bones. The memory of the moments when she had held him in her arms swept over her, obliterating everything else. She dropped her eyes, and a hot blush rose from her neck to her hair. Through a daze of confusion she heard the sick man's voice rap out a few words in some language she did not understand, and Shal Ahmi answered him in the same tongue, smooth and cool, yet sharp and authoritative.

For a moment there was a tense silence in the room. Then, swallowing the last fragment of his bread, Shal Ahmi said pleasantly:

"Mevrouw, one final favour. Restored as he is, my patient is still weak and he has a journey before him. Could you provide a little more brandy?"

"Oh, easily," she said, thinking of the forced lock on the cupboard in the dining room.

She took up the candle and moved swiftly to the door. As she closed it behind her she heard the stranger say, "Was that necessary, you devil?" And Shal Ahmi's voice answered him laconically in the foreign tongue.

When she returned with the brandy bottle the atmosphere in the room had changed again. Shal Ahmi was standing with his basket on his arm as though prepared to depart; the other man was eating, without appetite, some of the food from the napkin.

"I shall return as soon as possible, Mevrouw," Shal Ahmi

said. "I go now to make ready a prahau. Perhaps you will be so kind as to close the door behind me and await, as usual, my tap on the window."

When she had let him out and returned to Evert's room, the sick man had abandoned his pretence at eating and was sitting with his elbows resting on his knees and his head propped between his hands. It was an attitude of despair or of great weakness, and love and pity wrenched at her heart as she looked at him.

"Whatever he says, you're not fit to travel," she said. "Stay one more day. We've managed so far. We could manage one more day."

He had dropped his hands hastily and now raised his head. The bittersweet lines of his hard young mouth struck at her imagination anew.

"Mevrouw, I was only thinking. Please don't worry about me. I am unbelievably well, considering." He stared at her and his eyes confused her so that she took refuge in an anxious flutter of hospitality: "You haven't touched the brandy. He said it was necessary for you."

"That will do later. I was trying to think. And being still a little—shall we say feeble?—I was afraid of muddling my head. Mevrouw . . ." He spoke the last word on a rising note and then hesitated, looking miserable and dubious.

"My name is Annabet."

He seemed not to notice, but with the slightly desperate air of a man who is sick of debating with himself and has at last taken a decision and means to stick to it now for better or for worse, he blurted out, "It's you I'm worried about."

"Me? Oh, please don't. Once you are gone I shall be taking no risk at all."

"It'll be some days before Evert is back. And didn't you speak of a glove marriage? Does he love you?"

She was startled into frankness. "No. When he went away I think he hated me."

His haggard, bitter young face took on an even harsher expression. His stare slid from her face, uneasy, discomfited.

"I asked because Evert might have protected you if—— But in that case—— And anyway, he isn't here. You stood by me. You saved my life. By God, I'm going to tell you. Listen. Evert and Shal Ahmi and I do business together. I'm English; I live on an island called Gadia. They smuggle nutmegs out to me and the fellows who work with me, and we ship them to England and America. That's a desperate business, and we're all desperate men, Annabet. And Shal Ahmi is ruthless and incalculable as well. You heard what happened to Vehk. . . ."

A feeling of deathly cold came over her.

"You mean—he was—killed?" The question was a faint thread of sound in a horrified silence.

"I'm sorry. I shouldn't have blurted it out like that. But I wanted you to know that I wasn't talking idly. You see, you let that brown devil know that you didn't believe my story about the fighting cocks. And I have it in my mind that except for the fact that you've been indispensable—that once I've gone he might—— We've got to think up something quickly. We've got to think of a story you can appear to believe. Oh God, if only my head were clear. I think I will try the brandy after all."

She sprang forward to pour it for him. As the glass changed hands his burning fingers brushed against her icy ones, and the touch made her heart leap even at that moment.

"Look," he said, "could you act like a giggling fool who had discovered a silly secret?"

"I could try."

"Then when he comes back, take him aside and pretend to be angry. Say that I told you the truth. Say that I deceived you. Say I drank too much brandy and lost my head. Tell him that I told you I came to visit a native girl and was stabbed by a rival. Could you say that with a kind of mixture of anger at being deceived and giggling interest at having found out a secret? You could say that I was afraid that if the young man found out through your servants that I was still alive and in Banda he might try again. Run that through your mind, Annabet, look at it critically. Does it cover everything? My eagerness for secrecy, my deceiving you in the first place? He's not an easy man to deceive, God help you. And he could set Evert against you. Their hides are at stake, you know. If this passes over you must never, never, as long as you live, show that you know what I've just told you."

"I won't. I won't. I promise you," she said, anxious to ease his agony of apprehension.

"The devil was in this damned business from the start," he said in a calmer but extremely doleful voice. "We don't meet a patrol once in a hundred times. And if only that window hadn't been lighted; if only you hadn't let Shal Ahmi see that

you thought I was lying about the fighting cock. I shan't
sleep of nights thinking about you and wondering——"

"I shall think and wonder about you too."

He looked at her sharply, and she felt the blood flame in
her face.

It was true, then, the thing which he had put down to his
own delirium. She had held him in her arms, had called him
darling, had kissed him. He accepted the knowledge with a
fresh onslaught of sick despair. Love belonged, with so many
other things, like codes of honour and clean linen and good
manners, either to the past, which one tried not to
remember, or to the future, the remote future, about which it
was better not to think too much. But, given the right time
and place . . . Even now, when the only thing his body craved
was rest and ease from pain, and his mind must be driven by
force of will to the contemplation of practical things, he
could realise her sweetness; had indeed done so in what he
had thought was his last moment. That gentle, delicate face
with its expression of pitying concern had floated in a haze of
candlelight before his failing sight and he had thought of
angels. Then, of course, he had come to his senses and
thought that she was the Isa about whom Evert had boasted
with such regrettable lack of reticence, and he had been
astonished, as he had been when he first saw Evert's new
house, that such an ordinary fellow, such a clod, in fact,
should have such taste and such luck. And then he had
known who she was and there had been the dreams.

But there was nothing that could be done, save what he
had already done, take what steps were possible to ensure her
safety. He thought wryly of the risks, the secrecy, the squalor
that were the very fabrics of his life. What part had women,
or the love of women, in that?

"There is one thing more I would like to say," he said
abruptly. "If anything ever happens to you, if you get into
danger or trouble of any kind, send for me. I've given you a
great deal of inconvenience; you're in danger at this moment
because of me. If you'd let that poor little man chuck me out
you'd have run no risk at all. So I'm in your debt, and if you
send for me and I'm alive and in the islands, I'll come.
There's a fisherman called Gariz, a tall, villainous-looking
fellow with one eye; he has two boats painted red and black
and he lives in a hut at the extreme south end of the harbour. He'd find me for you."

"I don't even know your name."

The simple, straightforward sentence had a plaintive sound.

"I'm a fool," he said. "I told you my head wasn't clear. It's Ayrton. Christy Ayrton." He half rose and bowed, swaying. "Very much at your service," he said, and sat down again hastily.

She tried the strange, foreign-sounding name over in her mind, longing to say it aloud, afraid that in its very strangeness it might elude her. She had wanted something more personal than "he" and "him," and now she had it. Christy; a little name, endearing. Lest she might betray herself, she looked about the room with busy, unfocussed eyes, avoiding his face.

"If you are to be drunk when he comes back we should do something about the bottle. Will you drink some more, or shall I empty it?"

"A shrewd thought," he said. "A finger more for me." As she poured it he asked, "You think you can convince him that this time you are thoroughly deceived?"

"I think so. I'll try." Standing so near to him, she was conscious of an aching thrill through all her nerves. If only she could call back the moment when she had kissed him! But she mustn't think of that; she must think of deceiving Shal Ahmi. She pulled herself away and carried the bottle behind the screen which, with its panels of cherry blossoms, flowery bamboo, and water lilies, concealed Evert's basin and ewer and slop jar. Within its frail privacy, hidden from Christy's eyes, she wanted to cry, to shed in two seconds the tears of a lifetime. He was going out into the dark to an unknown place. He would be lost forever. And the only moments they had spent together or would ever spend must be wasted in anxious planning. It was cruel, unbearable. But she mustn't be weak, mustn't add to his anxiety. He was so ill, and so brave. She pressed a finger to her trembling lip and steadied it. Then she remembered the minute dribbles of brandy which Truitje had poured from a cherished little bottle in times of faintness or shock. And here she was, pouring a whole bottle away. She lifted the bottle and tipped it against her mouth, gasping.

"When I go," he said as she emerged from the screen's shelter and set the now half-empty bottle in a conspicuous place near the candle, "I shall have to pretend to be drunk. Above all things, he mustn't suspect that there is any connivance between us. So I will say good-bye now. Please believe that I realise how much you have done for me, even to calling in that old devil and endangering your own life— and all the little things besides. I shall remember you always with very lively gratitude. . . ." So much, at least, he must say. Of the nostalgia, the sense of enchantment, the feeling that if things had been otherwise than they were—of these, naturally, no word.

Resolutely he rose from his chair and stretched out his hand. "Good-bye, and thank you, from my heart."

She put her own hand into his, the formal gesture, the handshake, used every day, friends, acquaintances, enemies . . . The last touch, withdrawn even as you held, last hold on hope, on life . . .

"Good-bye," she said, and the word, forced through the ache in her throat, brought the blinding tears with it. "Take care of yourself. Oh, Christy . . . God bless you wherever you go."

Shal Ahmi's cane tapped at the window, gently, relentlessly.

The burning hand tightened on hers with quick nervous pressure.

"You know what to say?"

She nodded. He bent his head and raised her hand toward his lips, but she lifted her face instead and their mouths met.

The jewelled moment, wrenched from the dull matrix of time, was theirs until the cane tapped again, imperatively. Shaken and breathless, Christy put her away, gently but with firmness.

"Darling, you must go. For your own sake . . ."

He watched as she turned obediently and made her blind way to the door. Then he sat down heavily and gripped the arms of his chair, fighting for self-possession and calmness. An old memory stirred and he thought fiercely, Not again! He remembered how he had parted from Betsy Harrison on that teeming August morning when he had ridden out to join the King at Nottingham. He had never seen her again, but his memory of her lint-white hair and soft brown eyes and wild-rose face had added the final touch of bitterness to his first three or four years of exile. He had recovered at last, and between Betsy and Annabet stood a long line of shadowy women of many kinds and colours. He would have said, as he stumbled onto the verandah at Coenpark, that he had outlived and outgrown sentiment about women. They had their uses; everything else was poetic fancy, pleasant enough

in the right circumstances, but a useless burden of life lived
as he must henceforth live it. Nevertheless . . . I could
have loved her, he thought; and then switched his mind to
wonder, with a cold sweating sense of anxiety, how well, or
how badly, she was telling the story which he had put into
her mouth.

At the foot of the stairs Annabet wiped her eyes gently so
as not to redden them and composed her face. Now that she
must open the door to the man whom she knew to be Jean
Vehk's murderer, both the brandy glow and the excitement
of that long bittersweet kiss were swamped by a cold tide
of fear. Vehk, who at worst could only be suspected of guess-
ing at the secret, had been killed in the interest of its
preservation. *She* knew everything, and as she opened the
door she felt that her knowledge was written upon her face.
The story which Christy had concocted for her sounded
suddenly frail and incredible. She was horribly aware of
facing an adversary who recognised only his own laws.

But Christy had told her what to say, and she must say it
with confidence. Turning the key, she remembered the times
when she had helped Klara elude Mamma's lynx-like eyes.
How small and innocent those deceptions seemed now.

As the door opened she burst straight into her story,
hoping that the nervous breathlessness of her voice would be
set down by her hearer to excitement over her discovery.

"Oh," she said as Shal Ahmi silently crossed the threshold,
"I'm sorry you were obliged to tap twice, Shal Ahmi. But I
was hearing the *truth* about that man at last."

She had raised the candle, as she always did when opening the door, and instead of lowering it, satisfied, as on other
nights, she continued to hold it high, so that the light fell
levelly upon Shal Ahmi's face. There was no change in
his expression; his face remained bland and unconcerned,
though she watched him close enough to notice the
contraction of the pupils of his eyes in the candlelight.

"And what is the truth, Mevrouw?" he asked politely,
with no more than perfunctory interest.

She lowered her voice conspiratorially and stood still
halfway across the hall.

"You told me to give him brandy, didn't you? Well, he
drank more than he ought and told me everything. How I
wish I'd known sooner, before I put him into my husband's
room and bothered you about him and taken such trouble

myself. But I must say, though I didn't for a moment believe those tales about fighting cocks with black tails and suchlike rubbish, I did believe that *somehow* he was connected with my husband. How shall I ever explain to him?" She pretended to look onto the brown face piteously, as though searching for help and reassurance, but the interest and curiosity which she sought did not appear.

"And what was his business, Mevrouw?"

"I hardly know how to tell you—and you going to such trouble over him. He's nothing but a common philanderer, Shal Ahmi. He came sneaking into the compound to visit a *girl,* and some other man—on the same errand, I expect— stabbed him. Of course I realised that he had to go *some- where*—he was bleeding to death—but it was impertinent, to say the least of it, to come here and pretend to be Evert's friend. It hasn't been easy for me, Shal Ahmi, to sneak about in my own house, but I had the satisfaction of feel- ing that I was considering my husband's interests. Now I learn that the reason for the secrecy was that if the serv- ants knew he was here and alive they'd gossip and the man who did the stabbing would make another attempt. . . ." Had she overdone her part? Explained too thoroughly? There was nothing upon that smooth brown face to guide her. "I'm almost distraught, Shal Ahmi. What will my husband say when he knows that I took a person like that into his house, into his very bed? And I did try to act for the best."

Deliberately she allowed her mind to dwell for one second upon the thought which she had been keeping at bay: He's leaving me now, and I love him. Genuine tears—and a feeling of shame that they should be used as a means of self- defence—shot through her, instantly filled her eyes.

Shal Ahmi waited until several of them had brimmed her lids and slid over her cheeks. He watched her take out her handkerchief and fight for control. The fight was as genuine as the tears, for once she started to cry the pent-up emotions of the last few days seized at this chance of release. Finally he said, still coolly, but with a certain kindness in his voice:

"I see no reason for your distress of mind, Mevrouw. You acted hastily but from good motives. I do not think Myn- heer Haan would blame you. But if you prefer not to tell him anything of the affair, well, nobody shares your knowledge but me, and I—I am not given to gossip." Some slight shifting of the planes of his face which might have been a smile changed his expression at last.

"Oh," she said, struggling again to master her tears, and thought, There will be hours and days and nights in which to cry, now you must feign delight and relief. "If you *would* just say nothing, Shal Ahmi. It sounds very deceitful, doesn't it, but I—you see, I haven't been here long and I don't want my husband to think I'm stupid and credulous and careless with his lovely house, taking in such riffraff. Later on, when he knows me better, I will tell him, I promise you."

"Very well, Mevrouw. The thing is as though it had never happened."

"Shal Ahmi, I've said before that I can never express my gratitude——"

"Time is short, Mevrouw," he interrupted her, and began to make his silent way towards the upper floor. She followed, holding the candle.

"It is to be hoped that you can walk," Shal Ahmi said coldly as he entered the room.

Christy laughed drunkenly. "Walk! Of course I can walk. Why not? The brandy was just what I needed. But you wouldn't expect a woman to understand that, of course."

Shal Ahmi threw a glance towards Annabet that was almost apologetic. Christy Ayrton, seeing it, knew a great lifting of the heart. So she had convinced him. And she was safe. Oh, thank God for that.

"You would do better to save your breath. You will need it," Shal Ahmi said smoothly.

They were in the hall, across it. Annabet opened the door. Outside in the darkness something moved, came forward. A big, strong-looking fellow. Thank God. Once the door was shut and she had no longer to be deceived, they could probably carry him between them; Shal Ahmi would drop his mask of disapproval and be kind.

"But I must say good-bye to my hostess. Until this last moment she has been kind."

Swaying on Shal Ahmi's arm, he turned to Annabet and stretched out a hand. Her own would have flown to meet it, but Shal Ahmi was watching. Reluctantly, with a he-is-drunk-and-must-be-humoured glance at the brown man, she laid her free hand in Christy's. Some virtue, a secret reassurance, flowed from it.

"Mevrouw, I salute you. I kiss your hand. Your mind may be narrow, but your heart is warm. I shall remember you and your kindness until my last day. I kiss your hand again. Good-bye, farewell, *au revoir, arrivederci*. Take your choice.

And now, come weal, come woe, I'll tell whom you've had
the honour of entertaining: you wanted to know that, didn't
you, Mevrouw? As of course any lady would. Shamus
O'Flaherty, Mevrouw, as good an Irishman as ever said,
'The curse of Cromwell on ye.' Good-bye, Mevrouw, and
thanks for your hospitality."

Between the drunkenly jerked-out words his lips travelled
over her fingers. She felt her hand twisted and the warm kiss
laid upon her palm, her wrist. Never, never in the whole
history of the world, did lovers part in such a fashion. Desperately she racked her brain for some last ambiguous word
which would, while deceiving Shal Ahmi, convey her understanding, her love, her unfailing pledge of remembrance.
But her mind failed in this final test of inventiveness.

Shal Ahmi plucked him away. At the bottom of the wide
shallow steps the faceless, shadowy figure closed in and took
Christy's other arm. Then they were gone. In less than a
breathing space the darkness of the moonless night had
engulfed the three linked figures. Was the third man Gariz?

Before she closed the door she whispered, "God keep
you," into the darkness. The heavy handsome door swung
into place, and its thud of finality echoed through her mind.
She leaned her arm against the door and lowered her head
and wept. So this, after all the dreams and the imaginings,
was love. Coming so unexpectedly, hurting so much, so soon
wrenched away.

Evert, at the end of the last stage of his journey by prahau,
was inclined to hurry things by bullying his boatmen to
greater effort. He had made the awkward journey many
times before and had never been annoyed at its slowness, but
for weeks now he had been racked by impatience and
uncertainty, and as the journey reached its end he was
almost demented. There had been moments—for instance,
when the woman who kept the inn at Bandogar had rustled
towards him, bright with recognition and respect, or when
lot after lot was knocked down to him in the market,
"Mynheer Haan, of Banda"—when he had been brought
up short by the realisation that he, Evert Haan, known and
respected, had conspired with Shal Ahmi, a coloured man, a
native, to make away with his wife. It was an incredible
thought. But then, so was the thought that Evert Haan's wife
should be a stiffly moving skeleton whom he was ashamed to
acknowledge, even before those he regarded as his friends.

An incredible thing had happened to him, and he had taken an incredible way out. And there would be no rest, no peace of mind for him, until he had returned to Banda and heard for himself what had happened.

To Annabet, as a person apart from a problem, he gave no thought at all. She had ceased to exist before he left Banda. Once there had been an Annabet, born of Piet Odshoorn's drunken babble and quickly brought to full stature by Evert's own imaginings, a thing of golden, wild-rose beauty, to be enjoyed; a thing of pride, to be humbled; a thing of value, to be displayed. But that Annabet had died in the cabin of the *Java*. For the sorry substitute, the last effrontery of the Van Goens towards Evert Haan, he had no feeling, no pity. There was only one thing he wanted now—to be met by Dr. van de Lijn on the quay of Banda Neira and to hear him say, "She died, despite everything I could do." Or, since this was impossible, since no one, not even Van de Lijn, could know the exact moment of the prahau's arrival, he would have liked the first man he saw to look at him with sympathy—real or false—lower his eyes, and mumble out something about being sorry for his loss. Then he would know that he was a free man again.

As Evert's prahau bumped against the steps of the quay three sailors from the *Trade's Advance* were being hauled ashore. Their mates laid them carefully upon the three stretchers held by native bearers and with rough, good-humoured valedictions turned back to their boat. Dr. van de Lijn, with his big straw hat tilted over his eyes and his notebook already in his hand, was studying the three supine bodies. Scurvy, Evert thought automatically as he climbed to the quay briskly despite his cramped limbs, and far gone at that; any fool can see that with half an eye. No need for him to lean over them and study them so attentively. Look up, can't you, you ass, and tell me what I want to know.

He went forward and touched the doctor on the shoulder. Van de Lijn, jerked back from some fascinating train of thought, looked at him blankly for a moment, and then gave a slight smile.

"Ah, So you're back. And anxious about your wife, naturally. Well, I've good news for you. She's perfectly well. As I suspected from the first, it was all a question of diet. You look surprised. But, Mynheer, you do not—nobody—— Look, look at these poor devils."

He took Evert by the arm and swung him round so that he

had no choice but to look at the seamen. But the piteous, puffy, scrofulous faces made no impression upon his mind. That was wholly engaged by a vision of Annabet, that stiffly moving skeleton. Perfectly well. What did the fool mean? Able to eat and sleep? God damn her, she had been able to do that when he left. She'd said it herself, maddeningly, "I'm not ill, you know."

"In three days," said Dr. van de Lijn, taking Evert's silence for interest, "there'll be an unbelievable difference. Goat's milk and fresh meat, goat or chicken, fruit, green vegetables—that's what you need, my lads. Take heart. I've seen dozens as bad as you and had them walking in less than a week." He lowered his voice. "Dying of salt port and salt herrings. Yet, God in heaven, they're both food. What makes the difference? If only I could find out what makes the difference."

His eyes took on a faraway look. Evert could have killed him.

"When did you last go to Coenpark?"

The doctor blinked. "Oh, a week—no, more, twelve days ago. She was in no need of any attention, I assure you."

Evert pushed back his hat and mopped his head. Twelve days ago; that was quite a long time. Was it possible that Shal Ahmi had feared to begin before the doctor was finished? If so, for once his wits had failed him. It would have been better for the scarecrow to have died while in the professional man's care.

A hearty slap on the back made him stagger. Vehmeer, who had spied him from his office window, was welcoming him back, his vast face shining with pleasure.

"Good to see you back, Evert. Have a pleasant journey?"

"Slow, but uneventful. I'm glad to stretch my limbs." Now—now he would hear.

"Come in and have a drink. How's Bandogar? Do much business?"

"I want to get home," Evert said abruptly. "I've got some papers for Kaerko, and then I must get along."

The smile which had faded for an instant when his invitation was so bluntly rejected returned, wider than ever, to Vehmeer's wide face. He struck his fat hand on his thigh.

"God bless me, old man, I was forgetting. Somebody waiting for you at Coenpark this time! Of course you must get along. Oh, and by the way, I'd like you to know that my wife did call, visit of welcome and all that. But your lady wasn't up to seeing visitors. Though," he hastened to add at the sight of something in Evert's eyes, "she was getting on. Oh, yes, she sent down a message to say she was better, doing nicely."

"When was that?" Evert asked.

"Oh, quite a long time ago, soon after you'd left. Jehane ought to have gone up again—I told her so only yesterday—but she said she'd leave it until you were back and could send word when visitors would be welcome."

"Yes, I will. I'll let you know. I'll look in tomorrow and have that drink with you." Evert's words were pleasant, friendly, but his manner was a little strange, Vehmeer thought.

So there were still the twelve days unaccounted for. Why in God's name hadn't Shal Ahmi devised some means of letting him *know?* He strode around the corner and into Kaerko's office. The agent was aboard the *Trade's Advance* and his office was empty save for a young half-caste clerk who was dozing away the last hour of the warm afternoon. Evert laid the papers on the table which he knew was sacred to important business, and then, almost jumping down the steps, he turned into the street that was shadowy between the houses and began to hurry towards Coenpark. Away from the sea and the houses it was warm. The path was dusty, and even the dust seemed to smell of nutmegs. Hundreds of marauding doves guzzled and mourned amongst the nutmeg boughs, ceasing their soulful lamentations in order to snatch off the ripe fruit, wrestle with it until the hard nut was separated from its luscious covering, and then, swallowing the fruit, dropping the nut like a pebble; that done, they would cry again in voices that were the very negation of greed.

Evert, striding along hot and angry, made a mental note about bird lime.

Then, rounding a clump of trees which hugged the curve of the path, he came upon Shal Ahmi seated upon a boulder, his back comfortably pressed against a tree trunk. His hands were folded in a manner which suggested infinite patience; his dusty feet in their toeless sandals stuck out across the path. He looked as though he had been waiting for an hour, and it would have been hard even for Evert to believe that the brown man had watched with sardonic amusement his conversation with Van de Lijn and Vehmeer on the water front.

"The return of a traveller is always an occasion of joy," Shal Ahmi said softly as Evert drew level with him. Despite his urgent desire for news, Evert looked up and down the path and into the groves of nutmeg trees as far as he could see on either side before halting and speaking. He had always been careful in his dealings with Shal Ahmi and now, more than ever, was care essential.

"Tell me quickly," he said.

"Your trust in me was justified, Mynheer. It is pleasant to think that such complete trust has met with such complete justification."

"I don't want any of your riddles and crooked answers," Evert snapped, relieved to be able to show his ragged temper. "Is she alive or dead?"

"But alive, Mynheer. What else did you expect?" His dark eyes widened as his hairless brows, climbing his forehead, wrinkled it in simulated astonishment.

Evert was speechless for a moment. When he could shape his lips and control his tongue he spluttered out, "But you—I trusted you. You said you would—could; may the devil take you, you yellow traitor, you promised you'd rid me of her."

No sign of annoyance showed upon the bland brown face. Only the eyes twinkled briefly; the corners of the thin mouth twitched.

"I have rid you of her, Mynheer—as effectively as though I had throttled her. Go along. Go up to your house and see for yourself."

He rose from the boulder and gathered his garments about him with dignity, flicking off with a fastidious finger a fragment of bark which had caught in one of his many folds. Evert, lowering his head like an angry bull, moved to face him, prepared, it seemed, to oppose his going. Shal Ahmi stared at him without speaking. Then as Evert fell back he moved forward and turned his face towards the town.

He had taken six of his pompous, noiseless steps when Evert called him.

"Shal Ahmi, I'm sorry I spoke as I did. Listen, I—I—— Damn it, man, I asked you not to speak in riddles. I lost my temper. I apologise."

"Sometimes I wonder," said Shal Ahmi placidly, "how, with a temper so easily lost, the head is kept." Then, seeing that the significance of the rebuke had not been lost upon the white man, he softened. "Mynheer, I have many other things to tell you. Life has not been uneventful in your absence. But all that will do later. Perhaps tomorrow night. I think that then you will greet me as a friend."

He turned his back resolutely and moved away. Evert stared at the wide white back for a moment, and then, impelled by such curiosity as he had never known before, swung round and ran along the path towards Coenpark.

Everything in his beautiful house was ready for him; upstairs and down, from the whitened steps of the front door to the last tile of the passage that led to the kitchen quarters, everything that could be polished and scoured and dusted shone with cleanliness.

Annabet had attempted to share in this work of preparing for the master's return, for she was in that state of nervous tension that would have found relief in some physical activity, but Josef, without actual rudeness, had soon made it plain that even by taking an interest in the arrangement of the flowers she was insulting him; and when, tired of aimlessly fidgeting about the house and the garden, she had passed through the green hedge with the archways, intending to retrace the steps of the one walk she had taken with Evert, Katje, breathless and cross, joined her within four minutes. "It is not a right thing for Mevrouw to go out of the garden unaccompanied."

She had walked for a little way and then turned back, taken a leisurely bath, and put on the blue gown with the ruffles of lace which had come from Mamma's wedding dress. Then, with a towel pinned over her shoulders, she sat down at the dressing table before the silver-framed mirror and coloured her cheeks and lips carefully. The result was not like a painted death's-head any longer; some of her own natural colour was coming back, and confidence was returning, too, so that she painted less desperately, to enhance, not to hide. When she had finished Katje came forward and took up the brush and comb. She brushed vigorously, a hundred strokes, as she had been taught to do, and then wound the curls, one by one, about her fingers. They had grown since Annabet's arrival and, clustered upon each temple, shining behind each ear, added to the increased fullness of her face.

Throughout the lengthy toilette, as indeed throughout the hours of every day and night which had passed since she had made her momentous decision, little tremors passed at intervals along her nerves, making her heart flutter as though a butterfly had been trapped in her chest, making her face go red and then white, making her fingers unsteady. Sometimes she had a sharp clear vision of Evert's look of cold hatred, a memory of the contemptuous way in which he spoke the few words he had addressed to her. Anger flamed in her then, and a feeling of reborn confidence came with it. At least her looks were coming back. Still too thin, of course; and since Christy's going she had not continued to fatten as she had been doing. But her head sat squarely on her shoulders once more, and all her limbs were supple.

And that was Evert's doing! Nothing must be allowed to obscure that fact. It was Evert who had fetched Shal Ahmi to see her. In a very special way this new beauty of hers belonged to her husband. Well, she was doubly bound to deal honourably with him; and that she was prepared to do.

She looked at the French clock and rose from the dressing table. She had no idea of the exact time of Evert's arrival, but it could not be long delayed now. Josef had said that Mynheer always returned from such trips before dark. It would be better for them to meet in the parlour; bedrooms were always invested with an idea of intimacy.

She was halfway down the stairs when the heavy front door was flung open and Evert, pushing back his hat and mopping his forehead as he came, strode into the hall and towards the staircase. His shirt was unfastened at the collar and its ruffles hung limply. His face was red and hot and his breathing was quick and heavy.

After the sunset brilliance of the outer world the hall was dim. He slammed the door behind him with a backward thrust of his arm and hurried towards the stair foot, finding his way more from habit than from actual sight. He had reached the bottom step and had his foot on it before he saw her. One of those nervous spasms had come upon her at the sight of him, and she had gripped the bannister, standing still, waiting for it to pass.

For a moment he looked upwards with a stunned, stupid look on his face. Through the back of his guilty mind flashed the thought that Shal Ahmi had murdered her and that this was her ghost on the stairs. For, altered as she was, so very, very different from the crooked, ugly, starveling creature he had left, he recognised the hair and the dress. The submerged artist in him, which made him so ruthless and so susceptible, which had driven him to collect loveliness as a miser collects gold, gave him a sharp, unerring eye for detail; and even in that confused, uncertain, terrified moment he realised that standing there on the stairs, one hand gripping the bannister, the other pressed against her bosom, she fulfilled all the dreams he had ever cherished about the lovely woman in the lovely house.

"Annabet?" he said. And it was more a question than a greeting.

"Yes," she said. "You see, I am better."

The stupid superstitious fear—God, he could laugh at it now—fled away at the sound of her voice. Hastily he removed his hat; his other hand flew to the open neck of his shirt, pulling the ruffles together.

"I ran all the way from the quay," he said. "I saw Dr. van de Lijn, and he told me he hadn't been near you for twelve days. . . . I couldn't wait to see how you were."

The tremor had passed; the moment of compensating confidence had come. She began to descend the stairs. He watched her take two supple easy steps and then, tossing away his hat, leaped towards her, hand outstretched.

"You're better. I could hardly believe my eyes," he babbled, raising her hand to his lips and then letting it fall. The heavy warm arm went round her shoulders; the hot red face pressed against hers. "Now," he said between kisses, "I can give you a proper welcome. I was afraid to touch you before. Afraid of hurting you. Well, haven't you a kiss for your husband? Not shy of me, are you? You'll soon get over that." He was a like a great blustering boy granted at the last moment a longed-for treat which he had thought withheld.

"I'll go and tidy myself," he said at last, releasing her. He clapped his hands together loudly, and Josef came running. "Wait for me in the drawing room. You'd laugh if you knew how often I've pictured you in that room. I'll be down in ten minutes. Josef, you rogue, bring me some hot water and a long cool drink. And I want a clean shirt. And light all the candles. And tell them in the kitchen that I want dinner in half an hour, and see that it's good."

He went leaping up the stairs, two at a time. From the top he looked back and saw the straight slim figure of his wife in the doorway of the drawing room which he had furnished and planned with only his eye and his imagination to guide him. Lovely, exquisite. Just what he had hoped for. Bless Piet Odshoorn, and bless Shal Ahmi. What had the old devil said? "I have rid you of her, Mynheer, as effectively as though I had throttled her." And he hadn't even guessed.

As he washed and changed his clothing his blood cooled
and it occurred to him that his behaviour on the stairs
had been crude and boisterous. Well, what of it? he asked,
shrugging his shoulders under the fresh linen. He had
perhaps been a little carried away, but that was a good thing,
because if he had been given time to think he would have
remembered his behaviour towards her on her arrival, and
that would have made him uncomfortable. She had probably
forgotten it; she had been ill and would now remember only
that he had conducted her to a comfortable bed in a
beautiful room and had left her in good hands, Katje's and
Shal Ahmi's. Ah, the cleverness of the old stoat, to cure the
infirmities, to see that hasty action would result in the waste
of good material. There wasn't a white man to match him.
But to go back to that meeting on the stairs when, hot and
dusty, he had drawn her close and kissed her—wasn't that
the kind of thing he had planned ever since Piet had said,
"Two Van Goens girls, lovely as lilies"? From that moment
he had planned the subjection of Van Goens beauty and
subject the Van Goens pride. And, by God, he had done it.
In one instant. Hot and dirty, he, Evert Haan, had kissed a
Van Goens lady. A dizzying thought. And even more
dizzying was the one that if she had arrived upon the *Java* as
she was now, some semblance of diffidence and respectful-
ness would have hampered him. Heavens how carefully he
had dressed himself that morning, how mindful of his
manners he had been as he had descended the companionway.

Better so, he thought. It's worked out for the best after all.
The familiar sense of being lucky, almost elect, came upon
him. Now, he thought with a pint of well-cooled arrack
inside him, I will go down and show her that I know the way
to behave. I'll give her two glasses of my best Madeira—
that's a lady's drink—I'll pay her a few compliments—and
then I'll take her to bed. . . .

She had accepted the Madeira. She had managed to eat
her dinner. It was, after all, despite anything Father Vincent
believed, food and drink which kept people alive, gave them
vigour. And the kind of thing which she had to say needed
vigour. The big red-faced man who was her husband was
obviously so delighted with her that it was hard to believe
that he was the very same person who had said, "So that's
what they'd planned to do with you, is it?" and "This is a

very distasteful position." Had he forgotten those words as completely as he appeared to have done? Yet there was to his credit, and she must not, *must* not forget it, the fact that he had sent Shal Ahmi to cure her.

Therefore, as the long meal ended she called up all the courage that was in her and said:

"There is something that I must say to you. Shall I say it here or in the drawing room?"

He laughed unrestrainedly, like an excited boy.

"We'll not trouble the drawing room tonight, my dear. I've had a long journey. I intend to retire early."

His eyes ran over her with cheerful possessiveness. In his mind he thumped himself upon the back with hearty congratulations. He, Evert Haan, had actually said those words, with all they implied, to a Van Goens. Never had his vanity savoured a sweeter titbit. But the realisation was unlucky, for the mental process lent to his possessive stare another quality, less frank, less excusable, and there came to his face a look with which Annabet was familiar, a covert, sheepish lecherousness. Occasionally young yokels had worn it in Heydberg, meeting Klara and her in the street or on a field path.

"Then I must say it now," she said. Her voice was almost icy in its extreme clarity, though one of those nervous spasms had set her heart fluttering and her cheeks reddened and whitened behind the thin cover of paint.

"I told you when we first met that I would try to make up for my ugliness by being a good wife to you, didn't I? I meant it. I owed you that—if only in the material sense. You had sent money to my mamma. You must have known that what you sent was far more than was needed for my expenses. And though I know, I could see, that you felt yourself cheated—and I *was* sorry for you—you hadn't really been. There was no clause in the marriage contract about my being beautiful, you know. But now——"

"Look," said Evert, interrupting her, "let's forget all about that, can't we? If there was money over and your family found it useful, I'm glad. And if I was a bit stunned that day, well, partly it was because you looked so *ill!* I proved that, didn't I?" His voice, embarrassed to begin with, grew truculent. "Didn't I get you to bed with every comfort? And call in Shal Ahmi, who did what all the grand doctors in Holland had failed to do?"

"That was what I wanted to say. Because of that I feel that

I owe you a *different* sort of loyalty. And since I have been here I've come to realise that being a good wife means something more than I meant on that first day. *Willing* isn't enough. There should be some feeling behind it. And so I'm forced to tell you that I don't *love* you."

He looked at her, amused, enjoying the little scene.

"That doesn't bother me a bit, my dear. How could you love me? You don't know me. We'll talk about this in a month's time—eh?"

"But I shall never love you, not in that way. That's what I've got to make clear, even if it means that you drive me off, out of the house tonight. *Because* you asked Shal Ahmi to cure me, and therefore I am grateful to you, I must make clear that never, not in twenty years, should I ever be able to love you properly."

"Because," said Evert, as though speaking for her, "you love *somebody else?* That's it, isn't it?" He smiled with good-natured tolerance, almost smugly.

"Yes," she said, and was glad that he had understood so quickly; and she had a sharp painful memory of Christy's lips on her wrist.

Some dressed-up, flowery young sprig of nobility who hadn't the guts to take her without a dowry, Evert thought delightedly. There were people like the Van Goens in every village in Holland, families who thought themselves too good to breathe the same air as people like himself—as he was. Now with one stroke he had humbled two of them instead of one. He hoped the young fool was eating his heart out!

"I don't care," he said, pushing back his chair, rising, and going round to the place where she was sitting at the other end of the long table. "I don't care whether you love—as you call it—one other man or twenty other men." Standing above her, he could see the sheen on the soft hair, the fluttering shadow of her long lashes. "You belong to me," he said, his voice hoarse with genuine emotion. "That's enough for me. You're my wife."

He loomed over her, making her feel small and helpless. She rose hastily and turned to face him.

"But, Evert, you should listen and think about this. I shall love this other man until I die. . . ." She could hear her own voice losing its assurance in the face of his sustained, amused, misunderstanding tolerance. Falteringly she brought out the final awkward words, the words that she had promised herself she would say because she was grateful to him. "And if—if ever I saw him again, or if it ever happened that he—he sent for me, I'm afraid I wouldn't let anything stand between us."

Of the whole speech only the words "if ever he sent for me" made any real impact upon Evert's mind. So the luckless young gentleman had been left in Holland. And still she thought that he might send for her! What a forlorn hope! His hard thin mouth curved with amusement. Other men might have heard those words with anger or dismay or pity, according to their nature. To Evert they brought only an enhanced sense of triumph.

"D'you think I'd let you go?" he asked good-humouredly. He put his right arm around her, cupping her breast in his hand. "You'll forget all about this girlish hankering," he said thickly. The warmth and softness of her flesh under the thin silk sent the blood pounding through his veins. With his left hand he tilted her face and, bending his head, sent his mouth against hers. And even as he stopped with kisses her last vain bid for understanding, an emotion sharper and more dizzying even than lustfulness rocked his being: a consciousness of his own unfailing luck in life.

He dropped his head until his lips moved against the edge of the lace of her bodice. And he altered his hold, swinging her from her feet into his arms. "You talk of love, but you don't know what you're talking about," he said. "I'll show you what love is."

But Father Vincent, adored so long and then discredited and now never to be thought about without a guilty pang, had come into his own. He had dragged his poor little cousin back from the brink of madness with his talk about the supremacy of the mind over the body. And half a world away, the poor little cousin, restored to health and sanity, more lovely than ever, petted and pampered, wandered through her cool, lovely house or walked in her flowery, lovely garden, brooding over the truth of his words, twisting their truth to fit her case.

For if the flesh mattered, she should have been the most enviable woman living. She lacked nothing. And there remained with her enough of the memory of the bleak years in Heydberg to sharpen her appreciation of the luxuries she now enjoyed. From the moment when Katje drew the curtains, creasing the blue dragons into indistinguishable

blobs of colour amongst the folds and letting the bright
morning light into the room, until the moment when she
said, "Good night, Mevrouw," and padded away to her own
sleeping place, every one of Annabet's moments was hung
about with comfort, with wishes granted or forestalled, with
leisure, beauty, adulation.

And after that—when the night, so cool after the day's
heat, so spicily scented, flowed into the room—there was
Evert, changed in a moment's space from a good, indulgent
husband to a lover, not only ardent but skilled. She was often
amazed by her own lack of response to Evert. Night after
night, when he had gone back to his own room or had fallen
asleep beside her in the big blue-and-white bed, she lay
awake, wondering at herself, thinking of Father Vincent and
of Christy.

Here she was, bound by vows and by gratitude to Evert,
who was kind, generous, amorous. Every bit of food that she
put into her mouth, everything she touched or used or wore,
was provided by him. She belonged to him, as he said,
always with pride, if a little too frequently; and yet so soon
as he had left her or fallen asleep she was thinking of
Christy again—living through the experience just past, but
with Christy in Evert's place. And then, by a trick of
thought which had become a habit, thinking of Father
Vincent, remembering what he had said about the flesh and
the spirit. And knowing, knowing, that he had been right.
The passage of love, the kisses, the most intimate caress of
Evert were nothing, less than nothing, compared with the
lonely, unreturned, unrecognised kiss which Christy had laid
in her palm under cover of that drunken leave-taking.

Sometimes, with a feeling of panic, she wondered whether
she was simply in the grip of another infatuation, similar to
the one she felt as a girl. If that was so, then she was spoiling
her own life, and the life of the man who appeared to love
her, by her blind chasing after a dream. And at those
moments, sharply aware of the passing of the days which
piled up so quickly into weeks, which in their turn became
months, she tried with all the vigour of her mind and body to
forget Christy and love Evert. But that was no good. Such
efforts were always followed by a feeling of degradation, as
though she had been a traitor. And finally, when she had
been in the islands for about six months, she resigned herself
to a life which held two sharply divergent realities: the one,
her smooth, rounded, normal existence as Mevrouw Haan of

Coenpark; the other, her secret hungry existence as the yearning lover of Christy Ayrton.

And at exactly the same time, when the actual marriage was half a year old, Evert began to experience his first serious feelings of dissatisfaction with it. Perhaps he sensed her final withdrawal into compromise; or the first joy of possession was staling, his sense of being almost miraculously lucky sinking into commonplace acceptance. For six months he had been delighted with his bargain; then suddenly he began to see flaws in it.

Outwardly everything had gone exactly as he had planned during that boastful, self-congratulatory interval between the arrival of Mevrouw's letter and the arrival of Annabet herself. As soon as possible after his return from Bandogar he had reissued his invitations to dinner and had the satisfaction of seeing Annabet take her place at the end of his table around which were gathered all the most important people of Banda. The postponement of the dinner, the period of speculation, rumour and counter-rumour which had elapsed since Mevrouw Haan's arrival had heightened the feeling of curiosity provoked by Evert's complacent boasting; and although it took all Annabet's training in composure to face and ignore the stares, frank or covert, which were directed at her throughout the whole evening, Evert enjoyed himself thoroughly. There wasn't a woman in the room to touch this woman who belonged to him. Even Jehane Vehmeer, hitherto the undisputed belle of the white community, looked faded and a trifle overblown compared with Annabet. And that was as it should be. Evert Haan was the cleverest man in the islands; he had the best plantation, the finest house, and now the prettiest wife.

"I've never seen a first dinner party go off so well. Her mother reared her for better things than Evert Haan and his Coenpark," said Mevrouw van Heem later.

This pronouncement reached Evert's ears quite quickly and did not surprise him. Trudi van Heem and he had lived in a state of undeclared war for many years. Nor did it displease him. On the contrary, it flattered his vanity so much that there and then he decided that if things turned out well he would send Mevrouw van Goens a token of his gratitude for her training of Annabet. A piece of jewelry, perhaps, or another draft on the Bank of Amsterdam.

But the gift was never despatched, for as the days ran into weeks, and the weeks, with incredible swiftness, mounted into months, his vast complacency and satisfaction with his bride began to shrink and collapse.

It was not, he told himself furiously a hundred times, that he cared whether she was in love with one other man or twenty other men. But at the root of this non-caring was the certainty that, given complete possession of any woman for six months, he could bring her, if not to a state of infatuation—though that was almost certain—at least to a state of subjection. And with Annabet that was just what he had failed to do.

How he knew that he had failed puzzled him. There was no proof, no evidence; but he knew it just as he knew that a blue thing was blue, not red or green. She was, in every way a man could name, a perfect wife, always amiable, agreeable to his wishes. She had never once in six months withheld a smile, failed to respond to his nod, repelled a caress. When he gave her presents—and he loaded her with gifts in those first months—she thanked him prettily, kissed him, admired the offerings, and praised his taste.

But something was lacking, and though he could not have given a name to the thing he missed, the lack of it piqued his vanity and his egotism. You goddamned fool, he would say to himself, you've got everything you wanted. What's the matter with you? Why aren't you satisfied?

The artistic strain which ran through his hard nature like a flaw in a rock would lead him sometimes to think, Suppose this had happened to another man, Kaerko, Van de Lijn . . . What should I tell them to do? The answer came easily: Take the wench to bed and let her see who is master there. And that should have been the answer. But it wasn't.

And at last, on one of those occasions when he was soothing his vanity with the reiterated assurance that he had, after all, got the wife he wanted, a question fell like a drop of icy water into his mind: But have you got her? And he knew the answer to that. Knew that between kiss and kiss she eluded him; knew that, even from the most intimate embrace, something escaped, unpossessable, unpossessed.

He began to think seriously about that stupid young gallant back in Holland, that imaginary young man over whose failure he had gloated. He had hardly listened on that evening of surprise and delight to the words which Annabet had spoken; yet now they came back to his mind, clear,

significant, barbed: "I shall love this other man until I die."
And he remembered how, for a night or two, the thought of
that futile, robbed love had lent an extra zest to his own
love-making. But now, quite gradually but inexorably, the
despised young man began to gather strength and substance.

The complete single-mindedness which, combined with a
growing ruthlessness, had been so largely responsible for
his spectacular success in life rendered him singularly easy
prey to obsessions. There were emotions to which he was
a stranger, for the compass of his mind had swung almost
entirely between two points, his wants and his hatreds. Now
he found himself wanting something more than this
nominal, outward possession of a woman and hating the
nameless, unknown man who, simply existing, balked him.

The imaginary young Dutchman became his companion
in all those moments of the day when his mind was not
actively engaged upon some practical problem. He would
have given a thousand English pounds to have that puppy's
throat between his hands.

It never occurred to Evert to wonder *why* the complete
subjection of Annabet mattered so much. He would have
rejected with scorn that notion that he was, at last, in his
middle age, as much in love as his nature permitted him to
be, and that his feeling of frustrated possessiveness was
actually simple jealousy.

In his blindness, instead of realising that he was in love
with his wife and longed merely to be loved in return, he
concentrated upon this unknown young Dutchman as an
enemy who stood between him and something that he
wanted rather than as a rival who had been given something
which he himself could never attain. When finally he
blurted out a question about him he was not conscious of
any absurdity.

He had flung himself, baffled again and furious, from the
blue-and-white bed, and Annabet had said, as usual, "Good
night, Evert." And then suddenly he turned, his hands came
down heavily upon her shoulders, and he blurted out in a
thick tense voice:

"Who is he? I will know. Tell me his name."

She was startled, but not at all bewildered. She knew at
once what he meant. But the question, shot out with such
vehemence at such a moment, left her speechless. She had
tried so hard to behave as though she had come straight from

the cabin of the *Java* to Evert's bed, with no enlightening experience between. How had she failed? Through what unsuspected crack had Evert glimpsed her secret life?

Thrusting against the pressure of his hands, she rose on one elbow.

"Who is who? Whom are you asking about?" she said.

He shook her as though she were a talking doll.

"That man you spoke of. The one who stands between us. That puppy you left in Holland. Tell me his name."

She raised her hands, gripping his wrists, forcing him away.

"Evert! Stop shaking me. What do you mean? 'Stands between us.' Was anything between us just now? Or last night? Have I given you any reason for saying such a thing?"

"Yes," he said savagely, and repeated the word even more loudly. "Yes. You told me about him yourself. You said you loved him and would love him until you died. What do you expect a man to make of that?"

She pushed against his hands again and threw herself across the bed, scrambling to her feet on the far side of it. Standing upright in the voluminous white bedgown, she felt better, less overwhelmed now that the flushed red face and pale angry eyes no longer loomed over her.

"You made what you liked of it then, Evert," she said, her voice small but steady. "I told you because I felt I must be honest with you. I hoped you'd send me away. But you laughed and said it didn't matter. Why does it matter now?"

"Because you still love him, don't you? *Don't* you?"

Say no and end this scene. Say no, since I have come to know you better, Evert, I have ceased even to think of anyone else. So easy. Why not?

The word was there, ripe, thrusting, ready for birth, just behind her teeth, when the memory of Christy, swaying with weakness and saying, "Darling, you must go," bore in upon her. This was different; this was important. If she hoped ever to see him again upon this earth she must be honest now. Unheeding that the move brought her once more within the reach of those heavy hands, into the glare of those coldly angry eyes, she walked around the foot of the bed.

"Yes, I do," she said. "You see, I am still honest with you. And I'm speaking the truth when I say that I'm sorry. I have tried, Evert, not to—not to let it make any difference. But if I haven't been satisfactory, you must get rid of me. You could say what you liked about me. I wouldn't contradict."

The pang which he felt at the very mention of getting rid of her might have warned him, but he was without self-knowledge. Fury made him blind and senseless.

"You talk like a fool," he said. "You're my wife; you belong to me. I'd never let you go, not if the devil himself had a claim on you. So you're honest, are you? That for your honesty!" And Evert, who never gestured, made a gesture of ineffable contempt. "And you don't need to tell me," he added in a sharper voice. "I know. I don't have to be told whether a key fits a door or not. I can feel that for myself. I've tried not to let it make any difference," he repeated her words contemptuously, "but every time you've kissed me you've grudged it, every time I've——"

"I never grudged you anything," she said sharply. "That's a lie. You must know that." A hot wave of colour mounted from her neck to her hair. "It's the other way round, Evert. Very often I think—afterwards—that because of the way I—because I am so weak—*he* should be the one to be jealous. If he knew."

He had no idea that these starkly honest words were the pronouncement of his own doom; that they could never have been uttered save by a woman whose absent lover seemed real enough to have established rights. He could not read behind the faltering words their intrinsic meaning: "Evert Haan, it often seems that I have committed adultery with you."

Instead he was pleased, delighted. His fury evaporated. Vanity and passion took its place. Somehow, without conscious movement, he was there at the foot of the bed, his arms around her, his lips moving over her face and neck. Between kisses he muttered, "I'll make you forget him. You're going to belong to me. Forget the things I said. I didn't mean them. I was angry."

Accepting the sudden change of mood, the kisses and the apology, Annabet in turn had no notion of their real significance. After six months of marrige she still knew too little of Evert's character to realise that he was behaving in a way completely unlike himself. It was only afterwards that she could look back and understand that this scene—which was to be repeated, sometimes identically, sometimes with slight variations, many, many times—was the result of a genuine passion coming late in life to a man in whom were blended a fiery temper and a cold, stubborn selfishness.

Evert appeared to have forgotten the scene by the next morning. But at some time during the day he ordered from the ubiquitous Wang Fu a silk coat, deep blue in colour, embroidered all over with dragons which imitated in their posture the pattern of the curtains in her room. Six of Wang Fu's countrywomen worked for five days and nights, stopping for rest only when they could no longer see their needles, crouched in the stuffy cramped room in the rear of the Chinaman's house in the back street of Banda. On the evening of the sixth day Evert carried it home, and only a shrewd observer indeed would have seen that a thread of wistfulness ran through the complacent pride with which he watched Annabet array herself in the beautiful garment. He was pleased by her expressions of gratitude and by her praise of the design which had been his own idea, but a little disappointed because after one glance at herself in the mirror she had turned away from her own quite dazzling reflection. (Isa, given some trifling ornament, would have admired herself for hours.) But later on, alone in her room, Annabet put on the coat again and turned to the mirror, searching with half-reluctant curiosity for the confirmation of the knowledge which that earlier hurried glance had conveyed. The fleeting impression had been only too accurate. With the stiff embroidered folds of the silk falling about her she had lost all identity; she looked like an image, like a dressed-up doll.

She thought suddenly of the crushed eggshells which old Truitje used to drop into soup "to clear it." The Chinese coat was like them. It laid clear the fact that, petted and pampered, living with one man and loving another, the memory of whom was sometimes sharp and sometimes clouded, she was losing reality.

Still wearing the coat, she sat down on the stool, put her elbows on the white dressing table amongst the silver things, and stared, almost unseeing, at her own reflection. A body— a pleasing arrangement of bone and flesh, and hair; bathed, scented, fed, brushed, kissed, taken to bed, caressed. That was what she had become. And that was happening to Annabet, who had once been called back from the brink of the grave, or of madness, by words which proved that the flesh was unimportant, the soul all that mattered. A shattering, awful thought.

But it was only the rarest, strongest soul, she reflected dismally, which could survive the wearing process of daily pretence. For the others, the ordinary people, of whom she was one, the constant practice of pretence must be the slow death of reality. And one day the moment would come when she would offer to Evert the words his vanity demanded. "I love you," she would say. And that would be the end of Annabet. After that she would be as good as dead, though the years and years might elapse before they buried her.

Why was that such a dismal prospect? The answer came in the nasal whine which had so often announced the texts in the Heydberg church: "What shall it profit a man if he gain the whole world and lose his own soul?" And it's so dreadfully true, thought Annabet. I am losing my soul. Because Christy, and loving Christy, is part of it. Though that is very hard to understand—because, to be honest, that love started with the flesh too. It was his face, as poor little Vehk turned him over, that made it impossible for me to let him be turned adrift to take his chances in the prahau. His face then; and later on his body when I held him in my arms. Where's the difference? Why is living with Evert, and pretending—and sometimes not so much pretending— making me less myself, whereas just remembering that I love Christy makes me more myself and more real altogether? The right, the *moral* thing would be for me to pretend to love Evert until I really did—and then I shouldn't exist at all.

And sitting there in the coat which Evert had given her as an apology, the coat which had made her look like one of the images carved over the door of the Hindu temple, she accepted with a sad certainty that, cut off from Christy and spending all her days and nights under the impact of Evert's personality, she was like a leaf on an autumn tree, cut off from the flow of sap and exposed to the merciless buffeting of the wind. It might hang tenuously, deteminedly, for a time, but at last the stem would snap and the leaf, dry and lifeless, would go whirling away, the plaything of the wind.

If only, she thought desperately, I could see Christy sometimes; just see him, even from a distance; or hear his voice from behind a closed door, as I sometimes hear the voices of the men who come to talk to Evert in his office. Or if I could hear some news of him, as I used to hear news of Father Vincent when his mother wrote to mine. Anything, any little thing which would bring him near, make the whole of those three days less unreal and dreamlike.

She got up restlessly and slipped her arms out of the wide

silken sleeves, letting the coat drop to the floor for Katje to put away with reverent, envious hands. As she did so something happened within her mind, less a matter of slow constructed thought than a blinding flash of revelation. Within her orbit, she suddenly realised, there were two people who knew of Christy's existence—Evert and Shal Ahmi. The perilous business in which they were partners must involve some meetings, some conversation. Openly Evert had no dealings with the brown man. Shal Ahmi himself had said that when he arranged for his visits to be made so secretly, and since she had partaken of the social life in the islands she had heard in a dozen drawing rooms the Banda ladies end a discussion about the "queer creature," as they called him, with the words, "Of course my husband is like yours, Mevrouw Haan—detests the very name of the man." Over and over again she had been given to understand that Evert, like most of the other husbands, had nothing but derision for Shal Ahmi.

So now she thought logically, Then Shal Ahmi and Evert meet secretly, and what meeting place is more likely than this house? And if Christy does business with them, perhaps he comes too. He knew the way to the office window; he expected to find Evert there. Perhaps . . . Perhaps . . . Her heart began to thump as she dwelt upon the possibility that on many an evening when Evert had left her with her embroidery in the drawing room and gone to his office Christy had stepped onto the verandah and tapped at the window and been admitted.

Her wits, once wakened, showed something of their pristine sharpness. Twice during the next day she mentioned the heat, three or four times complained of the stuffiness of the drawing room after the candles had been lighted. Evert, remembering with some difficulty the discomfort which he had felt during his early days in the islands, was sympathetic and full of helpful suggestions. Would she like Juan and Abbas to take turns with a fan? A fan of peacock feathers, he suggested. His eyes swept around the pale-coloured room and his voice was eager, with something that was almost greed in it, as he said, "Yes, peacock feathers—and a blue sarong and a jacket the colour of apricots." Aware of her indifference to these suggestions, disappointed, he spoke of the tryingness of the climate just before the rains broke. "In three weeks or a fortnight there'll be a change. Not like the winter in Holland, of course; but I bet there'll be evenings when you'll be glad to have a shawl."

"But *now*," she said relentlessly, wondering whether her voice betrayed her obstinate determination, "couldn't we sit on the verandah? I'm sure it would be cooler there."

"We'd be bitten to death," he explained tolerantly.

"I'd rather be bitten than stifled, Evert."

"You'll learn," he said, losing his patience suddenly. But he raised no further objections, and before the week was out, Annabet, with a gauzy shawl over her neck and arms, the oil lamp placed at a distance because it was found to attract a swarm of little buzzing insects, was spending her evenings on the verandah just outside the dining-room windows. And upon the evening when Evert said, "I shall be busy for an hour or two; don't go to bed unless you're very tired. I shan't be late," she was seated in what had become her usual place, with only the corner of the house between her and the window of the little office.

As soon as she was certain that Evert would be in the office she pulled her chair forward until it was around the corner, and with the lamp no longer visible her eyes became accustomed to the darkness. Midway between the place where she now sat and the office window was the flight of steps leading to the garden. And before she had been in her position for ten minutes a figure, looking quite vast in its white wrappings, moved like a pale shadow noiselessly up the steps and towards the window. She heard the gentle tapping, the sound of the shutter opening and being closed again. So she had been right. Shal Ahmi did come to Coenpark under cover of darkness. And Christy might come too.

Now that the moment might at any beat of the heart be upon her, a dreadful quaking emptiness came over her; for some seconds she felt as though there was nothing between her madly racing heart and her unsteady knees. If Evert had at that moment opened the study window and stepped onto the verandah she could not have pushed back her chair as she had planned; if Christy had walked up the steps and by some miracle had become conscious of her presence and held out his arms to her she could not have taken a step towards him. But as time passed and nothing happened her nerves steadied themselves and the wild beating of her heart changed to the dull beat of disappointment. She waited until the pale silent shadow which was Shal Ahmi had rolled down the steps and disappeared into the shadowy garden, then, swift and nervous, she pushed her chair back to the place where Evert had left her. And there, three minutes later, he found her, apparently asleep.

Any thought of eavesdropping by the study window had not gone through her mind on that evening, nor at any previous time. If Christy had appeared she would have been irresistibly drawn to listen on the chance of hearing his voice. But the details of the business which lay between Evert and the native whom he pretended to hate and despise, interesting as her intelligence told her they must be, had at that point no intrinsic attraction for her. And it was as well that upon this occasion she had maintained her watch on the garden and the steps, for behind the unglazed shuttered window Evert, having disposed in a few sentences of the business which had brought Shal Ahmi on one of his clandestine visits, had turned to the subject which interested him almost, if not quite, so closely.

The hardheaded Dutchman who had made his way in a hard world was not precisely superstitious. But his mind's armour had chinks labelled with other names. He laughed at the suggestion that Shal Ahmi was a spell maker, yet he trusted the brown man's medicines. And it was with some idea of pill or potion in his mind that he approached Shal Ahmi on the subject of Annabet's failure to produce an heir.

Shal Ahmi listened attentively, his face giving no sign of the cynical amusement, the half-pitying scorn which the story roused in him. When Evert had finished he moved his heavy shoulders under the voluminous wrappings. "I think that I can help you. By midday tomorrow there will be upon the table of your office in Banda a little package. Place a pinch between the fingers, thus, and no more, in the bottom of a cup and fill it up with good wine. Towards evening. If within a month you do not greet me with a shining face, there are other devices. And now, with your mind easy upon that matter, let us return to business."

Wine had been almost unknown in the Heyberg household. Egbert, when he came home, would bring his own supply, and there had been Truitje's cowslip, and dandelion and blackberry for occasions like birthdays or Christmas. But aboard the *Java* Annabet had drunk wine every day, for it was as plentiful as—and in the later days, since it travelled better, healthier than—water, and in Banda she had accepted without question the Madeira or light Rhenish which Evert poured for her each evening. Except that it lightened her spirits and helped the flow of easy chatter which was one of the wife's duties to provide, it had had no noticeable effect. But on the evening following her abortive vigil outside the study window she was appalled to find that she was intoxicated. She rose from the dinner table feeling light as a bubble; the automatic censorship which lies between the conceived speech and the audible word went out of action, and she talked and laughed with abandon; for the first time she found herself meeting Evert's stripping, desirous stare with something like boldness, and when on the way upstairs he put his heavy arm around her she leaned back against it amorously.

Once alone with Katje in the blue-and-white room, she had a sudden reversal of feeling. She began to think about Christy with a depth and darkness of passion of which she would not have thought herself capable. Her flesh, her very entrails, crawled with desire. She sent Katje away hastily and went dizzily to the window and leaned out into the sweet night air, trying desperately to command her thoughts and hoping that Evert would not come tonight.

But Evert came. Her drugged mind laid down its arms and slept. It was a night of triumph for Evert and the flesh.

In the morning she woke from heavy slumber to an instant sense of disgust and remorse and betrayal.

And thank God she knew the remedy. Abstinence and thought for others. All the good women of Heydberg engaged in acts of what they called "charity," which meant a care for the poor. Even Mamma, who, heaven knew, was poor enough herself, visited a few cottages regularly, carrying some of Truitje's horehound cough cure, a jar of soup, a flannel petticoat past further mending, even a spoonful of hoarded brandy for an old woman not expected to last through the night. And Annabet, her daughter, had lived here, amongst people infinitely more degraded, people openly referred to as "slaves," for more than seven months, without once giving a single thought to their welfare.

The compound lay between the kitchen quarters and the edge of the nutmeg plantation. It consisted of a number of mud-and-thatch huts ranged in a rough circle around a well. When Annabet stepped onto the hard-trodden space about the well there was no one in sight except a small boy who sat on its rim, busily whittling a stick. He stared at her for a moment with enormous eyes and then called shrilly in his own tongue. From one of the doorways a skinny old woman with big brass earrings slapping against her withered cheeks emerged. She, too, stared at Annabet and then said in a high, quavering voice:

"Mevrouw has mistaken the path. See, I will show you." She began to shuffle, barefooted, towards the path Annabet had just trodden.

"No. I wanted to see the compound." In the face of the old woman's frank astonishment explanation was not easy. "I mean—I wondered if there were any sick—or anything that was wanted—whether I could do anything to help."

Did she imagine it, or was astonishment tinged with disapproval?

"It would be better if Mevrouw returned to her own place. The sick are attended. I myself am skilled in such matters." Professional pride overruled caution. "The boy called me from the bed of a woman whose baby was born two days ago. She does not mend." There was no sorrow in her voice.

"Perhaps I——" faltered Annabet, dismally aware of her ignorance in such things.

"Mevrouw, the gods forbid! She is not for your eyes. Come." She made another shuffling movement towards the path, and Annabet was tempted to follow her. But she knew that if she did she would lose the last poor remnant of her self-respect. Turning her back on the old woman, she ducked her head and entered the cabin. It was small and filthy and stuffy and cluttered with objects not immediately recognisable. At the back of it was a hole roughly knocked through the outer wall, and from the space beyond a low, piteous moaning made itself heard.

"The sick woman—is she through there?" asked Annabet, looking with horror at the low opening and the dark cell beyond.

The old woman, who had entered, apprehensive and defensive, said simply but firmly, "Where else? Childbirth defiles the house, Mevrouw."

Crushing down a feeling of nausea, Annabet, on her knees, crawled through the opening. The stench of the place was nauseating. Very dimly, on a heap of straw or rags, she could make out the body of the woman who was moaning.

"Anybody, however healthy, would die in this atmosphere," she said, addressing the old woman over her shoulder. "Help me to get her into the air where we can see."

"And defile the whole dwelling?" asked the crone incredulously. "She will die, yes. But it is her own fault. With my own eyes I saw her kill a hen to make broth when her husband was sick. She has broken the law of the gods, and so neither medicine nor charms avail her."

"Help me," said Annabet.

"If she enters here, Mevrouw, neither the man nor his brother can eat rice or sleep within again."

"Then they must go elsewhere," said Annabet between her teeth. "Lift when I tell you. Gently now."

The outer cabin, which had at first seemed so dark and malodorous, seemed light and airy when at last Annabet, stretching her cramped limbs, looked down upon the woman. Almost the first thing she noticed was a thin red cord so tightly tied about the woman's waist that it had eaten into the flesh.

"Give me a knife," she said. The old woman handed it to her without protest, but as it was severed and thrown aside she gave a cry in which fury and consternation were blended.

"And where is the baby?"

The woman reached into the cave at the back and brought out the little body.

"If she had fed it," she said accusingly, "it would have been a fine boy, a blessing to his father." She laid the child with a gesture of awful finality beside his mother.

"You should have fed him," said Annabet, peering at the child and seeing with astonishment that he still breathed, lightly and slowly.

"With what, Mevrouw?"

"Goat's milk."

"They own no goat."

"A wet nurse, then. Is there no woman in the compound who has milk to spare?"

"Two, Mevrouw. One is a follower of Mahomet and the other a wild woman caught from the head-hunters of Borneo. Should the son of a Hindu drink from such sources and be defiled?"

"I will send for milk and for Dr. van de Lijn," said Annabet, and stood up and went to the door.

The compound, which had seemed so deserted a little

while ago, was now humming like a hive. A throng of women, most of them old, several pregnant, some deformed, and one blind, leaning upon another's shoulder, had gathered around the cabin. As though the mere sight of them gave her confidence, the old woman sprang forward and burst into passionate speech. Turning her head from one to another, she gabbled out a sentence or two in the language which meant nothing to Annabet and then repeated her complaint in swift broken Dutch. Mevrouw had defiled the whole house; she had cut the sacred cord; she had suggested feeding the child on milk from a heathen's breast; and finally, most awful heresy of all, she had threatened to send for the doctor—a man, the white man doctor—to attend a Hindu woman in childbirth.

At each spluttered sentence a kind of hissing groan went up from the assembly. But on the fringe of the crowd there were a few women who muttered approvingly. A low clear voice called musically in bad Dutch, "The Mevrouw is right. The woman has been in agony for two long days. Our God Himself touched the sick and healed them, men and women alike."

Pandemonium broke out then. Women began to gesticulate and scream; those on the edge of the crowd pushed forward, and some nearest the door turned and began to push back.

"Go away," Annabet cried. "This isn't your business. What I have done is my own responsibility; nothing for you to quarrel about. Clear the way. I want a boy to run to the house and fetch milk. Be quiet, be quiet, remember the sick woman."

She might as well have cried to the wind; the old racial and religious prejudices, so long suppressed, must seize upon this outlet.

And then suddenly there was a deep full-chested shout, followed by immediate silence. The women nearest the door parted, pressing on either side against the walls of the cabin, and at the end of the path thus cleared Annabet could see Evert.

She had never seen him pale before; usually all emotions served to heighten his colour, but now his face was the colour of spinet keys and his grey eyes were clear and colourless as glass.

She ran towards him.

"Evert, you came just in time."

He flung his arm around her shoulders. "Are you all right?"

"I'm all right. But, Evert, there's a woman in there dying. And a starving baby, and I wanted——"

Without a word he spun her round towards the house. Still keeping his heavy arm across her shoulders, he glared around the compound, his head lowered like a bull's about to charge. But the women had gone. In that second the whole crowd had become invisible.

"You little fool," Evert said, propelling her along. "What on earth possessed you to go there? You gave me the fright of my life. I heard the shindy and then *your* voice! I wonder I didn't have a stroke."

"I'm sorry, Evert. I didn't mean to cause a commotion. I just went because I realised that I'd been here a long time and never had a thought outside myself. And I could have done something for the woman and the baby."

"You could have started a riot that would have set all Banda ablaze. If I hadn't arrived just when I did some hothead would have struck a blow and then their menfolk would have been involved and God knows what it would lead to. As for you . . . My God!" She could feel the shudder that went through his big body. "Promise me never to go into the compound again."

"I promise. But, Evert, may I send milk for the baby?"

A most curious look came over Evert's face.

"You liked the baby, eh?"

She felt her face go hot with embarrassment. She said stiffly, "To the extent of not wanting to think of it dying of starvation while we have milk to spare."

"What you want," said Evert, tightening the clasp of his arm, "is a baby of your own. That'd give you something to think about."

It is true, she thought. I do want a baby. I knew that this morning when I looked at the one in the cabin. But it's yours I want, Christy, yours, yours. . . .

But later on sense asserted itself, together with the memory of Jean Marie's talk about resignation and acceptance. If I could give Evert a baby, she thought, everything would be different. He would be pleased and I should have something to love and live for—apart from Christy. If only I could have a baby; please, God, forgive my folly and my sinfulness and let me have a baby. I didn't go to County Down, O God, because I hadn't a vocation. I came here instead, and even if that was wrong, please do try to forgive me and let me not spoil Evert's life too. Let me have a baby and I will try to forget those moments with Christy. I'll try to be a good wife and mother. . . . I'll try. . . . I'll try. . . .

Book Three

Book Three

PIET, LIKE MOST captains in the Company's service, disliked all agents on principle, and the fact that Kaerko, since the discovery of his relationship to Evert, had treated him with unusual civility merely served to tinge his dislike with contempt; so he watched without sympathy how Kaerko's hands fluttered as soon as he had taken in the contents of that sealed cargo list and how his face changed colour and how his rather prominent yellow upper teeth caught at his lower lip.

Neither man made a comment upon the unusual nature of the cargo, but awareness of it lay heavily between them throughout the routine business of checking; and Kaerko's face still bore marks of concern when he left the ship to go up to the Fort to carry to the governor his despatches and to make arrangements for the unloading of the surprising items. Evert, rushing out to see Piet immediately, halted at the sight of Kaerko's expression and asked anxiously, "What's the matter? Plague aboard?" Kaerko shook his head and muttered, "No, perfectly clean bill of health," in as glum a voice as he would have used if the answer had been the exact opposite.

Evert, bent upon his own business, showed no further curiosity. He would not have rushed voluntarily into the range of infection, but, short of that, nothing would have stopped him from getting hold of Piet and taking him home to dinner with him. For weeks now he had been looking forward to Piet's next visit to Banda. Piet would know the name of the fellow whom Annabet had wanted to marry; he would be able to give the phantom a name; and although he might be stubborn and reluctant to part with his information, Evert had had proof that Piet's tongue could be loosened by a sufficiency of liquor.

Piet had seen Kaerko down the ladder and with the thought, Well, that's given him something to think about,

191

had turned back to his own cabin, where his best shirt and
breeches lay on his bunk side by side with two sealed
packages addressed to Annabet. He had promised both
Mevrouw and Klara that he would deliver the letters with his
own hand and that he would at the same time see for himself exactly how far Annabet's report of her health was to be
believed.

It had been such an easy, obvious thing to promise, but
now that the *Eastern Venture* actually lay at anchor in
Banda Harbour he found himself wishing that he had not
done it. He was, in a way, anxious enough and curious
enough to see Annabet, but something deep within him
shrank from the prospect of seeing her in Evert's house, in
Evert's presence, in Evert's possession.

The girl seen across the Heydberg church had been young,
immature, dressed in made-over, earnestly contrived garments, and as remote and beautiful as an angel; the girl in
the Heydberg parlour had been very ugly, emaciated, stiff,
grotesque, finely dressed, and so friendly and intimate that
he had actually dared to offer money for her support. Now,
in the oddest way, the woman who rose from the low chair in
the lovely room at Coenpark combined the most seductive
qualities of both.

He was paralysed with shyness as he handed her the letters
and replied with a few wooden words to her animated
greeting and enquiries. Annabet, standing with the letters in
her hand and feeling for a moment very near to Mamma and
Klara and Truitje, near to the cold bare house and the flat
landscape and the coolly flowering cherry tree and the stiff
tulips, remembered very sharply the details of their last
meeting and put his shyness down to embarrassment. She
had been overfrank with him then. And he had been very
kind. So she restrained herself, though her fingers ached to
open the letters and her mind hungered for news of home,
especially for Klara's news, and she exerted herself for a
moment or two to set him at his ease. Before Evert himself
could suggest it she said, "We must drink to this happy
reunion." And Evert threw her a sardonic glance, and she
was momentarily embarrassed and driven to say, "Oh yes,
I'll risk a headache tonight. This is an occasion." Evert
poured wine for her, schnapps for Piet and himself, and she
raised her glass and said, "Many lucky voyages, Captain
Odshoorn," and then after a moment, seeing that Piet, with a

glass in his hand, had relaxed a little, she set hers aside and said, "Now please don't mind me; I must just look at my letters."

Despite her eagerness for Klara's news, she opened Mamma's letter first from an almost automatic sense of fitness. But after scanning the first few sentences she laid it down and ripped open Klara's. The hasty, blotted, jubilant words sent stab after stab into her heart.

So happy I can't tell you. Don't mind anything Mamma writes; she sees only my outside. Just think, by the time you have this I shall have my baby, our baby; I am so looking forward to it. I do so hope it will be a boy with Jan's eyes and the same funny little nose. Jan would rather it was a girl, like me. So any way one of us will be pleased. Nab, I love him more every day, he's so kind to me. I'd do it again, a hundred times, if I had to. Though it was awful when I first knew what had happened, and there was no one to tell, and for six weeks, Nab, six whole weeks, I couldn't even get out to tell *him*. Suppose he'd found another girl in that time? Truly, darling, that six weeks aged me by six years. . . . The house is small and rather poky, but cosy and comfortable compared with ours. All the furniture has been there since the Flood, I think, and Jan and I have the old people's bed. I did protest about that, but Jan's mother said, "Bless you, child, where Klaus and I sleep now doesn't matter." But if the harvest is good this year Jan says he will build another room. . . . Mamma passed me in the street the day before yesterday, not looking, and with a face like stone. I suppose I should mind. But I don't. I didn't begin to live until I found Jan, and I was never happy until I came here. . . . I'm learning to milk a cow; you would laugh to see me, but I do want to be as good a wife as any farm girl he might have married.
. . .

On and on, reiterative, incoherent, but vital and ecstatic, the account poured itself over six pages of poor thin paper. Annabet read to the end and then folded the sheets carefully and put them aside. Klara had married for love; she was spending her days and her nights—oh God, her nights—with somebody who roused in her the feelings which Christy had roused in Annabet. I'd have lived in discomfort too; I'd have learned to smuggle nutmegs, just as Klara is learning to

milk a cow, she thought. And I would have been happy too.
I understand now all the things about Klara and Jan Mulder
that puzzled me before. The one person. Nothing else
matters. But I mustn't think about that now. I have a guest
in my house.

She glanced quickly through Mamma's letter, with its
fierce, derogatory, coldly scornful sentences about Klara, its
smooth civilised dealing with less painful subjects, its warm
enquiries and good wishes. Then she laid that aside too.

"My sister Klara is married," she said to Evert. And to
Piet, "I suppose you haven't happened to see her since."

Embarrassment had made Piet reckless, and he had drunk
three glasses of schnapps while Annabet was reading her two
letters. He felt the better for them. But the question was
awkward. He had seen Mevrouw Mulder; she had brought
the letter to his cottage herself. She had been wearing the
cloak and the hood and the wooden shoes of the ordinary
tenant farmer's wife, and she had been pregnant as the devil
and as sleek and shining and happy as a woman could well
be. And the whole of Heydberg had been talking about her.
But young Mulder had come with her as far as the gate and
had hovered while she gave Piet her letter and asked him to
see for himself how Annabet was, and when she had
clattered away down the path in her wooden shoes he had
taken her arm—very loverlike.

But they were made for love, and that was the truth of it.
Annabet and Klara too. Any man . . .

"Oh, yes, I've seen her. She looked well and happy," he
said cautiously.

"We must send her a present," said Evert in his genial,
blustering way. "Who's the lucky man?"

"His name is Jan Mulder, and he's a farmer," said
Annabet clearly, seeing that Piet looked confused and
uncomfortable. "Mamma is disgusted by the match, but if
Klara is happy that is all that matters."

"Well said," said Evert, dropping his heavy arm around
his wife's shoulders. "Now, Piet, tell me. How do you think
she looks? Does Banda suit her better than Heydberg?"

"Mevrouw looks very well," said Piet stiffly. "And so do
you, Evert."

But that was a lie. Evert looked less well than he had done
when they parted. It wasn't, Piet thought puzzledly, that he
was obviously aged; the year or so which had passed had
touched him lightly if at all. But his expression had altered.

Complacent was a word outside Piet's range, otherwise he might have reckoned that the complacent expression had been wiped from Evert's face. As it was, he finally wrestled through to the thought that Evert looked as though somebody had given him a good rap on the nose.

They went in to dinner, and Evert kept Piet's glass well replenished, cunningly varying the liquors. Towards the end of the meal Piet had got the better of his nervousness and could look at Annabet calmly. The liveliness, the frank look, the friendliness, which the angel of the church had lacked and which had so startlingly shown themselves in the piteous wreck of the parlour, were still there, now set in beauty. And the beauty itself had increased. The full, immature curves of girlhood had gone, replaced by something even more subtle and breath-taking. And the lovely hair had grown a darker gold. But now and then, when she had sat in silence for a moment and Evert had held Piet's attention, turning back to her suddenly, Piet surprised a look of not sadness, exactly, but of something almost as disquieting upon that lovely face. And then, turning back to Evert, he realised vaguely through a haze of liquor that Evert wore much the same expression. A kind of hungry, yearning look.

He was blissfully unaware that every time he looked at Annabet his own face wore the identical expression.

Annabet went away with a whisper of silk, and Evert pulled his chair closer and poured brandy into two glasses.

"Go steady, Evert," he said, thinking of Kaerko and Gijs and all he had to do tomorrow.

"I'll see you safely aboard," Evert said amiably, and leaned back in his chair, planning his next move.

A lightness of touch was essential; he didn't want Piet's sympathy. Better begin by thanking him for having made the match and then go on: "And I'm the more indebted to you for taking the proposal so promptly, because if I hadn't grabbed her just then it'd have been too late, wouldn't it?" That would start Piet's gossiping tongue, and within a few minutes Evert would have what he wanted.

"You know," he began, "I never thanked you properly, Piet, but I hope you'll believe that I'm damned grateful for all you did. I often look at Annabet and think that but for you . . . Well, you know what I mean. We aren't the sort to make flowery speeches to one another, but if there's ever a chance for me to do anything for you, remember I'm in your debt." That was good. The word "debt" would lead on easily to the other thing he wanted to say.

"Aw, nonsense," said Piet, twirling his wineglass violently and bringing his rust-coloured brows together in a frown. "The boot was on the other leg." He spoke sincerely. In his present mellow mood he was capable of seeing Evert as an unrewarded benefactor. He had helped Piet in a matter of life and death; Piet had only done for him—and that with extreme reluctance—a thing which anyone else could have done equally well.

"I'm going to tell you something," he said, leaning forward suddenly.

"Yes?" said Evert in a carefully controlled voice. By heaven, Piet was going to blurt it out on his own accord. He wouldn't even have to ask.

"Something you ought to know. Something secret. Might be useful to you."

"Yes?" said Evert again.

"There's going to be a war. Here, in the islands."

The colour went out of Evert's face, and Piet heard his gasp of astonishment.

"Are you sure? How d'you know? Who told you?"

"I brought the stuff. Cannon, muskets, powder, and shot. They mean it to be a surprise this time. They swore me to secrecy, and everything was packed to look like something else. But Kaerko knows now, so does His Excellency. And I don't see why you shouldn't know too, Evert. In business a little bit of information in good time sometimes comes in handy."

"By God, you're right," said Evert. He had recovered his colour and his eyes were clear and steady. "It's a bit sudden, but it was bound to come. Been brewing up ever since the Navigation Act."

"The smuggling," Piet corrected him.

"What smuggling?" Evert asked sharply.

"Out here. Oh, I know they don't admit it; always talking about the patrol boats and the care they take. But at the other end they make no bones about it. Why, just three weeks before I sailed this time a ship reached the port of London with nearly a million guilders' worth on board. They knew in Amsterdam within three days, prices dropped so steeply. The English market dropped to nothing. The Company's been forced into action."

"I'm glad you told me. This'll send the price up. Look,

Piet, I'm going to act at once. I was sending in a consignment in the morning. Now I shan't. I'll hold it back and take advantage of the price later. And I'll split the profit with you, old man. I must go out. Now. You go and talk to Annabet about Heydberg. Tell her I was called away for a few minutes. I won't be long."

He stood up and drained his glass. Piet, glad that his bit of information had proved so immediately useful, sat back, contented.

The house to which Evert hurried stood by itself outside the town of Banda Neira on the side opposite the Fort. It was Shal Ahmi's house. Its one door and single window looked out upon a deserted strip of beach. Farther to the south, where the land grew fertile, Byskin's plantation began, and Byskin's landing stage ran out into the sea.

The little one-roomed house was perfectly clean, and the only scent in it came from the handfuls of mysterious herbs and other substances which the occupant flung upon his little charcoal brazier as soon as he had completed the cooking of his simple meals.

Shal Ahmi opened the door himself. He showed no surprise at seeing Evert upon his threshold, though in the whole course of their long dealings Evert had visited the house only twice before. Most of their business had been transacted during apparently unplanned meetings upon the path to Coenpark, or in the seclusion of Evert's study.

"You save me a journey, Mynheer. I was about to visit you."

Evert, passing into the enclosed space, became aware that he was out of breath. He had walked too quickly after eating a heavy meal. He sat down heavily upon a box and opened his mouth and breathed deeply before he spoke.

"The prahau," he said after a moment. "Has it gone?"

"It goes with the tide, Mynheer. Two hours yet."

"Of course. I need not have hurried." He breathed deeply again. "It mustn't go tonight, Shal Ahmi. Apparently their suspicions were aroused by a bit of news the *Eastern Venture* brought in and they're doubling the patrols. We mustn't take any risks. The load will keep until this activity dies down."

"So," said Shal Ahmi, dropping down upon his haunches. "And thus the game ends."

Evert, through whose mind the very words had been passing, looked startled.

"What d'you mean by that?"

"I told you, Mynheer. I was about to visit you. I had news—not of doubled patrols, Mynheer. I was coming to ask your advice and assistance. You have often had mine."

There was, for the first time in Evert's experience, a glimmer of expression on the bland brown face. The light of the little brass oil lamp which stood on the shelf amongst the bowls and jars fell full upon Shal Ahmi's countenance, but the expression, though plain and noticeable, was unfathomable.

"What news have you had? What advice did you want?" It couldn't be that Shal Ahmi knew what Piet had whispered.

"Tell me first, Mynheer, why was it so urgent that the prahau should not sail tonight?"

"I told you. Didn't you hear me? They're doubling the patrol. Think of the risk."

Shal Ahmi made a gesture with which Evert was familiar. He turned his hands, palms upwards, in his white lap and studied them closely.

"Mynheer, for many years now we have done business together—business of many kinds—for many years. I ask you to consider this: Have I ever failed in discretion; ever betrayed your trust; ever uttered a word when I should have kept silent; ever grudged you the utmost service within my power to render? Answer those questions, Mynheer, and then tell me—why should the prahau not leave tonight?"

"I have already told you twice, Shal Ahmi," said Evert, beginning to bluster.

"Twice you have lied to me, Mynheer. Unwittingly? One of the patrol boats is dragged ashore, being caulked. The other has not yet returned from its search at Tal Arin. What liar spoke to you of double patrols, Mynheer, when such a thing is impossible?"

"I had reliable information. My kinsman, in today on the *Eastern Venture* and with the agent all afternoon, told me that the smuggling was causing alarm in Holland and that as a result of the orders he carried patrols were to be doubled. I didn't ask any questions or test his information. I just hurried straight to you."

"He forbore to mention that many extremely heavy pieces of furniture—bulky, too—had lain in his forehold? Spinets and harps in large wooden cases to enliven the tedium of the ladies in the Fort. Boxes of great weight labelled 'cooking pots,' and bundles of tools wrapped in straw and sewn in sacking. Of these he said nothing?"

"He never mentioned such things."

Shal Ahmi raised his eyes and looked at Evert in a way which made the big man strangely uncomfortable. Then he studied his hands again, saying in a gentle, reminiscent voice, "Mynheer, it is many years now since the Dutch came to Banda; many years since I saw muskets in any number, or cannon dismantled and carried ashore piece by piece. But so clear is my memory of those distant days that if the weapons of war were nailed into coffins draped with flags and followed by a hundred weeping mourners I should not be deceived. The coolies believed that they carried tools and musical instruments and cooking pots ashore this afternoon. But I know differently. Mynheer, war came to the islands today. And the moment has come when you and I must face our obligations."

In the quietude the little flame of the oil lamp flickered and began to subside. Shal Ahmi rose silently and padded across to the shelf and replenished it. He did not sit down again. Folding his arms in his wide white sleeves, he stood and looked down upon Evert.

"I was coming to you, Mynheer, to discuss this situation. The English in the islands have been our good friends. Now they are threatened———"

"Well?"

Evert's cold stubborn stare met Shal Ahmi's inscrutable one. For a moment neither man spoke. Then Shal Ahmi gave an almost imperceptible shrug of the shoulders.

"So," he said, and there was a wealth of finality in the one small word. "Their gold has lined your pockets; their offences against your honourable Company have been directly aided and connived at by you. I have been your trusted associate and friend. But the first breath of war has fired all the Dutch blood in your veins, Mynheer. When I speak of obligations you pretend not to understand me."

"I understand you." Evert obeyed the impulse to stand up and take advantage of his greater height in order to look down upon the brown man. "You're suggesting that now, because we have traded with them, we should warn them of an impending attack. And I tell you straight away that I wouldn't do it for anything in the world. Granted I've smuggled out nutmegs and thereby cheated the Company of some thousands of guiders—that doesn't make me a traitor. They were my nutmegs, produced on my land, by labour I'd paid for and supported. But that's a very different thing from warning the English now. That'd be treason."

He threw out the ugly word truculently, expecting argument. But Shal Ahmi, after regarding him thoughtfully for a second or two, nodded his head.

"You have convinced me, Mynheer," he said at last, dropping his hands from his sleeves in a gesture of resignation. "It now remains to cancel the prahau's orders and return its load. The English will all be dead before it could reach the market, and if the home prices rise——"

"That's it exactly."

Shal Ahmi went to the shelf and lifted from it a square of ruby-coloured glass. He propped it upright upon the ledge of his window and stood the little lamp behind it. The prahaus carrying the contraband always set off from the desolate, dangerous strip of beach that fronted his house, and the boatmen coming down to make ready could not fail to see the warning signal.

"That's settled then," said Evert.

As he walked away Evert broke a twig from a bush beside the path and walked along, slowly stripping off the leaves and tearing them into little shreds. The action helped him to think clearly.

Shal Ahmi knew what the Company evidently intended to keep secret for a time. He wished to pass on his information. He had allowed himself to appear to be argued out of the intention, but—and this no one in Banda knew better than Evert Haan—Shal Ahmi was a very devious creature. He had been supremely useful. If it had ever occurred to the Company to tackle the business of the smuggling at its root and every native in the island had been put to the torture, with the idea of extracting information, not one, in an extremity of pain, would have gasped out the name Evert Haan. Within the island Shal Ahmi had organised the business, made plans, issued orders, and paid out the piteously small rewards. Evert had made the original contact with the English and organised all the outside business. He had also handled all the money, receiving it from a French tavern keeper in Bandogar who was content to exact his ten percent and ask no questions. Evert had also provided the one thing without which the business could not have even started—the precious nutmegs.

And that, Evert thought, reviewing the whole situation, had been growing increasingly difficult. Year by year the Company had grown more possessive, more inquisitive, more restrictive. Almost before the storehouses were cleared there was Kaerko with his papers, demanding the estimated prospect for the next consignment; and woe betide the planter if the actuality did not match the forecast. The Company knew just how many young trees were planted each year, how many of those no-longer-profitable ones were destroyed, and just when each young tree would come into full bearing. For years Evert's keeping of accounts had been a matter of juggling. Now it was over. He had made a great deal of money, had had a great deal of excitement, and had enjoyed to the full the reflection that the Company, which thought it was exploiting Evert Haan, was actually being exploited by him. Now it was over, and there remained only the problem of Shal Ahmi. If the old brute succeeded in warning the English it would be because he had been Evert's associate in the smuggling, so Evert would feel responsible, and when Evert had pointed out the difference between smuggling and treachery he had spoken from his heart. Walking away and leaving Shal Ahmi in possession of that dangerous piece of knowledge made him acutely uncomfortable.

Quite suddenly a thought struck him. The idea it presented was so akin to the practical jokes he played upon Piet long ago that he burst out laughing. It was safe enough, too, because if anything went wrong before the culmination of the scheme he could easily say he was merely playing a joke on old Byskin.

Cornelis Byskin reared the decorative white fowls of Cochin China as a hobby. Evert, through Wang Fu, had actually procured the original cock and hen for him. Their progeny now lived in an enclosure at the end of Byskin's garden and were quite as dear to him as any children could have been. To praise his eggs and to admire his fowls were a sure way to the old man's heart.

They were tame and used to their master's handling, and although when Evert reached into the roosting place and withdrew the nearest fowl that came to hand they squawked and shuffled a little, they made nothing like the outcry that a similar number of ordinary barnyard fowls would have made in like circumstances. Once over the wall again, Evert wrung the neck of his captive inexpertly, but with a certain clumsy despatch and skill. He scattered a few of the distinctive white feathers in a trail leading back along the path towards the deserted beach. At a turn in the path he dropped a few more. Then, scattering feathers, he began to move cautiously towards Shal Ahmi's house. He approached it from the rear this time and dropped the half-denuded body of the dead fowl upon the edge of a rubbish dump nearest the blank back wall. It would look, he thought, as though Shal Ahmi, leaping ahead of his pursuers and certain at last of discovery, had thrown away his prize upon the last inch of safe, neutral ground.

Back in Byskin's garden, he reached into the roosting place again, this time bent upon disturbing the fowls. He threw them roughly from their perches, flapped his handkerchief amongst them, and made hissing, snakelike noises. Once their lethargy and pampered confidence were overcome, they screeched and squawked like mad. The cock, making a noise like an unoiled winch, launched himself at Evert's face and pecked at his eyes. Evert beat him off and retreated. As he leaped the wall again he heard sounds of a very similar commotion emerging from the house. Cornelis's voice, a little reedy now but loud enough, was raised in furious shouting; his boys yelled; his dog barked. Evert, rubbing his hands with his handkerchief, sprinted back along the path towards Coenpark. He hadn't thought of the dog!

But old Byskin had seen the trail of feathers and had held the hound's nose to them for a second. The pursuit went off in the direction Evert had planned. Presently he slackened pace and wiped his hot face. Not a very clever plan, but it might just possibly serve. Byskin would be vicious enough. The circumstantial evidence was there, and Knol was not the man to give Shal Ahmi the benefit of the doubt. And anyway, he, Evert Haan, had done what he could.

With one of those sudden switches of his whole attention which had helped to make him so successful, he stopped thinking of the war and the English and Shal Ahmi and reverted to Annabet and Piet. *I never asked him what I meant to. No matter. I'll ask him tomorrow. A man can't think of two things at once.*

After Evert had left him Piet sat on in the dining room. He had imagined that Evert would just step down to the sheds and lofts by the jetty, give an order, and walk back. Twenty minutes, perhaps. He poured himself another glass of brandy

and sipped it slowly, intending to make it last until Evert's
return. But the reckless, greedy demon which waked in him
after the first few drinks was soon in full charge. He filled
and emptied the glass again. Then he remembered that Evert
had entrusted him with a message for Annabet; she would be
sitting alone, wondering. And he was in no state to go and
talk to a lady. But he must. He took another drink to give
him courage and then, after another period of desperate
waiting during which he almost prayed for Evert's return, he
rose and, lurching, made his way into the drawing room
where Annabet sat with her embroidery.

She saw that he was drunk but gave no sign of her
concern. With a smile as sweet and almost as false as
Mevrouw's she said, "Come, come and sit down, Captain
Odshoorn, and tell me some more about Heydberg. How is
your mother? I should have asked that before, but I was so
engrossed in hearing about Klara."

"My mother's very well," said Piet carefully, lowering
himself into a chair and fixing her with a disconcerting stare.
"And are you glad now that you came? It was my fault, you
know. I put the notion into Evert's head. But for me he'd not
have heard of you. It was my fault you came here."

"But I'm glad to be here, Captain Odshoorn. I got better
here. I've been very fortunate. I'm extremely grateful to you
for any part you had in bringing me here."

"I'm very glad to hear that," said Piet. "You see, I can
never make up my mind about Evert. Things that happened
a long time ago make me inclined to think badly of him
whenever I get half a chance. And you know, I used to sit in
church the times I was home in Heydberg and sort of make
plans for you. I never reckoned then that I'd open my big
mouth when I was drunk and set Evert Haan to marrying
you, and that's the truth. I'm a little drunk now, you know."
He added the last sentence by way of explanation.

She had a curious flashing feeling about destiny, gone
before it could be crystallised into such a slow thing as a
thought. Herself going to church, cross because she must
appear in such makeshift finery, and—purely on Father
Vincent's account—resentful of the Protestant service. And
somewhere, unseen and unnoticed, this big man gathering
up his impressions and coming across the seas and getting
drunk and talking about her, and Evert asking to marry her,
so that she came here and saw Christy. . . . A curious
sequence, leading where? Her young, romantic mind could

provide only one answer. To Christy. Sooner or later, by some means or other, she and Christy would meet again and all would be well. Why else had she come to Banda?

The next day began as any other day. Evert went by prahau into Banda Neira as soon as he had made his morning rounds. Acutely aware of his moods, as she always was, she thought that he had seemed silent and preoccupied that morning, but he had come into the house again on his way to the landing stage, had kissed her, and had said that he would be home by five o'clock. When he had gone she went into the garden, as she usually did, catching at the short time of early morning freshness, so soon to be lost in the scorching heat of the day. Hassan, the gardener, was already at work, busy with the interminable job of rooting out the fast-growing weeds from a border. As she came near he straightened himself and stood nervously shifting his bare feet, nervously plucking a weed into shreds between his big earth-soiled hands.

"What's the matter, Hassan?" she asked when she was close enough to see the flutter of his heart behind the prominent bones of his thin brown chest. He looked from side to side before he answered.

"Nothing, Mevrouw. In the garden, nothing. But I have a message for Mevrouw. Just a message. Mevrouw will please understand that I pass on what was told me. As I was bidden." He looked at her with eyes in which terror showed plainly.

"All right, Hassan. You were told to give me a message. I understand. What is it?"

For no known reason her own heart had begun to flutter too.

Hassan looked right and left again, then, lowering his voice until it was the merest thread of sound, said:

"Shal Ahmi is in the gaol, Mevrouw. He sent you a message. It concerns a fighting cock with a black tail and an Irish name, Mevrouw."

"Yes, yes. I understand. Go on."

"He has news of the bird. Also, he is anxious about your health. If you would visit him, Mevrouw, and ask his advice upon your sickness, he would give that and also the news."

"Is that all?"

"They are the words as they were given to me, Mevrouw."

The old man drew a deep, steadying breath. "Mynheer is no friend to Shal Ahmi. That is known to Mevrouw? And eyes are everywhere."

"I know. Thank you, Hassan. I will be very careful."

She turned away and walked quickly back to the house. She was trembling with excitement and agitation. Shal Ahmi, in gaol of all places, had news of Christy. To get it she must go to the gaol, and eyes were everywhere. Even Hassan had felt it necessary to warn her of that.

News. What could it be? Had Christy enlisted Shal Ahmi's help to arrange a meeting? Would there be a message for her? Why had Christy chosen Shal Ahmi, whom he distrusted so profoundly? Was there some trick in it and she too blind and excited to see it?

Speculations were just a waste of time. She must take the risk and go to the gaol at once. But she had been repeatedly forbidden to leave the house alone. Take Katje to the gaol? Take Katje into her confidence? Pretend to be seeking Shal Ahmi's aid for some complaint as yet undisclosed to Evert? Oh no. The very idea was distasteful. Must get out of the house. Must get rid of Katje. Must get to the gaol. News. News of Christy.

Katje was dawdling about the bedroom. At the doorway Annabet steadied herself and forced her quivering lungs to take their fill of air.

"Katje, I want you to pack my yellow muslin with the slashed sleeves. Stuff the sleeves with paper and pack it carefully. Mevrouw van Heem wants to take a pattern of it. We're going there this morning. You can help Nina with the cutting out and basting while I talk to Mevrouw."

Trudi van Heem was friendly and sensible. And her house was close to the Fort, though Van Heem's plantation lay on the other side of the island. Told some feasible story, Trudi would keep Katje occupied and allow Annabet to slip away; and although Evert did not personally like Trudi, he approved of her as an associate for his wife. A sudden, spontaneous visit to her house would cause no comment.

"I was a fool ever to ask you for the pattern," said Trudi when the yellow dress and the pattern paper were laid out on the big dining table. "I shall look as broad as I'm long in a gown like that. But it was sweet of you, Annabet, to bring it and to come yourself and offer your girl to help. I do appreciate it." She put her soft, warm, fat arm around Annabet's neck and kissed her.

"I want you to do something for me in return," said Annabet, trying to speak lightly. From a distance it had seemed a good idea to half confide in Trudi and ask her help; but now, face to face with the woman, misgivings made themselves felt. Trudi had been from the very first both friendly and gracious, but she could at times assume a frightening dignity and at other times make remarks that were lacerating in their frankness. Something within Annabet said, Suppose, when you had blurted out your request, she chose to be affronted by your assumption that she would lend countenance to deceit; or roundly told you what she thought of your folly; or, worst of all, sent for Evert and handed you over? But the risk must be taken. Shal Ahmi had news of Christy.

"Come along," said Trudi van Heem, slipping her arm through Annabet's. "We'll leave the girls to their work. Now, what do you want me to do for you? Don't look so worried, child. If it's humanly possible I'll help you." Her small bright eyes dwelt upon Annabet's face with a look of kindness mingled with intense curiosity. Homesick? Evert? Pregnant? Lover?

It was no use beating about the bush, Annabet thought. That would be just a waste of time. If Trudi would help, she would help; if she refused. no amount of pretty preparatory speeches would serve.

"It's just this. I want to consult Shal Ahmi. And he's in gaol. I've got to go there and I don't want Katje to come with me. Do you mind if I go while I'm supposed to be with you? You know how Evert feels about Shal Ahmi."

"It's about the only thing your husband and I have in common," said Trudi brusquely. "Is the rogue in gaol? I didn't know. I'm glad. I hope they keep him there. But that's all by the way. What do *you* want with that brown devil?" She saw the embarrassed colour mount in Annabet's face and jumped to her own conclusion. "My dear," she said earnestly, leaning forward and laying her hand upon Annabet's knee, "has somebody been telling you how to get a baby? Jehane Vehmeer, I'll be bound. Don't, I do beg of you, listen to her. Oh yes, I know it works. I know of two cases. But I know how it works too. Nights of vigil at that old shrine of his, prayers and fastings and spellbinding. Then an opium dream timed to coincide with a ship's arrival, and a drunken sailor earning two guilders very easily. There, now I've shocked you. But it's true, Annabet. As God's in His heaven, that's the kind of thing Shal Ahmi does."

To lie to this kind, earnest woman was horrible. But there was nothing else for it.

"It isn't that, Trudi. I'd like a baby, of course, but I'm not worried about that *yet*. It's just my hair. I lost it all when I was ill, you know, and Shal Ahmi made some stuff that made it grow again very quickly. Now it's beginning to fall again."

"But, my dear child," said Trudi, her eyes on the thick, lustrous cascade of golden curls, "that's not a thing to go pushing into the gaol to see *him* about. He'll be out in a day or two. Captain Knol loathes him and is always trumping up charges against him, but nothing ever comes of it. Besides, do you really have faith in him? To my mind he's a charlatan. And dangerous."

"Dangerous he may be. But he isn't a charlatan, Trudi. I don't like him. But he did do me good in other ways besides my hair. And I do want to see him."

"But, my dear child, you can't just walk up to the gaol and ask to see that old devil and think Evert won't know. It'd be all over Banda in fifteen minutes. And look, I've got some real rosemary water in my room. I'll give you some for your hair."

"You're so kind. But, Trudi, I must see him. Nothing else——"

The stout little woman's kindly expression faded. Irritability brightened her eyes. And something else. Suspicion. Well, who could wonder? Annabet asked herself. Falling hair seemed such a trivial excuse for such obstinacy.

"I believe there's something behind all this," said Trudi van Heem with one of the devastating flashes of frankness which Evert found so intolerable. "You're not a superstitious fool like Jehane Vehmeer. Come along, tell me. Did that old devil treat you unbeknownst to Evert and then blackmail you? That's another of his tricks. Are you taking money to the gaol for him?"

Annabet felt dizzy. And all this time the news of Christy was waiting! She could have screamed with impatience.

"No, it isn't blackmail; it isn't money; it isn't anything to do with his spells, nor with my hair, if you must know. More than that I can't tell you. I'm sorry I ever mentioned the matter. I shall just order Katje to go home alone and go to the gaol by myself. If you think you ought to tell Evert, well, you must. I have to see Shal Ahmi today, as soon as possible."

Trudi was silent for a moment. Then she said:

"In that case you must wait until evening. The gaol is in the Fort, and from this door to the gate you could be seen by everybody in Banda. I'll send word to Evert that you are staying to dine here, and he can come up and fetch you. At dusk, in cloaks and veils, we might pass unnoticed."

"You are—you will come with me?"

"Of course. I may not see eye to eye with Evert upon many subjects, but I agree with him about Shal Ahmi and about your walking about alone. Now, shall we see how those two idle wenches are getting on?"

By the time they set out Annabet was resigned to failure, apathetic, almost dumb with resignation. If Trudi insisted upon accompanying her into the actual presence of Shal Ahmi she must bear the torture of being so near to the source of news and still not hear it. She must waste the precious interview in trivial, false talk. Trudi, she decided, could not be trusted fully; not because she was malicious or likely to tell Evert or for any of the more obvious reasons, but because her concern for Annabet's welfare would impel her to further argument and interference. And dimly she realised, now that it came to the point of making confidences, that this infatuation would not stand up to the test of facing Trudi's practical common sense.

With their faces hidden the two women turned through the rapidly deepening twilight and made for the Fort. Trudi seemed to know the way, avoiding the big guarded entrance and making for a side door. Annabet was content to follow, to stand aside, to remain silent; even glad that the ordeal of facing the Dutch sergeant who was on guard, of announcing the desire to see Shal Ahmi, of discreetly slipping the sweetening coin from palm to palm had not been left to her to bear alone. But once they were actually inside the place, following the guard down the long, malodorous passage with cells on either side, her resentment against Trudi quickened. At this point a true friend would have paused and said, "I'll wait here, you go on alone." But Trudi actually went ahead directly behind the guard until he paused at the farthermost door and rapped his knuckles on the grille which composed its upper half.

"He sleeps all the time," he explained genially. "There you

are, Mevrouw. I can't let him out or you in because I don't
carry the cell keys. But you can ask him whatever it is you
want to know."

Almost indiscernible in the faint light, Shal Ahmi's dark
face appeared behind the grille. Then, and only then, did
Trudi step back. Annabet, still undecided as to the exact
nature of the "secret" errand she must pretend had lain
behind her feigned concern for her hair, stepped forward
and, swallowing the stiffness in her throat, said in a low
voice, "Good evening, Shal Ahmi. I am Mevrouw Haan."

"Ah yes," he said in his smooth thin voice. He looked not
at her but at Trudi lingering in the background but well
within earshot. "Let me see, Mevrouw Haan. Forgive me. . . .
Much has happened since you sought my help and advice.
. . . As you see, my own life has suffered some disturbance.
But I recall it all now. Ah yes, Mevrouw, I used all my skill
and all my influence in an endeavour to trace the missing
articles. But I failed. I am afraid that you must allow good
sense to overrule your kind heart, Mevrouw, and tell your
husband and let justice take its course."

"But justice is so harsh, Shal Ahmi. And the offender so
young."

"More hope of his benefiting by a sharp lesson, Mevrouw.
However, since your heart is still tender towards the rogue,
there is one road of enquiry which might lead to results. I
thought of it only this morning after I was incarcerated here.
Too late. If you would really rather take further trouble than
hand over the matter to your husband I could outline what
you should do. But I still hold to the opinion that you are too
kind, Mevrouw."

"I would do anything. Please tell me what you have in
mind."

He stepped back from the grilled door, and Annabet
caught sight of his little charcoal brazier, dimly red, burning
away in the far corner.

"Excuse me, Mevrouw. We prisoners cook our own food,
and my supper is ready to stand aside to cool. That is well,
for now I can sweeten this foetid air. Mevrouw, you force
from me the remark that no other Dutch lady in Banda
would visit this pesthole, this plague spot with its lice and its
stinks, in order to save a little thief from his just punishment.
This in your honour, Mevrouw." He took a handful of
something and laid it on the glowing charcoal, and almost
instantly there burst from the grille of the cell a thick cloud

of vapour, pungent, stinging, choking. Annabet caught her breath and her eyes filled with tears. Behind her Trudi began to cough like a cow with the husk.

"It is nothing; it will pass; it sweetens the air," said Shal Ahmi, fanning the cloud past Annabet and into the passage.

"Mevrouw, if you intend to let your kind heart rule you, the best thing to do—— Dear me, this is really a little over-powering, even to me. In the poor light I must have thrown on more than I thought. I ask your forgiveness, Mevrouw." He fanned energetically, and Trudi, turning to protest, took the cloud full in her face.

"I must—get some—air," she gasped. "Come, Annabet." She turned and hurried, gasping along the passage. Out of range of Shal Ahmi's air sweetener, she stopped and, leaning against the wall, mopping her steaming eyes. Foul old devil, she thought. How could Annabet *breathe?* Well, anyway, it didn't matter. She had heard enough to rest assured that Annabet wasn't playing with fire, seeking a love philtre or a fertility charm. Just trying to protect a horrid little brown thief from Evert's just wrath. She'd have something to say to her about native servants and their ways!

"Now, Mevrouw," said Shal Ahmi, coming close to the grille and speaking rapidly, "we must waste no more time. Your presence here speaks of your interest in the young Englishman whose life we saved. He is in danger again, great and deadly danger. I have here"—he fumbled amongst his crumpled white clothing and produced a folded paper bound with red twine and sealed with great blobs of beeswax—"a letter of warning. If you would take it, Mevrouw, and write upon the cover the man's real name and give it to Gariz to carry, you may save his life. You would wish to do that, I think. I regret that I must drag you into this business. But first, he did not entrust me with his name; and second, though I managed, on my way to the gaol, to whisper a message to you, it is not possible for me to find a willing and reliable bearer of the letter. You will take it? Turn your back to the passage and lean towards me. It will pass unobserved."

"But my husband—he is the one the Englishman sought. He could act so much more quickly and freely. You see"— she jerked her head backwards—"how I am placed."

"Your husband," said Shal Ahmi, "has worked with me and the English. Now he is content to see them taken and murdered. I cannot explain. He has made his profit and does not mind if the patrol overtakes them. But I care, Mevrouw. And so do you, for the sake of the one man. I was not deceived, Mevrouw. I witnessed your parting. The Dutch take fierce vengeance. They torture before they kill. This paper, despatched by Gariz, the boar-man, who has the boats striped red and black, will save the young man. The patrol, when it pounces, will find the English islands deserted, the victims flown. Turn your back, Mevrouw, and lean forward as though I gave you information. There. That is well. He will owe you his life again, Mevrouw. Such debts the gods are eager to honour." He raised his voice. "That is all I can suggest, Mevrouw. If it fails you must let justice take its course." Then suddenly the expression of the brown face pressed against the grille changed from conspiratorial guile to something real and urgent. "One thing more, Mevrouw, and now I speak from the heart. By all the signs there is unmistakable evidence that the Fire Mountain will shortly spout again. If it could be arranged, it would be well for you to take a holiday. A little visit to Batavia, Mevrouw, while the earth shakes and the lava pours. Good night." He turned abruptly and was lost in the gloom of his cell. The little brazier was extinguished.

Trudi, still a little breathless, pattered along the passage and took Annabet by the arm. "Really, my dear, you're a bigger fool than I suspected. Making all that mystery and dragging me here to this foul place and getting half choked yourself for the sake of some wretched little thieving boy."

Suddenly Annabet thought, I know how to change the subject and make her quiet.

"Shal Ahmi talked of something else," she said brutally. "He says the Fire Mountain will spout shortly. All the signs point that way."

She had lived in Banda long enough to know that any inadvertent mention of the volcano would provoke silence in any gathering. The Fire Mountain, for those who lived within range of its fury, must be resolutely ignored, otherwise its terror would dominate the thoughts of everyone in its vicinity as inescapably as its physical presence dominated the landscape. Now and then some careless person would speak its name, often in tracking an elusive date—"just before, or just after the last eruption." And there would be a shocked silence before everyone within hearing shrugged away the memory and the fear as deliberately as

they would have moved a source of physical discomfort.
The Fire Mountain must be ignored. That was the only
attitude which made life supportable in such a place.

Thoughts of these things went through Trudi's mind for a
moment or two, while Annabet, with other things to think
of, blessed the little interlude of silence. Then Trudi said
sturdily, "How should he know? All the signs are favourable
this year." As they walked the few remaining yards towards
the house she recounted the good signs. Annabet did not
listen. Good or bad, she could feel no concern over them.
She must think out some way of conveying her message to
Gariz, and then in a few hours Christy would be gone. Never
until this moment had she realised how large a part hope had
played even in her moods of despair and resignation. Always
there had been a chance, frail, farfetched, but still a possible
chance, that the unexpected, the almost incredible, might
happen. Now that last, most forlorn link was about to be
broken. Gariz would carry a message out into the vast of
blue water; and the glow which had rested upon that
unknown island, Gadia, would fade. Christy would be lost;
her mind, searching for him, would wander the whole world
undirected.

She forced back the despair and the tears which the
thought brought, and tightened the arm which was still
linked in Trudi's.

"Thank you so much for coming with me, Trudi. I'd have
hated going alone."

"I only came from vulgar curiosity," said Trudi.

Evert came back with Gert van Heem, and the four sat
down to dinner. Despite Trudi's efforts, it was a more silent
meal than the four usually shared. Evert was less easily
provoked by Trudi's sallies than usual, and Annabet had
reached that stage of mental exhaustion where she heard
everything she said before she said it, analysed it, and
decided that it was not worth saying. Her inward agitation
was not soothed by the sight of Evert in a thoughtful, almost
glum mood. It wasn't possible, it couldn't be possible, she
told herself, that he had heard already of her visit to the gaol.
Of course not; only a guilty conscience could suggest such a
thing. But he was brooding over something.

However, though rather silent, he seemed amiable
enough, and on the way home she was glad of his silence.
Once inside the house, she made an effort to banish her

melancholy by thinking of practical things and was glad to
find something which ought to be dealt with at once.
Klara's wedding present.

"Evert," she said, taking up the piece of embroidery which
she had put down last evening when Evert returned, last
evening which now seemed such ages ago, "would you mind
very much if I sent Klara some of my clothes? For a wedding
present? You give me so many; I don't need them all. And
silk is very expensive at home." Klara has never had nice
things since she was old enough to appreciate them; and,
loving her young farmer, wouldn't she rejoice to be seen in
such shifts and petticoats and nightdresses as Annabet
owned in such plenty?

Evert had poured himself a glass of schnapps and was
sipping it with less than his usual enjoyment, almost absent-
mindedly. Was it possible, she wondered, that he was
secretly worried about the situation between the Dutch and
his erstwhile partners?

"Do as you wish," he said. His voice was genial but lacked
some of its usual bluffness. "As a matter of fact, I'd been
thinking about a present. I looked in on Wang Fu and
ordered a set of things for a dressing table. Silver. Like yours,
but plainer. More suitable for a farmhouse bedroom. Piet
can take them back. They'll be ready at the end of the week."

"Oh, Evert, how very kind. I wasn't thinking of anything
so grand. She'll love them."

But that wasn't true. Any woman who knew about being
poor would know that the steel comb and the worn brush
could be concealed in a drawer, whereas drab and shabby
underclothes . . . But a man wouldn't know, and obviously
Evert had meant to make a spectacular and generous
gesture. Still, he had said, "Do as you wish," so perhaps she
could send the silk things as well; and though they would
wear out in time, the dressing-table set would last—could
even be sold if Klara ever found herself in need of more
money than her husband could give her.

"It really is extremely generous of you, Evert. Such a gift
to somebody you've never even seen."

He looked at her and saw that she was genuinely moved by
gratitude, and he thought of all the presents he had show-
ered upon her and of all the times when he had been disappointed, thinking that her reception of them had been cool
and forced. His mind slipped away to the narrow, stuffy
cabin of the *Eastern Venture* and the interview which he

had forced upon Piet. But he must make some reply before
he began to brood and remember and plan again. So he said:

"She's your sister. I'd like you to send her a present that
was suitable." Then he was silent again.

He had gone out to the ship at the end of the day, and Piet
had not seemed very pleased to see him, despite the fact that
they had parted on friendly, indeed intimate, terms on the
previous evening. Piet had recovered his senses as he grew
sober again and was in the mood to regret his breach of the
Company's confidence. But Evert was not to be deterred
from his purpose. It had taken a few hours for his mind to
absorb and accept the news about the imminence of war; but
as soon as it had done so there had come to him, side by side
with immense satisfaction that the cargo of contraband had
been saved, the realisation that all this was Company's
business, not Evert Haan's. Startled by the news, he had
rushed out to Shal Ahmi, and at once regretting his haste
and alarmed by Shal Ahmi's attitude, he had made his plot
and had gone home. There he had found Piet maudlin and
almost incapable and had taken him back to his ship without
broaching the subject which had regained its pre-eminence
in his mind.

He stepped into Piet's cabin, determined to rectify his
mistake. And this time he would allow nothing to divert him.

"I've come to drink with you for a change, old man," he
said in such a way that Piet, who had spent the hours of
daylight in renewed vows of perpetual abstinence, was
bound to bring out a bottle.

After his second glass—for a man must drink with his
guest, particularly if the guest has been noticeably free with
his liquor on previous occasions—the sharpest pangs of
Piet's alcoholic remorse were deadened, and he could look at
Evert without regret and even think that, had the warning
not been given last night, he would have spoken now.

"Well, one more, then I must be getting back," said Evert,
accepting an invitation which had not yet been given, and
Piet filled the glasses again.

Evert began to work round to the speech he had prepared
last night.

"You really thought Annabet looked well—and happy,
Piet?"

Piet, already a little befuddled, remembered that Annabet
had said that she was happy and that Evert was kind to her;

that she had thanked him for having been the cause of her coming to Banda. You couldn't believe your own stupid drunken eyes against a lady's given word!

"Indeed I did. What's more, Evert, I asked her, as an old acquaintance, whether she was happy and she said she was. She thanked me for my part in the business. More than I deserved—but I didn't go into that." He gave a foolish laugh.

"Ah," said Evert. He set down his glass and put his finger tips together while his eyes went meditatively to the porthole. "I was lucky, thanks to you; and a good many people would think Annabet lucky too. The one I can't help being sorry for is that poor young sod she deserted. How did he take the business?"

Oh, admirable. Casual, gossipy, perfect.

"What poor young sod? Who d'you mean, Evert?"

"The name has slipped my mind, if I ever knew it. But you'd know it, I reckon. I gather that he was very devoted."

Piet knit his brows and ran his hand over his beard. The lure of gossip and a slight mystery, allied to three glasses of schnapps, made him an ideal collaborator in Evert's scheme. He would have been quite prepared to tell what he knew had he known anything. But he didn't.

"I don't believe there was anybody else," he said firmly after five minutes' slow reflection. "Nobody special, that is. There was a dozen or so used to look at her with calves' eyes through the service. Like me!" He added the last words jocularly, with a burst of schnapps-born laughter which ended as abruptly as a severed string. Nothing to laugh about in that; the thing wasn't a joke any more.

Evert laughed, too, accepting the joke. But he went back to the point stubbornly.

"All the same, there was somebody special. She as good as told me so once. I didn't pay much attention at the time, and it's not a matter I'd care to raise with her again—she's probably forgotten him now herself. But it stuck in my mind somehow, and I felt sorry for the chap."

Suddenly Piet laughed and slapped his thigh. "I've got it. By God, Evert, I know who she meant. But you needn't worry about taking her away from *him*. He couldn't have had her if there'd been no other man on earth."

He laughed again while Evert looked at him with scarcely concealed impatient hatred. But Piet's tongue was loosed again, and he must hand over his information in his own long-winded way.

"Mevrouw was a Sieberg, wasn't she, from Brussels? Well, her sister had a boy, nice-looking, fair-haired boy, the image of the old Padroon. Jean Marie, they called him. He used to stay at Janshaven and later on at Heydberg. My mother used to grizzle and say that he looked hungry all the time he was there because Mevrouw starved him, having had only girls to feed."

"Yes," said Evert, and with difficulty refrained from adding, "Get on, you garrulous blockhead."

"Well, maybe she did like him a lot; you know what the Van Goens are for marrying their cousins. And just now when I said, 'I've got it,' I saw the whole thing clear. Their old Truitje told my mother that when your Annabet was ill and looked like dying she kept crying and asking for him. But bless your soul, you didn't take her away from him. He'd given her up getting on for ten years before that."

"Why, had he married? What made them send for him then?" Evert asked sharply.

"Didn't I make that plain? He'd gone into the Church. He's a priest. They don't call him Jean Marie any more. He's Father Vincent, all shaven and shorn. *Now* d'you see why I laughed?"

"Of course," said Evert, and laughed himself. For a few moments the cabin was filled with a strong Protestant savour.

"Well," said Evert, ending the session, "I won't worry about *him* any more."

But the knowledge of the identity of the man who stood between him and complete possession of Annabet had not brought the relief which he had anticipated. The phantom now had a name—two names, in fact—was both Jean Marie Seiberg and Father Vincent. And the phantom was a priest, tonsured, emasculate, ludicrous. And immune.

Walking home, eating his dinner, sitting opposite Annabet in the drawing room, Evert understood with a feeling of utter frustration that long ago, when she was only a child, all idea of physical contact must have been purged from her mind. In one thing, and only one, he had been right. And that was in seeing the unknown as a phantom and as a barrier.

All these thoughts and memories and angers rushed through his mind during the moment which followed Annabet's words of gratitude concerning Klara's wedding

gift. And with them ran the poignant realisation of how
sweet she had looked with that warm, surprised, delighted
expression on her face. No reserve, no barrier just then. If
only it could always be like that!

His mood turned two wild somersaults. For one moment
he wondered whether he hadn't imagined his own frustra-
tions. After all, there wasn't a thing he could put his finger
on and say with any truth: "There she has failed me—or
there." He couldn't honestly accuse her even of coldness.
Wasn't his best plan to ignore the whole business and be
thankful for what he had, a lovely, kind, acquiescent wife of
the kind he had always wanted, dismissing everything else as
the product of his own fancy?

Next moment he was philosophic. Well, suppose it wasn't
all fancy; allow that in all their intercourse, even at the most
intimate moments, she was looking beyond him, hankering.
What was she hankering for? A priest, all shaven and shorn,
vowed to continence? Couldn't Evert Haan, who had got
everything he wanted out of life, afford to pity and smile?
Poor bastard, what good would Annabet's thoughts do him?

But in the next moment the real Evert came to the surface
again; the weathercock of his mind steadied and swung
between the old fixed points of his hatred and his desires. The
egomania which had made the Janshaven farm boy fight his
way into the ranks of the nutmeg princes and eclipse them all
forbade that he should now accept the second best. He
wanted Annabet, the whole Annabet, with no reserves and
no evasions. He'd never had that yet. But he must have it.
Even at the risk of losing what he had—the kindness, the
affection, the gratitude—he must make a bid for all the rest.
He would, by sheer force of his will, root that damned priest
out of her mind. And that, he realised with a suddenness
which shook his heart a little, would be, in a double sense,
the triumph of Haan over Van Goens. He saw a little dimly,
misted by the experiences of their months together and his
own changes of feelings, all those plans he had made for this
girl's humiliation and subjection. Somehow, for some reason
which he did not clearly know, not one of them had been put
into action. If anything, he had been the humiliated and
subjected one. Now he would put that right.

He looked at her again. The soft golden light of the lamp
made a halo of her hair as she bent over her embroidery.
Below it her face looked shadowy, delicate oval of cheek,
sweet sensitive mouth, long lashes fluttering over the down-

looking eyes. Mine, mine, Evert shouted to himself greedily,
all mine; it must be, it shall be, entirely mine.

He got up so abruptly that Annabet thought he had
sighted a mosquito or some crawling pest and had leaped to
kill it. He paused by her chair and laid his hand for a second
on her head, feeling the silkiness of her hair, the warmth of
her scalp.

"We'll send Klara the silver and as many silk things as you
like. But there's one thing we didn't do. We forgot to drink
her health. We'll do that now!" He looked down at her quite
fiercely. "You'll risk a headache to drink your own sister's
health, I suppose?"

"Why, yes. Yes, Evert, of course."

And I'll drink to Christy's safe escape and wish him well
wherever he goes.

Evert marched into the dining room. He swallowed two
glasses of schnapps hastily and filled the glass again. Then
from its hiding place he took the powder which Shal Ahmi
had given him and placed a generous pinch in the bottom of
a fresh glass. He thought for a moment and added another
portion. He filled the glass with Madeira and was annoyed to
see that the liquid turned cloudy. But it cleared almost at
once, and, carrying the two brimming glasses, he returned to
Annabet.

"Well," he said in a loud bluff voice, "here's to your sister.
I don't know her, but I admire her spirit. All for love and the
world well lost, as they say."

"I hope she'll be happy," said Annabet, rising and raising
her glass.

"If she loves him she will." Evert spoke aggressively.

"Oh, she loves him," Annabet said, bursting into nervous
chatter because Evert seemed so strange tonight. No harm,
anyway, in telling it now, with Klara safely married and
Mamma powerless. She told him the story of Klara's
clandestine love-making, her own share in it, the escapade to
Whitwater with its well-nigh tragic result.

The story, when she started it, had lain clear and plain in
her mind, like a road often travelled or a song often sung.
But before the end her mind had clouded. Identities merged,
and Klara slinking out to meet the young farmer had become
Annabet slinking out to keep tryst with Christy. *Then*
I didn't know how she felt; I wondered at her. I thought I
knew about love because of the way I had felt about Jean
Marie, but of course I didn't. I never thought of Jean Marie

in that way at all. That was why I couldn't understand Klara.
Now I do. And I am glad, glad, glad that I helped her. In my
ignorance I helped her. Oh, if only there were someone to
help me now. If only someone would scheme and plan and
lie so that I could say good-bye to him. Just good-bye.

Very hard, after a brimming glass of wine, to talk about
one thing and think of another. Once, in saying "Klara," she
heard her tongue slip; the soft *l* hardened, and she almost
said "Christy."

And Evert had been prepared to let Christy be killed by
the patrol. Evert had been colder-hearted, less honourable
than Shal Ahmi. Evert became a patriot as soon as his pocket
was lined.

Evert is my husband, and presently we shall go upstairs.

"And that's where I got my rheumatic fever."

"And Klara her husband. Well, well, what a story," said
Evert tolerantly. "It's getting late and I must be up early in
the morning. Come along."

The night seemed cool after the burning brightness of the
day, yet enough of the swooning warmth remained to make
covers unnecessary and clothes merely an adornment. Inside
the room was the stored scent of spices and flowers, outside
only the soft rustling of the nutmeg leaves and the distance-
hushed soughing of the sea.

And here, in the heart of the night, was that closeness of
flesh, that mysterious sharing of feeling in a relationship so
unique, that when the early Fathers sought for some way to
illustrate the unity of Christ and His Church they could find
nothing better than the metaphor of the Groom and Bride.

Here are the two oddly shaped collections of corporeal
matter, recognised to anybody as man and woman, known to
their little world as Evert and Annabet, joined by the blessing
of the Church, by the custom of the law, by their own
recognition of their unity. And here are two minds, housed
in heads which share a pillow, operating in brain cells which
are at the moment only separated by two thin cases of
contingent bone, yet so opposed, so irrevocably at odds with
one another, that even out upon the open common ground of
speech they miss communion.

"D'you remember what you told me that night I came
back from Bandogar?"

"Oh, Evert, need we go over all that again?"

"Well, *need* we? Not if you've changed your mind."

Give in now, lie and surrender. Always before the truth

has seemed vital and important, concerned in some mysterious fashion with the possibility of seeing Christy again, a bribe to God: See, I am truthful when it would pay me to lie, reward me! Tell the lie now, boldly; it will make Evert happy and your life will be easier. But why should I wish him to be happy? He was willing to let the patrol pounce upon Christy unawares. Ah, but to you he has been kind; only this evening, over the matter of Klara's present, he startled you by his kindness.

"Does it matter so much? It didn't at first, Evert. You laughed when I told you." Gain time to think. Think quickly.

"I'm not laughing now," Evert said unnecessarily. "I had to give you a chance. I took you for what you were, a raw young girl with a head full of fancies. It's different now. Oh, I know we've been over this time and again. You always say you grudge me nothing; you're grateful; you're affectionate. What's that worth? What woman wouldn't be, treated as you are treated? There's hot blood in you too. But it doesn't work for me. I'm not foxed. I can feel the change come over you. I know when I stop being myself. And I know how you feel afterwards. That surprises you, doesn't it?"

She was indeed surprised by his perspicacity into unguarded retort.

"Then why do you ask if I've changed?" She was ashamed of the sharp, bickering quality in her own voice.

"Because something has got to be done about it."

"I'll do whatever you suggest, Evert."

She spoke meekly in an attempt to make amends for the sharp question a second since. But the acquiescence was genuine enough. At the beginning she had almost hoped that Evert would send her away; had he done so, she would have taken a chance with Gariz, gone to Gadia, and said simply, "Here I am if you want me; if not I'll go away." But now there was no hovering halo of hopeful light over Gadia, and Gariz had gone on his errand and Christy was lost in the dark. Yet still, if Evert was dissatisfied, she would accept banishment. She was indifferent to what happened to her now.

Evert sensed the genuine, bleak acceptance of the statement and was silenced. His twin passions of wanting and hating made tumult in his mind. Some physical outlet became essential. He put his hands—large peasant's hands softened by years of easy living—around her throat. He could kill her so easily; it would have been an assuagement to kill her, an end of the thing that defied him. But it would have been bereavement too. Even as his fingers tightened a little he could see the years stretching ahead with no Annabet, no conflict, nothing to hope for. In real agony of spirit he cried out:

"What's the matter with you? Why do you hanker for something you could never have? You must be crazy. Even if he hadn't been a priest, what could he ever have given you that I haven't? I want you; he didn't. He chose God, didn't he? Doesn't that show what sort of husband he'd have made? Maybe he was your cousin, and maybe it's in your family to fall in love with your cousins, but you're too good to be caught up in that sort of old-fashioned jumble. He left you; I married you. Haven't I done everything a man could? Can't you forget him and love me, me, me?"

Talking to Piet Odshoorn. Poor Evert. Jealous of Jean Marie, who, more than anyone else, had been instrumental in sending her here. It would have been funny, if anything in the world was funny just now. Jean Marie, Father Vincent, with his talk about the flesh and the spirit which she had finally interpreted so capriciously. Jean Marie, the flowering cherry, the green sunsets, God, and the cold stiff tulips.

There was no end, no escape. Christy was gone and all hope. Even her own mind was clouding and failing. The whole of the world and the whole of life were narrowing down to the physical nearness of this big, fleshy, heated man with his wrongly directed jealousy and his insatiable demands. And now that nothing mattered to her, now that life held no hope, what did honesty matter? Honesty was a tribute to one's self-respect. When one's self didn't matter any more . . .

"Do *you* love *me*, Evert?"

So many answers—"Haven't I proved it?" "How can I when you're engrossed with this self-made eunuch?" "By God, I do. Damn you, I do"—rushed into his mind that, choosing among them, he hesitated.

"I shouldn't have asked that," she said penitently. "I've never done anything to make you love me, have I?" Ah, but now she was speaking Evert's language, using the word as he understood it. The initiated knew that love could neither be bought nor exchanged nor willed; like the wind, it blew where it listed. "But I will try again, Evert. It's all past and done with. I know now that I shall never see him again. And I will try to forget. I'll be a better wife, I swear I will."

When I arrived I said I'd try to be a good wife; now I'm vowing to be better. Good, better, best, like the grammar books. But I'll never be a best wife; I'm lying at this moment, and cheating. What else can I do? This is the only thing left to me in the whole world; there's nothing else I can do with my life except try to make this man happy.

With Shal Ahmi's aphrodisiac at work sharpening her senses and dimming her mind, the job seemed very easy. Only the small indestructible core of her spirit pressed out into the night. Oh, Christy, where are you now? I love you. Good-bye.

Sometime during the next day the governor's circular reached Coenpark. It demanded, in the name of the Company, that Mynheer Evert Haan should forthwith send up to the Fort at Banda Neira any number up to twenty of specially selected slaves. They were to be male, between the ages of twenty and thirty, physically sound, with good eyesight, not natives, nor descended of natives, nor married to natives of Banda, Lonthoir, Ay, Lu, or any adjacent island. They were to be provided with food for one day, and before leaving Mynheer Haan was to make certain that each one knew the purpose of their call-up, which was: The Company's standing forces in the island having fallen below the level deemed necessary for safety and the keeping of order, one hundred recruits were being sought. Those of the slaves whose response to training and general demeanour rendered them most suitable for military life would be, at the end of a month, manumitted and enlisted. The accompanying pamphlet set out the conditions of service and the rates of compensation to be paid to the owners of the slaves thus removed from the plantations.

Evert, taking the papers from the hand of the smart young lieutenant, suppressed a smile. Very clever, he thought. Had I not known, I should not have guessed. Some such scheme was put into operation every second or third year, but ordinarily the number demanded never exceeded five, and the rate of compensation was always exactly based on the Bandogar market price. Now Knol wanted twenty, and the compensation was calculated to induce the planters to send their best men. Usually the recruiting station received those who, outwardly conforming to the letter of the demand, actually could well be spared; men, in fact, for whom the market price was unlikely to be obtainable elsewhere. There was one other difference. The paper setting out the rates of pay referred to Colonel, not Captain, Knol. And that in itself was significant. Quick, easy promotion was one of the fruits of war. And although the islands were still unaware of it, the Company had been at war with the English ever since that shipload of spices had reached London.

"Very well. I'll attend to it. I'll send my batch along in the morning."

"The selection takes time, Mynheer," the lieutenant ventured. The least time any other planter had asked for this inspection of nationality, antecedents, and matrimonial tangles had been forty-eight hours.

"Oh, I know mine like the palm of my hand," Evert said casually, and it was true. Some of his knowledge he owed to the fact that he was the Company's agent in the matter of purchasing slaves; a good deal more from his association with Shal Ahmi, who could look at a hundred new arrivals and divide them into racial and religious groupings without hesitation and without error. Even that miserable, long-necked deformity whom Evert had taken as a "makeweight," and the like of whom even the slave dealer in Bandogar admitted never having seen before, presented no puzzle to Shal Ahmi. "Burmese," he had said after a fleeting glance. "She was stolen, doubtless, and much mourned."

Also, in addition to his knowledge of his slaves, Evert had had at the back of his mind the possibility of a call-up. The regular soldiers would be sent to attack the English strongholds, and the new ones would, with a few of the others, serve to uphold the authority of the Company in the islands. He had already selected his men. The highly inflated rate of compensation would induce him to make a few re-arrangements, that was all. The young lieutenant, however, was much impressed and, being earnest and efficient himself, was pleased to observe that Mynheer Haan's reputation as the most successful planter in the islands rested upon actual, inimitable qualities.

And now how long before we are informed and taken into confidence? Evert wondered as he went to collect and address the men he had selected.

It was less than a fortnight.

Before the last load of nutmegs and the last cask of water had disappeared into the hold of the *Eastern Venture* three little schooners, taking advantage of their shallower draw, sailed in and anchored between her and the quay. They were, Piet noticed with interest, in tiptop condition: all their paint was fresh; every inch of canvas, every thread of cordage about them was brand new. The brasswork of their cannon—they carried three apiece—glistened in the sun. The Company's pennant fluttered at each masthead. Even if Piet had not had knowledge of the nature and significance of his late cargo he would have suspected something, for the schooners were of the kind reserved for work of importance and imperative nature. The Company maintained nine of them; their headquarters were at Batavia, and they were used for the transport of important officials, the overhauling of suspected vessels, and, more rarely, as troop carriers. No doubt, Piet thought, they carried the final orders.

Later in the day he received a request which, politely framed, was nevertheless a command. Would he make it convenient to return by way of Java and carry back one of the officers who had brought the schooners to Banda? Despite the loss of time which the diversion would cause him, he was pleased. His time was the Company's, and he had friends in Batavia.

On his last day in the island he went to dine by invitation with Evert and Annabet, and although the food had obviously been chosen with the greatest care and generosity as an offering to one who would very shortly be faring monotonously, there was very little to drink, which showed great thoughtfulness on Evert's part. Piet, with his erratic faculty of observation unimpaired, thought that his half brother seemed happier, to have regained the full measure of that blustering, overwhelming confidence and self-esteem which was either admirable or abominable, according to whether you were liking him or hating him. Annabet was a little less animated, but that Piet put down, in his simple way, to reserve. Perfectly sober, in full possession of his senses, liking Evert, who was so generous and hospitable and yet thoughtful, glad that he looked happy, envying him more than ever, hating him like hell and loving Annabet like a crazy man, he spent a mad, miserable, but delightful evening. When Annabet had left the table, Evert and he, over their single glass of wine, talked about the war and about the schooners, agreeing that the secret had been well kept. The English would be taken completely by surprise. The whole thing would be over in a few hours. They talked as all men talk, all the world over, before the first shot is fired.

"But if—mind, I'm only saying *if*—it doesn't turn out to be so easy, Evert. If they start to look up old soldiers and so on. Have you made any plans? Have you made any use of my giving you the nod?"

"Indeed I have," Evert said firmly. He was willing that Piet should go away happy about his breach of confidence. Piet was his friend. He had brought him Annabet, and he had given him the key to the knowledge which, used discreetly, had made a vital change in her. The last ten days had been the most triumphant (he meant the happiest) of his life. And it was all due to Piet. But towards avoiding military service in the case of the standing army's failure, Evert had made no move. His faith in his star was so strong that he would have welcomed rather than feared another call to arms. It would have offered him a further chance to distinguish himself. If anything, he was sorry that his age and his importance as a planter precluded his taking part in the actual physical assault. He would have enjoyed showing Knol and the rest of them how Gomarus had waged war. He was, in fact, too vain, too much in love with life, too unimaginative, despite his artistic eye, to fear death or maiming. He would have plunged into a fight as confidently, as insensitively as he had plunged into marriage.

"I won't waste your time by describing my precautions, Piet, but they're made, and they're watertight. I'm very grateful to you, old man. And as I said, if I make money on that withdrawal I spoke of, I'll remember you."

They parted on the warmest terms, and next morning Piet upanchored and sailed for Java. In the afternoon Evert, with other planters all over the islands, was summoned to the Fort, ostensibly to take dinner with the Government, actually to hear that within twenty-four hours the assault against the English in Gadia, Ay, and Lu would be launched.

The governor was thin, dry, old, unsociable, acutely but not unhappily conscious of being nothing but a figurehead, the puppet of the remote Board of Directors in Amsterdam and of the more closely revealed powers in Batavia. He knew, and he was aware that everyone in the islands knew, that Mynheer Kaerko, Colonel—he must remember not to call him Captain—Colonel Knol, Mynheer Haan, Mynheer van Heem, and probably half a dozen others were actually far more irreplaceable than he was himself. He knew nothing about business, nothing about soldiers, less than nothing about growing nutmegs. He was here in Banda, treated with respect, ostensibly deferred to, because in the islands there were the Company's direct representatives like Kaerko, the soldiers represented by Colonel, *Colonel* Knol, and the men who actually grew the nutmegs. Left to themselves, each might think himself primarily important. So a governor was appointed, a kind of perpetual weighing machine, a thick blob of quietening oil cast upon the turmoil of the active waters. He had no illusions, no ambitions.

He gave his guests an indifferent dinner, nothing like the meal Kaerko or Knol or Evert would have offered to him, and at the end of it he said in his dry, old voice, "Gentlemen, doubtless you have guessed that there is something behind this gathering. Some of you know already, and the rest of you are still to be informed that the Company has decided to clear out the English. The operation can hardly be dignified by the name of war." Knol bridled like an insulted girl; he had been waiting for a war for six long years. "The presence of the English on the islands of Gadia, Ay, and Lu constitutes a perpetual threat to our trade. I have been asked to call you together and explain the circumstances. The Company does not, for one instant, doubt your allegiance and your co-operation. Your own interests are at stake. That is all I have to say. Colonel Knol has, I believe, something to add."

Knol, with his wrinkled brown nutmeg face alight with fervour, rose as soon as the governor ceased speaking. He was enjoying his moment. But his speech was practical and to the point. He explained that when the schooners sailed tomorrow there would be left in the islands only a few regular soldiers, the recently enlisted draft, and the planters themselves. The one thing to be aware of was trouble amongst the slaves.

Knol paused and went on in a crisp voice: "Some of you gentlemen have lived in the islands longer than I have. I cannot speak to you out of greater experience. But I have studied my trade, and amongst the things I have read is Colonel Kraemer's own account of his campaign against the Moorish pirates in Sulaya twenty-five years ago. During that campaign, gentlemen, he was obliged, no fewer than four times, to cease his operations against the enemy and return to quell disturbances at home. The campaign, planned to take a few weeks at most, lasted, on this account, for eighteen months. I am not anticipating a repetition of this catastrophe. Things are very different from what they were in Kraemer's time. But I do ask you very solemnly to be alert and wary. Overlook nothing, however trivial, that is at variance with the usual routine on your plantations. Lieutenant de Klerk"—he turned towards his subordinate, the smart young man who had presented Evert with the circular which called in the draft—"will be at the Fort, ready for action, at the slightest sign of trouble. And each of you, I know, has his own methods of keeping order. I do beg of you gentlemen not to call me and my men back from Gadia to save you from being burnt in your beds." He sat down, smiling.

Evert, like every other planter at the table, began to reckon the number of men who could, in an emergency, be trusted. He made his reckoning with all the confidence of his boisterous temperament. Why, he and Josef, Toeg, the foreman, and Hassan, with a musket apiece, could keep the whole mob at bay. It was just like Knol to make mountains out of molehills.

Piet and the young naval officer talked about the war all the way to Java. There was no need for secrecy now, and added to the delight of discussing the campaign as such was the pleasure in talking openly of what had been a matter for brooding inwardly. The young officer was of a thoughtful, slightly pessimistic turn of mind. He distrusted, not wholly without reason, the ability of his immediate superior to whom the seafaring part of the expedition had been entrusted; and even more he doubted the wisdom of the Company in recalling him to Java and allowing his place to be taken by somebody from the Fort at Banda. So his favourite topic of conversation was the welfare of the schooners, and for hours on end he conducted a kind of nagging, fretting dissertation upon the little vessels' idiosyncrasies and the peculiar perils of the islands' sea roads. But occasionally he indulged in wider speculations. Sometimes he wondered, he said, whether the English were as unprepared as the Company imagined. "After all," he would say, "they knew that someday or other we would take action. They must have some defences. One cannon, say. Surely they'd have one cannon, Captain. Well, say they did. A cannon, properly mounted and skilfully handled, could sink one of those schooners. Look . . ."

He drew on the table with his forefinger and indicated to

Piet exactly where a well-directed cannon ball could strike one of his little darlings with fatal results. His long, big-nosed face turned pale. He was, Piet thought, like a father who had left three beloved children in a dangerous place. He worried until it became a habit, and the scope of his worry widened, like the ripple of a stone flung into a pond. It reached the matter of native risings.

"I had to read Kraemer's report of his campaign when I was training," he said one evening. "D'you know, as soon as the soldiers left the island the damned natives rose and carried bloody murder and fire through the whole place. Women and children slaughtered and burned in their beds. Suppose that happened again?"

Piet, who had listened with equanimity to the naval officer's dire forebodings about the fate of his schooners, felt his heart turn over. Annabet, he thought. For a moment the whole of his big body was subjected to a wild prickling impulse which, if it could have miraculously been translated into action, would have resulted in his flying through the air and landing bodily in the house at Coenpark with a pistol in either hand. Since action was impossible, he was forced, as all men are forced with an intolerable thought, to argue it down.

"Nonsense," he said sharply. "There hasn't been a rising in Banda since Coen rooted out the last of the native strongholds. The coolies there are noted for their good behaviour, and if my kinsman is a fair sample, the planters are pretty wide awake. I mean to say, if you and I can see the danger, surely they will, too, and be on their guard."

Oh, Evert, use your head now, and all your cunning; be alert for Annabet's sake.

"Oh well, there's no use worrying," said the young officer, using his favourite phrase, the favourite phrase of all congenital worriers. "There may be news in Batavia. These prahaus skirting the coast lines and doing short relay trips travel very quickly. Or, if things went really wrong, they'd send a schooner back. *Greta's* the fastest of the three; she'd move landward of us all the way and could be in Batavia now, this minute. If anything went really wrong they'd send *Greta* back for help." He seemed to take comfort in the thought of the beloved schooner's speed. Then his brow darkened. "Unless of course the English have rigged that cannon," he said gloomily.

From that moment Piet did not draw a completely easy

breath, taste anything he ate, or think a comfortable thought. Over and over again he saw Annabet with her gown and her long hair afire; he saw her with her throat cut; he saw her raped. The whole business of the war, which had been at first merely a secret to be kept and then a secret to be confided—in order that Evert might wriggle out of any connection with it—became suddenly the most urgent and personal problem of his life. It was he who was directly responsible for taking Annabet to Banda; and this consciousness of responsibility, which had hitherto been mild, semiromantic, concerned with a man's behaviour and a woman's happiness, now became savage and practical, concerned with wounds and pain and danger and life and death, things which Piet's mind understood.

The crowded, lively harbour of the capital presented a picture from which one would have thought it difficult for any man to pick out instantly any particular detail, but the young naval officer, eagerly leaning out over the rail of the *Eastern Venture*, had a lover's eye. His cry, "There she is. There's the *Greta*," was compounded of relief and anxiety and triumph. At least the beloved schooner was safe and sound; but her presence here implied ill news from Banda, and he had been right in saying that she could outsail the big East Indiaman. Piet could share in one emotion only. The six words fell like lead upon his spirit. Bad news from Banda. Bad news. What news? How bad?

The young man, politely trying to conceal his impatience, made his adieux. "I'll get your fellow to wait," he said, moving towards the boat which was just about to be lowered, "and I'll send you word how things are."

"Damned if you will," Piet said roughly. "I'm coming with you."

The young man looked at him, startled, and saw that just above the line where the reddish-brown growth of beard began an edging of dirty pallor showed on the broad tanned face. Of course, he thought tolerantly, he spoke of a kinsman in Banda; naturally he's anxious. He said with an attempt at lightness which sat uneasily upon him:

"Don't attach too much importance to her being here, sir. Maybe the whole thing was over in half a day and she's brought the good news."

"Don't talk bloody rot," said Piet. "We both know what it means." He dropped into the boat.

"I know where to get the news; that's one comfort," said the young officer, leaping ashore and starting to run. Piet lumbered after him, across the quay, round a corner, down a narrow cut between two warehouses, and in at a little low doorway. They clattered up a flight of dirty wooden stairs and burst into a small room with a wide, ink-stained counter dividing it in two. Behind the counter on the far side another young naval officer, with his cuffs pushed back nearly to his elbows, his fair hair in wild disarray, and a smear of ink on his forehead, sat hunched on a high stool, laboriously scribbling away with a squeaky quill.

"For God's sake," he exclaimed irritably, finishing a line at great speed. Then he looked up. "Why, Hein! You! Stand there a minute, don't speak. I thought you were some swine come for the copies. I won't——" He ducked his head and scribbled madly, threw down the quill, dashed sand over the wet ink, and then, suddenly leisurely, read through what he had written. Bundling the papers together, he opened a little hatch in the farther wall and pushed them through. "Take them along," he said, and slammed the hatch. "Why, oh, why did I join the Navy?" he said lugubriously, smoothing his hair with inky fingers. "Six copies in half an hour. It isn't human. What they want is a writing machine." He turned a brilliant sunny smile upon his friend and Piet. "It's good to see you again."

"What about *Greta*? When'd she get in? What news?" Hein asked abruptly.

"About an hour ago. That's what all the hurry was about. She brought a report from Colonel Knol, and somebody thought it would be a good idea to send a copy of it home. Some damned ship was expected to put in today for a few minutes. They don't care if I get hunchbacked and blind."

"What was in the report?"

"Oh, nasty news as usual. Knol's wounded, but he wrote the report himself, and it made me squint-eyed to read it. They went to Lu first, found it deserted, went on to Gadia, found that deserted too, proceeded to Ay, and found that apparently deserted; and then hell broke loose. The English swine had got platforms in trees and fired down, and pits in the ground and fired up; they'd got God knows how many cannon, all hidden in bushes. They sank the *Margarete* and hit the *Sanje*. They cut the two landing parties to pieces. And when poor old Knol got back to Banda, somebody'd started a little private fire, and all the powder magazines had blown up. Write that out six times in half an hour and see if it doesn't make you dizzy!" He smiled disarmingly and rattled on.

"Looks as though you'll take *Greta* back, Hein, my lad. Poor old Albert lost half a hand—pity it wasn't half his head; I'll say it for you, you heartless rougue—and thought he'd rather go to hospital here than in Banda. Who wouldn't? And Van Holk is going to take Knol's place. He didn't say how bad he was, but, judging by his scrawl, he's dead by now. They're going to cram fifty men on the *Greta* and send her back immediately. *Seabird* will follow with a hundred. Now is there anything else I can tell you and your friend? If not, you'd better skip. This is the very core and centre of our great administration; everything that goes on in this sanctum is very, very secret. I'll see you before you go, Hein, if you go." He smiled, hopped onto his stool again, and drew another sheaf of papers towards him.

"I'd better report at once, if I'm expected to take *Greta* back," said Hein soberly, turning to the door.

"So had I," said Piet, wooden-lipped. "I reckon mine's the ship they want to take back that report. This is a bad business."

"No worse than I expected, really. Thank God I got back in time. I'd have hated to hand *Greta* over again."

Oh, you and your *Greta*, Piet thought furiously. Can't you see beyond your long nose?

They parted casually, each preoccupied with his own thoughts, at the mouth of the passage, and Piet hurried along to the agent's office. The sunny street was filled with a crowd of chattering, jostling people. Piet hated them all because either they had not heard the news from Banda or were undismayed by it. All right for them, snug in the centre of things, giddy, frivolous, like that young fool upstairs, he thought. If they'd left somebody—somebody very—somebody they cared about in Banda . . . Oh God, two landing parties cut to pieces; that'd mean practically all the standing force. And the powder magazines blown! And all the things gloomy young Hein had said about native risings . . .

The agent was frivolous and uncaring too. He had sent out to the *Eastern Venture* for Piet and now complimented him upon the promptness of his appearance.

"We want a report carried," he explained, offering a chair and thrusting a glass of Marsala into his hand. "It's bad news from Banda today, but a bad start is a good augury in any campaign. And it won't do the directors any harm to realise that we have our difficulties out here. Make yourself comfortable, Captain Odshoorn. I won't keep you long. The report should be here any minute."

The agent's office seemed as busy as a street. Men came in and out. And here, within the circle of the initiated, Banda was on every man's tongue. Some came in search of news; others, already informed, came to discuss it. The general tone was lighthearted. Obviously Knol had bungled the thing. The English would find what they had tackled when Van Holk set about them. He should have been sent in the first place; it was silly to play about with such an affair, even when victory looked certain; mustn't let anything interfere with the nutmegs.

One stout—and, to Piet's mind, very overdressed— gentleman did express a more pessimistic view. "I don't like the look of it," he said. "It was supposed to be a strict secret, but by all accounts the English had got wind of it. How? That's what I want to know. It looks to me as though there'd been a leakage. After all, somebody's smuggled out nutmegs. Maybe information travelled the same road."

Eventually somebody bustled in importantly and handed over one of the copies which Piet had seen in the making a few moments earlier. The agent read it through, made some trifling alteration in the punctuation, enclosed it in a bundle of papers which he had ready, and sealed the cover.

"These were to go by the *Indian Star*, but they'll get there a fortnight sooner if you take them. She'll carry better news, I hope."

Piet took the bundle and put it into his inside pocket. He set down the glass which he was surprised to find empty, for he had no memory of drinking the wine. He found his hand being shaken; heard his voice replying to the agent's good wishes for the voyage. Then he was in the street again, alone with his thoughts.

He tried to make them rational. He told himself that every woman in Banda was in equal danger with Annabet and that every woman on the island had been taken there through somebody's agency. If anyone was to be blamed for Annabet's presence there, it was Evert. He himself had opposed the idea from the very beginning. A man couldn't be held responsible for a few words spoken in jest when he was drunk. But logic and common sense could not soothe the frenzied anxiety of his spirit nor lighten the sense of heavy responsibility which lay on his heart. In a few moments now he would be on his way to the West. Not another breath of news from Banda would reach him for six months at the very least. Six months of this suspense. I can't bear it, he thought simply; I can't bear it.

His stomach had sickened as the frivolous young man had given the gist of Knol's report; now he found that the single innocuous glass of Marsala had turned to acid in his throat and lay sour and uneasy behind his collarbone. As he stood looking across the crowded harbour, picking out his own ship and looking at her for the first time in his life without fondness, he belched violently, and some low level of his mind, immune from the anxiety, noted dispassionately that what he needed was a glass of schnapps. The door of a tavern, invitingly open upon a shadowy interior suggestive of coolness, was close at hand. Thrusting aside resolutions and scruples, he entered.

The first measure eased the sour discomfort in his chest but did nothing to disperse the agony in his mind. He contemplated ordering a second but discarded the idea. Drinking wouldn't help. If he soaked in schnapps until he was unconscious his last thought would be of Annabet and the dangers around her. If he got roaring drunk he'd—he knew what he'd do. He'd turn the damned ship back to Banda. The *Eastern Venture* was a peaceable trading vessel, but she was no negligible fighting craft. A good crew . . . do anything he told them . . . pistols . . . cutlasses . . . and the cannon. That's what he'd do if he were drunk. So he mustn't get drunk. By heaven, did he need to get drunk?

He was stunned by the daring and violence of his thoughts. He stumbled out of the tavern and stood again in the blinding sunshine, shaking his head a little like a man pestered by a cloud of insects. Gradually his face hardened. The healthy colour seemed to drain out of it. All expression—even bewilderment—deserted his eyes. Slowly, like a man walking in his sleep, he turned towards the place where his boat waited. Behind the set, wooden, doomed mask of his face a tide of half-petulant tears came pressing. What a way to go downhill, when the climb had been so long and arduous.

Not lightly are the loyalties and disciplines of twenty-five years discarded.

Book Four

ANNABET HAD GONE down to the quay with Evert to see the schooners set sail. Evert had insisted upon it. He had been strangely excited during these last few days, boisterous and noisy to an extent which sometimes threatened to undermine his dignity. Was it, she wondered, that that midnight scene had pleased him, set his mind at rest, restored his pride? Or was that too personal, too feminine a view to take? Were his high spirits actually due to the nervous excitement which radiates from the prospect of war as heat radiates from a fire? On the morning when the expedition set out she inclined to the latter view, for almost every man and woman upon the quayside seemed to share Evert's mood. Annabet, immune from the contagion by virtue of her secret knowledge, was an interested spectator at a scene the like of which she had never witnessed before. The planters, the merchants, and their wives usually conducted themselves with an almost oppressive dignity; easy living, the absence of any mental stimuli, a relaxing climate, and intermittent bouts of fever combined to make all the white people in Banda slothful, slow-spoken, ponderous. Part of Evert's charm for his fellows lay in the fact that with his greater resistance to circumstances he had retained a healthy vigour and bluster which would have passed unnoticed in his native Holland. But this morning they were all Everts; the women waved flags and flung flowers; the men slapped one another's back, shook hands vigorously, threw up their hats, and cheered lustily. And doubtless, Annabet thought, to anyone who did not know that the English islands had been left to the jungle, the monkeys, and the birds for a full fortnight, the scene was a stirring one. Knol's miniature army was smartly turned out and well equipped; brown or white, the men bore themselves well; and the new draft, with its stiffening of trained soldiers, did vast credit to its fortnight's training. The inexpert eye could not have told which group was about to embark and which was to turn back for holding duty at the Fort as, with fife and drum at its head, the brightly coloured column wound down to the shore.

Annabet thought comfortably, And they'll all come back. No ghastly wounds, no dead. Does anyone else know that? She scanned the faces about her. Here and there a woman wept furtively or openly; here and there a man looked serious. But there was no sign that anyone else knew the thing for a farce, a concerted action whose reason had been quietly cancelled. Shal Ahmi? But he was not there. Gariz? She could not identify him apart from his painted prahaus. Did he know the import of the message he had taken?

"Lu today; Gadia tomorrow; Ay the day after," a man shouted in her ear. Oh, thank God that Christy had told her how to find him; thank God that she had enough credulity to believe Shal Ahmi's story of the impending arrests. Suppose she were now as ignorant as all these laughing, flower-flinging, weeping women. What unthinkable torment, what agony of mind she would have been enduring now.

Trudi van Heem threaded her way through the crowd and put her plump warm arm through Annabet's.

"Come up and visit with me. You'll be tired with standing and I can do with your company."

This morning, between the downward-beating light of the sunshine and the upcast glare from the sparkling water, Trudi's wide plump face looked grey; and the corner of one of her heavily lidded eyes twitched regularly, a little beating pulse. She was conscious of it, for she laid a finger against it as she talked.

"I'd like to do that," answered Annabet. "I'll just tell Evert."

They walked up to Trudi's house, past the little Hindu temple, deserted at this hour, with its images, its little dishes of rice, its wilted flowers and bits of rag in the forecourt. Walking like this with Trudi reminded Annabet of their visit to the gaol. Only a fortnight ago, yet the whole of life had undergone a subtle change in the short time. There had been the public announcement of the war and her own dazed realisation of the fact that Shal Ahmi had lied to her and used her. But she had quickly resigned herself to that thought. If it were good for Christy and his fellows to run from a mere arresting party, how much better that they should escape from a serious war.

The other difference which the fortnight had brought was in the relationship between herself and Evert. Evert was happy now and content. Perhaps rightly so. For the moment when she had realised that there was nothing left in life for her but to be Evert's wife had coloured the whole of her attitude towards him. Not that she did anything now which she had refrained from doing before, not that she had altered her behaviour in any way; but her spirit no longer looked beyond the bounds of Coenpark for happiness. Evert knew the difference.

She was aware, when she stood in the hall of the Van Heem house, that she had spent the walk in silent thought, utterly undisturbed by Trudi, usually so garrulous. And that grey tinge under her sallowness, that poor twitching eye which made one's own try to flicker in sympathy. Was Trudi ill?

As they took off their hats and loosened their damp flattened hair she asked gently, "Are you feeling quite well, Trudi? Was standing in the sun too much for you? Would you like to lie down?"

"God forbid. I'm glad to be up. I didn't sleep last night, that's all." She put her finger to the twitch again. For a moment she stood still, staring blankly at the wall; then she roused herself.

"We'll have some tea, shall we?"

She rang the bell, and the houseboy, an elderly Chinese, appeared. He came in very quietly, and Trudi gave a kind of startled jerk and swallowed audibly before she gave the order.

When the tea came Trudi lifted the pot and put it down again.

"You pour, dear. I'd only spill it."

She held her right hand out straight before her, and Annabet saw that it was shaking with a steady rhythmical vibration, not exactly a tremor, more like the form of palsy seen sometimes in the heads of very old people.

"Trudi, something is wrong with you. Has anything happened? Would you like to tell me about it? Is there anything I can do?"

Trudi stared at her for a moment, and then horribly her face crumpled; she put her hands over it and began to cry.

"I'm a coward," she said in a voice of the bitterest self-contempt. "I'm a coward, and I'm frightened out of my wits."

"What of, Trudi? What's frightened you?"

Trudi did not answer. She drew a long shuddering breath and checked her sobs. She took a handkerchief out of her sleeve and dabbed at her face. There were queer dusky patches on her cheeks and forehead. Her humourous long-lipped mouth was loose and tremulous.

"It's just that I'm frightened. You see, I was here—at least not here, in Lonthoir—when Kraemer went to Sulaya. It was just like this morning, Annabet. The flags and the flowers and the cheering. It might have been the same morning all over again. And then—you know what happened."

Annabet nodded. There had been enough talk during the last fortnight of Kraemer and his unfortunate campaign to make her familiar with the story.

"It'll happen again," said Trudi.

Despite herself Annabet felt a cold prickle run along her spine and lift her hair.

"Oh no, Trudi. Things are so different now." She repeated, with all the confidence she could muster, the things she had heard Evert and other men say; neat little arguments about the contentedness and placidity of the coolies, their mixed nationalities and religions, their lack of leadership.

"But you don't see! That's what they said then. Gert says these things. All men say them. My father said them. I was twelve, Annabet. I can remember everything about that day. It began just like this one. And at night my sister and I—she was eight—were allowed to stay up to dinner, to celebrate, to mark the occasion. I heard my father saying those very things, and the men who dined with us said them too. To comfort my mother, who was nervous. In twenty-four hours my father was dead. They cut off his hands before they flung his body in the fire. My mother was stabbed to death, but first—— Oh, it's too horrible to talk about."

She put out her unsteady hand and snatched up the teacup. It shook so that a thin yellow stream slopped over her chin and onto the bosom of her gown.

"When I first heard about the war," she went on in a slightly calmer voice, "I wanted to go away. I wanted—oh, I know it sounds crazy, but I wanted to ask you and Rita Byskin to come with me to Batavia. I spoke to Gert and he laughed at me. At least, not laughed exactly, but he said things about running away and how it would look and how there'd never be any spread of civilisation or any nutmegs grown or any trading posts or anything if people ran away. 'And why should three go and the rest stay?' he asked. There isn't any answer. Except that my nerve is broken. I saw things so awful—just like the worst kind of hell you can imagine."

"You poor little thing," said Annabet, speaking across the years to the small frightened child Trudi had been. Had been? Rather, was still. The years had added layer upon layer of fleshly growth, of wealth, of dignity and experience around the core of Trudi's being, but beneath them all cowered the frightened child, haunted by her nightmare memories.

"Oh, I was lucky, if being saved was lucky," said Trudi bitterly. "We had a Chinese houseboy. My father had bought him in Bandogar from a very cruel master who was trying to teach him acrobatic tricks. He was faithful and grateful. He carried me and my sister out of the house in a sack. Literally in a sack. All the natives who weren't killing and raping the whites were carrying off loot, so nobody noticed. The screams, Annabet. I hear them in nightmares still. There's one particular——"

"And afterwards, what happened to you afterwards?" Annabet asked quickly, trying to forestall that glazed look of horror.

"Afterwards? Oh, we got away in a prahau. To Java eventually."

For a moment the terror upon Trudi's mottled face was replaced with a sly cautious look. Then with a gesture of her shaking hands that implied that nothing mattered any more, she said, "We were orphans and penniless. The Company adopted us and sent us to school. And when we were sixteen they sent us East again. I'm a Company's daughter. Nobody knows that in Banda, except Gert, of course."

Even at that moment Annabet was conscious of surprise. Everybody had heard of the Company's daughters, that sentimentally named, practically exploited body of girls, raw human material of one of the Company's schemes for keeping men contented in the East Indies and for ensuring the continuity of the white race there. They were mostly girls of poor or unknown origin, orphans, some of them picked up in the gutters, slums, and stews of the ports and cities, given a little education, some smattering of social training, and then despatched to marry any planter, merchant, or clerk who had failed to provide himself with a wife. At a time when unrest and uncertainty in the islands had made it unlikely that any woman with an alternative to choose would want to go there, the scheme had had its advantages. Some of the marriages had turned out well and happily. But there had been scandals too. As the plantations became settled and marriage with a "nutmeg prince" a thing to seek after rather than avoid, the Company had adopted no more daughters. There must have been, amongst the women in the islands, several who had been shipped out, like slaves or cattle, under the scheme, but Annabet had never heard of one until Trudi van Heem, the most respected, the worst-feared woman in Banda, made her startling announcement. And nobody in Banda gave more clearly the impression of sound Dutch background and gracious upbringing. But then her father had been a planter. More than any of them, perhaps, she was at home. That thought begot another.

"Didn't you hate coming back? Wasn't it rather cruel of them to send you?"

"I loathed and dreaded the idea." Trudi's voice was harsh with remembered torment. "I can't tell you what I suffered when they told me where I was bound for. I begged and prayed to be allowed to stay. I would have scrubbed floors in the orphanage, done the meanest, hardest work all my life, if only they'd let me stay. For the last six months there they kept me in the kitchen always, for fear I should say something that would frighten the others. Not that I would have. And once I tried to run away. . . . But, you see, they'd spent money on us. We were trade goods." She paused and then said in a softer voice: "I was lucky to get Gert. He's been a very good husband to me. He laughs at me about my feeling against the natives, but he understands—or at least he's humoured me. He found me Nina because I couldn't bear a brown face in my bedroom, and all our boys indoors are Chinese. I don't like them either, really, which is very unfair. I can't help it. They remind me of Ho and that night." She shuddered. "Not that I need anything to remind me. Even at home, where I was safe and never saw a brown face, I had those dreadful dreams." She closed her eyes and two tears squeezed out and ran down her cheeks. "I shouldn't talk to you like this. It's vile of me. Don't despise me too much."

Suddenly Annabet knew the right thing to say. Why hadn't she thought of it before?

"Trudi, the past is over. You've outlived that, haven't you? What worries you now is the thought that it might happen again. Today. Darling, I can assure you that Colonel Knol isn't going to repeat Kraemer's campaign."

"That's just what he will do. This morning was a—an echo."

"But I know something about this war that nobody else in Banda knows, Trudi. If you could promise not to ask me how I know, or to tell anybody what I tell you, I would tell you something that would make you feel a great deal happier."

"What could you know about the war, Annabet? But tell me, tell me. I promise not to say anything or to ask you questions."

"Well—I just happen to know that the soldiers and Colonel Knol will come straight back home. Because the English have gone away from the islands. So there won't be time for anything to happen. Here, I mean. There, does that make you feel better?"

"It would if I could believe it, Annabet. But I don't see how you could know. I mean, dear, if anybody else knew— well, the men wouldn't have set out this morning. Have you been listening to compound gossip?"

"No. It's genuine fact, Trudi. They left a fortnight ago."

"Then, my dear girl, if you have by some means got hold of a secret—— No, no, I'm not asking how you did it, but having done so, why in the name of wonder didn't you tell Colonel Knol?"

"I don't know," Annabet said slowly. "I've thought about it a lot. For one thing, I doubt whether he'd have believed me—you don't quite believe me now, do you? And I couldn't give a soldier news like that without saying whence I had it myself. And that I couldn't tell. It was—it is—very awkward. Besides, it hasn't done the soldiers any harm. Going prepared to find an enemy and finding nothing isn't expecting nothing and finding an enemy, is it? They'll just come home, all safe and sound."

It was the first time she had put the argument into words, but the words had run along a well-worn groove in her brain. Night after night, ever since she had learned that it was war, not arrests, which had been planned and circumvented, she had debated the ethics of her position.

"The optimists," Trudi said, "were reckoning Lu today, Gadia tomorrow, and Ay the day after. If they did find Lu deserted they could easily reach Gadia today too. Then Ay tomorrow, with no fighting. Good heavens, with any luck they could be back tomorrow afternoon." She looked at Annabet with an expression which told how much she would have liked to believe her; how nearly, in fact, she did believe her; and yet how wide a gap lay between nearly and quite. But the news had brought her some relief; her skin was resuming something of its natural smooth sallowness, her eyes brightened, the twitch was less apparent.

"Oh, Annabet, if only you could be right. If only I could go to bed tonight knowing that the soldiers were back in the Fort, how happy I should be."

She moved across the room to the left-hand window. Annabet, watching, saw her eyes go to the great black structure at the top of the artificially heightened mound of the Fort. It was ugly from every point of view, stark and angular, with the grey dusty ground sloping before it and all signs of vegetation pruned away. But Trudi was looking at it with love.

"I know the colonel's rooms," she said over her shoulder. "I shall look out tonight and tomorrow to see if they are lighted. . . . Oh, Annabet, you have cheered me. I still can't quite believe, but I can hope now." Her whole body stiffened suddenly and she said in a different voice, "Annabet, come here. Is that smoke?"

Annabet hurried across and stood shoulder to shoulder with her hostess. The window gave a full, foursquare view of the Fort and little else, but by standing at the side and craning one's neck, one could also see a portion of the town, the white and pink and yellow houses with the hyacinth blue of the harbour behind them.

She looked at the Fort and then at as much of the town as was visible. She could see no smoke.

"Where, Trudi? Where do you mean?"

"Straight ahead. Low on the Fort wall. That piece sticking out at the foot. Yes, it's the gaol. Can you see it now? There—now you can. It's blazing." As she spoke, Annabet, to whom the drift of smoke had been invisible against the black bulk of the main building, saw the red-and-yellow spears of the flames shoot upwards.

"Oh yes, I see it now," she said.

Trudi van Heem swung away from the window, blindly grasping at the back of a chair for support. Her face was ashen; her white lips parted as she panted. Annabet moved forward to support her into a chair, but she shook herself free. "The door," she gasped. "Lock it. Lock it." Better humour her, Annabet thought; she was beyond reason, almost dead of terror. Annabet turned the key in the door. As she did so Trudi stumbled to the window and tugged at the long white shutters. Her breathing was rapid and noisy.

"I'll close them," Annabet said, and ran across the room. Before she fastened the shutter she looked out and saw the Van Heem gardener placidly taking the dead heads from the roses.

"It really is nothing, Trudi," she said. "There's your gardener at work just as usual. And the fire is out now. Yes, they're taking away the buckets. It was just an accident. They cook their own food in gaol, don't they? On those rickety little charcoal stoves. Probably one overturned." As she spoke she saw a thin streak of fire, like a comet, race across the drill ground before the Fort and dart downhill towards the town. What was that? Was she wrong and Trudi right? Was something queer afoot? As though in answer, there came a short sharp rattle of musket fire, ping-ping-ping. Hastily she closed the shutter and the room was dimmed, lighted only by the thin lines of sunlight which stole in at the tops and bottoms of the long windows and the places where the halves of the shutters met.

"It still could be nothing, Trudi. Perhaps in the confusion of the fire a prisoner got away."

"I want to move this chest in front of the door," said Trudi, refusing to be comforted. She staggered over to a great Chinese lacquered chest which stood against the wall, six feet or more from the doorway, and reluctantly Annabet helped her. "I've just remembered. In my dreams it's always this room. The worst, the most dreadful thing always happens in this room. And now I am here and I daren't move to leave it."

A fresh burst of musket fire, this time from the direction of the town. "Oh, my God," said Trudi van Heem, almost soundlessly.

Was the town ablaze?

"Trudi, I'm just going to open one shutter a tiny crack and

have a peep. I want to see if your gardener is still there. It gives me confidence to see him."

"Be careful. For God's sake, be careful," said Trudi. But she got out of her chair and went with Annabet towards the window and took hold of the shutter's edge, wary, frightened, ready to slam it home at a second's notice.

The old man was still at work. Craning her neck, Annabet looked beyond him, sideways, at the town. Yes, a great cloud of smoke now hung over the houses, blotting out the line of the sea. Despite the comforting evidence of the gardener's placid, plodding figure, something was wrong in Banda. She was just about to close the shutter again to hide the smoke pall from Trudi when she saw a little boy, naked save for a strip of loincloth, vault the gate and come flying towards the house. He bore every sign of having urgent news.

"There's a little boy," she said over her shoulder. "I think he has a message."

The muted sound of voices came from the hall; then there was a tap on the door, the handle was tried, and the tap was repeated.

"Don't speak. Don't answer. It's a trick," Trudi whispered.

Annabet began to feel that the position was ridiculous. Not entirely immune from fear herself, she was reasonable enough to have taken courage in the sight of the gardener working, the little boy vaulting the gate, from the ordinary sound of the doorbell, the tapping on the inner door. Her patience with Trudi's fears frayed slightly.

"If we don't answer," she whispered back, "they'll be justified in breaking down the door to see what has happened."

"Mevrouw," said a voice from the other side of the door. And the handle was tried again.

Annabet rose and walked over to the door. "The door has stuck. Something wrong with the handle. What is it you want?"

"Mevrouw, I can't open the door."

"No. It's stuck. What do you want?" she bellowed.

"Mevrouw, is anything the matter?"

"This is ridiculous," she said, and turned to look at Trudi. "I'll go out by the window and talk to them."

Trudi got up and clutched at Annabet with shaking, impotent hands. Annabet, pushing her off, thought irrelevantly, She's mad; I'm the one who should be frightened, locked in here with a madwoman. She opened one half of the shutter, pushed open the window behind it, and stepped through the narrow opening into the garden. To the last moment Trudi had followed her, clutching, imploring, past coherent speech, mouthing, gibbering. The garden was full of drifting smoke and the acrid scent of burning. From the window it looked as though the whole of Banda were ablaze. Trudi, as Annabet stepped out of the window, caught sight of the smoke, smelled the old nightmare scent of unleashed fire. She slammed the shutter with a scream. Annabet heard the bar fall into place.

She hurried round the side of the house. The little boy, breathing deeply, stood on the top step. He rattled off his message: "Mynheer says Mevrouw is not to be alarmed at the fires and the shooting. It is only three bad men trying to get their brother out of gaol. Mynheer will be home in an hour. Mevrouw is not to worry."

"You may go," said Annabet. What had this attempt at gaol breaking to do with the town being ablaze? No good asking the child. He turned and sped across the garden, vaulted the gate again, and disappeared.

She went back and tapped on the window and called loudly, "Trudi, it's me. Annabet. The boy brought a message from Gert. Everything's quite all right. He sent word you were not to worry." Not a sound came from behind the shutters. She cried again, shouting the news of comfort. Still no sound, nor any sign of life.

For Trudi van Heem had realised as soon as she barred the shutter behind Annabet's back that now the very worst had happened. She had seen the smoke and the flames and heard the shots, and she had deliberately barred her friend, a woman who had been kind to her, out into the world of danger. And the worst was not that she herself should be killed or maimed or frightened, but rather, the thing she had always dreaded, the thing that for years had lain just upon the other side of nightmare, that she should know that she had acted like a rat—craven, coward, selfish, treacherous. The last faint remnant of sanity and reason reared its head in her demented brain; the last voice of self-preservation made itself audible. It was Annabet's fault, she thought. Annabet would insist on opening the window and being a party to what Trudi knew was a trick. It was Annabet's fault; she

might have stayed in the dubious safety of the barred and
barricaded room. Ah, but that thought was no good. She
shouldn't have barred the shutter. At the very least she
should have stood with it in her hand so that Annabet,
tricked and aware of the trick at last, could have had a path
of retreat.

With that thought in mind she staggered to the window
again and lifted her arms to the bar of the shutter; and her
heart, insidiously weakened by years of nervous strain and
now racing madly with terror, refused the effort. She
dropped where she stood, collapsing like a bundle of cloth
upon the floor at the foot of the window, and so lay, never to
be frightened of anything again.

Evert's reception of the news of Mevrouw van Heem's
death showed Annabet how strait and confined were the
limits of his sympathy. He had never liked her. As soon as
Annabet and he were alone on their way home, he threw off
all pretence at grief and obviously expected his wife to do the
same and join him in his jubilant mood.

The morning's occurrence had excited him. He had played
a foremost part in putting out the fires on the quayside and
had, spectacularly but at some real risk to his life, entered a
blazing building and dragged out a clerk who had been
trapped and overcome by smoke fumes. Afterwards men had
slapped his back and wrung his hand and said the
incoherent, complimentary things which come easily even to
the inarticulate when moved by some display of courage or
skill. Presently he would find a way to tell her, without
immodest boasting, of his own exploits.

"The silly brutes fired the gaol, you see, thinking that in
the confusion they'd get this brother of theirs out. But it
didn't work out. That'd be the fire you saw, and you saw for
yourself how smartly the soldiers put it out. Then two of the
mad beggars ran in to the town with their torches, setting fire
to places as they went. One was shot almost at once; the
other started about a dozen fires before they shot him. But
the third did the most damage. He crept round the Fort,
setting fire to anything combustible, and one fire touched off
a powder store. There're several magazines scattered about,
some distance apart, in case of accident; but you can't stop
sparks flying once explosions start, you see. They just went
off one after the other."

"Yes, I heard them. Does it matter? Losing the powder stores, I mean."

Talk about anything, think about anything, except that moment when the houseboy tried the key which did fit, and the key upon the inside fell with a clatter to the floor, and you saw Trudi lying there by the window, and the first of the crackling booms shook the shutters as you fell on your knees and tried to lift her.

"It's a loss, of course," Evert said cheerfully. "But it doesn't matter much. Knol has got enough for his job."

"But, Evert, suppose what Tr-Trudi feared *does* happen, and the few soldiers that're left haven't anything to shoot with!" Her fingers, lying lightly on his forearm, closed suddenly in a nervous grip. "Suppose she was right, Evert? This might be the beginning of something——"

"My *dear* girl, you've spent the day with a crazy woman and had a nasty shock or surely you'd see that you're talking nonsense. There isn't a brown rascal in the islands who could ever think up anything so clever. There'll be no slave rising here, believe me. They're over; things of the past. But when they happened they didn't begin with clever foresighted planning. Three or four silly bastards would lose their heads, generally at a religious festival, and go for the nearest white man with whatever happened to be in their hands. Then the rest would follow. The idea of blowing up the powder stores on one day and then attacking sometime later is one that no native mind could possibly conceive. I know 'em."

Perhaps fear *was* catching. Or was it merely because Trudi was dead that the thing which had lain behind her fear now seemed so actual and possible? Anyway, even as Annabet thought of the argument against what Evert had just said, her heart jolted and she wished she had not thought of it.

"Shal Ahmi is clever," she said, and her voice was small.

"That I grant you." He glanced at her with indulgence, as though she had been a petted child who had uttered some words of precocious wisdom. "Fancy you thinking of that. Real smart. I must tell Knol that. You see, he had the same idea. And for safety's sake, some days ago—before the war was made public, in fact—he raked up some excuse and put Shal Ahmi under lock and key for the duration."

He broke off as they stepped into the open space between the line of offices and warehouses and the jetty. There, just

ahead, was the shell of the burned-out house where he had
made his rescue that morning. He wanted to tell Annabet
about it, but his vanity was too complicated to allow him to
say simply, "I saved a man's life in that house this morning."
It wasn't enough that she should think him brave; his
modesty must exact tribute too. And at that moment he had
another proof of his own astonishing luck. From the
doorway of Vehmeer's office, Vehmeer, Hoogenbeet, and
Vanderbosch, in the hilarious stage of inebriation, emerged.
They hailed Evert with loud excited cries, and Hoogenbeet,
who had only an hour before arrived from Lonthoir in a
state of pitiable apprehension, must offer his congratulations
and thump Evert upon the back, and Vehmeer must explain,
"We've got a hero amongst us, you fellows; I hope you
realise that." He thumped Evert again, violently. And Evert
moved out of reach, saying—for one must be modest; all
truly great men are modest—things like, "I just happened to
be nearest. By God, if I'd known what an inferno it was I
shouldn't have ventured. Anybody else would have done the
same. . . ." All the proper things.

But Annabet was hardly listening, and she was remembering Trudi van Heem, thinking, To the right person I
could talk about it. I long to talk about it—sensibly, under-
standingly—probing the mystery of how a person who
dreads something can be frightened to death by quite
another thing which happens to resemble it. Like a person
who fears ghosts being driven to an extremity of terror by
what anybody else would see is only a stick with a sheet over
it. But I couldn't make Evert understand. Is that because he
is a man? Would Christy have understood? Could I have
talked to him about it? I don't know. I never really knew
anything about him as a person. He was concerned for my
welfare, but then so is Evert. Evert was just angry with
Trudi for shutting me out. So might Christy have been.

Annabet continued her thoughts as they all moved on,
laughing and talking. They emerged upon the water front
just as Knol, with his broken arm supported in the front of
his jacket and a bloody clout tied about his head, stepped
from the boat which had brought him from the *Greta*. In the
eerie white light of the moon his wrinkled brown face was a
mask of anguish and fury, and the evidence of his wounds
was plain. So there had been fighting after all. The English
hadn't gone away. They had stayed and fought. Christy!

Suddenly Evert felt her whole weight upon the arm on which her hand had rested so lightly, so conventionally.

"Hi, hold up," he said, slipping his other arm around her. "It's nothing to faint about. He isn't hurt much." Vehmeer, Hoogenbeet, and Vanderbosch surged forward, crying, "What news?"

Knol said briefly, "Bad. One of you fetch the governor; and you, Vehmeer, give me a hand to Kaerko's. I can't manage to get to the Fort." One of his legs had been injured, too, Evert saw. And he was being led off to the agent's house, and in a few minutes the governor would arrive and the door would be shut. He must, he simply must, know what the bad news was, how bad. He looked down at Annabet indignantly and then, on an impulse, swung her into his arms and walked to where the prahau waited. He bundled her in unceremoniously and told the man to wait. Then he ran towards Knol and elbowed Hoogenbeet aside. "You're hardly capable of supporting yourself," he said rudely. Well in the centre of things, with his strong arms around Knol's battered little body, he asked, "What happened, Colonel?"

"They were warned and armed. And we were ambushed. That's all. And what in God's name has been happening here?" He jerked his bandaged head towards the shell of the house where Evert had effected his rescue.

Vehmeer, Hoogenbeet, and Evert began simultaneously to tell him what had happened. Evert was the one who checked the spate.

"What does it matter, Colonel? This morning's affair was a mere drop in the sea. What happened to *you*?"

"I'll tell you when we're all together," said Knol faintly. Evert felt the body stiffen within the circle of his arms. "This wasn't going to be worth calling a war. This was a punitive expedition against unarmed men. I tell you, Haan, it'll take six months and a major campaign to root out that rattlesnakes' nest."

At the very back of his mind Evert was conscious of Annabet. Poor little thing, she'd had a shattering experience, and there was no doubt that Trudi van Heem had bequeathed her a legacy of fear. She'd be very scared if she came to and found herself alone with the boatman, not knowing how she got there. But he couldn't, he just couldn't, turn back now and go to her without hearing all of Knol's story and learning what steps the governor intended to take, faced with this reverse. Annabet must wait.

And when only three quarters of an hour later he pounded across the quay and jumped into the boat, Annabet, conscious again, gave no sign of thinking herself ill treated. She did not mention the moment of extreme panic she had known when she opened her eyes and found a brown face leaning above her. She spoke to Evert as though she had herself despatched him in quest of news.

"What happened? What did he say?"

Evert put his hand on her arm and pressed it lightly, warningly. "Oh, splendid news. A good fight and a great victory. The colonel looks a bit shattered, but all his wounds are superficial. He says our casualties have been very light."

He was not speaking from natural caution. The words had been put into his mouth by Knol himself. For in Kaerko's office, after the whole dismaying story had been told, Vanderbosch, struck sober, had reverted to the state of terror in which he had arrived in Banda earlier in the evening and had voiced his fears as to the effect such tidings would have upon the natives. Nobody just then, not even green-gilled Hoogenbeet, had found his terror ludicrous. Knol had said bluntly, "Best not to tell them. If the *Greta* goes back at once we'll have reinforcements and fresh powder before any rumours can be confirmed. I'll have my wounded taken into hospital and absolutely segregated. They'd better be landed tonight." He had looked at the governor and then at Kaerko. "Perhaps you could see to that for me. Lieutenants Voss and De Klerk will handle it. I'm done in. And I must send a report by the *Greta*. I want to make something clear."

They had looked at him inquiringly.

"I know," he had said heavily, "I know what you're all thinking; what they'll think in Batavia and everywhere else, and go on thinking and saying long after I'm dead. But it isn't true. The third landing was conducted as carefully as though we had had the enemy in sight. Two blanks hadn't made us careless or overconfident. But they'll blame me till the end of time."

His voice had quavered, and every man in the room had felt uncomfortable, the more so because every man recognised the truth of the statement. Knol had steadied himself and gone on: "I'm not whining. The ambush was fair enough and the fight was fair enough. What sticks in my craw is the fact that we've an enemy in our very midst. Somebody had warned them. Those pits and platforms and cannon hadn't been rigged in a day——" He had broken off as Dr. van de Lijn entered and bustled forward, full of professional importance. "No Dutchman," he had said in a lower voice, "and that leaves only natives under suspicion. And the secret was so well kept. There was so short a time . . ." He had mused for a moment, grey-faced, gnawing at a finger. "And I had Shal Ahmi, whom I'd suspect of anything, safe under lock and key . . ."

Van de Lijn had begun to remove the bloody bandage, and Evert, feeling that he had learned as much as there was to be learned at the moment, unostentatiously took his leave.

So now, following Knol's advice, he spoke with false cheer and squeezed Annabet's arm to warn her not to ask any more questions. She sat quietly, thinking. The English had not gone from the islands. There had been fighting after all. Christy might be wounded or dead. Had that folded paper never reached him? Had he and the others ignored the warning which Shal Ahmi said it carried?

As soon as they had left boat and boatmen at the landing place she burst out with her questions. "What really happened, Evert? What did Colonel Knol have to tell? Was there much fighting?"

"Wait till we're in the house," said Evert cautiously.

Never had the distance seemed so long. But at last they were safely inside with the door closed, and then, without further prompting, Evert burst out, "Knol was fooled. Completely fooled. Cover it up as he may, he can't hide that fact."

"What happened, exactly?"

"I'll tell you. But we must have something to eat first. You're so empty you faint and I'm yawning my head off." He clapped his hands and roared for Josef. The ill news had not marred his appetite; on the contrary, he felt hungrier, more vigorous, more active, more himself altogether.

"You do look mortally ill," he said, leading Annabet to a chair in the dining room. "This has been a bloody fine day one way and another, hasn't it?"

"I'm all right, Evert. I'm not even hungry. I just want to know what happened to Colonel Knol and the soldiers."

"You shall hear," said Evert, snatching up a piece of bread from the trencher in the centre of the table and breaking a crust. "They went to Lu first—it's nothing but a speck of an island—it was deserted, but there were signs that the English had been there at some fairly recent date. They sailed across to Gadia and reached it before noon. That was deserted too. Not a soul, but again signs that the English had been there and had apparently left in a hurry. Knol says there was a lot of stuff, some of it quite valuable, left about. Even some food, not much decomposed. In less than half an hour they'd combed the place thoroughly and were on their way to Ay. He *says* that he landed at Ay, after some preliminary cannon fire, as carefully and suspiciously as he had landed at the other islands. I doubt that. I'd wager that by that time the men were laughing and joking about a day's outing, walking anyhow and not looking for anything except loot.

"There was the usual ramshackle collection of huts; there were the signs of men having left hurriedly. Behind the huts, inland, there was a clearing, and beyond that, Knol says, evidence that somebody had tried to start a nutmeg grove: a fifty-foot belt of saplings about shoulder high. Behind that again, the jungle. Not a sight or sound of human life. Just as he and his men reached the nutmegs, bullets began to hail out of the jungle—literally hail, because they came from above. They'd got properly built platforms up in the trees. And then firing began from underground; they'd got trenches running through the nutmeg grove. And then, behind them, all the huts burst into flame, and cannon began to pound away at the schooners. You see what had happened. They'd had warning of the attack, somehow, from somewhere, and they'd all gathered in Ay. They'd got plenty of muskets, plenty of ammunition *and* cannon. Voss, the second-in-command, took every man he could collect and made a second landing party and found himself between two concealed cannon and the blazing huts, just as Knol was between the musket fire and the huts on the other side. Devilish clever. I oughtn't to say so, I suppose, but it was a piece of strategy worthy of old Gomarus himself. I can remember——"

The arrival of the food interrupted him. He insisted upon Annabet piling her plate high with the rizplatzen and helped himself greedily.

"And were many English killed too?"

"They never saw them. Never got near them. At least that's how I understand it. Those who could run or crawl made for the boats. When those who could get away were on the schooners there was more cannon fire, and the *Margarete* was sunk and the *Sanje* hit. And so back home they came. . . . Don't look like that, my darling. It's only a temporary setback. Eat your food. It's been kept waiting too long. But it's good."

Only a temporary setback! This morning men had been talking about a punitive expedition that would last three days; this evening, after a bloody beating, they were talking of a temporary setback.

That would have been all right, that would have been admirable, if it had concerned only the fight between the English and the Dutch in the islands. Cut off as they were on their tiny island, the English (and she remembered with a shudder of apprehension that that meant Christy too!) were bound to be defeated sooner or later. From Batavia would come fresh troops, supplies of ammunition, other schooners with their bright brass cannon. But what of the enemy at home? The enemy who had sent that warning message? The enemy that only she knew by name? The enemy whom she had aided and abetted? What of him? Wasn't a temporary setback just what he had desired and planned?

Her head was heavy and dizzy from the turmoil of her thoughts. She pushed away the hardly tasted plate of rizplatzen and looked at Evert with sick eyes. At the moment when the moonlight had showed up the bloody bandage upon Knol's head, she had felt that the time had come for her to make a cruel, shattering decision; and inch by inch the trap had closed in on her. Remain silent and preserve your secret and jeopardise the lives of all the white people in Banda; or tell what you know and give them a chance, at least a chance, to defend themselves against the real enemy?

The dizziness in her head increased as her thoughts whirled round like the axis of a cyclone. Why should this happen to me? I mean no harm. I just didn't want the patrols to pounce on Christy and hang him. So I passed on the message. I was just a pawn in a wicked man's evil game. But now I'm not a pawn. I can see what his game was. It is in my power, partly at least, to defeat it; if I speak now. If I pay the price of earning Evert's scorn and hatred.

"Come along," said Evert, starting up from his chair, the last piled forkful of food still in his mouth. "If you won't eat you must go to bed. I'm sorry I told you so much of what

Knol said. But take heart, the folks in Batavia won't see us come to harm; we're too valuable. They'll have fresh troops and powder here in no time. So there's not a thing in the world for you to worry about. Come on. You're exhausted, and upset about Trudi, naturally. A good night's rest'll set you right."

He spoke brusquely but kindly, concerned for her well-being. Still munching vigorously, he came to her end of the table and slipped his hand under her elbow. A sick pang went through her as she realised that her next words would be an end to everything but loathing upon his part. She let him pull her to her feet, and then, twisting free of his hand, she seized the back of her chair and leaned on it for support as she gasped out the dreadful words.

"Evert—I know who sent the message. Shal Ahmi wrote it and I despatched it for him." Brutal, irrevocable.

Evert looked as though somebody had struck him a stunning blow in the face. He actually stepped backwards, recoiling from her as he would have done from a self-confessed leper.

"Are you raving?" But he knew the answer to that.

"I wish I were. I had to tell you, Evert, because it means that he wished us harm here in Banda. You must warn everybody."

"Why, in God's name, did he pick on you?"

Cutting the story to the bone, without explanations or excuses, remembering that time was short, she told him the whole truth. When she reached the point where Shal Ahmi sent for her to go to the gaol, Evert, unable to keep silent any longer, broke in with, "That'll do. So you went. To save Ayrton's hide."

The hatred and fury in his face and in his voice surpassed anything she had imagined.

"But I didn't know anything about the war," she said shrilly. "I did wrong, I know. But, Evert, I love him. I couldn't let the patrol take him and hang him. Shal Ahmi said the patrol was after him because of the smuggling. I didn't know about the war, Evert; I didn't know about the——"

Evert had forgotten the war; had shoved aside the impersonal significance of her story; had overlooked the reason for telling it at this moment. His curiously single-tracked mind had seized only fact, and the name "Christy

Ayrton" danced in a red mist before his eyes. Annabet had
not spoken the name, but he knew the one Englishman who
would have found his way to Coenpark in an emergency, and
he had heard that Ayrton had been hurt in an unfortunate
brush with the patrol. It had been Ayrton all the time.

In blind fury he reached out towards Annabet, who leaned
trembling, frightened, half fainting, yet relieved that the
moment of speech was over, and laid his hands on her
shoulders. He shook her as a child, mad with temper, might
shake a rag doll. He shook her until she hung between his
hands, her mouth open, her head lolling, and her last
fragment of consciousness ebbing away in the thought that
he would kill her. But he mustn't forget Shal Ahmi. She
clawed at his iron wrists with weak, desperate hands and
tried to find sufficient breath to utter the two words loudly
enough to be heard through the stream of awful words Evert
was shouting at her. "Don't forget Shal Ahmi," she gasped,
and the sound was shaken out of her as the last few drops
might be shaken out of a bottle.

"I'll attend to him too," said Evert and, pulling her once
more towards him, thrust her away violently, at the same
time loosing his hold so that she fell backwards, tried to
catch at the chair, missed it, and crashed to the floor,
striking the side of her head on the table as she fell.

The madness seemed to go out of Evert then. He stood for
a second looking down at her. Then she heard his tread,
heavy and rapid and purposeful, in the hall and the thud of
the door behind him.

She lay on the floor, too spent and battered to make the
effort to rise yet. This was the end of everything. But she had
done what she could to undo the evil she had unwittingly
done. Evert would know what to do, and whatever it was
Shal Ahmi had planned might be forestalled. It might even
be that on picking on her to help him Shal Ahmi had
committed a fatal mistake. If he could have found a brown
accomplice . . . But he couldn't. So there was no solace in
that thought.

And again she wondered, Why should all this have
happened to me, brought up so coolly and correctly, trained
to do and say and even think the right things? I came here
with such good intentions, meaning to repay Evert for saving
me from Ireland by being a model wife. The whole thing
seemed so simple then. Life lay out as smooth and plain as a

skein of silk; now it is all spoiled and tangled, as though an idiot's fingers had been in it, knotted and complicated and useless, past any human skill to put right. And empty. Trudi, my one friend, dead. Christy dead, or doomed. Evert estranged.

She gripped the edge of the table to pull herself to her feet; and then suddenly she was on her knees, her arms along the table edge, her head bowed down upon them. And she was praying, not in the formal set phrases of happy childhood and easy churchgoing, but in the bitter, self-accusatory outpourings of the soul that feels it has lost both its way in this world and its hold upon the one invisible.

The violence with which he had handled Annabet had relieved some of the pressure of anger within Evert's mind. Ten minutes of hard walking eased him still further, and before he reached the first pale glimmering house in the town he was able to push Annabet and Christy Ayrton to the back of his mind and to think about his errand.

He must go carefully now, not make a fool of himself, not appear to have caught Vanderbosch's terror, not betray Annabet. It was going to be difficult. His pace slackened as he thought, and by the time he reached Kaerko's house he was walking slowly and ponderously.

Lights were bobbing about on the quay. The wounded from the _Greta_ had already been brought ashore; the report had been taken aboard her and already she was headed for Java, her white sails catching the moonlight as she breasted each wave. The wounded from the _Sanje_ were being unloaded and taken to the hospital within the Fort. Voss and De Klerk were in charge of the business, and it was being conducted in silence and as speedily as possible. By morning all the injured men and all those who had seen them would be immured within the frowning fortress, cut off utterly from the outer world. There would be rumours, naturally. Evert's own boatman, for instance, would whisper that he had seen the colonel back in the island with a bloody bandage on his head; but until fresh troops and ammunition arrived no native would know for certain that the Dutch arms had met with a defeat, and before they had time really to act upon this information—if they actually intended to act—the English would be defeated and the troops back to deal with any sign of insurrection. What then? asked Evert, coming to a standstill and watching the wounded stumbling along on their own legs or being helped along by comrades or being carried upon improvised stretchers. What are we worrying about? Even if Shal Ahmi did warn the English, even if he is planning some deep devilment, what can he do from his cell in the gaol, while the rest of the brown swine are kept in ignorance?

Once again he decided to feel his way very carefully.

Kaerko was still up and about. Perhaps in deference to the governor, who had not stopped to dress when summoned to the office, Kaerko had removed his coat and donned a long thin dressing-robe of brightly coloured silk. His nondescript features were twisted into a mask of anxiety, and his greeting of Evert's return betrayed his expectation of further bad news.

"Come in," he said, opening the door. "The governor is still here and the doctor. What brings you back? More trouble?"

"That depends," said Evert cautiously. "How is Knol?"

"Very poorly. He insisted upon writing his report himself and fainted as soon as he'd finished. Van de Lijn is with him now. He's given him opium and hopes he'll sleep."

The governor, looking very old and brittle, was seated in Kaerko's most comfortable chair. A tray nearby bore signs of an impromptu meal having been served and picked at without much relish.

"I had to hurry away earlier," Evert explained, "because my wife was waiting. But there was one little matter I wanted to bring up." He divided his glance fairly between the agent and the governor. "When we heard of the ambush and were discussing from whence the warning might have been sent, why did no one think of Shal Ahmi?"

Kaerko's face reddened slightly and took on a truculent expression.

"Why Shal Ahmi?" he asked. "I've said before and I say it again that Shal Ahmi, without position or salary, is one of the most loyal servants the Company possesses in these islands or anywhere else."

"Shal Ahmi," said the governor dispassionately, "was safely in gaol before I made the announcement which conveyed to you the Company's intention. Colonel Knol preferred a charge against him—fowl stealing, a very trumped-up charge. There is no harm in my telling you that, for the colonel himself would be the first to admit it. He should have been released, but, with this matter brewing and Knol feeling so strongly upon the subject, I decided to let the charge stand. So you see, unless he really owns the magical powers he lays claim to, he could hardly have sent the message."

"Perhaps not," said Evert, humouring Kaerko, who was bristling like a turkey cock. "On the other hand, messages have been got out of gaols before this. And it sticks in my mind that gaol breaking was attempted this morning. Because Seth Aranda's kin carried the fire we all assumed that it was Seth Aranda's escape that was intended." He took one of the blind leaps in the dark which had so often landed him at a desired point and, turning to Kaerko, said sharply, "I suppose he is there still? I suppose he didn't get out in the general confusion?"

"How should I know? I am not the keeper of the gaol. If I were——" He remembered the governor's presence and checked himself. "With all due deference, Your Excellency, the man should never have been imprisoned at all. In a thousand ways he has served the Company, and just because Knol is prejudiced——"

"Send up and ask," Evert cut in abruptly.

"But even if he isn't there, if he did escape this morning," Kaerko said, "does that prove that he warned the English? That was your original suggestion, wasn't it, Haan? That the English had been warned by Shal Ahmi. If—and we'll soon find that out—he did take advantage of this morning's rumpus to escape from unwarranted confinement, does that make him guilty of the other charge?" He rang a bell furiously, and to the sleepy servant who came in answer he gave an order to run to the gaol immediately and ask after Shal Ahmi.

"No—wait," said the governor, rising stiffly. "Go back to your bed." As soon as the man had retired he explained, "We agreed, didn't we, to keep the wounded away from the natives? They may not all be in yet. I'll go myself. I was only waiting for Dr. van de Lijn to come down and tell me about the colonel. I shall be glad of the walk. But before I go, Haan, I must say that I agree with Kaerko. Shal Ahmi's disappearance wouldn't prove anything."

Smug and stupid, Evert thought; two officials sticking

together against a mere planter! Oh, if only my information
had come to me with equal certainty but from a different
source, how I should enjoy ramming it down their throats!

"No," he said quite pleasantly, "even his disappearance
from the gaol wouldn't prove anything. But allied to what I
heard this evening, it might point the way to something. I
don't as a rule pay much attention to women's gossip, but my
wife was with Mevrouw van Heem today just before she
died, and——"

"Mevrouw van Heem dead?" asked the governor in an
astounded voice.

Evert nodded. "She died this morning. My wife was with
her and swears that she died of fear. And before she died she
told my wife something—I think you will both admit that
Mevrouw van Heem was shrewd enough. And her house
overlooks the Fort." He paused.

"Well?"

"Mevrouw van Heem said that she saw Shal Ahmi
intercept, on the slope up to the Fort, the coolies who were
carrying what looked to be musical instruments and tools.
After he had intercepted these coolies he seemed disturbed in
his manner and proceeded to the water front, where he was
seen in conversation with a boatman who immediately put
out to sea, though it was just on dark. In the light of what we
know, does that seem to you a significant story, gentlemen?"

"I'll go and see what Shal Ahmi has to say about that," the
governor said.

"He'll lie," said Evert.

"He may lie, but we do have methods of extorting the
truth."

"Oh, that," said Evert, lightly dismissing the thought of
the instruments of torture, known to be rusting away in the
Fort dungeons. "So many other lies will come out with the
truth, Your Excellency, that we shall probably all find
ourselves implicated."

Even then Kaerko put up a feeble but loyal defence. "I
have never caught Shal Ahmi out in a lie," he said solemnly.

Evert laughed.

Almost as soon as the governor had gone, a dignified errand boy, Van de Lijn entered the room, pulling down his
sleeves and shaking his head.

"His injuries are such as would make it seem incredible
that he could have walked from the beach, talked to us, and

written his report," he said gravely. "I have done what I could, but I fear for his life. Especially as his heart is broken as well as his head. I find it very significant that he wrote his report, then fainted, as though his spirit had braced itself to make his defence and then succumbed."

"Did he include in his report tht fact that he was now useless?" Evert asked brutally.

"His Excellency added a word or two to that effect. The colonel merely mentioned that he had been wounded. His Excellency was anxious that another experienced man should be sent—in case of accident."

"Huh!" Evert made a noise that showed that he was not impressed by this piece of forethought. "That'll mean either Van Holk or Boender. Neither of 'em, to my mind, the right man for the job. What we want is an adventurer, not a soldier hidebound with rules for conducting a campaign. I was thinking a little while ago that if Gomarus had been in charge today he'd have guessed two deserted islands meant a trap on the third. He'd have landed in the unlikely place and attacked from the rear. By God," he said, warming up to his subject, "I could do it myself. Tonight. A hundred good men, that's all I'd ask. I'd make an attempt with fifty. Tonight, when they're patting themselves on the back and talking about their victory. I've got no patience with these tactics, going to the front door and ringing the bell and saying, 'Would you like to have a little battle this afternoon?'"

The doctor, who was not one of Evert's admirers, listened coldly. A professional man himself, he distrusted inspired amateurs; but Kaerko, naturally timid and unenterprising, found his blood moving more warmly as he heard the bold words. Haan was pigheaded on the subject of Shal Ahmi, but otherwise he was admirable; he lived, perhaps, a little out of his proper period; he would have been an excellent pioneer, overlooking his nutmegs for four days a week and engaging in guerrilla warfare on the others.

"There's a good deal in what you say," he said thoughtfully.

Van de Lijn yawned. "Well, I'll just have another look at my patient. Then I'll get along to the hospital. There'll be work for me there," he said grimly. He disappeared and in a moment was back in the doorway. "He seems to be sleeping. I'll come back when I've dealt with the worst up there. Good night."

Evert wandered over to the tray of food and without waiting for an invitation selected a pasty and set his teeth into it.

"I've had nothing since breakfast, and then my supper was disturbed by what my wife told me about Shal Ahmi," he explained. Inwardly he was a little surprised by the upwelling of vigour and spirit within him. Bad news all round—bad news from Ay and shattering news at Coenpark—and yet he was far from feeling dispirited. The spell with which Annabet had bound him had snapped, and he realised that for more than a year he had been in danger of limiting his world and his outlook to the narrow radius of a swaying petticoat. He had wanted Annabet and had hated whoever, whatever, it was that had barred him from full possession. Now he knew, and he could hate both Annabet and her lover. It was easy now, for that knowledge that Annabet had hankered for a man whom she had met after she had seen Evert Haan stung his vanity. Christy Ayrton! Well, he could have her. If it hadn't been for the war he'd have tied a label round her neck, stripped her to her shift, and told a boatman to row her over to Gadia. He couldn't do that now, but he had a very sweet revenge in mind. As soon as this business was settled he would go back and put it into action. And he would be avenged, not only for her mental unfaithfulness, but for all the weakness with which he had treated her in the past.

The governor returned. Bless the man, he had been running! He was blown, and it took him so long to recover his breath that both Evert and Kaerko knew what he would say when he regained his voice.

"He's gone," Evert said, not as one who asks a question but as one who answers it.

The governor nodded, gasped, broke into speech.

"Somebody's been very remiss," he said. "Until I asked after the rogue nobody had noticed that his cell was empty. One gaoler swore that he was there at ten o'clock this morning, and that's the last anyone saw of him. He's gone now. I've sent a party to his house, but he'd hardly be there, would he? As soon as it's light we'll comb every house on the island."

"And I trust, Your Excellency, that the searchers will be given orders to shoot at sight. I don't suppose he'd dare show his face at Coenpark; I've never encouraged his mumbo-jumbo in my compound, but if I see him I shall shoot first and let him explain afterwards."

"Such hasty and unwarranted action might easily precipitate the very situation we hope to avoid," said the governor, but his voice was uncertain, unrebuking.

"If what's afoot is what we think it is," said Evert, flicking away a crumb, "there'd be no situation with him dead. Shoot at the head is always a sound rule." He swept his eyes over the governor and the agent. Neither of them useful, neither of them men of action, neither of them men at all by his standard. "Well, what other steps are we going to take?"

"There isn't much that we can do, is there, until Shal Ahmi is found and brought in for questioning?"

"With all due deference," said Evert, and his tone made the perfunctory phrase almost insulting, "I should suggest that word be despatched immediately to every planter. Tell them what we suspect and ask them not only to keep a sharp lookout for Shal Ahmi himself but to look over anybody with whom he had any connections—any slave he's doctored or been talking to or had any business with. You"—he turned towards Kaerko—"could help there. All these thousands of loyal actions he has performed, whom have they concerned? Who's been the source of any information he's sold you? Who's been entangled in any muddle he's straightened for you? For those are the men he'll use now."

"Very cogent suggestions," said the governor, looking at Evert with half-resentful admiration and then shifting his gaze to Kaerko, who looked frightened and baffled and stubborn. "Do you, Mynheer, keep a record of such happenings, or do you rely upon your memory?"

"Come along, Kaerko," said Evert jovially. "You've been fixed by the old bastard, but so have other people. It's beyond being a matter of prejudice or policy now. Give us a list of the people you *know* have reason to be grateful to him. Blast it, man, if half what we suspect is true, it's a matter of life and death for all of us. This expedition has started like Kraemer's; we don't want it to go on."

"What Haan says is only too true," said the governor. "If you have any information . . ."

Kaerko went slowly to his big desk, juggled with some keys, and opened the bottom drawer, from the back of which he took a small notebook bound in black and red and ruled like an account book. The front page bore, in excellent copperplate handwriting, the words:

> *Account of Moneys paid out to Shal Ahmi in return for Services Rendered*

With it in his hand Kaerko stood still for a moment. "You will understand, Your Excellency, that these sums were paid out of my private purse. No penny of the Company's money is involved. I have kept the account as a matter of interest."

He handed the book to the governor, and Evert, taking another pasty as he passed the tray, came and stood behind the chair in which His Excellency sat and read over his shoulder. The little record covered several years, and although never, for any service, had Shal Ahmi received more than two guilders, the sum involved in the aggregate was quite considerable. The entries were very varied.

> For information leading to the recovery of Mevrouw Byskin's necklace without scandal.
> For keeping watch on Captain Moeller for four days.
> For reporting conversation overheard at Park Helgers.
> Sick woman hidden at the Dyke; suspect plague?

And under each heading, as though prepared against just such an occasion as had caused the little book to be brought to light, was inscribed in Kaerko's beautiful hand a list of people, Dutch and native, who were involved in each case. Evert caught sight, before the page was flicked over, of an entry which concerned him although his name was not mentioned.

> For information averting the arrest of Captain Piet Odshoorn on the charge of smuggling unlimed nuts aboard the *Eastern Venture*.
> Manuelo Cortez
> Ramjit Sita Singh.

A wry smile curved his mouth as he noted it. Shal Ahmi had asked only two guilders, one apiece for Manuelo and Ramjit; he himself had received, according to the book, two more from Kaerko's private purse. Four guilders had

changed hands and Piet had carried the papers! How cheap!
But dear at any price!

"Well," said Evert, coming out from behind the official
chair, "with all that settled, I will go home. I pass Byskin's
and Jenner's on my way. I think I'll wake them and warn
them of what we know and what we suspect. Good night,
Your Excellency. Good night, Kaerko."

When he had concluded both his errands, Evert stood on
the path back to Coenpark and laughed to himself. All this
fuss about warning the fellows, really it wasn't necessary at
all. They were all not only aware of, but definitely looking
for, danger. Byskin had greeted his nocturnal visitor by
poking a loaded blunderbuss through an upper window and
bellowing, "I'm armed. What do you want?" And at
Jenner's, Evert had found the house patrolled by two
enormous hounds, one of whom bayed menacingly beside
him, ready to take his arm in its jaws at the slightest
provocation.

Well, that was Shal Ahmi and the rebellion disposed of.
Now for Mistress Annabet.

The amusement faded from his eyes. In the waning
moonlight they took on a cold frosty glitter. Walking slowly,
he reviewed in great detail the history of his married life. He
skirted round the first episode—her arrival, his shock, the
calling in of Shal Ahmi—tossing self-accusation aside and
thinking eagerly, Well, that cured her, didn't it? He dwelt
lovingly upon the material things he had lavished on his
bride; upon his abandonment of all his ancient plans for
humiliating her and so getting his own back upon the Van
Goens. Damn it, he thought, if I'd been a raw schoolboy, in
love for the first time, living with the woman I'd chosen from
a thousand, I couldn't have given her more or treated her
better. He dismissed the memory of those nights when he
had emerged unsatisfied from her embrace and had
attempted to wring from her the name of the phantom. I
tried, he told himself, I tried to understand her; I was patient,
kind, tolerant. And when I thought I'd found the man, that
cousin of hers, and she told me that the past was over and
she'd try again, by God, I met her more than halfway.

The sweetness of the days and nights which had followed,
he regarded now with distaste. It was the sweetness of
rottenness. Then, more than at any other time, he had been
deceived. That was true. You're not really, wholly cheated

when you feel that you are being defrauded. It is when the cheating is subtle and sweet that the real deception begins. If for nothing else, he owed her a grudge for this last month.

He followed the main road out onto the quay. The lights had gone now. It was all deserted and silent save for the soft hiss of the rising tide. He turned into a narrow passage between two warehouses and stopped by a little low house, the whole of its frontage occupied by a wide, unglazed window, now closed by cane shutters, and a door over which projected a sign gaily painted with Chinese letters. He rapped on the door and waited. After two minutes he rapped again, more loudly. Suddenly impatient, he cursed and would have made a more violent assault upon the door had not a little shutter let into its upper half opened. Wang Fu's wizened yellow face, fitfully lighted from below by the rays of a tiny oil lamp which he had waited to kindle, showed in the aperture. Without greeting or a word of apology for rousing the old man from his bed at such an hour, Evert stated the nature of his errand. The Chinese unbolted the door, and Evert stepped inside.

Katje had found her mistress in the dining room and escorted her to bed. Mevrouw had been weeping a great deal and was talking to herself in a very strange voice when Katje, impatient for her own bed and anxious because of the silence in the lower part of the house, had crept down to investigate. Mevrouw had let herself be undressed like a child, weeping again and hardly speaking at all.

In the morning Annabet, waking from the deep, sluggish slumber that follows a wakeful night, opened her eyes to find Katje, bearing the breakfast tray, with tears running down her brown impassive face.

She braced herself against the onslaught of misery which was launched with her first return to wakefulness and asked kindly:

"What is the matter, Katje?"

"I am dismissed, Mevrouw."

"Dismissed? Who said so?"

"Mynheer. He said that you would have no further need of me and he would ask Mevrouw Byskin to take me into her service." She gulped and fixed her beady, red-rimmed eyes upon Annabet's face. "Mevrouw did not know of Mynheer's intention?"

Be careful now. Every word of this conversation would be repeated in the Byskins' kitchen and compound before the day was out.

"I didn't know that you were to go today, Katje. But for some time now Mevrouw Byskin has wanted you for her maid. And I—well, I never thought you seemed very happy here."

"Mynheer said I was to go at once. But," she added magnanimously, "I will lay out the dress for the morning if Mevrouw will tell me which one. And Juan and Abbas will carry the bath."

"Oh yes, Katje. I shall manage, thank you. I'll have the lilac dress with the plain collar. Thank you. . . . I hope you'll be happy, Katje. Good-bye."

So ended a relationship of peculiar intimacy. Annabet had a swift vision of Trudi's Nina howling like a bereaved dog as she crouched by her mistress's body. I have failed even to endear myself to Katje, she thought dully. Not that it matters now. Nothing does.

She drank some coffee and set the tray aside. She missed Katje's aimless fidgeting around the room, much as it had sometimes annoyed her. The silence seemed to grow oppressive. Each of her thoughts was as uncomfortable as the one that went before it. The war, Christy, Evert, Trudi. Especially did she dread facing Evert again. Nights like last night should really be the end of things. When she fell against the table she should have died. Or she should have died as she knelt by the table, praying for forgiveness for her sins and for Christy, wherever, in this world or another, he might be. Nights like that should not be followed by a bright morning, with the sun streaming in at the window and the doves cooing in the nutmeg grove and the scent of flowers coming up from the garden. Once a life had ended, the person who lived it should not be left alive and sentient, given breakfast, asked what dress she would wear, just as usual.

She heard Evert's step in the gallery and leaped from the bed, pushing her arms into the sleeves of her dark blue wrapper. He opened the door abruptly and stood in the doorway, not speaking at first, just looking at her coldly. She forced herself to return his stare, but the attempt failed. Her gaze wavered and averted itself.

"Evert—please don't look at me like that. I'm sorry. I was wrong, I know. But I am sorry. . . ."

"You're going to be sorrier," Evert said gloatingly. "I've sent Katje away. I engaged her to attend my wife, not Ayrton's mistress."

"Evert, I was not his mistress. You know that."

"I'd have respected you more if you'd gone the whole hog," he said untruthfully. "Don't wag your virginity in my face, madam. Whatever you care to call yourself, you played the traitor to save his hide. Perhaps there's a word to describe you, but I don't know it."

"I wasn't deliberately a traitor. I didn't even know about the war. I thought I was sending a warning about the patrols." She was conscious of a wild impulse to add that she was no more a traitor than the people who had smuggled out the nutmegs to the English and then left them to the mercy of the patrols. But there was no point in angering Evert further, and nothing to be gained by argument.

"Will you collect precisely the things you brought from Heydberg, nothing more, and carry them to the end of the gallery? This room, also, was intended for my wife."

He had expected some protest. From things she had said out of a desire to please him in the early days of their marriage he had gathered that the room and the pretty things in it and the unique, incomparable bathroom were dear to her. He was disappointed to see no flash of resentment in her eyes; angered afresh by her meek words.

"Very well. I will do that."

"You bet you will," he said roughly. "You'll further oblige me by staying in that room except when I ask you to come out. You'll come to know which side your bread was buttered on, my fine lady. My God, when I think how I've pampered you! Get along now. . . ."

He stood overlooking her hasty, muddled effort to sort out what remained of the things she had brought from those he had provided in the first place or subsequently bestowed. The pile of belongings, when finally assembled, was pitiably small. Dresses rotted so quickly during the rains, and she had rashly given so many things away. After each of Evert's munificent offerings Katje had carried away a bundle of superseded garments, to wear, to give away, or to sell. There remained of Mevrouw's secretly grudging but honourably just provision merely a nightgown and a change of underclothes, saved and cherished for sentiment's sake, for Klara and Maria and Mamma and Truitje had all had a hand in their making, and a gown of yellow muslin sprigged with little green sprays. The colour had reminded her of the primroses in the woods beyond Whitwater, and although it was faded and rotting she had hung it in the back of her cupboard and had looked at it sometimes when her eyes were tired of the brighter colours and more flaunting blossoms of this new home.

Apart from the silver articles upon the dressing table, she did not possess even a brush and comb. She had given her own to Katje, who had craftily expressed vast admiration for them.

She refrained from mentioning this deficiency. She gathered the few things into her arms and said, "I am ready."

"Come along then," said Evert, resolutely repressing his surprise that she should own so little.

He moved the key from the inside to the outside of the door and locked it. He didn't feel so elated as he had expected, and he attributed that fact to her behaviour. Too proud to show that she minded, pretending not to care about possessions. Wait till tonight, he thought. She'll be stung into speech then. And I shall have something to say as well.

He stepped ahead of her and opened the door of the room he had mentioned. It was nothing more than the dressing room of the guest room next door. The communicating door was locked, and Annabet's new domain was a narrow oblong, nine feet long, five feet wide, with a little truckle bed pushed against the inner wall. There was a cupboard and a chest of drawers upon which had been set a basin and ewer and a tiny heart-shaped swing mirror no bigger than a plate.

"It's luxury compared with what Ayrton could have given you," Evert said. "The boys will bring you food at midday, and I shall hope for your company at dinner."

He closed the door but did not, as she had expected, lock it. Annabet, laying her possessions on the bed, remembered with a stab of irrepressible irony that both the nightgown and the wrapper which she wore had been given her by Evert. If he had thought of it, would he have made me walk along the gallery stark-naked? Oh, dear, was that anything to be amused about?

Evert found Josef clearing away the breakfast things. He pushed the door shut with his foot and signed to Josef to stop fidgeting with the dishes.

"Listen to me," he said brusquely. "Katje's gone, and unless you want to follow her you'd better swear by your Prophet's beard or anything else you hold holy not to mention a word about some other changes I'm going to make in this house."

"Mynheer, have I ever——"

"I'm not talking about the past; I'm talking about the future. Are you going to swear?"

"But certainly, Mynheer. By the beard of the Prophet I swear not to mention any of Mynheer's affairs."

"All right. I'm having Isa back tonight."

Josef gave no sign of his unbounded astonishment or of his sharply piercing curiosity.

"Yes, Mynheer."

"She'll help you with the work. Abbas and Juan are not to come inside the house again. If there isn't enough to occupy them in the kitchen they can start work outside. They're both too old and neither of them good enough to be houseboys anyway. So if a breath of this business gets abroad I shall know where it comes from, and you'll be sorry. Do you understand?"

"Perfectly, Mynheer. But——"

"But what?"

"Katje, Mynheer. Is she not to be replaced?"

"No, except by Isa. Mevrouw is persisting in a very foolish course of action, Josef, and I must show her that I am not a man to be trifled with. You would do well to remember that too."

"Yes, Mynheer."

Business in Banda that day was at a standstill. Behind the closed doors of offices and in corners of quiet warehouses, out of the hearing of clerks and porters, men gathered in little groups to talk over the news and voice their opinions, the cheerful trying to encourage the pessimists, the pessimists endeavouring to discourage the cheerful. Within an hour of leaving his house Evert had forgotten both Annabet and Isa. As the person who had been present at the moment of Knol's return, and present also at the midnight meeting in Kaerko's house, his contribution to every conversation was eagerly welcomed, his opinion constantly invited, his blustering, sanguine view of the situation extremely popular.

The news itself was bad. Knol had died at dawn. Shal

Ahmi had not been traced. Twelve, then fifteen, then nineteen, and finally twenty-three of the wounded men, hastily operated upon by Van de Lijn in the reeking hospital inside the Fort, succumbed during the day. Their names were sent down to Kaerko so that he might register them in his book of deaths, and he made no attempt to keep the white population in ignorance. He was anxious himself and willing for others to share his burden.

Evert called upon him shortly before noon and asked bluntly whether his suggestion of following up the people mentioned in his account book had borne any results.

"So far nothing," the agent replied with less complacency than Evert would have expected. "At least"—he consulted a slip of paper—"on the Vanderbosch estate—following a clue presented by the fact that one of the coolies had begged Shal Ahmi's intervention in a matter of criminal carelessness— the man, Manuelo Cortez, was found to be in possession of a pistol. At first we thought we had made a discovery, but he swore that Mevrouw Vanderbosch herself had entrusted him with it. And that was the truth. Mevrouw Vanderbosch, apparently, had taken it upon herself to select six men and arm them in case of trouble. If many other ladies have taken similar precautions, the natives know more about our fears and suspicions than we do ourselves. I took it upon myself to point that out to her, and Vanderbosch, to my surprise, was most offensive. He said that if the performance of the soldiers yesterday was any gauge there was little to be hoped for in the way of protection from official sources and it was every man for himself." Kaerko swallowed, and his Adam's apple jumped convulsively. "Haan, where *could* Shal Ahmi *be?* I'd have gone bail on his loyalty and integrity. But you must admit that his getting out of gaol and disappearing just now looks very fishy."

"*I* admit it! My good fellow, it was I who first pointed it out to you."

"Oh yes, yes, of course. Last night. Really, I'm so confused I hardly know where I am or what I am doing. This is a horrible business." He looked at Evert miserably. "What's the matter with this place, Haan? On the whole they're well treated. I don't have much to do with the plantations, I admit, but the natives who come in to Banda on errands and the ones who live and work here always seem happy enough. They laugh and sing and loaf about at the slightest opportunity. Now the moment when we're in trouble we've got to treat them as if they were enemies too. It's like building your house on what looks like solid rock and then seeing it turn into a quagmire."

"No, no," protested Evert cheerfully. "It's not quite so bad as that. It's like having a straw stack near your back door. Perfectly harmless so long as nobody throws a taper at it. All we're doing is seeing that nobody gets a chance to throw a taper—and keeping a bucket of water handy."

"I'd feel better if I knew that Shal Ahmi was under lock and key again. D'you know, Haan? It struck me last night. After you and the governor had gone I sat down and added up what I'd paid him. I've never paid him more than two guilders for any single service, and it was quite a year before I discovered how very useful he was. But what do you think the sum totted up to? One thousand two hundred and fourteen guilders. What's he done with it? He lives in a hovel, he owns nothing, he has no dependents, he lives so meagrely that he's always glad of a bite at the back door. Where've one thousand two hundred and fourteen guilders gone? That's what I should like to know."

Evert, who had sometimes paid Shal Ahmi twice that sum in a single year and sometimes asked himself the same question, gave voice to a supposition with which he had often satisfied his own curiosity.

"I believe he owns property in Bandogar. Once, after a tornado struck there, he asked me on my next trip to place an order for a new roof on a house there. That's all I have to go on. He may have been acting as a landlord or as a charitable friend. Or the people in the house may have been his relatives. I don't know."

"No. That's just it, Haan. Nobody knows anything about him, really. It seems incredible that he should have lived in the midst of a small community like ours, so open to inspection and so ridden with gossip, and yet retain his mystery. Isn't it queer?"

"Everything about him is queer if you ask me. And the sooner he's found and locked away again, the better."

Kaerko looked relieved. Outside the routine duties of his post he liked being told what to do. Now Knol, who had enjoyed directing and even mildly bullying him, was dead; and the governor wasn't positive enough. From that morning dated Kaerko's dependence upon Evert. More and more frequently during the next days and nights was he to say, "Let's send for Haan," or "I should like Haan's opinion on that."

Evert spent a longer day than usual in Banda and did not attempt to return to Coenpark until dusk. Nothing of note had happened since his visit to Kaerko. Shal Ahmi had not been found; no further signs of revolution had been uncovered. At four o'clock in the afternoon the governor had issued a proclamation, forced out of him by the flying rumour that Colonel Knol, seriously wounded, had been carried ashore during the previous evening. The proclamation, written in Dutch, Malay, Chinese, and Tamil, merely stated that the war was going well. Colonel Knol had returned to Banda in order to report upon the day's fighting in Lu and had then proceeded to Gadia as arranged. Further bulletins would be issued as soon as reliable news arrived, and in the meantime it would be to the advantage of everybody if work went forward as usual.

Evert, passing the door of a warehouse upon which a copy was nailed, halted and stood at the edge of a little knot of coolies, porters, minor clerks, and boatmen who had gathered round it. A honey-coloured boy with so severe a squint as should have precluded him from reading at all had just gabbled out the Dutch version and had started upon the Malay, showing off, very proud of himself, pausing now and then to shush with great firmness those of his elders and betters who, having profited by the Dutch reading, were now trying to discuss it, to the detriment of those of his hearers who still awaited the translation.

"Brave," said Evert loudly, when for the second time the boy raced through the final sentence and spread his hands to show that he had finished. "Very clever, my boy," he said with the geniality which so often sweetened his casual contacts. "I'll wager a guilder you can't twist your nimble young tongue round the next lot."

"Mynheer will lose his guilder," said the boy with a cheeky smile which, momentarily obliterating the squint, made him oddly attractive. Hardly looking at the paper, trusting his memory, and with his crooked gaze shifting between Evert and the Chinese members of his audience, he rattled through the proclamation again in fluent Chinese.

"Splendid," said Evert, tossing the coin expertly. "Five if

you can master the Tamil." He looked around and noted the faces of those few who were still waiting, patient, unenlightened.

"Five, Mynheer. Never in my life did I earn money so easily. Listen."

This time he turned his back to the paper and in a loud clear voice gabbled the governor's message for the fourth time. Evert saw one or two of the hitherto blank faces lighten with understanding. The boy wasn't cheating.

Good-humouredly he handed over the money.

"I doubt if there's another boy in Banda who could have done it," he said.

"Necessity loosens the tongue, Mynheer. My mother is Malay, my father from Coromandel, my master is Chinese, and my native tongue is Dutch." His good eye looked at Evert, and his other seemed to turn a derisive glance at the oblong of paper. "What is more, Mynheer, a lie is a lie in any language."

"Hi! What's that? What the devil do you mean by that?" Evert demanded. But the boy, with a final pert glance, had slipped through the little gabbling crowd and was gone.

I shall know him again; that eye and the Chinese master will make him easy to find, Evert thought. I'll have him safe by ten o'clock tomorrow morning. Cheeky little devil. Maybe I ought to do something about it now. But I told Isa sunset. And though he seemed to be looking at the paper when he said "lie," that may have been just his affliction. And the damned natives love making wild wide-sweeping statements like that. He may not have meant anything. All the same, I wish I'd got my hands on him.

The memory rankled in him halfway to Coenpark. Then he forgot it. The sweet treat he had prepared for himself was about to begin.

A whole day spent in complete silence and solitude in a room nine by five, with nothing but a loathsome bit of embroidery and one's thoughts for company, is a wonderful clarifier of one's mind. By the time Evert returned Annabet had settled exactly what she must say to him, with dignity and restraint, but with assurance; and for quite a long time she had been looking forward to his arrival. She was not frightened of him any more.

She heard him enter; there was nobody else who would

come straight in at the front door, and nobody else ever pushed the door closed with such a careless, backward thrust. But some time elapsed before he flicked his fingers across the door of her dressing room and called in quite a cheerful voice, "Are you ready for dinner? Don't keep me waiting. I'm hungry."

Annabet herself was empty rather than hungry. She had had no dinner, no breakfast, and the boys had not arrived with the promised midday meal. No one had come near her all day, and she was too miserable as well as too proud to go out and demand attention.

Now she smoothed her hair as well as she could with her hands, pinched up the pleats and the sleeves of the old faded, rotting yellow dress, and stepped out to the gallery. Despite her cultivated calmness of mind, her heart began to thud quickly and audibly as she made her way down the stairs. All the flowers in the tubs and vases had been changed; they were all scarlet now, some kind of lily, with stiffly curving petals and great yellow stamens, thick with dusty pollen. She had never seen or smelled anything like them before. Their perfume was overpowering, heavy and sweet and languorous.

The candles were lighted in the dining room and the door was open, an oblong of warm yellow light. She could see the middle section of the table from where she stood on the stairs, and it held more silver and more flowers and more candles than usual. Evert surely wouldn't have asked guests tonight, knowing that she must come to the table in this old gown, without even having been able to brush her hair. Or—wasn't that just the kind of thing he was capable of? If this were part of her punishment, she must bear it.

She straightened her back and lifted her head and walked into the room with that peculiar gentle dignity which had made Piet prefer her to Klara in the church at Heydberg all those months ago.

Evert was sitting at one end of the table, his plate already piled, his glass filled. Josef, with his back to the room, was moving dishes about on the sideboard. And somebody was sitting in Annabet's chair at the other end of the table. A third place was laid on one side. As his wife halted just inside the doorway Evert pointed to it with an oddly uncouth movement of his knife handle.

The situation needed no explanation. This is one of the

things I must bear, Annabet thought. It doesn't matter. To fuss would be ridiculous. Having forfeited all claim to Evert's esteem, I mustn't mind his behaviour.

She slipped into her place, saying quietly, "Good evening." The little golden-brown girl choked over a mouthful of food. Evert took a noisy gulp from his glass. Josef's usually careful hands let a plate fall with a clatter.

Everybody is as uncomfortable as I am myself, Annabet thought.

Josef placed a plate of fish before her and she applied herself to it for a moment or two, not knowing, despite her hunger, what she was eating.

The silence in the room became a pain. Desperately, irrationally, she sought for some word which would end it. But what could she say? Was there a single phrase that would be acceptable? And was it for her to speak at all? Neither hostess nor guest . . . When Evert had planned this, for planned it must have been, had he envisaged the possibility that her intended discomfiture would be shared by everyone, even by Josef? Evert himself seemed to be trying to cover the silence by noisy manipulations of his knife and fork; the little brown girl ate like some dainty animal, sometimes using her fingers. Her small pretty face wore a look of frightened malevolence such as might, indeed, have been seen upon the face of a small wild creature held captive in unnatural surroundings.

Josef, tray in hand, went out of the room. Had he to fetch the next course of the meal himself? Where were the boys?

As soon as he had gone Evert brought his heavy mocking look to bear upon the girl.

"Well," he said, "you're making slow work of it. What's the matter? Isn't it to your liking?"

"It is very good. But I am not hungry."

"And you," said Evert, switching his glance to Annabet, "have you lost your appetite as well as your tongue?"

"I was hungry," Annabet said, laying down her knife and fork, "but I am satisfied now. I think, if you don't mind, I'll go back to my room. I had—I had something I wanted to say to you, but it will do later on."

"You'll oblige me by staying where you are and taking a little notice of my guest. You were always one to point out the beauties of nature and you've hardly looked at her. Look at her. Don't you think she's pretty?"

Isa, after another flashing look of malevolence, stared down at her plate. Why, Annabet wondered, was Evert so anxious for her to study the girl? One glance was enough to reveal all that was of significance—that she was a woman, that she was attractive, that she was brown, and that she was in the place of honour at the table. Probably most women, after one glance, would have turned and walked away; and they would have been wise. Was that what Evert had expected and wanted? And if she had retreated would he have ordered her back, made a scene?

Then she realised why Evert had ordered her to look at the girl. Hung in the little brown ears were the emerald-and-diamond earings; the matching necklace sparkled upon the slender, round, honey-brown neck; the ring flashed from the thumb of the little brown hand—too big for any of the slim red-tipped fingers.

Oh, Evert, she thought, how pitiable, how puerile! As though I would mind. And again she wondered what he had hoped for, what he had expected. Was she supposed to scream now, or rave, or fling herself upon that little childish creature and try to snatch back her possessions?

Isa raised defiant eyes. Annabet looked straight at her and said quietly, "You are, very, very pretty. And the trinkets suit you extremely well."

The bitch, Evert thought furiously. All pose, all pretence. At heart, of course, she would like to dash at Isa and scratch her eyes out. But she wouldn't give him the pleasure of knowing that he had provoked her; too proud; too much a Van Goens. Subtlety was wasted on their thick-hided conceit. He should have taken a stick and given her a damned good thrashing.

And the other little trollop was pretty well equally as annoying; instead of sitting up and making the most of herself and throwing herself in Madam's pasty, sick-looking face, there she sat, looking like a cornered monkey, half scared, half savage.

Josef, with the vast, devout, injured dignity of a high priest condemned by circumstances to scour the floor of his sanctuary, bore in a tray of food and began to change the plates. The strained silence lay hold upon the room again. But the crisis was past. Annabet knew now what Evert had hoped for. Evert knew that his plan had failed in its purpose. And she won't flinch, he thought, at the idea of Isa and me in that room. God damn her, she's had me jealous for two years, but she'll never be jealous of me. Not that I care, he told himself, ignoring a strange stab at his vitals. I've finished with her. And I shall have Isa. . . .

He looked along the table and let his eyes dwell upon the brown girl, trying by anticipation and the memory of past delights to spur himself into a comfortable state of about-to-be-gratified lechery. But there was no response. In his mind he could strip Isa naked; no nerve, no muscle moved. With something very much like dismay he realised that Isa had lost her power.

Against his will he looked at Annabet. Yellow hair a little tousled, pale face a little sunken, eyes reddened with tears, long neck and fingers unadorned, body quiescent within the faded, shabby dress . . .

With a blinding flash of revelation he saw what had happened to him; knew what had lain behind his tolerance, his patience, his discontent, his jealousy, behind last night's fury and spurious sense of freedom, behind the glee with which he had planned his revenge. Stunned and dumb, he realised that in one respect he was no more immune than other men, and no luckier. Too late he knew that he could no more humiliate Annabet than he could possess her. He could only love her.

His new knowledge, once assimilated, served only to infuriate him further. When the wretched meal was at last over he sent Isa away, dismissing her with a few brusque words. Then he turned towards Annabet in much the same tone. "Well, you said you wanted to speak to me. Out with it; but I warn you, if you're thinking a few soft words will put you back where you were, you're going to be disappointed."

"I wasn't thinking of that, Evert. I've been over and over it in my mind all day, and I just wanted to explain something to you and then ask you to let me go back to Holland."

"You can go back to Holland when you can pay your own passage," Evert said brutally, and was lashed to further anger to find that hurling insults into that sad white face brought pain as well as pleasure. "I've wasted enough money on you," he added.

"Then perhaps I could go elsewhere; or perhaps I could find someone who would take me. I could—cook and mend." She brought out the last words with extreme diffidence. Such small and uncertain tools. "You mean that if I can find a way to go you will allow me? You don't want me here any longer?"

"What I want or don't want has never been your first consideration in the past. We won't discuss my feelings now. I am waiting to hear what you please to call an explanation."

"It is more an apology. Evert, if I talked for an hour I couldn't tell you how sorry I am that it has turned out like this. I was so very ignorant. I'd no idea what love meant when I came to Banda. When I was very young I imagined that I was in love with my cousin, but that was just girlish fancy, and then he became a priest. It was he, in a way, who sent me here, although he didn't know it. When I first realised what had happened to me I was almost mad, and then he came and told me things that are half true and half false about the spirit being more important than the body. And then there was Mamma; she said no husbands and wives were in love before they married, and that if I tried to please you and minded my manners and kept your house well everything would be all right. And I might get better. I didn't come to you in the wrong spirit, Evert. And what Mamma said might well have been true—if Christy hadn't come." Her fingers moved in the pleats of her faded dress, wrenching and pleating nervously; the red colour washed over her pale face, but she went on steadily, aware that Evert was, at least, listening attentively:

"Honestly, Evert, I couldn't help falling in love with him. It's the last thing I would have chosen. I never—you know, Evert, you must know that I—that we—— I only kissed him before he went; and I knew really then, in my heart, that I should never see him again. It was mad of me to tell you what I did. But I was grateful because you'd had me cured and I wanted you not to be disappointed, because, you see, knowing how I felt about Christy, I knew I should never feel like that about you or any other man. I did give you the chance to send me home then. Didn't I?" Evert stared, unspeaking. "And about what I did for Shal Ahmi. I'd no idea then that it was war he was warning them of. I couldn't do nothing and let Christy be killed when I had the means to warn him in my hand. Evert, if you've ever been fond of anyone in your life, put yourself in my place and try to understand. I'm not asking you to take me for your wife again. I realise how horrible I seem to you. But if we could——

part—without hatred . . . If I needn't feel that I'd ruined your life as well as my own . . ."

"And that's all you have to say?"

Annabet nodded. There had been other things, little frail silly things that could not be spoken in the face of Evert's cold, scornful stare.

"You make out a very good case for yourself, poor little innocent. But you must know in your heart that it's all sentimental rubbish. Look at my side for a moment. I married you, beggared, crippled, a bag of skin and bones; I overcame my own prejudices in order to give you the last chance of recovery; I gave you everything you wanted and a lot that you'd never have thought of; I treated you with respect; I was faithful. In two whole years I never gave a thought or a glance to another woman. And what is my reward? You turned my house into a stew; day and night you were pining and fretting for your lover, and finally you turned traitor to save his worthless hide." The words seemed to wake an echo, and he realised that they were just a repetition of what he had said only that morning. A kind of sick weariness came over him. Round and round we go, over and over the same bit of ground, getting nowhere, he thought; it's like a fencing match against somebody who will stay out of reach. If only she'd acted as I thought she would when she saw Isa, we'd have had a blazing row and I could have thrown her own jealousy in her face as proof that she did care. But it's no use. She doesn't. Nothing will make her. And arguments are just a waste of time.

"Colonel Knol died this morning; twenty-three soldiers died during the day. There'll be more deaths tomorrow. Half those men would be alive, celebrating the shortest and best-planned campaign in history, but for you. Take that thought to bed with you. Your friend Shal Ahmi is still at large, and God only knows what devilry is going on under the surface. Maybe we'll all perish in our blood before this thing is done. But perhaps you think that a small price to pay for the safety of Christy Ayrton's carcass. Love like yours must be worth having, my lady. You make me sorry that I could never attain it. Good night."

That did break her. She turned and went stumbling out of the room like an old woman, her hands over her face, her shoulders shaking with sobs.

He had an irrational impulse to call her back, to say,

"that's all rot—soldiers expect to die in a battle; it's what
they're paid for—and as for Shal Ahmi, he'll rot in gaol; and
reinforcements will come and we'll grind the English into
powder." They were the things he would have said if she had
brought this tragic situation about through any other reason
than a desire to save Ayrton. How stoutly he would have
comforted her! How madly and unreasonably he longed to
do it now, even now, knowing why she had acted. Really, he
must be a little crazy. And could you wonder?

The sun was quite high next morning when Isa tapped on
the dressing-room door and called softly, "Mevrouw, I have
brought your breakfast."

So there was another day to face. She had spent most of
the early hours of the night in tears and frantic prayers, at
first for forgiveness and then for death. When at last she had
lain down upon the little truckle bed she had felt too ill and
so utterly exhausted that it had seemed possible that her
latter request might be granted. Of forgiveness she had no
sign. Mevrouw van Goens, who had abandoned the practice
but retained the ideology of her own faith when she left
Brussels to marry her Protestant cousin, and Father Vincent,
who had seen in young Annabet's earthly affection an
opportunity to sow seed which might later come to flower,
would have been pleased, perhaps, to know that in this
extremity her distracted mind had adopted a strongly
Catholic bias. She had prayed for the souls of all the men for
whose deaths she felt responsible. That they had died with
their sins upon them she begged might be reckoned against
her, not against them. She had prayed not only to God but to
the Virgin and to those of the saints whom she could
remember by name. For herself she had begged forgiveness
not only for unchaste thinking and worldly behaviour but
for having voluntarily abandoned the opportunity of leading
a devout and dedicated life. Not going to Ireland was the first
and the most heinous of her offences; all the others stemmed
directly from that. And when at last she had fallen into
exhausted, leaden slumber, whose precincts were like the
precincts of death, she had expected to wake to the pains of
purgatory, which she thought of not as the sterile process of
punishment but as a blessed chance of the ultimate
attainment of forgiveness.

And now there was Isa with a breakfast tray.

She opened the door and stood in the shaft of light from the gallery. She had slept in the yellow dress. Her unbrushed yellow hair was wild and tangled, her face hollower and whiter than it had been even on the previous evening, and her eyes were sunk in lilac-coloured shadows. She looked ill and mad, Isa thought.

The little brown girl was bright and flowerlike in her scarlet jacket and sarong of clear apple green. Her own gold earrings were in her ears this morning, and her jingling collection of coloured bangles glinted upon her slim arms. But her beautiful brown dove's eyes were heavy-lidded, and she wore an expression that was at once sulky and troubled.

Annabet said, "Thank you," and put out her hands to take the tray. Isa did not relinquish it, however. She entered the room and, pushing back the basin and ewer on top of the chest of drawers, set down the tray, taking in every detail of the cramped apartment as she did so. It was rather strange, Annabet thought, that Evert's new favourite should be waiting upon her, and she said, "Thank you," again humbly. Isa flashed her one of those queer glances and then looked at the tray.

"I hope I have done it right. There was no one to ask except Josef, and he was busy and would not help."

"It looks just right," said Annabet gently. "You won't—you mustn't mind if I leave some. I'm not hungry. But I am grateful for the coffee. It smells lovely."

Isa backed away from the chest of drawers and stood in the tiny space between the foot of the bed and the door.

"Mevrouw," she said, and the word was jerked out nervously, "I want to say something. It is this. I did not ask to return. It is not because of me it has happened thus."

"Oh no. I know that. I never imagined for a moment——"

"In some way you have made him very angry, Mevrouw." Difficult to tell whether that was a question or a statement. The girl's lilting little voice made either possible. If it were a question, perhaps one ought not to reply. There was such a thing as dignity, though in the circumstances . . .

"Yes. I have made him very angry."

"And it was for your punishing that he brought me back." Again that doubt as to whether she was bent upon giving or extracting information. But this time Isa did not wait for an answer. She rushed on, and as she spoke something very curious seemed to happen within, or rather

behind, her eyes; it was almost as though a red flame had
waved back and forth and then gone out. "That was a bad
thing. And to give me the jewels and pretend they were for
me alone. And to pretend that it would all be as it was before,
but better. Mevrouw, that is what he did. I did not know. I
would not have come to be made sport of."

There was nothing one could say to that. To offer pity
might seem insulting; one knew too little of her circumstances to say, "Well, why not go home?" She might not
have a home. Her whole past life and her background were
beyond the reach even of imagination. At some past time
she had lived at Coenpark and been Evert's mistress, that
much was clear; and then she had disappeared so entirely
that Annabet had never heard even a breath of rumour
as to her existence. Now, out of that obscurity, she had
emerged again, a tool in Evert's hand for Annabet's punishment. And human enough to feel the ignominy of her
position. Not to be blamed, or pitied, or advised.

The silence had fallen again. Annabet moved to the tray
and poured a cup of coffee. Standing there, she caught sight
of herself in the tiny heart-shaped mirror and was appalled,
first at her own appearance and then by the greatness of her
horror. Having renounced the world and prayed to die, it did
seem ridiculous to feel so violently about one's hair. Quite
clearly there was something peculiarly worldly about hair; in
convents they cut it off! Her eyes turned towards the little
case which held her needles, her thimble, and the sharp-
pointed scissors which had been old Truitje's parting present.
For a moment the balance of her mind hung undecided.
Sense of guilt, despair, exhaustion, self-abnegation upon the
one side, nothing but youth and vanity upon the other. Then
impulsively she turned to Isa.

"Do you think you could lend me a comb? Your own
comb?"

"I have none of my own, Mevrouw. He said I need
nothing. Everything, he said, I should find in the place
prepared for me. And that was true. I did not know then that
all the things were yours. But I will fetch it."

"But I—perhaps——" Oh, wasn't it an awkward thing to
put into words? Isa flashed a look of complete understanding.

"Just the same, I will fetch it."

Was that anything to be amused at? Wasn't it awful, final

proof of her entirely graceless and degenerate nature that at such a moment she should find anything funny? But it was. And as Isa pattered in with the silver comb and the silver-backed brush as well Annabet gave vent to something that was very like the conspiratorial giggle which had so often sounded through the bleak Heydberg house; and Isa's silky, sulky lips parted in a smile that held more malice than amusement. In that moment a bond, frail, frangible, but real enough, was forged between them. Except in moments of rivalry over a man there is a curious free masonry amongst women.

Van Holk arrived in Banda in a mood of self-confidence and self-importance calculated to restore cheerfulness to the community. Foolishly, since no man can foresee the future with certainty and what he has said against a predecessor may so easily be said again against himself, he laid the whole blame of the original expedition's failure at Knol's door.

Convinced that Banda's premier soldier had been stupid and lacking in precision, Van Holk did not expect much from the governor and the agent; and he saw in them exactly what he expected to find. The governor was dithering, indecisive, nervous, and the agent was fussy, nervous, dithering, and indecisive. Voss, whom Knol's death had left in command of the remaining soldiers, was, in his new superior's opinion, little short of imbecile. Instead of drilling his new draft and getting them ready for action, he had spent his time hunting for some wretched native who had broken out of gaol. And not even found him. In an island the size of a pocket handkerchief. It was ludicrous; it was pitiable. And if the English were half as strong as Knol's written and Voss's verbal report made out, the wonder was that they hadn't swooped down on the island and followed up their victory in Ay by the conquest of Banda, where the poor silly sods had even let their powder reserves be blown up by three natives with torches.

This last fact stuck in Van Holk's mind like a burr in a sheep's fleece. Again and again he referred to it, sometimes as a joke, sometimes seriously. And when, within a short time of his arrival, he discovered that the chief men of Banda were at least equally concerned with the possibility of a native rising as they were with the English war, his immediate mental reaction was to think: And no wonder! If

they let three coolies destroy all their powder, how can they
hope to hold down thousands?

He himself, straight from long-settled Batavia, regarded
the settlers' fear as grossly exaggerated. He—to use his own
expression—got to the root of the business about Shal Ahmi
within his first twenty-four hours of control. Why had Voss,
with so much of importance to do, wasted his time combing
through the alleys of Banda Neira and the compounds of the
plantations? Voss explained; Kaerko explained; His Excellency explained. In such explanation the name of Evert
Haan was prominent. Van Holk sent for Evert and within
five minutes had angered him so profoundly that only the
most iron self-restraint prevented Evert from bursting out
with the stark, awful truth. How would Van Holk's boiled-
pudding face with its gooseberry eyes look if Evert rapped
out, "I know Shal Ahmi warned the enemy because my wife
carried his message. Ask her if you doubt my word"? Not to
be able to say it—God, it was enough to make a man mad. It
was like holding a master card in a game and not being
able to play it. But he stuck to his story about Mevrouw
van Heem's last words to Annabet and made much of the
significance of Shal Ahmi's escape from gaol under cover of
the raid which was supposed to free Seth Aranda, and
relieved his temper by barking at the great man in a manner
which even the governor himself did not dare to use.

"If you're so clever, then, tell us poor fools who the hell
did send the warning if he didn't?" he asked.

"I don't think they were specifically warned," Van Holk
replied, not in the least offended. "Because Knol didn't find
them at breakfast, you all begin to talk of treachery, and
Voss wastes his time hunting the supposed traitor. And what
is more, some idiot from Lonthoir—what was his name?—
Banderbosh or something like that—actually forced his way
into my presence this morning, demanding that before I
move against the English I make sure that everything is safe
at home. He suggested that I leave a posse of picked men to
patrol the islands. I sent him off with a flea in his ear."

Evert, who had actually no patience with Vanderbosch
and no fears for himself and no doubts as to the docility of
the Coenpark natives, belied his own feelings and retorted:

"Vanderbosch is old enough to remember Kraemer's
campaign. And he knows more about native behaviour than
you and I will ever learn." He looked into Van Holk's face as

he delivered this rebuke, and then, satisfied that he had done his duty by his fellow planter, added truculently, "Not that we want any men left. Vanderbosch happens to be nervous. You go ahead and pound Ay into powder and we'll take care of things at home."

Van Holk, for some reason, liked Evert better than he liked anyone he had met so far in Banda.

"Leave that to me," he said in a friendly way. "I'm leaving Voss in charge here. I've replenished his powder stores. If you can keep the natives from running amok with torches you've ample supplies to keep order." He grinned sardonically and Evert squirmed. If Von Holk knew what he, Evert Haan, knew of Shal Ahmi's resource and cunning he wouldn't find anything funny in three natives blowing up the entire powder reserve. But, alas, that source of information was also sealed. Nobody in Banda except Evert Haan knew the depths and reach of Shal Ahmi's guile; and he, Evert Haan, was battling against it singlehanded.

The fresh powder had been stored all together, at Van Holk's suggestion, in the ground-floor room of one of the gatehouses of the Fort. The place had two prime advantages: It was easily accessible from the inside of the Fort, and from the outside it was under the constant surveillance of the sentries who guarded the gate. In his last interview with Voss, who felt very ashamed and angry at being left behind this time, Van Holk had said in the gibing manner which covers the greatest insults, "Don't, even if the governor himself suggests it, go chasing any gaol breakers; and if you see any natives with torches hanging around the gatehouse, set your terrier on them."

Voss, who had been aboard the *Margarete* when the previous powder stores were fired, resented this gibe and with youthful lack of caution retorted in a manner which was going to do him very ill service when Van Holk returned to headquarters. And then, because he was young and had failed with his second landing party to extricate Knol, whom he had idolised, from that death hole between the musket barrage and the blazing huts, and had failed again in his search for Shal Ahmi, and had failed yet a third time when he tried to persuade his new commander to take him on the next expedition, he went back to the Fort and straight to the board which bore the list of names of the trusted white soldiers who were picked for sentry duty. He scratched out one name of every pair on night duty and substituted his own. Then he had his hard camp bed moved into the doorway of the powder store. He would go on guard all night; he would work from eight in the morning till two; from two until six he would sleep in such a position that if the powder were blown up he would be blown up with it and Van Holk, returning victorious—as he would; his sort always did, and he had poor old Knol's experience to profit from—shouldn't have any chance to taunt him.

Van Holk sailed at sunset. He planned a dawn attack. This time, by his own orders, there was no crowd upon the beach to see the *Greta,* the *Seabird,* and the refitted *Sanje* set sail; and the new bulletin from the governor, in Dutch, Malay, Chinese and Tamil, informed the islanders that evening that fresh forces under General Van Holk had gone to relieve the victorious soldiers of Colonel Knol from the wearisome task of rounding up the English survivors who had taken to the jungle. The squint-eyed boy with his pentecostal gift of tongues was no longer there by the warehouse door to delight his listeners with his virtuosity. Evert had reported him first thing in the morning after his performance, and when the new paper was nailed to the door he was safely in gaol.

At two o'clock in the morning after Van Holk's departure Lieutenant Voss and the sergeant who had admitted Trudi van Heem and Annabet to Shal Ahmi's cell were on guard together. The sergeant, usually an amiable man, was sulky. Night guard was boring and deadly at any time, but generally you knew perfectly well that at midnight, and perhaps—but not certainly—again at about four o'clock, the officer on duty would stick his head out of the gateway and enquire whether all was well. Between these two moments he and Dirk (it was generally Dirk; that wasn't too difficult to arrange) were able to sit down in comparative comfort, backs against the wall, and talk or play Nobbin or drowse as the fancy took them. Now, instead of Dirk, Lieutenant Voss, bolt upright, deadly serious, was sharing the night duty; and the eight-hour spell long enough at any time, stretched out interminably.

There was no moon that night, but the stars, except when hidden by scudding clouds, were brilliant; and there were two lanterns, one on either side of the main gate. At intervals, to ease the tedium of standing and to keep themselves awake, Voss and the sergeant turned right or left and marched to the end of the wall and back again. They took turns, and the gate was never for a second left unguarded.

The sergeant took his turn, walked to the end of the wall, and, since Voss stood in the circle of light thrown by the lanterns and a cloud just then blotted out the star glimmer, was momentarily lost to sight. Voss found himself almost automatically counting in time to the man's paces, just as he counted his own, for lack of something better to do, when he walked his beat. Ninety-six, turn, and ninety-six back again. But this time after the ninety-sixth pace there was a pause, a moment, perhaps a little more—it might be less—it was difficult to reckon exactly. Then the steady pacing footsteps began again and the sergeant walked back to the edge of the circle of light and took up his regular position. It was not difficult to account for that momentary pause, and it went through Voss's head that he would make similar use of his next second of privacy. Might as well go now. He turned, and immediately a heavy body hurled itself upon his back and there was an excruciatingly sharp pain in the nape of his neck. He opened his mouth to shout, and no sound, only a gush of blood, came from it. He fell forward on his face.

Seven minutes later there was a great blinding flash and a roaring explosion that seemed to shake the whole island. Van Holk, with his scorn for what he called "piddling little dumps, impossible to guard properly," had, by insisting on hoarding the powder all in one place, played straight into the hands of whoever it was who was so anxious that there should be no ammunition in Banda Fort. And this time the damage was not confined, as on the previous occasion, to the powder and the isolated buildings which had housed it. All the main gateway of the Fort was blown up. The governor, whose palatial suite was immediately over it, was killed in his bed; and the hospital, which was directly behind the place where the powder had been stored, was entirely wrecked.

Voss's body, with its head half severed from behind, was not recovered until long after, when a new governor, planning a new front to the Fort, ordered the heaps of stone from the old one to be moved. The flesh had all gone from the bones by that time, but the knife which had killed him— a curved-bladed Malay kris—was still there, buried in the vertebrae of his skeleton. The sergeant's body, however,

stripped of its distinctive yellow shirt but clad in its breeches,
was found at the end of the wall. And nearby was a worn and
shabby coat of rust-coloured velvet, old-fashioned even
when judged by the standards of the gentlemen of Banda
who must wait a year for any news of a change in cut, and
then perhaps five more before they could take advantage of
it. But it was not the old-fangledness of the garment, nor its
worn silver-gilt buttons and obstinately clinging shreds of
tarnished lace, all so suggestive of past glory, which made it
significant in the horrified eyes of those planters and
merchants privileged to view it. For the coat had three
pockets, two in its skirts, one in its torn and dirty lining. And
in each pocket there was something which only a very
careless person—or a very cunning one—would have
discarded with the coat. In one was an English Book of
Common Prayer, in the edition sanctioned by Archbishop
Laud and made the subject of one of his acts of uniformity;
in another a simple leather purse, greasy from long usage
and containing fifteen shillings and fourpence in English
money; and in the small inner pocket was a letter, also
greasy, and frayed and worn very thin in the folds. It bore a
date, January 1648, and began, "My Own Dear Edward."

When Evert saw the coat and the contents of its pockets
they were laid out on the biggest desk in Kaerko's office. It
was still very early in the morning and the room faced west,
but Kaerko had drawn the shades over the window because
he had been crying and wished to hide the red rims of his
eyes. But this morning everyone's eyes were red-rimmed, for
nobody had slept much after that explosion, and certainly
nobody was in a mood to be critical.

"Well, what d'you make of that?" Kaerko asked; and
although Vehmeer and Van Heem and Lieutenant de Klerk
were all in the room, together with half a dozen others, he
looked straight at Evert.

"I can tell you what I'm intended to make of it," Evert
said. "It's all laid out as plain as print. I'm to think that an
Englishman came ashore last night, stabbed the sergeant, put
on his shirt and chucked away this coat, disposed of Voss,
somehow, and touched off the powder. I know English
money when I see it, and according to you, the book and the
letter are in the English lingo. All the same . . ."

"Well?"

"I may sound daft, but to my mind it's a little *too* plain. As though somebody said, 'Look in all my pockets and you'll see the same thing!' Do you see what I mean?"

"That it was put there deliberately to mislead us? That the guard was killed and the powder fired by—a native? But where, in the whole of Banda, would any native find these?" Kaerko pointed to the things upon the desk.

"They're all old," Evert said. "And we haven't always been at war with the English." He pondered for a moment and went off on another tack. "There's no sign of what happened to Voss. If, as De Klerk says, he would stand by the gate while the sergeant walked, it's easy to guess that he's now under the stones. But suppose the sergeant cried out and Voss ran to him? Has the ground around there been searched?"

"Thoroughly," said De Klerk. "There isn't cover for a rabbit, and the ground is sandy. There was no sign of a scuffle or of a body being dragged. I thought of that," he went on defensively. "As soon as I found the one body and knew that Voss was missing I searched with that in mind. Voss was my friend as well as my comrade in arms."

"Yes, yes, of course. Well, Voss is either under the stones or kidnapped. And if he was kidnapped by the English he's gone; but if it was a native job he's in the island somewhere. We must search."

"Shal Ahmi, by all accounts, is in the island somewhere," said Van Heem.

"But there is this difference. Shal Ahmi wants to remain in hiding. Voss, I take it, doesn't. I suggest that, just for the sake of making sure, we beat over the island again and yell his name in every alley, every compound. It may seem just a waste of time; it may *be* just a waste of time. But if Voss were alive and could be found he could tell us what we want to know."

Well, Evert thought, looking at Kaerko, if we're all agreed on that, give the order. Send me, go yourself, but for God's sake do something.

"Well," said Kaerko, "are we agreed on that, Then perhaps——"

"Perhaps Lieutenant de Klerk would collect a party and set out at once." Evert smiled at the smart young soldier and said disarmingly, "You must forgive me if I'm taking too much on myself, Lieutenant; it isn't for me to give you orders. But all at sixes and sevens as we are, and poor Kaerko here with everything on his hands——"

"You couldn't have given me a job more to my liking. If Voss is alive and in Banda I'll find him."

"I'd like to say we'd get the stones moved and make sure that way," Evert said. "But it'd take a week no matter how many men we turned onto it. And if he's under there he's dead and can't tell us anything."

De Klerk hurried away. A curious silence fell upon the roomful of men. Kaerko fingered the velvet of the coat and stared at it as though he hoped to learn something from its texture. Then suddenly he lifted his head and spoke.

"I suppose," he said, "the Company never imagined a situation like this when they sent us here. But now you see the weakness of their arrangements. Our world has fallen apart. We're at war with the English and have horrible reason to suppose that all is not well at home. The military authority, vested first in Knol and then in Van Holk, is busy elsewhere, the civil authority, in the person of His Excellency, has been blown to pieces. What is left? Sometimes I think," he said with a wild glance at Evert, "that I shall go mad."

The silence which he had so suddenly broken fell again. So much of what he said was so terribly true. Every man in the room had been obsessed with the production or the marketing of nutmegs. Now, in the face of danger, they were left without a rallying point. Dogs without a master. Sheep with no shepherd. Votaries of the sacred guilder, learning for the first time that money was nothing but a symbol.

"Nonsense, man," Evert said heartily. "We've lost our figureheads—but what are they except a decoration? We all had a shock last night, but we're none the worse for that. The governor, poor soul, is dead, and so are those poor crocks in the hospital. But all the real men are still alive. We've had sense enough to ask ourselves about *that*." He tapped the velvet coat with his finger. "If last night's business was the work of the English, Van Holk is paying them for it now; and if it was the work of the natives, we're ready and waiting for them. We're here, Kaerko, all of us, to plan the best means of defence. We're all free Dutchmen ready to defend ourselves. Isn't that so? We don't need anybody to tell us what to do or how to do it."

"I grant you," said old Cornelis Byskin in his reedy voice,

"that the governor and the wounded men in the hospital are no great loss materially. But the powder! Evert, doesn't your heart fail you when you realise that *twice* in so few days we have lost our powder?"

"Our powder? The public supply. The soldiers' powder, you mean. Did you ever stop to think, Cornelis, that if the Fort had been stuffed solid with powder and riots had broken out at places as far apart as, say, Vanderbosch's place and mine and Hansen's the soldiers, for all the good they'd be, might as well be armed with snowballs? Haven't you got powder of your own? And muskets? And pistols? Haven't you *three* men you could trust? Didn't you come out here with an idea that you might have to fight, as you worked, for yourself and your own? Don't you think I can't see danger as clearly as any man? I'm not a fool. Shal Ahmi warned the English; he broke gaol; he's still at large; and that coat with all its paraphernalia stinks of him, to my mind. *But* I've made sure that there isn't a firearm anywhere in Coenpark except in my house, and if the whole lot come against me with sticks and knives and torches I'm ready for them. They'll get a warm welcome. And if you all go home and take the same precautions we shall hang out until Van Holk comes back."

Cambellis, a merchant who lived in Banda Neira and who had actually been the first to throw himself into Kaerko's house, demanding wildly, "Now what shall we do?" spoke up in desperation.

"That's all very well for you, Haan, but we haven't all got compounds full of trustworthy natives. What about the town rabble? Did you happen to notice as you came along? Mobs of them, gossiping and staring. The secret is out now. They know that our backs are against the wall. All riots start in towns."

"I'll give them something to riot about," Evert said after a moment's reflection. "They can start clearing up that mess outside the Fort. A good day's work stone-carrying for everybody who shows his face in the street. What d'you think of that for a cure?"

Every member of the hastily assembled council approved of the idea, but it was Evert who went out into the burning day and shouted the orders.

Panic mounted by steady, almost imperceptible stages all

through that day. De Klerk, drawing blank after blank in search of Voss, sent a report to Kaerko from time to time, and the agent was secretly relieved that this new combing of the island had revealed nothing which called for immediate action. As the day wore on he went, at shortening intervals, to an upper room of his house where the window looked out over the harbour, and with his glass to his eye scanned the littering, dancing waters for some sign of Van Holk's return. It had taken Knol only sixteen hours to visit three islands and lose a battle; how long would it take Van Holk to attack one island and gain a victory?

By midafternoon the wretched little man was facing a new problem. From the outlying plantations of Lonthoir and other islands a trickle, and then a growing crowd, of frightened people began to pour into Banda Neira. The story of the finding of an English coat had spread rapidly and gathered a snowball layer of rumour and supposition as it travelled. The later arrivals fully believed that Van Holk's forces had been dispersed, that the English had attacked the town during the night and had been beaten off but would shortly attempt another landing at some unfortified spot. Planters, with their wives and their families, most of them accompanied by houseboys and maids, stewards and foremen known to be faithful, besieged Kaerko's house, avid for information, for advice, for comforting words. Kaerko was not without sympathy for them, but, as the Company's agent, he was much concerned for the safety of the plantations they had abandoned. Even at a moment like this he could not happily resign himself to the thought of work stopping in the groves, of ripe nuts falling to the ground to rot, or being left to the rapacious doves. And apart from that, a compound full of idle natives, left without direction or discipline, constituted a special danger at such a time.

Putting aside his ordinary human feelings, he forced himself to speak as agent to planter. "But the houses and the plantations are your property, held in trust for the Company. It is your duty to protect them. Who will if you don't?" Several of the men, relieved to find the true situation less serious than flying rumour had portrayed it, regretted their precipitancy and said they would go back as soon as they found accommodations for their families. Then their womenfolk cried and some refused to be parted and some said they would go home, too, if they could leave their children in safety, and at that the children cried too. And Kaerko scampered up the stairway and looked out towards the harbour again and prayed that he might catch a glimpse of the returning schooners. If only Van Holk could come back with news of a smashing victory and take charge!

By sunset, when Evert gave the signal for the stone-carrying work to cease, even he was exhausted. Four times during the long hot day he had gone home to Coenpark and found everything going on as usual. He was not surprised by that. Behind his cheerful, blustering, confident exterior he was suffering from a curious schism of mind. He *knew*, better than anyone in the islands, that Shal Ahmi was up to something, was in league with the English, was hidden somewhere and doubtless planning fresh devilry. Yet he could not, for the life of him, believe in the logical outcome of Shal Ahmi's plans and action. The blessed lack of imagination which had been such an asset to his career in the past prevented him, as he looked upon his placid slaves going about their work, from seeing them as anything but peaceful slaves. He had gone through all the motions of credulity and preparation. Josef, Hassan, the foreman, Toeg, and half a dozen others had been partly taken into confidence and armed; Isa, pretending to be taking Katje's place, went to and fro between house and compound, warned to keep eyes and ears open. Not even the most frightened, most suspicious man—not Vanderbosch himself—could have done more. Yet as he looked at his big, lovely, silent house dreaming away the afternoon within its circle of shrubs and flowers Evert could no more imagine it with its windows smashed, its doors battered in, its walls charred by fire, than he could have imagined himself as a feeble, drooling invalid. All the same, his own sense told him that Shal Ahmi hadn't organised that ambush on Ay or twice had the powder reserves destroyed in order that everything in Banda should go on as usual. It behoved a man, even if he couldn't quite believe in a threatened danger, to be wary and careful. But as after his fourth visit Evert had himself rowed swiftly back to town, intending to send his mob of labourers home—too tired, if he knew anything, to get into much mischief during the night—and pay a last visit to Kaerko and then return to look after his own house and plantation, he found himself wishing that something definite and irrefutable would happen. Something to clear the air. Something which would point to a focus for attack. The nervous strain to which even he had been subjected in the last few days took the form of impatience, unlike Kaerko's which evidenced itself in a prayer for a delay, for the deferment of the moment the threat ceased to be academic.

He dismissed his gang of involuntary labourers cheerfully, yelling at them in Dutch and Malay that they had worked very well and that there was food for all who wanted it at the bottom of the drill yard. He had commissioned Van Heem and Vehmeer to collect food during the day. "Good stodgy stuff, as much as possible," he had said. "And no liquor. We don't want an orgy. I reckon that tired limbs and a full belly'll keep 'em quiet till morning anyway." Van Heem and Vehmeer had amassed a great quantity of food, and as Evert saw the men, women, and children trail away, tired, grateful, cheerful, he thought: And *they* don't look dangerous either! Then he looked behind him, across the drill yard to the Fort, smashed like honeycomb, and felt another stab of impatience at the intangibility of the danger.

"Let's go and see Kaerko," he said, laying a heavy arm on his companion's shoulders.

"There's no news," Van Heem said heavily. "I looked in less than an hour ago. The Hansens were there then, the whole family. Kaerko was suggesting that you should put them up, but Mevrouw Hansen said she hadn't left the Dyke in order to go to Coenpark, which was just as isolated. So they're up at my place now. That makes sixteen."

"We've got twenty-two," said Vehmeer. "Old Graef of Lonthoir arrived. He'd remembered all his bastards and rounded them up from the compound. Twelve of them. You never saw such a collection of dirty, ugly-looking little devils. Jehane is madder than a pye-dog. But when old Graef tackled me he'd got just his wife and his white lot with him then; the rest were round the corner somewhere. I offered him hospitality and he went off. Then, just as I was weighing out the rice, Jehane sent for me to come home at once, and there were all those little brown beggars. What could I do? The poor old chap had tears in his eyes. 'They're as much mine, Mevrouw, as these,' he kept saying. Nice for Mevrouw Graef with her own pretty little brood. And the old beggar old enough to be her father. Funny, though, how blood counts for more than colour at a moment like this."

"I can't understand these fellows at all," Evert said. "As soon as I've seen Kaerko I'm going home, and if there's any trouble that's where I shall stay. I look after Coenpark and Banda must look after itself."

"That's senseless. You'd do far better to bring your wife in and stay here until it's all over. Here at least we might hold out until Van Holk returns, if we all stick together. One man, even a bold one, Evert, doesn't stand a chance all alone."

"I shan't be alone," said Evert shortly. "And I'm not sure yet that anything *will* happen. I've been thinking about things all day and I—— By God, I believe I see through it." He brought his hand down on Van Heem's back in a blow that almost felled him. "I see now. It *is* the English at the back of it all—not Shal Ahmi. He's just a tool. Their tool. I'll bet they fooled the old boy who boasted that he couldn't be fooled. They told him they were going to land and drive us out of here and promised him everything under the sun if he dropped them a word in season and saw that the powder was kept short. And here we've been thinking of nothing but bloody rebellion. Slave rebellion, my backside! Where'd we get that into our heads from?"

"From past history," said Van Heem dryly.

Evert gave a grunt of scorn and disgust. "Folks remember too much, too long," he said, and, releasing his hold upon his companions, leaped ahead of them up the steps of Kaerko's house, eager to lay the result of his cogitation before somebody who would be glad to hear it.

De Klerk was with the agent. His round boyish face was drawn and tired and flushed with dark dry heat. Kaerko, who seemed to have grown smaller and greyer in the few hours since the morning, was perched upon the edge of his desk, his feet in the seat of his chair. De Klerk was blurting out some story in a hasty, shamefaced manner.

"There's not a sign of Shal Ahmi," he said. "I've searched everywhere and made a proper fool of myself, but he's still not found."

"Well, unless the English actually land here," said Evert, going back to his own inspired train of thought, "I don't think we need worry about the natives or Shal Ahmi. I can't think there's riot planned; we'd have found some sign during all these searches. If there were any chance of an English landing, maybe we might be stabbed in the back. But Van Holk will see that doesn't happen."

"He's already been away longer than Knol was," said Kaerko drearily.

"Burning them out. Knol simply bounced back. There's the difference," said Evert cheerfully, forgetting that he disliked Van Holk intensely. "Well, if that's all, I'll get home. Look, I came by prahau, but I'll walk back. If anything should happen—of interest, shall we say—one of you give my man the word and send him home. . . . Thanks. Good night, Kaerko. Get some sleep, you look as though you could do with it. Good night, Vehmeer. I hope your lodgers behave themselves. If you see Cambellis, Van Heem, tell him that we've overworked and overfed his mob, and they're all sleeping like pigs. Good night, De Klerk, and don't you worry." He nodded and grinned to each as he spoke, then strode away, slamming the door as was his habit; and something of cheer and confidence went with him. Every one of the four men he left was conscious for a moment of the length and the loneliness of the path to Coenpark—and it was dark now, and things were unsettled, to say the very least.

Before Evert entered his house he made a round of the compound. Everything was just as it had been on a thousand nights before. He looked in upon Toeg, ostensibly to give some orders about the work in the morning, and heard with his ears what his eyes had already seen, everything peaceful and quiet. He stopped Josef on his way to the kitchen and told him to serve dinner at once. Then he entered the house. And at once a curious feeling of flatness came upon him.

In the old days Isa had always been waiting like a faithful, yearning little dog, or like a child. She would hide behind a bank of flowers, or just within a room, or on the curve of the stairs, and then call or jump out upon him, welcoming him with little cries and clasps and kisses. In more recent times there had been Annabet, beautiful, silky, smooth, and scented, waiting for him in the drawing room, or coming downstairs towards him with a smile and words of welcome, with a readiness to hear his news.

Tonight, as for several nights past, there was no welcome. Isa had changed; probably she was jealous and couldn't understand why he kept Annabet in the house if he had finished with her, or, more likely, she was shy of showing her feelings before the white woman. And Annabet was like somebody dead. Last night he'd kissed Isa at the dining table and Annabet hadn't even looked away. He could neither hurt nor provoke nor shame her. She looked like a dead woman too. In another few days, if this state of affairs went on, she'd be as scraggy as she had been on her arrival.

All day he had been too busy, both in mind and body, to give a thought to his domestic cares. But now, coming into the quiet house, he knew that he wanted somebody to talk to. There was so much to tell. His own cleverness about the English coat, his day's work, his final seeing through the whole business, De Klerk's failure to find Shal Ahmi. And Isa was no good as a listener.

He mounted the stairs more slowly than usual. He was very tired. All this business was a strain on a man—and when things were wrong at home too! And everywhere he went there were the miserable beggars gaping at him, wanting to be cheered and bolstered up.

He was conscious of a sudden, unfamiliar feeling of depression. What's the matter with me? he asked himself. I've been in worse straits than this and never felt downhearted. Short of sleep and empty-bellied, that's what it is. Feel better when I've fed.

He went into his own room and washed his hands and splashed the cool water against his face. Something tinkled in the next room—Isa at the dressing table. Surly little beast, prinking her damned face and letting him come into a house that felt like a tomb.

He sat down on the side of his bed, and his eyes lighted upon the brandy flask on the bedside table. A good drink, that was what he needed. If Kaerko wasn't a watery-blooded codfish he'd have seen to it that there was some liquor in his damned office. We do his work, Evert thought crossly, and he won't even wet our whistles for us. And he'll get all the credit.

He drank from the flask and waited for a moment, hoping to feel better. Then he rose and went out to the gallery, halting outside the door of the blue-and-white room. "What's the matter with you? Are you sick?" he shouted. "You've had all day to get ready."

Isa opened the door and stood there, sulky, seductive, a little defensive, as she always was these days. Why in hell, he demanded of himself, had he been fool enough to think that he could get any pleasure out of putting her in Annabet's place?

The door of the little room at the end of the gallery opened quietly and Annabet stepped out. She looked ill, very pale and wasted, but her hair was smooth and shining and the old rag of a dress had been washed and pressed during the day.

"So you're ready too," he said roughly, angered by his own mixed feelings. "Nobody to greet me, oh no," he went on, forgetting he had forbidden her to leave her room. "But both of you ready at feeding time. Worse than a couple of dogs. Even monkeys'd show some signs of welcome."

Isa flashed one of her curious inscrutable glances and did not speak. Annabet, after a second's hesitation, said quietly:

"I was actually very anxious to see you, Evert. Is there any news?"

"Maybe," he said grudgingly. Why should the prospect of telling her about his day give him pleasure? Did she deserve to be taken into the confidence of decent men? He looked at her and all at once felt quite sick with self-pity. At a moment like this, when there was danger and uncertainty outside, if only he'd been sure of his wife. I'd have shed my last drop of blood for her, he thought melodramatically.

The odd trio went down the stairs and into the dining room in silence. Then something in the quality of Evert's speechlessness told Annabet that he was longing to talk. As she lifted her knife and fork she called up the memory of Mamma's training. Pretend that Evert is a stranger, she thought, pretend that there is nothing between us save the necessity of dining together and making agreeable conversation.

It worked. Her voice came out clear and steady and gracious.

"What have you been doing all day, Evert? What has been happening in Banda?"

He told them both about the English coat; about the killing of the guard and the destruction of the Fort—all the things which everyone in Banda knew by that time. Then, with a cold imperative glance, he dismissed Isa. "Go and help Josef make the coffee, Isa. You do it better than he does."

And then, with a sweet sense of relief and home-coming which he did not recognise for what it was, he told Annabet about his own inspiration as to the true position between the English and Shal Ahmi. Almost against his will he went on:

"I reckon that if you hadn't helped him it would have made no difference. He'd have found somebody else."

It was no longer an impersonal discussion of outside news; no longer a mere dinner-table conversation. How could it be? The very silence shouted "Christy Ayrton" in a voice louder than thunder. Evert wanted to cry out, "Oh, why did you do it? Why must you love somebody else? Why wasn't I enough for you?"

Isa sidled in with the coffee.

A meal and a rest restored Evert's body, and talking to Annabet disturbed his mind and he decided not to go to bed. His boatman might come back with news—that was the excuse he gave himself. Twice before midnight he walked down to the little jetty and stood staring along the narrow inlet of water between the nutmeg trees. Tonight there was a slip of moon like a tendril of hair in the sky and no clouds over the multitudinous stars, and the little night wind with its burden of spices crept about in the open spaces. Evert's incongruous susceptibility to beauty was heightened and quickened by the tension of his nerves. As he walked he dreamed. Van Holk would come back victorious and all this nonsense would be forgotten. All the English would be killed, and that would dispose of Christy Ayrton. He would punish Annabet for a little while longer and then he would send Isa away. All would be well.

Each time as he turned back from the inlet of sea he took the path which led to the compound. Everything there was quiet. Before the huts the little fires or the smouldering charcoal braziers which had been used for the cooking of the evening meal were damped down under handfuls of leaves whose smoke kept the voracious insects at bay. It was all as he had seen it on a thousand nights before. There was even the baby wailing softly in the cabin nearest the cluster of kendri trees. For a full five years there had always been a baby there.

He went back to the house, snuffed the candles, drank a glass of schnapps and chewed a hard biscuit, and visualised for a moment both his women sound asleep upstairs: Isa snuggled in the luxury of the blue-and-white bed, Annabet stretched upon the hard mattress of her tiny one. Once again he was surprised to find that he felt no pleasure in the contrast; once again he admitted to himself that fetching Isa back had been a mistake.

But in this state of unusual physical exhaustion, awake alone in this unfamiliar night hour, he realised that he had been mistaken in his treatment of Annabet from the very beginning. He should have had sense enough to see that in the ugly twisted scarecrow thing which the *Java* had brought him something very special and precious lay hidden. She'd been friendly and intelligent then, eager to please, his for the taking. If only he'd waited. I was as much to blame for things going wrong as she was, he thought, and on the day when she says she loves me I'll tell her so.

Lighting a candle and drawing it close, he looked once more to the priming of his pistols. Thinking of those days after Annabet's arrival had brought Shal Ahmi into his mind. He lingered over his belief that Shal Ahmi was harmless unless the English came to Banda, which they could never do, never in a thousand years. But at the same time he thought, with comfortable assurance and some pride, of his own canny arrangements in case of trouble. Of Josef and the four picked men sleeping in the kitchen beside the harmless-looking bread bin packed with arms and powder; of Hassan and Toeg and his two brothers, armed and warned in the cabin in the very centre of the compound; of himself, so wary and clever. One more prowl round, he thought, and then he would try to get a little sleep.

There was still no sign of Tas, the boatman. But no news, in this case, was good news, because if Van Holk had run into trouble as Knol had done they'd have heard in Banda by now. He waited by the jetty for some moments, more in idleness than expectation; then for the third time he walked through the compound and saw nothing, heard nothing. He looked into the kitchen, which seemed for a moment to be in inky darkness but which presently lightened into shades of grey of varying density. He could distinguish the five sleeping forms. As a test he said, "Josef," quite softly, and instantly one body stirred, rose on an elbow, and said, "Mynheer" in the same suppressed tone.

"Everything is all right, Josef. I'm just having a last look round."

He went back into the house and dragged a long chair into the passage that ran between the living rooms and the kitchen. He set his little oil lamp beside the chair and laid his pistols beside it. He kicked off his boots and loosened his collar and the top of his breeches. He intended to doze lightly, keeping one ear open for any sound of Tas, whom he had told to come to the back door.

He was just about to stretch himself in the chair when the door handle moved. Tas! News of Van Holk! Bootless, empty-handed, he ran to the door and wrenched it open. As it swung back a musket went off in his face. In less than a second he had time to feel a scorching, searing pain somewhere in the region of his right ear, to think, So it's started, and to know that he was not much hurt. His hands shot out and closed upon bare warm flesh. A musket clattered as it fell. The man within his grasp wriggled, and Evert felt the point of a knife pierce his left arm at the wrist. He freed his right hand and swung it in a great blow. He felt his knuckles split against hard bone and heard, with atavistic pleasure, a sharp crack. The body he held turned heavy and slumped downwards, almost dragging him with it. He let it fall.

Ah, he could see now. He snatched up the musket and brought the butt of it down twice upon the face of the man who lay at his feet. Tried to kill me, did you? he thought. Wonder who it was; ought to have looked first. Can't recognise him now, just a bloody mash. Where're my brave chaps in the kitchen? They must have heard the shot. Ah, they're moving now. Must get my boots on; a man's helpless without boots if he's used to them. Damn this blood, you'd think I'd been pig-killing.

He stamped his feet into their boots, took up his pistols, remembered the dead man's musket, and tucked it under his arm. One more gift from heaven, he thought.

As he turned towards the kitchen Josef came out. He had a musket under his arm, a pistol in one hand.

"Mynheer, it has begun."

"I know, somebody just tried to kill me. Come on."

"Yes, Mynheer."

Josef's voice and manner were as calm as though Evert had merely asked him to put some forgotten thing upon the dining table. They belied the secret sickness of his heart. Josef was not brave; he had not even the optimistic recklessness of youth. He had always lived softly, and he hated the sight and the thought of blood. But the whole of his life had been spent in obedience to his white masters, and for fifteen of those years Evert had been his master, and now, in war as in peace, he was prepared to come and go and do and speak exactly as Evert directed. Of the four men with him, two were old and had lived at Coenpark ever since Evert had owned it, and two were boys whom Evert had destined for the recruiting draft and then withdrawn. Disappointed at being soldiers in the ordinary professional sense, they were keen to prove their value as amateurs. These four, with Hassan, Toeg, and his two brothers across the compound, comprised the whole of Evert's secret force. He had argued that, the more people were let into a secret, the less the chance of its remaining one, and that nine men, all trustworthy and properly armed, were better than a mob.

In this, although he did not know it, Evert's instinctive common sense had led him to precisely the same conclusion as Shal Ahmi's wily, convoluted reasoning. There were at that moment in the Coenpark compound only nine revolutionaries. There had been ten, but the tenth lay dead now on the path outside the house door, his mission unfulfilled. Shal Ahmi had depended more upon strategy than upon numbers. The numbers were there, a vast horde of stupid coolies, flaccid as seaweed, ready to sway with the tide. But every one of Shal Ahmi's selected men was a fanatic, carefully chosen, sternly tested, and every one was a direct descendent, either son or grandson or great-grandson, of one of those pure-blooded Bandanese women who had been brought back from Java to work as slaves upon the soil that their fathers had owned and died to retain.

Out of this revolutionary nucleus one man had been chosen on every plantation to perform the most dangerous and difficult task of all, the striking of the first blow. And there again Shal Ahmi's and Evert's utterly dissimilar minds had shown a kinship. Evert had said, "I believe in shooting at the head." Shal Ahmi had arranged for the quiet assassination of every planter. Once that was done, his few tried adherents could take charge, overcome any dissentients, and stop the outbreak of trouble between the ill-united factions, who, as soon as the white control was removed, would take the opportunity of avenging their age-old grievances and grudges.

The methods for the assassinations varied and had been left fluid. Evert, whose house servants slept apart, was to be killed indoors if entry could be gained to the house. Byskin, whose slaves slept all over the house, even along the upper passages, was to be killed on his regular night visit to the earth closet in the shrubbery. Van Heem's intelligent, embittered bastard son had been entrusted with the task of avenging his discarded Bandanese mother's wrong and the slur on his own birth. Boender's deathblow was to be struck by a house slave who, five years earlier, had been shipped and temporarily degraded to plantation work for stealing. He was not a thief, and when the truth was discovered, Boender, a sentimentalist where natives were concerned, had made a public proclamation, restored the man to his old position, and bought the Chinese girl whom he wanted for a wife. But the injustice had rankled, and Shal Ahmi had taken advantage of it. Nothing had been arranged hastily; no trouble had been spared. Over the whole of Banda and Lonthoir his nets had been spread, and some of them had taken years to lay. Since the day when he had conspired with Mynheer Haan to smuggle nutmegs to the English, Shal Ahmi had known that the day of vengeance would dawn; but it would not be only, as the Dutch fondly imagined, the vengeance of the Dutch upon English.

But Evert, alienated from Annabet and tired of Isa, had chosen to sleep on a chair in the passage and had been expecting Tas, the boatman, with news. The door which his assassin had softly tried had opened unexpectedly; the musket had been fired wildly; the knife blade had only provoked reprisal. And the nine conspirators, awake, waiting for Fernando's return with word that the job was done, had still to reckon with Evert himself.

The compound was humming like a beehive. The single shot had wakened a number of the lighter sleepers, and they had wakened the others. Here and there men had come to the low doorway; here and there women had lighted the little oil lamps. Shal Ahmi's men, with their brand-new muskets and pistols and knives, stood ready in their secret, separate places. Tani Amani, malaria-ridden, an old man of fifty, whose mother had served a princess in the palace upon whose ruins Kaerko's office now stood, and who had been appointed the chief of the Coenpark revolutionaries, drew long deep breaths and counted them, waiting for the moment of glory.

But it was Evert's voice which roared through the compound; roared in Dutch, and then in the Malay, which he had never mastered properly, that the first person to poke a head out of a hut would have his brains blown out. Roared for Ramjit Singh to step outside and ordered that everything he said be repeated in Tamil, clearly, audibly. Roared for four little boys from the cabin under the kendri trees to throw twigs upon the smouldering braziers.

Then Tani Amani knew that the moment of glory had come, but in shape other than he had hoped. As soon as the flames leaped and the starlight was dimmed by the glow of the little fires he pushed aside the mat that covered his doorway, lifted his musket, and fired at his master. The bullet actually tore away a piece of Evert's shirt sleeve. I'm lucky, Evert thought. Aloud he said, "Get him," to his two young men. "Don't give him time to reload."

But Tani Amani had a new pistol too. He waited until the young men were within a few paces and then fired it into the face of the taller one. The young man's cheek was blown away. He was stunned for a second and then remembered that his master's face had been horribly injured, too, but that hadn't stopped him. His hands were sharing the burden of Tani Amani when they brought him over to Evert.

"We'll be scarred on the same side," Evert said, and whipped round like a snake to fire into the unglazed window of another hut, from which one of Tani Amani's confederates was taking aim. Evert had felt, with the seventh sense of an old soldier, the danger behind him and, turning, had seen the glint of light upon the barrel of the musket.

"Get him," he said to Josef and the other older man. And to the two youngsters, "Chuck Tani into the well." Then, seeing them hesitate, "Go on. He tried to kill you, didn't he?"

Tani made no outcry, but as the splash sounded a woman somewhere began to scream, and in several huts the noise was taken up.

Josef and his companion made for the hut from which the threatened rebel shot had failed to be fired. And then for a few seconds it did seem that hell had broken loose in the compound. No one human eye could take note of all that happened, and the noise confused the ear. From the hut upon which Josef was bearing down a frightened screaming woman emerged and threw herself on the ground, clutching at the houseboy's knees. Simultaneously three shots rang out from the other side of the compound, and the boy with the wounded face fell flat, squealing. Evert took the unfired pistol from his hand and aimed it at the man who had shot the boy. Toeg and his brothers closed around a third hut, while from a fourth a man emerged on his belly, crept like a snake to the rear of it, and from there fired at Evert again. The bullet struck the front of his leg and emerged at the back, missing the bone and the main artery by a hairsbreadth. Stung by the pain and mad with the lust for battle, Evert yelled, "Missed me! Try again!" And though the words were lost in tumult, the man seemed to obey him. He showed half his face around the hut, taking aim with one eye. Evert fired and blew his hand off.

And then suddenly it was all over. In the grove the birds, disturbed by the tumult, settled down again with a flutter of wings and little cries. In the compound there was only the sound of screaming women and the yelling of frightened children. The smoke and the stench of the gunpowder sullied the spicy air.

Evert sat down upon the wall of the well and lifted his leg to the same level. As an older soldier, he knew the danger of leg wounds. Expertly, with steady hands, he took out his knife, slit the seam of his breeches, pulled the cloth aside, and tied his handkerchief tightly about the wound. Then deliberately he looked over his little force. The boy whose face had been hurt lay where he had dropped, felled by his second wound. Josef had been shot through the shoulder, and dark streams of blood were streaking his brown chest, but he was holding fast to his prisoner. One of the older men stood with his foot on the small of the back of a fellow who lay prone, but alive and groaning. The younger man held a wriggling captive by the neck. Three. One down the well. One still lying behind the hut from whose cover he had shot Evert. Five. There had been more than five enemy shots.

"Turn out every hut from which a shot was fired," said Evert to Hassan. "Down the well with those. Then reload. There may be more trouble."

Two of the prisoners screamed as they went over. Evert, sitting within a foot of their passage from life to death, never even looked their way. He was reloading his pistols and at the same time keeping his eyes upon the huts in which he suspected rebels to be lurking still.

"Now," he said. "Everybody out of there, and there, and there." He pointed. "Go boldly. I'm covering you."

Only one of the four remaining showed any fight. He shot Hassan as he kicked the door open, and immediately after

was picked off by Evert. The other three allowed themselves
to be led out. One man was followed by a little crowd, two
young women, an old one, and a horde of children. As they
were rounded into the centre of the compound, towards the
well and the cold-eyed man who sat upon its rim, the women
and children screamed like banshees and threw themselves
upon the ground. The man to whom they belonged ran
forward, not waiting to be kicked and prodded towards his
doom. With clasped hands he flung himself at Evert's feet.
"Mercy for my women and little ones. They knew nothing.
They had no share."

"I may consider that. On conditions," said Evert stonily.
"Stand aside with your brood. Over with the others,
Hassan."

Even the screaming women fell silent, listening to the
splashes. Even the children hushed. There was a deadly,
horrified silence in the compound.

"Now," said Evert, "make up the fires. All the fires. And
you, Ramjit, repeat this order. Everybody is to come out and
sit on the ground immediately in front of his cabin." He
bellowed the order in Dutch and Malay himself.

One by one the cabins opened and the mutual crowds who
had crouched with indoors listening to the shots and the
screams and the orders crept out silently and seated
themselves exactly as Evert had bidden them.

"Now, listen to me, all of you," said Evert loudly. "There
has been a plot afoot. But for my vigilance and the valour of
these few with me, you and I, with our families and dear
ones, would have been slain in our sleep before this night was
out. Ten of your comrades, ten of my people, have been
possessed by the devil and were bent upon murdering us all.
Repeat that, Ramjit."

The man who had so far been spared moved and looked
as though he were about to speak. Evert glanced significantly
at the cluster of women and children and then at the gaping
mouth of the well. The man stiffened.

"I will now find out for you the name of the devil who
planned this thing. Kari Adoad will tell us." He lowered his
voice, but in the tense silence every word which he addressed
to the man in an almost genial, conversational tone was
clearly audible. "Kari Adoad, who inspired this foul deed?
Who made this devilish plot?"

"Mynheer, I do not know. I never saw or spoke with him.
Tani Amani carried the orders. . . ."

"Come here," said Evert gently. "Look into the well. See the end of Tani Amani, the fitting end of all who carry the devil's orders. Would you join him? Who gave the orders? I know, Kari Adoad. I could speak the name now. But I want your fellows to hear it from your lips."

"Mynheer, I do not——"

"Lift the youngest child, Josef. Here." He jerked his head significantly over his shoulder. The youngest and prettiest of Kari's women screamed and grabbed at the child. Josef pushed her aside.

"I will speak, Mynheer," said Kari Adoad in a dead voice.

"Turn then to the others and speak clearly. Who gave orders for the murder of us all?"

"Shal Ahmi, but, Mynheer, he never——"

"That will do. You all heard what the man says, and remember, the truth, when wrung out of a man, is always the simple truth. Shal Ahmi, he says, ordered the massacre." He repeated the statement in Malay, and Ramjit Singh echoed it in Tamil.

"And what did he promise you and these"—he jerked his thumb towards the well—"when we should all be dead? With what promises did he bribe you to wickedness?"

"Mynheer——"

"I wait, Kari Adoad, and the water waits."

"Mynheer, he promised that things should be as they were in the days of our forefathers. He spoke of peace and plenty and said that we should be kings and princes, as were our fathers before us."

"You hear?" said Evert. "For the benefit of a handful of those whose forebears lived in the islands the rest of us were to be slain. You and you and you"—he pointed to a few men selected at random—"and me." He touched his own breast. "Our lives were of no importance if by dying we gave back the glory of ancient Banda. You and your wives and children, me and my wife must die that Kari Adoad might be a king and a prince." He allowed this piece of information to sink in and then turned back to Kari.

"Where is Shal Ahmi now?"

"Mynheer, that I do not know. By the graves of my ancestors I swear I do not know. Mynheer, be merciful. If you dropped them all into the well one by one before my eyes and then tore out my eyes I could not tell. I do not know."

"Try it," said Evert, and signalled to Josef.

The youngest child was a little girl. Great black eyes, wide with bewilderment, shone in her little brown face. Her long black hair streamed over Josef's hands as he lifted her. Her mother screamed again and called wildly to Kari to tell everything, anything, to think of nothing but the child. Tears and sweat poured down the father's face and body. As Josef held the little creature over the well, waiting for the final signal, Kari made a convulsive movement. "I cannot tell you what I do not know," he cried in a terrible voice, and lunged forward. Evert, aware of his precarious position upon the well edge, moved to set his injured leg on the ground. Toeg made a dive for Kari and caught him, but at the same time Josef put out a hand to steady Evert; and the child, feeling some support withdrawn, screamed and twisted, trying to put her small arms around Josef's neck. She slipped and with another piercing, dreadful scream disappeared into the water. Her mother, with a cry that set all the birds in the grove fluttering from their perches again, pushed her way through the ring of guards and jumped into the well herself.

Nobody in the outer circle moved or made a sound. Kari sobbed aloud. Evert put his leg up again and adjusted the handkerchief which had been disturbed.

"That was your doing, Kari Adoad," he said calmly. Then, sweeping his eyes around the compound, he went on. "There are now ten bodies in this well; you see the fate of those who aim to be kings and princes," he warned. "The devil is strong and still at large; tomorrow or the next day he may be here again, promising to make kings and princes of more of you who will pay the price in blood. On that day remember the end of Tani Amani and of Kari Adoad, for as I live, I swear that such shall be the end of any man who dares to take an order from anyone but me." He signalled to his men again and Kari went to join his wife, his child, and his former conspirators.

He rose then, concealing with difficulty a grimace of pain as he put his foot to the ground. "Nail up the well," he said to his foreman. "They must fetch water from the spring until we can dig anew. The old will serve to keep the memory of this night alive."

He turned and was hobbling away when a middle-aged woman ran out from the seated ranks and knelt before him. She was the mother of the boy who had been first wounded and then killed by the conspirators.

"I may take his body, Mynheer?" she asked, and pointed.

"Assuredly." He put his heavy hand on her shoulder. "Your son died honourably, having fought like a good soldier." He peered at her in the firelight. Hindu. "There is no doubt that in his next life he will be a great warrior. As for you and any other of his kin, the bread of idleness shall be spread for you in my compound for the rest of your days. May they be many."

Annabet had heard the first shot and leaped out of bed without any very clear idea of where to go or what to do. As she dragged on her gown and thrust her feet into her slippers she heard a door open along the gallery and a series of heavy bumps. She tore open her door, expecting to find Evert dragging out muskets and powder pouches. But it was only Isa, quite calm, surrounded by bundles of various sizes which she was carrying a short distance towards the stairs, dropping, and then going back for more. Incongruously Annabet thought of backstitching.

Isa stiffened when she saw Annabet, but she did not pause. "They were given to me," she said defensively. "And now that this has come you will never need them again."

She threw a heavy bundle wrapped in a towel towards the head of the stairs and dashed back for another, slightly smaller, knotted in one of Annabet's silk petticoats.

Annabet had seen that Evert's door stood open; a glance showed her that the room was empty. Ignoring Isa, she ran towards the stairs, thinking, I could load muskets if I were shown. . . . I must help. . . . I must help. . . .

Downstairs the house was in darkness and she felt her way along the hall and as far as the door at the head of the passage to the kitchen. It was locked. She imagined that upon the farther side she could hear movement and voices, and she beat on the door and shouted, "Evert!" at the top of her voice. But Evert was at that moment mustering his men and had forgotten her very existence. As she stood there she heard the outer door slam. She turned and felt her way into the hall again, turned down the shorter passage which led to Evert's little office, and found its door locked.

The hall was dimly lighted when she returned. Isa had set a candle at the stair top and was now getting her bundles down. Some she merely threw and they fell limp and heavy, like dead bodies. Others she carried down and then raced lightly up the stairs again.

"I don't think you'll get them any farther," said Annabet. "We're locked in."

Isa paused halfway up the stairs. "Every door?"

"Yes, look." Annabet tried the door of the dining room and of the parlour. "The office, too, and the door behind the stairs."

"Then I shall throw them out of the window and jump out myself," said Isa, and she ran down the stairs and seized the towel-wrapped bundle in arms that looked too frail to lift anything a quarter of its size.

A burst of musket and pistol fire sounded from the compound.

"They'll be here," said Isa, anxious, but not frightened. "They'll take some of my things." She looked at her scattered bundles as a flustered mother hen might look at her chickens. And then suddenly her face changed.

"Mevrouw! They will rob me. But they will kill you." She clutched the bundle to her body and over it looked at Annabet. Her face was like a flower. "I would not wish them to kill you," she said simply.

"I'm prepared to be killed," said Annabet truthfully. And wildly melodramatic as the statement sounded, it was nothing more than the truth. Her recent moods of self-hatred, despair, and resignation had seen death as the inevitable—indeed, desirable—thing. And although at this moment there was sickness in her stomach and a cold crepitation pervading her flesh, they were only the physical reactions to threatened danger. In her mind she was as calm and detached as Isa. "I'm prepared to be killed. But I should like to help Evert first."

"Oh, no one can help him now," said Isa, without emotion but with great certainty. "They are too many. All day I have gone about the compound spying and have caught no word. That means that all are in it, since without sign it comes. He is dead now, Mynheer Haan. Listen."

There was another burst of firing and then silence. "All is over. Soon they will remember the house." She dashed to the top of the stairs and threw the bundle along the gallery. Then she ran back and, looking down, said, "The thought has come to me. Help me to carry away the things that were given me and you shall be safe. Come, come quickly." She skipped down the stairs again and dragged Annabet by the hand upstairs and into the blue-and-white room, where now nothing seemed to remain except the immovable pieces of furniture and a few discarded native clothes tossed into a corner. Her little red-tipped fingers that looked so indolent and helpless fell upon Annabet, hard and rapid as a monkey's paws. Off with the dressing gown and the night robe and on with the tattered dirty finery which Isa had not thought worth while to carry with so many more valuable things to care for.

Annabet stood neither helping nor hindering the flying hands. She had not thought of escape. She had wanted to help Evert, but every door had been locked. My life will end as it has been led, she thought, in futility. Nothing I ever started has reached its appointed end. Even my death will be silly. And if Isa but knew it, she will be bound to lose every bit of loot she entrusts to me. But let it go. Christy is dead by this time, and Evert. Let me serve as pack horse to a little native girl. . . .

Isa slit a garment with a sound like a shriek. "It'll cover your face," she said, dropping it upon Annabet's unresisting head. "Pretend to be old, stoop. That is, if anyone sees us. Now."

She abandoned her dressing of Annabet in native clothes as abruptly as a child might cease dressing a doll. "Help me with the bundles!" She ran to the open windows and flung back the curtains.

Annabet picked up the towel-wrapped bundle and dropped it into the rose bed beneath the window. How often had the scent of those short-lived roses come up into the room while she was dreaming of Christy—or trying to give Evert his due—or confusing one with the other. . . .

There was no sound now from the compound, but there were fires. Trudi van Heem had spoken of the shots and the screams and the fires; she had said that it was like hell. Perhaps hell started without any loud announcement, like love or growing up. Perhaps this was hell itself, silly and meaningless. Perhaps one's hell was like one's life, silly and meaningless without being really bad. Dressed like a native girl, throwing bundles out of a window, with Christy dead and Evert. Christy and Evert, linked together at last in the chains of death. And she soon, uncaring, to join them. "No marriage nor giving in marriage." The preacher had said that in the Heydberg church. Suppose, purgatory passed, she should meet Christy and Evert again, stripped of their bodies, clad in their souls. I wouldn't know either of them, she thought, dismayed. And they would not know me. All along it's been body, body, body. Hair, eyes, mouths, hands, voices. All perishable as the petals on my cherry tree.

"It'd be quicker if I just handed you the parcels and you dropped them out," said Isa. Her voice was quite sharp and authoritative. "There, that's as much as we can hope to carry," she said, throwing across a bundle of what felt like shoes. "Now we must jump."

"I don't think I could," said Annabet, voicing the conviction that had seized her as she dropped out the first bundle.

"You must," said Isa. "There's no other way out. You'll be killed if you stay here. And I want your help." She came and stood by the window. "It's not far. Get up on the sill and put your feet out, then drop." Short of putting up violent resistance, Annabet could see that she would be pushed out as unceremoniously as one of the bundles. Just then a door slammed heavily in the lower part of the house. "Oh, be quick," said Isa, "they're coming, they're coming." She spoke with such urgency that one would have thought it was her life, not her loot, which was in jeopardy. She weighed the problem of whether to jump herself and run to and fro with the bundles, or whether to spend a few valuable seconds forcing the stupid white woman through the window and having the advantages of her services as a porter. She chose the latter and had actually heaved Annabet onto the sill and was about to thrust her forth when the voice that neither of them expected to hear again rang through the house. From the bottom of the stairs Evert was calling imperatively.

"Mynheer. He is alive still," said Isa with surprise but little joy in her voice. She stepped back, and Annabet lost her balance and fell into the room. Isa stood undecisive for a second while Annabet pushed past her and out to the gallery.

"I'm coming, Evert. I'm coming. What's happened? Are you hurt?" She sped down the stairs, calling as she ran. He wasn't dead. There was still a chance that she could do something, help in some way.

"Yes, I'm hurt," said Evert quite cheerfully. He put his grimy right hand over the wound at the side of his face, sparing her the first shock. "Not badly. I'm all right. Don't go fainting, now. I want you to see to me. Josef has got enough to attend to, or I wouldn't have bothered you."

"I'm glad you did. Let me look. Oh! And your arm too. And your leg. Oh, Evert!"

"I can't manage the stairs. You'll have to get water and bandages here." He hobbled to the door of the dining room and unlocked it with the key he took from his pocket. He sat down heavily in his usual chair and lifted his leg, setting his booted foot upon the edge of the table. A little pool of blood gathered immediately upon the shining wood.

"The others are nothing, but this might bleed me to death. Get some cold water and a stout bandage. Edge off a sheet if you've nothing else handy."

She ran upstairs and fetched down her own ewer, the sheet from her bed, and her scissors.

"Light some more candles and set them here," said Evert, pointing to the table. "It's all right. Take your time. . . . That's the way. I've had luck tonight." He looked at her as she held the wet cold cloth to each wound in turn, and passed his hand over his eyes and looked again. "What're you doing in those clothes?"

The makeshift veil had fallen off when she tumbled back from the window sill, and Isa's little jacket, being too small, did not meet across her breast. But she couldn't spare a hand to pull it. She said a little shamefacedly, "It was Isa's idea. She was so sure the worst had happened. . . ."

"A damned good idea, too. I'm afraid I hadn't thought about what you'd do. But then I didn't really expect anything like this." His voice was rueful for a moment. Then he went on, "Anyhow, the worst didn't happen. Though, by God, it was a near thing. If that swine had stopped to take aim . . . Pull it tighter. You won't hurt me. . . . That's the way. Now, look at this." He turned the side of his head towards the light. "It's still numb; I can't feel it much. Did he take my ear off?"

"Not—not the whole ear. The lobe and some of the——"
It was silly, but the mutilation which Evert said was not serious was worse to look at than the two holes in the leg had been.

"I shall look as though I've been cropped for thieving," said Evert. "Here, give me that rag. This isn't your job, I can see. Pour yourself some brandy. Give me some too. With plenty of water in mine."

"No, I'm all right, Evert, really. It was just your poor ear—and a great long gash along your jaw. You'll have a scar, I'm afraid."

"I shall grow a beard from ear to ear and wear my hair long. No, you can't bandage that to do any good without throttling me. It'll dry off by itself. Or I've got some alum somewhere, when I can remember where to look for it. Annabet—I'll have to have that brandy; you keep going a mile away and then coming close again."

She ran to the sideboard, and as she was pouring the brandy Josef came in, bringing with him a pungent scent of ointment. His chest was swathed in a piece of cloth dripping with yellowish-brown fluid.

"Mynheer, there is someone at the back door."

"Tas?"

"He says so, Mynheer."

"Then why didn't you let him in?"

"I thought I would ask you first."

"You could have told Tas by his voice, I should think," said Evert, lifting his leg from the table and cursing.

"I know his voice, Evert. Sit still. I'll know in a minute," Annabet said.

"I'll go. I'm all right," said Evert, snatching the glass from her hand and gulping from it. Tas might have good news. And, by heaven, that would make the whole thing practically perfect.

"Lean on me then," said Annabet. He put his hand on her shoulder and hobbled across the hall, down the long passage, and stopped at the door which, only an hour earlier, he had opened so carelessly.

"Who's there?"

"Tas, Mynheer. Let me in, Mynheer. Let me in, please."

Evert opened the door, cautiously this time, and Tas, the boatman, fell into the passage. He took one horrified look at his master and said, "Here too?" Evert put his bulk between Tas and Josef and manoeuvred the boatman along into the hall. As Tas walked he produced a crumpled piece of paper and kept trying to hand it to Evert. Annabet followed Evert and as soon as they reached the hall pulled forward a chair.

With the paper still unfolded in his hand, Evert sat down and stretched out his leg stiffly.

"Have you seen any trouble, Tas?"

"Yes, Mynheer. Mynheer Kaerko's clerk brought me the paper and said that Mynheer Kaerko himself had been shot at in his office. And there was shooting everywhere."

The few lines of scribble across the paper could not have

been recognised as the agent's meticulous hand; it was so nearly illegible that Evert guessed rather than read its import. He crushed the paper in his fist when he had scowled at it for a moment or so and then said easily and cheerfully, "Ah well, that's all right, Tas. Not so bad as it looks. Like me! Go along to the kitchen and get something to eat and send Josef and Toeg here to me."

"Is it bad news?" Annabet asked timidly.

He stared at her without speaking, and she realised that for the first time he was discouraged about the state of affairs. He had been exhilarated when Knol left for the war and cheerfully confident and resourceful when the first bad news came in; he had been boastful and angry, derisive and optimistic, in turn, during the interval of waiting. Tonight, wounded and tired, he had shown admirable resolution and fortitude; but now, for the first time, she saw desperation on his face.

"By God, yes," he said at last, clenching his fist over the paper, "the worst news yet. Van Holk's defeated and dead. Kaerko's most trusted houseboy tried to stab him over a cup of coffee. Byskin's killed, and Van Heem. All Banda is in an uproar. But the soldiers held, and Kaerko wants me to go and take charge." His face darkened with fury, and the patches of pallor around his nose and mouth were engulfed in a fevered flush. "That's always the way, I've looked after my own. I stopped the nonsense here before it got under way. All these goddamn fools. Fancy Kaerko writing at such a time, 'My houseboy handed me the coffee and then tried to stab me.' Doesn't that show? Fancy mentioning coffee! My God, if I——" He broke off as Josef and Toeg appeared.

"Well," he said cheerfully, "everybody didn't have the luck we did. In one or two places that old devil's followers got the best of it. We've got to call out the Army, and I, as an older soldier, am going to be commander in chief. How do you fancy coming with me, Josef, and showing the youngsters how to shoot, eh?"

"Me also, Mynheer?" asked Toeg eagerly.

"But if I take you, who's going to look after the nutmegs, Toeg? And the house, and Mevrouw?"

Josef and Toeg exchanged a long, significant look.

"Mynheer," Josef said, "at Coenpark I shoot well because I know what I am about, but for fighting in other places I have little stomach. But Toeg——"

"Toeg is like me; he likes a fight for its own sake. Is that so?" The big foreman nodded and grinned. "Very well. I'll take Toeg and leave you, Josef. Mind, if Toeg goes, you've got to keep everybody at work and out of mischief."

"My brother will help, Mynheer," said Toeg.

"Very well," said Evert again. "Now, Toeg, apart from those in the kitchen and us, who're the best six men on the place?"

Often in the past, in moments of bitterness, Annabet had attributed Evert's popularity to his unscrupulous use of humbug. "Here's the old ass now," he would say as the guest arrived, and the next second he would be in the hall greeting the man with every sign of affection and esteem. Or sometimes for two full days before they were due to be guests themselves he would complain of the impending boredom, deriding his host and raking up bits of malicious scandal about his hostess, yet during the visit he would be the most charming guest that ever stepped over a threshold. He never attempted to hide his double-facedness from Annabet, and sometimes she was flattered and sometimes frightened by the fact. On the one hand it implied a peculiar intimacy, on the other it announced clearly that he had little regard for her opinion of his honesty. But tonight, watching his swift change from despair to cheerfulness, hearing that carefully chosen but carelessly spoken "and us," she was bound to respect his tactics. He was clever. A list of his other virtues slipped into her mind. He was brave. He was generous. When not provoked he was very kind. He was good company. Ninety-nine women out of a hundred would be madly in love with him. Why had she to be the hundredth? If Christy had never come to Coenpark, I suppose I should be in love with Evert now, she thought. After all, I wasn't hard to please. I nearly kissed Jean Vehk. If Evert had come back that night . . .

But he hadn't, and now, though she remembered his virtues and thought that he might be killed and was conscious of all the wrongs she had done him, she knew, with a flat, deadly certainty that held a tinge of regret as well as great bewilderment, that she would not feel one tithe of the emotion she had felt when the door had closed behind Christy.

"All right," said Evert, ending the confidential talk with Toeg. "Fetch them. We'll take all the arms and powder we have. And tell Tas to have the boats ready. Now, you, Josef, you chose to stay behind and, believe me, you've picked the hard job. When I come back I shall expect to find——"

But feeling wasn't everything. There were obligations and duties. And penances. She waited until Evert had told Josef exactly what he must do in his absence and then she said quietly:

"Don't add me to Josef's responsibilities, Evert. Let me go with you. Honestly, I'm not frightened and I might be able to help. I'd rather go with you. Really. Truly."

Evert waved Josef away. Then, turning stiffly in his chair, he looked at her.

"I'd rather take you," he said heavily. "But I dare not. Here the thing is squashed. Everybody who had a shot to fire in Coenpark fired it tonight. In Banda the thing got out of hand and the fighting is still to come. And we may have to fight our way in. I don't say you'll be safe here. But I will say that you're safer here than anywhere else in the islands. I'm leaving Josef and several good men in charge. And I'll leave Tas too. He's proved his faithfulness tonight. If the worst should happen he'll get you away in his prahau." He looked wildly around the hall and up the stairs and along the gallery. "God knows," he said vehemently, "I never thought of this when I brought you here."

"If I hadn't helped Shal Ahmi," said Annabet, beginning to sob, "if Captain Knol hadn't been ambushed——"

"Don't talk bloody rot. If you hadn't helped him he'd have found somebody else. Stop crying, Annabet, and listen to me. My will's in the iron safe in my office. Take it out—here's the key—and keep it, whatever happens. I may be killed. Every white man in Banda may be killed. But if Tas gets you away and you have my will, the Company'll see you get your rights. They'll never give up Banda, and you have a stake in it. And there's money in the bank at Amsterdam as well. Remember, you can trust Josef and you can trust Tas, and there'll be no trouble in the compound unless Shal Ahmi's people overrun the island." He stopped abruptly. A spasm went over his face. "Even then—he might remember that you——"

She screamed at him, "Don't say it, Evert. I know it's true. I know it's all my fault. But don't say it. I wouldn't—— Evert, please let me come with you. You could show me how to load muskets, even if I couldn't shoot. I don't want to be safe. I don't deserve to be safe."

"But I want you to be safe; that should be sufficient. Besides, you'd be a nuisance. I've made everything here as safe as possible in the circumstances and I want you to stay here until the worst happens and then trust to Tas." Another spasm convulsed his face. "And now, fetch me a little brandy, please. And then, if you don't mind, my shaving things and a clean shirt. I won't attempt the stairs."

"How're you going to walk?" she asked when she came back with the brandy. "Couldn't you be carried? Between two men, on a chair?"

"It may come to that. But not tonight. It'd be a bad example, for one thing. My fellows are all wounded, more or less, and they've got to come, because really they're all I have. Those Toeg is collecting now are only for show. The others have been taught to shoot, and tonight they've been under fire. And if I walk they will. Help me into this shirt, will you?"

There was the sound of voices and of men mustering in the passage beyond the door at the back of the stairs. "Hurry," said Evert, hindering her efforts by his struggles. "Where's Isa? I'll tell her to keep you company."

"She's gone. If you hadn't come back just when you did I should have gone too. She wanted me to help carry her things."

"Your things, I suppose." He backed away from her and, unaided, tucked the shirt into the top of his breeches.

"I'm sorry, Annabet." He gave a bark of mirthless, half-hysterical laughter. "For two years you've driven me crazy. You're my wife, and you sold me and everybody else in Banda to save another man's hide. And here I am apologising to you for the loss of your truck." He swung round and put his hands on her shoulders. "Maybe I am crazy. I've got to go now. But I shall come back. We'll settle everything then. Kiss me before I go."

With his good arm he hugged her to him; his hard mouth moved over her face, eyes, hair, cheek, and lips.

"Be careful, Evert. Take care of yourself."

"I will. Don't worry. I'm coming back."

He released her so suddenly that she fell back against the wall. She watched him hobble to the passage doorway, saw him brace himself before he opened it, saw, as it swung open, the dim lamplighted passage full of brown faces and muskets slung at curious angles.

Then it closed, and she was alone with Josef, who said softly, "There are good men in the kitchen, Mevrouw. And I myself will sleep here at the foot of the stairs. Mevrouw need have no fear. Is there anything Mevrouw would like before she goes to bed? A cup of tea, perhaps?"

She looked at him blankly and then shook her head. "Don't worry about me, Josef. I'm not frightened and I'll ask you for anything I want. You give all your attention to looking after things."

Over Banda Neira, all night long, an orange-pink haze hung, and now and then a fresh column of blue-black smoke shot into the glow as a new fire started below. Then as the last-fired building was consumed the smoke column faded and was absorbed; the haze regained its colour and hung unstained until another conflagration broke out.

Annabet spent the night at her window, at first standing and then kneeling. Sometime before dawn she dropped her head on her folded arms and slept a little. When she woke, stiff and cramped, the fire haze was fading into the rosy dawnlight.

The sun rose just as usual, and, as usual, the tong-tong sounded. Hundreds of doves rose with a soft flutter of wings as the coolies went to work in the groves.

Annabet went downstairs and was met by the scent of freshly made coffee. Josef was just bringing the tray through the passage door.

"Could we send and find out how things are going?" she asked.

"Mynheer gave no orders about that, Mevrouw."

"But I am anxious, Josef. Wouldn't one of the boys run? A boy could slip in unnoticed, whatever happened, surely. Send Abbas to me."

When the boy came she explained what she wanted him to do. To run into Banda and gather all the news possible. To find Evert if he could, ask after his health, tell him that all was well at Coenpark, and see if he had any message for Mevrouw.

Abbas seemed to be delighted with his errand. He grinned and nodded and scampered off. But an hour passed and then another. He did not return. Annabet's suspense became unbearable. At eleven o'clock she sent Juan on the same errand, and when at the end of another hour the midday tong-

tong sounded and neither boy had returned she despatched a
third messenger, this time a boatman, who was to take a
prahau and try to get into Banda from the seaward side. She
was angry with the boys rather than anxious about them. She
had a fixed idea that natives could move with impunity
anywhere, no matter what had happened. The boys had
simply forgotten their errand and were hanging about
amongst the crowds or looking at the fire damage.

But the boatman, old and steady, did not return either.
The hot drowsy afternoon wound its way along slowly, and
Annabet, unable to remain still any longer, wandered about
the house, looking out of every window, listening at every
door. If night set in without news arriving she knew she
would go mad. What had happened to Evert? If things had
gone well, surely he would have sent word. Was he dead?
Was every white person in Banda dead? And she cut off
here, isolated, just waiting and waiting?

Towards the end of the afternoon she wandered into her
ravished bedroom and noticed, close to the window sill, the
length of material which Isa had ripped and arranged over
her head. She picked it up, pushed her hair back from her
face, and set the makeshift veil in place. If she rubbed earth
into her skin and walked with down-bent head, could she, in
the darkness, make her way into Banda and find out for
herself what had happened? If they were all dead she must
die with them.

She folded the veil and hung it over her arm and went
downstairs again, intending to gather a handful of soil from
the garden while it was still light enough to see. Just as she
set foot on the bottom stair pandemonium broke out, both
inside the house and without. A kind of muffled roaring
pierced with screams from the compound, and from the back
of the house shouts and the sound of blows and then six
shots fired in rapid succession. The door at the back of the
stairs was torn open, and Josef flung himself through it,
closely pursued by a tall native whom Annabet had never
seen before. Josef screamed, "Mevrouw, Mevrouw!" and
Annabet thought that he was running to her for refuge and
was filled with wild pity. In the next second she thought that
Josef had turned traitor, for as his eyes found her he levelled
his pistol and pointed it straight at her breast. But he
screamed in a terrible voice, "Mynheer's order," just before
he fired. The bullet passed over Annabet's shoulder,

ricochetted off the bannister behind her, and struck one of
the large pottery jars full of dead flowers. Water and
fragments of pottery and bits of twig rained down on
Annabet's head. The man who was following Josef shot him
through the back of the neck.

Annabet held the newel post at the foot of the stairs and
looked at the stranger. He held his musket and looked at her.
Then he turned his head indecisively and looked over his
shoulder.

Another burst of gunfire and the sound of shrill, demented
screaming came from the compound. Josef lay in his blood
on the tiles at her feet, the fingers of one of his outspread
hands twitching a little.

"Why don't you kill me?" Annabet asked in a shrill,
cracked voice.

"Shal Ahmi's order, Mevrouw," said the man, and turned
his head again to watch the door. She heard him draw a deep
breath of relief as another native, an old man with grizzled
hair and lined, hollow cheeks, came forward from the
passage door.

"You have her? That is good," he said, nodding his head
with an air of satisfaction. He turned Josef's body over with
his foot callously, as one would roll a billet of wood from
one's path. He nodded again. "It is over," he said, and
Annabet wondered whether he referred to Josef's life or to
the fighting in the compound. Certainly a deathlike silence
had followed the last outbreak.

"Take her to the others. I remain," the older man ordered.

The man who had shot Josef shifted his musket and took
Annabet by the arm.

For the first few hundred yards of the walk into Banda she
tried to question him, but to every question he returned only
one answer, "I do not know, Mevrouw," spoken in a civil,
quiet voice.

As they drew nearer to the town evidence of fierce fighting
met Annabet's horrified, fascinated eyes. Dead bodies lay
huddled in grotesque attitudes under the charred walls,
amongst the broken bushes, in the midst of trampled flower
beds. The big houses, with all their windows broken and
their doors gaping, stood like empty shells in the last slanting
light of sun. A curious, almost enchanted silence lay over the
precincts of the town. Nobody stirred. And with the

detached, active part of her mind Annabet noticed that although the houses, with their open doors and windows, were stuffed with possessions nothing appeared to have been touched or moved.

On the water front itself, when they reached it, some activity was in progress. Little groups of men, moving quietly and resolutely and obviously under orders, were collecting the bodies of the dead and dividing them into two heaps. One sort they handled reverently and gently; the other they tumbled roughly together. Ours and theirs, Annabet thought sickly. How could they tell? By what means did a dead native show to which side he had belonged? But her deduction had been right, for before her guard urged her forward with a gentle but relentless pressure on her arm she saw the body of a white man, clad in shirt and russet-cloured breeches, thrown onto the heap of roughly handled dead.

Evert's breeches had been blue, but there was no comfort, no hope, in the thought. Either he was dead, defenceless as the body she had just seen cast aside, or he was captured. And with Banda in Shal Ahmi's hands it was better to be dead.

They stopped by the doorway of Rykshalt's warehouse. The man on guard at the doorway watched them approach and grinned and spoke to the man who held Annabet's arm. He spoke in Malay, but her guide was as uncommunicative in that tongue as in Dutch. He replied in two monosyllables which made the man at the door shrug his shoulders. He raised the bar of the door, opened it about a foot, and pushed Annabet inside.

The lower floor of the warehouse had been cleared of its contents. It smelled of dust and nutmegs and mace and overcrowded humanity confined in airlessness and heat. At first all the pale faces swam together in the gloom, and then here and there Annabet recognised somebody. Jehane Vehmeer, old Rita Byskin and her daughters and daughter-in-law, pretty Marie Graef with her little children clinging to her skirts, Elsa Hansen wearing nothing but a nightdress and a shawl.

They crowded about her, beginning to weep afresh, as though her appearance deepened their sense of calamity. Well may you cry, she thought; if you knew all you would fall on me and tear me to pieces. I helped to bring you to this.

Now that there could be no good news, no hope in any news, there was news in plenty. True, some of the women had been struck silent with grief and terror, but others were voluble. They crowded about her, asking questions, not waiting to be answered, speaking with hysterical tears or bitter calm of their own losses and experiences. Jehane Vehmeer and Marie Graef had actually seen Evert. The Vehmeer house had been fired, and they had been trying to get the children away to Van Heem's when the battle had broken out in the street. Between the blazing house and the turmoil in the street they had been trapped, obliged to take shelter as well as they could in the bushes of the garden.

"I saw Evert quite clearly," Jehane said. "He was fighting to get through to some soldiers who were surrounded between our house and Van Heem's. He was magnificent, Annabet, but of course it was hopeless. . . ."

"What happened to him?"

"I didn't see. Some natives came searching through the bushes and found us and brought us here."

"All the men are dead," said Marie Graef positively. She looked with tear-swollen eyes at her children and added, "I wish to God we were all safely dead too."

There were no words of comfort. The bitter, despairing words were echoed in the heart of every woman in the room.

Annabet looked at the children. Tear-stained and di-shevelled, they were still more beautiful than flowers. And because Knol had not been able to carry out his surprise attack and return triumphant, they were all . . . The load of shame and self-hatred became insupportable. I must tell them, she thought wildly; I can't live here with them, accepted as a fellow sufferer, when it is all my fault.

The door opened noisily and two men entered, pushing before them two of the low open barrows used for transporting the sacks of nutmegs. One was piled with food, a miscellaneous collection, evidently the spoils of several larders; the other held about two dozen cups and two vast jugs of coffee. As one of the men straightened himself and released the handles of his barrow he said in an enquiring tone, "Mevrouw Haan?" Annabet stepped forward.

"You will come with me, if you please."

The women crowded about her again with renewed tears. They believed that she was being singled out for special, more speedy vengeance because Evert had so nearly made contact with the soldiers and won the street battle. She pulled herself free of their hands and said in the wild shrill voice over which she seemed to have no control, "Oh, please don't worry about me. Don't give a thought to me, I do beg of you. Whatever happens to me isn't half what I deserve."

The man interposed his body between her and the rest of the women, and she stepped quickly through the door, which the guard bolted again immediately. Her new guide was more communicative.

"You may be calm, Mevrouw. No harm is intended."

"Where are you taking me?"

"Only to the Fort, Mevrouw. To Shal Ahmi himself."

I'll ask him, she thought, to have me shot. Or, if he won't do that, to have me shut up alone in the darkest, foulest place he can find. I can't go on living amongst those innocent ones.

The gaping void where the great gateway had been and the heaps of stones which had been the gatehouse and the wall had been fenced off, and her guide led, her through another entrance, far to the seaward side. There were guards there, and more at some of the inner doorways, but that same strange quiet prevailed. There was none of the running to and fro, none of the bustle and transmission of orders, which one would have expected to find in the headquarters of a man who had just organised a bloody and successful revolution and made himself head of the island. Nor, when finally the tall double door of the Justice Room opened and she stepped inside alone, was there any sign of success about Shal Ahmi himself.

He sat behind the table across which the governor and his attorney had so often dispensed Dutch justice. Two wrought-iron candlestands, each holding twelve candles, stood on either side of his chair. Behind him his own little brazier, or one exactly similar, glowed under a handful of aromatic herbs. The polished table top held only a few sheets of paper, a silver inkstand and some quills in a little silver pot, and a small rough pottery bowl containing rice balls, smoking hot, at which he was picking with his fingers.

He looked up as she entered.

"Ah, Mevrouw. We meet again. Come in and be seated."

He nodded towards a chair on the opposite side of the table. She sat down, thankful for the support. Seeing him again, so exactly as he had been in the gaol during that fatal interview, unnerved her so that her knees quivered and she could not have spoken if she had wanted to. She could only sit and stare at him with sick eyes.

"I mean you no harm," he said gently. "On the contrary." He lifted a rice ball and then, with it poised halfway to his mouth, remembered something. "I disturbed your supper, Mevrouw." He dropped the rice ball back in the bowl and clapped his hands together so sharply that her half-whispered "It doesn't matter" was drowned. The door opened sharply and Shal Ahmi said quietly, "Fetch some cakes and a bottle of wine for Mevrouw."

"I couldn't swallow them," she said.

"Nonsense. You look to be upon the verge of collapse, and you need strength, Mevrouw. We have a great deal to do."

"We? You mean you want me to do something? To help you again? I won't do it, Shal Ahmi. I wouldn't lift a finger to do anything you suggested—not if you—not if you cut off my hands. . . ."

He looked at her with calm interest. "Your hands, Mevrouw? How strange that you should mention them. Your hands have for me a significance beyond all the other hands in the world." He looked at them, thin and white and tremulous, clasped against the front of Isa's soiled little jacket. "Why do you speak so vehemently?"

"Because I listened to you once, and I shall regret it to the last day of my life."

"To me, Mevrouw? Was it not rather to your own heart that you listened? And when you have heard what I have to say your heart will speak again. This time with many voices, not with one only." His eyes narrowed slightly. "You speak of regret. That is unnecessary and foolish of you. In the first place, you were deceived by me, and in the second place, although Gariz arrived with his message safely, it was only one of three and not even the first that came. From the very heart of affairs in Batavia a like warning had been sent, by whom, who can say? No, no, Mevrouw, I am not speaking from a desire to comfort you. Why should I? The days when I must lie and fumble my way are past. Ah well, cry if you wish; you will feel better afterwards."

"I should have liked Evert to know," she sobbed.

"Well, it may be that he does," said Shal Ahmi, biting his rice ball at last. "There are many who hold that after death

great wisdom comes. Mynheer Haan is dead. A slippery
man, Mevrouw, but one of great courage. . . . Ah, thank you.
Set it down here." His smooth brown fingers busied
themselves with the cork of the bottle, but his eyes rested on
Annabet without impatience, without sympathy, but with
close interest, as though he had never seen a woman in tears
before and had no idea of their meaning. He poured some of
the wine into one of the glasses which bore the Company's
badge, as did almost everything the governor had used, and
then said gently:

"Mevrouw, are you crying because of the crime you did
not commit or for the husband you did not love?" She made
no answer and went on crying helplessly. "Look at me," he
said with insistence. "Now, stop crying. Come, drink your
wine and listen to what I want you to do."

"I'm not going to do anything."

"You may think differently when you have heard my
proposal. You have spent a little time amongst my prisoners.
Did you count them?"

"No."

"There are twenty-eight women and thirty-four children.
Sixty-two in all. There are also six or seven men in another
place, but they are all badly wounded and need not, I think,
be considered. But the sixty-two women and children are
very important. There is at this moment"—he changed to a
casual conversational tone—"a little ship on her way to
Batavia with news of the defeat of the great Van Holk and of
the beginning of trouble in Banda. She bears a charmed life,
that little ship. Twice she has escaped; twice she has carried
back bad news. But this time, before she reaches port, a
humble prahau dodging amongst the islands and shallow
waters will outstrip her and carry bigger news to Batavia.
And if I have reckoned rightly, the little *Greta* will not, this
time, return with fresh men and fresh arms. Because my
prahau will carry word that I have won back my islands and
that twenty-eight women and thirty-four children, all of the
purest Dutch blood, are in my hands. You see, Mevrouw,
with the firing of the first shot against me, sixty-two innocent
lives will end bloodily." His voice took on edge. "This,
amongst other things, I wish to make quite clear to the
authorities. And the trouble is that, although I speak Dutch
at least adequately, I write it very ill. The spoken word is
easily acquired, but for writing one needs a teacher, a

copybook, some leisure. And I would not have the authorities in Batavia dismiss my ultimatum, thinking me an ignorant native of no account. I must make it very clear that I am a man to be reckoned with; no shade of meaning must be overlooked because the word which carries it is ill spelled or unclearly written. Therefore, Mevrouw, you must write the letter for me."

"I couldn't do that without the consent of the others."

"What others? The women in Mynheer Rykshalt's warehouse? Mevrouw, you have been amongst them. You know better than I that they would agree to any measure that ensured their safety and the safety of their children. Is it not written in your own Holy Book, 'All that a man has will he give for his life'? Are women less reasonable than men?"

"The women and children would probably endorse your letter." She reckoned rapidly; Marie Graef had six children, Rita Byskin four, Corrie Byskin three, Anna Rykshalt four; the children were accounted for before half the women were counted. "Those who have lost their men and have no children here might very probably choose death rather than deny everything their men died for. Besides, Shal Ahmi, the authorities in Banda would not leave you in control of the islands for the sake of a few women and children."

Shal Ahmi moved aside a paper and touched the one thus brought uppermost. "Perhaps not, Mevrouw. I am not in a position to argue about the humanity of your people. But here I have other arguments and, I think, very powerful ones. Today I went into Mynheer Kaerko's office and studied all his books. The best year that the Company has ever known was six years ago, in 1653. In the rough draft of the letter I wish you to write I have promised that exactly the same amount of nutmegs, mace, and kendri oil shall, without fail, be produced every year henceforth and so long as I remain in control of Banda. And I have pointed out that the administration will cost them nothing. No governor, no agent, no soldiers' pay. Will that move those who have no scruples against the shedding of innocent blood? Moreover, I offer them a monopoly—that is the sacred word, is it not?—twice as valuable as the one they now hold. I can swear that no one single nut will ever be smuggled out of the islands. And I offer security too. Each year they may send their inspectors to look everywhere and to see everything, as a proof that I am not deceiving them. You will agree,

Mevrouw, that such proposals will at least halt the progress
of hostilities. The authorities in Batavia will consider them
worthy of being referred to the supreme authority. And that
will gain me almost a year. Openly and with a free hand, I
can do much in a year."

Despite herself, she was interested and impressed. "But
wasn't that kind of arrangement tried long ago? I've heard
men speak of the old days at dinner parties. Contracts—that
was the name. Weren't there bargains between the people in
the islands and the Company? And didn't they all fail?"

"That was so indeed. And all the contracts were broken
and all the peaceable agreements failed because my people
were always looking backwards upon the old lazy days of
leisure and easy living; and the Company was always looking
forward to days of greater effort and greater power. How
then could they hope to agree? Now the trial has been made.
My people know that the easy days have gone forever; your
people know exactly what richness the powerful days have
brought them, and what burdens. I offer to match the
richness and diminish the burden. I think that now we may
come to a better understanding—if you write it all as clearly
as I speak it, Mevrouw."

She stared at him, half hypnotised by his confidence, by
the boldness and scope of his plan. And as she stared she
realised why it was that there was a difference about his
appearance. On the folds of his spotless white clothing,
above his left breast, glittered an enormous jewel. A single
diamond as large as a walnut, wide and rounded at one end,
tapering at the other. It rose and fell with his breathing,
flashing, sparkling, combining in itself the elements of fire
and water.

Shal Ahmi saw the direction of her eyes. "Ah," he said,
and touched the stone with the tip of one finger. "You are
admiring my diamond. It was once the centrepiece of my
father's crown. You are seeing, Mevrouw, what no other
white person has ever seen, the Sacred Raindrop of Banda. I
could not bring myself to sell it with the others. For
sentiment's sake I have preserved it through many vicissi-
tudes." His hand dropped back to the edge of the table and
his tone changed. "We must not dwell upon the past. The
future is ours. You will write the letter." He pushed some of
the sheets of blank paper, a red-feathered quill, and the
inkpot across the shining table.

"I won't write it," she said steadily. "You deceived me before. You said then that by acting as you told me I should save lives. Now you say it again."

"This time it is true. Sixty-two lives lie in the hollow of your hand, Mevrouw."

"Go to your prisoners," she said. "Ask them if they agree to your plan. If they do, get one of them to write the letter."

He leaned forward against the edge of the table and spoke with extreme earnestness.

"I will tell you something. I will explain why you, and you only, must write for me. Mevrouw, do you remember the time when you arrived in Banda? On the night of that day the man who had married you came to me for aid. Like all vain men, he imagined that the eyes of his world were upon him; like all vain men, he feared, above everything else, the ridicule of his fellows. And because you had come to him, twisted and ugly, in the place of the beautiful bride about whom he had boasted, he came to me, pitiable, abject, distraught in his despair. He said to me in simple words, 'Rid me of her.'"

He paused and studied her, watching for some effect of his words, and was disappointed to find none. She was listening to a story that was empty of all personal meaning, a story of two dead people long ago.

"Mevrouw, all white men and all white women are born my enemies. The life of one of them is less to me than the life of any leaf on any tree in the jungle. I could have killed you then so very easily, without danger to myself, without the slightest remorse. But on that evening I was most strangely aware of being upon the brink of an important decision, so I did what I always do at such a time. I appealed directly to the gods. When Mynheer Haan left me to go and make the way clear I took out my tela, the sacred stones which, when they fall, fall from the gods' own fingers, and I cast them for you. Astonished, incredulous, hardly able to believe my eyes, I read in the signs which can neither lie nor be misunderstood that you, a white woman, as yet unseen by me, would serve me and my cause. The tela told me clearly that by your hand you would help me." His bright, almost hypnotic stare bored into her.

"When you came to the gaol and the letter of warning was taken into your hand, Mevrouw, I thought, 'There, it is done, the will of the gods is fulfilled,' and I was willing then that you should go your way in peace. As clearly as I might then, I told you to fly from the danger that was to come. But later, when the gaol was broken for me and I reached Ay, I learned, again with astonishment, that the action of your hand had been unimportant. You had not, since a previous message had already arrived there, served me or borne out the prophecy of the gods. There are many gods, Mevrouw, and it may well be that their plans overlap. But my gods had told me that it was by your hand that my triumph would be finally established. Therefore, it was plain to me that your action was still to be performed. Now I understand. You did not flee to Batavia; the shot which should have killed you this afternoon, though fired at close quarters, went astray. *Because* you were to write that letter for me. Written by your hand, it will meet with the reception that I plan for it. You are young and foolish, Mevrouw. I am old and wise in these matters, and I say to you, very solemnly, the gods are not mocked. We may delay and deny, ah, we may protest and weep, but in the end we do their bidding."

"But your gods are not mine, Shal Ahmi. I have served my God very ill, but He allows me what He allows all His followers—free will. And I will not write the letter that will help you to keep Banda, which my husband and all the men I knew have died to save from you."

"Would that be so evil a thing, Mevrouw?" he asked with the patience which he had learned through thirty tedious years. His smooth bland face took on an expression of passionate intensity. "Since the very dawn of time these islands have always belonged to my people, the happy, harmless, laughing people of Banda. We interfered with nobody; we desired nothing save to live as our fathers lived, to adhere to the old customs, to raise our children as we had been raised, and to die and go to our fathers. But we lived where the nutmeg grew. We did not grow the nutmegs; they grew around us, making shade for our houses, wood for our fires, and the substance of friendly trade with our neighbours.

"Then white men came, deeming the nutmeg precious, demanding ever more and more. We did not resist them, Mevrouw; we laughed and said, 'Take the nutmegs you deem so precious and leave us alone.' But that they could not do. They must have our nutmegs and they must have our bodies, bound in contracts to labours that our fathers never conceived. Then they must have our souls. Even our gods we must abandon. First in favour of the white virgin goddess and her baby, and then in favour of the strict old man god and his rules written in the stone. But always the nutmeg was behind the altar, Mevrouw. Then, and then only, when we saw our gods, the laws of our fathers—everything we held sacred—in jeopardy, did we resist. 'Hold,' we said, 'this is too much.' With what result? Mevrouw, the blood shed last night is but a drop in the ocean to that which Coen and Gomarus shed. Even those desperate ones who took to the hills were hunted out or lured down with false promises and slain, not in anger, but as goats and sheep in the slaughterhouse. For the sake of the little nutmeg which can neither heal a broken bone, stop a flux, nor cure a sickness of the soul, the Dutch were willing to kill and kill until not one man of the Bandanese blood remained alive."

He folded his arms in his sleeves and leaned forward, resting his elbows on the table. "One did, Mevrouw. I escaped from Coen's bloody hands. I remained alive. I remembered. And I waited. The men of my own race, of my own age, had gone to their fathers untimely, and I must wait until the women who were driven screaming into the slave markets of Batavia and Bandogar were brought back to live as slaves on the very soil where they had lived as the children of free men. I waited until they had borne children of their own. Their fathers were of all colours, of many beliefs, and of many races. But I claimed them as my own, Mevrouw. I trained them, I armed them, and I waited. Had I time I would tell you of the thousand little dirty, shameful things I have done for a guilder, of the great dangerous things I did for many guilders. My children had children, and I claimed them too. Not one escaped my notice. To every one I offered the chance to avenge his mother's shame, to reclaim his grandsire's cherished, bloodstained land. I have borne scorn, calumny, shame, hunger, and imprisonment. And I have won back my islands." He paused, and then with a wave of his hand, one of his rare gestures, dismissed the subject. "Mevrouw, when you have written the letter you shall have your reward." He turned the backs of his hands upwards and studied them intently. "I was in Ay, amongst the English, as lately as yesterday afternoon. Your man still lives. He has been shot in the foot and will probably limp for the rest of his days. But what is that? When the letter is written I will send you to Ay."

Still ostensibly studying his hands, he glanced at her slyly from under his lowered, hooded eyelids. He had the almost unique experience, for him, of seeing one of his offhand, momentous statements ignored. No melting warmth came to the frozen pallor of her hard little face; no light quickened in her sick eyes. For a moment he wondered whether she had heard or, hearing, understood. And he did a thing which he rarely did, rarely had cause to do. He repeated himself.

"When the letter is written, Mevrouw, you will be free. I will send you to Ay."

Some submerged, moribund feeling stirred in her feebly, tried to resuscitate itself, and failed. Up to so short a time ago the idea of one day going to Christy had lain behind all thought, all action, all hope. And now, by means that she had never dreamed of, the idea had become an actuality. She had only to write a few words, be patient for a few minutes more, and she would be free to go to Christy.

But there was no resurrection of hope and desire. Appalled and astonished, she regarded her own lack of emotion. It was too late. One could not wrest one's own heart's desire out of a holocaust; one could not step across the bodies of all those dead men light of spirit because one man was still alive. With her world, Banda, happy and secure and thriving, with Evert alive and arrogant and possessive, it had been possible to toy with the idea of going to Christy and setting personal happiness and fulfilment before everything else. But Banda was ravaged and burned, Evert and the other men whom she had known were dead, and in that crowded, airless prison twenty-eight women were weeping for their loss. The mere contemplation of personal happiness against such a background was obscene.

And Christy? She had understood once, when she had held him in her arms, the terrible significance of one person. Now, sadly, but with an overpowering assurance, she knew that it was not paramount. There were things for which even love must stand aside. Or, rather, there were loves more urgent and embracing than the love between men and women.

The songs and the poems and the books denied that. If she had been a woman in a poem she would have been crying with joy now, ready to do anything—say, write, do anything—that would give her the chance to see Christy again. But I'm not, she thought steadily. I'm just an ordinary, wretched, bewildered woman, bound to admit that Christy counts for less to me at this moment than those sad women, those pretty, innocent children. Is that because I didn't love him enough? I shall never know. Such things have no measure. I would have left Evert and all the security and comfort of Coenpark; I would have gone hungry and barefoot with him anywhere. But I can't leave those women and children for him. I don't even want to. There is no feeling left in me. Only my mind remains.

"And the rest of your hostages?" she asked, breaking the long silence.

"They must remain, naturally. Until I have my assurance from Holland itself and have rebuilt the Fort and armed myself against the perfidy which the Company might show. They shall be treated well, Mevrouw. I may kill to rule, thereby following the example of those who call themselves my superiors, but I do not rule to kill. Moreover, strange as it may sound, I bear no grudge against the women of your race. Women are not, of themselves, dangerous. Even amongst your people there has never been a woman explorer, a woman soldier, or a woman perkanier. Also, of course, it is to my advantage to keep them alive. A dead hostage is no argument."

"In Batavia they will not know whether your hostages are alive or not. Or the numbers."

"They will have my word."

"They could have mine as well. It might count for more."

He looked at her sharply. "What are you suggesting, Mevrouw?"

"A bargain. Send those women to Matu, Shal Ahmi. Then, when they have been gone for one hour, I will write your letter and another as well. I will write a letter purporting to come from all your hostages, and signed by me, begging the authorities in Batavia to consider your terms and save our lives. They have no means of knowing that of the sixty-three only one will remain in your power. It will take months for the women to make their way from Matu to Batavia, and even then no one will know that they are not women who have escaped naturally. So many are dead that you could still hold sixty-three hostages."

She remembered what he had said about her hands, and as she spoke she folded them together ostentatiously and placed them upon the edge of the table. She saw his eyes follow them.

"My husband was esteemed by the Company. They will remember the name in Batavia. And you will have your answer before the women got back to Java. Matu is so small. Hardly one ship in a hundred stops there."

Shal Ahmi leaned back in his chair, and his smooth brown fingers moved slowly over the blazing jewel on his breast. After a long pause he said in a voice which, though smooth and bland as ever, held something cold and menacing.

"You are daring to offer me terms, Mevrouw?"

She felt her breath catch with fear. One's mind might be prepared for death; one might be so desperate, so sickened, that one longed and even prayed for it. But it was easy, painless death the mind envisaged. A cessation of being. The frail, shrinking flesh, so vulnerable, so susceptible, had strong instincts and dreads of its own. She had said wildly, "Not if you cut off my hands . . ." But suppose he took her at her word and said, "Write, or with this knife I will sever your hands at the wrists?" He was capable of it. Remember little Jean Vehk who had offered no provocations at all.

"You will lend your aid as soon as these women are out of Banda?"

"Yes, Shal Ahmi. That is my condition." Thank God her voice was under control again and rang out with firm assurance.

"Mevrouw, such a suggestion shows regrettable lack of faith in my integrity."

"Does that surprise you, Shal Ahmi, remembering how you tricked me before? Since the moment when I realized what I had done I have not passed an hour without wishing myself dead. You are not yet strongly established; an attack from Batavia could brush you aside. If I helped you to postpone such an attack and those women remained in your hands and you dealt evilly with them; or if, a year hence, an unfavourable reply came from Holland and you wreaked your vengeance upon your prisoners, the torments I have felt in these last weeks would be as nothing compared with those I should know. I understand you now. All your time, all your endeavours have been devoted to the restoration of Banda; nothing else matters to you. So you will be able to understand me. All my concern now is to save the poor remnant of my people. When they are safe I will help you. Not till then. Apart from their safety, nothing matters to me."

"Not even the young Englishman?"

"No. I will write your letter and my own letter. I will stay here and be your sole hostage. If things go wrong you may wreak your vengeance on me. One body or sixty-three, what does it matter?"

"Give me your right hand, Mevrouw," he said gently.

Unsuspecting, she stretched it across the expanse of shining mahogany. He turned it in his own for a moment, looking at it with interest. Then he bent her little finger, pressing the top joint down upon the bottom one and gradually increasing the pressure until the full force of his strength was brought into play. She had had no idea that such a simple thing could become such excruciating agony. The taut muscles cracked; the stretched nerves sent arrows of pain across her arm and into her neck. She wanted to scream, but she set her teeth into her lower lip and held back the sound. Jerkily she shook her head at him, dumbly informing him that if he broke all her fingers one after the other she still would not give in.

There was, mercifully, a limit to the amount of pain that could be consciously accepted. Still fast in the torturing vise, she felt her arm growing numb. Shal Ahmi's face, with its expression of fiendish interest, was washed over by a wave of darkness. She began to sag forward as she sat.

He released her finger suddenly and straightened it quite gently between his own.

"One should always test one's opponent," he said pleasantly, and then sat silent for a moment, thinking, while Annabet stretched and rubbed the pain-paralysed, rapidly swelling finger.

"Very well," he said at last, abruptly. "They may go. I will give the orders."

"No. Not you. You could so easily tell the men to row for an hour and then bring the boats back."

"How then shall we arrange it?"

Out of his presence, freed from the conflict of wills in which, miraculously, she had gained a victory, she could sort out her thoughts. There was a shred of hope now for the women and children at least. There was suffering ahead of them, but once in Matu they would be amongst friends and on the first stage of their journey to Batavia. She fingered that thought gladly. There was less complete joy in the knowledge that, even if she had never visited Shal Ahmi in the gaol, never carried that message to Gariz, the course of the war would not have been altered, the rebellion not averted. But her sense of guilt in the matter was too deeply ingrained to be removed by a few words. She still felt like a traitor.

About Christy she could feel nothing at all, except an impersonal relief that he was still alive—as though he had been a stranger whose life had been in danger—and a kind of muted sorrow that an emotion which had been so vivid and so engrossing should have been so mortal.

Over the piece of information which Shal Ahmi had thrown at her about Evert's intention towards her on her arrival, she skimmed without investigation. They had both been wrong so often, and now he was dead.

There was one other thing which stood out from that interview in the Justice Room, and that was this: Impregnable as Shal Ahmi appeared to be to ordinary human feelings, there was one noticeable chink in his armour. He was superstitious. And of that one weakness she had taken full advantage. It might even be that she could find some other way of using the weapon so suddenly and surprisingly placed in her hand. In her hand. Literally. She looked down at her own hand wonderingly. The little finger stood out stiff and distorted.

Annabet and one of Shal Ahmi's men had reached the warehouse again.

"See me safely locked in here, Julendi," Annabet said. "Then go and find six seaworthy prahaus, large ones. Man them with reliable men, three of whom at least have been to Matu before. Find somebody to help you and provision the boats—rice and water will do, enough to keep seventy people alive until they reach Matu. Do you understand?"

The man looked at her with wild astonishment. But Shal Ahmi, the master, had said that she must be obeyed; it was not for him to question or hesitate.

The air within the prison room was almost unbreathable by this time. A little office opening off it had been provided with two buckets for the sanitary needs of sixty-two people; but the small room had no proper door, just a swinging screen which started a foot from the top and ended a foot from the ground, and the noisome stench had pervaded the whole place. A brass oil lamp was flickering to extinction and exuding its own peculiar odour of burned wick, rancid oil, and hot metal.

Most of the women were sitting on the bare floor, resting their backs against the wall. Some had their children's heads in their laps or pressing against their shoulders. Older children either leaned against the wall or lay in the centre of the floor, their heads supported upon rolled shawls or petticoats. Almost all the children and some of the women were asleep when the guard opened the door, but a startled stir, amongst the women at least, testified to nervous alertness.

Jehane Vehmeer, whom Annabet had never liked, threw herself forward and cried, "Oh, you're back. I'm so glad. I never hoped to see you again. What happened? Why were you sent for?"

"Shal Ahmi has decided to send us all to Matu. The prahaus are being got ready now. It means days in open boats, in the sun. And they'll be overcrowded and short of food and water, but there'll be safety in the end."

He had been right, of course. Safety—the preservation of their own bodies from death and torment—that was what was uppermost in their minds. Relief shone on every face, even those upon which the tears of mourning were scarcely dry. In the final issue life itself was a very precious thing, the most important thing of all.

The barrow of food, with a good deal remaining on it, had been pushed into one corner.

"Eat before you go," Annabet said. "There will be little enough afterwards."

Those who had no appetite before were hungry now. Nobody wondered why Annabet Haan should be telling them all what to do. Nobody noticed that Annabet Haan, who said "Eat," now stood aside, eating nothing. The children, hastily roused, now stood about, sleepy-eyed, hardly troubling to lift to their mouths the food which their mothers almost fought to secure for them.

Old Rita Byskin hobbled forward. "Why is he sending us to Matu, Annabet darling? That's turning us loose."

"He did not explain anything. He sent a man to see to the prahaus and me to tell you. That is all."

A babble of speculation broke out. Shal Ahmi didn't want the trouble of feeding them. He couldn't spare men to guard

them. He was clever enough to see that the presence of a
group of white women, some of them young and pretty,
would cause trouble amongst his men. "Every native, in his
heart, wants a white woman *that* way." Annabet stood aside,
silent, and looked at her hand. "It was by your hand, by your
hand, Mevrouw, that my triumph would be finally
established." Obviously he believed it implicitly. There was
no living, breathing creature who did not believe something
implicitly. How very, very fortunate for these women,
flicking their tongues after stray crumbs. . . .

"Mevrouw, the prahaus wait."

"Tell the guard to open the door."

They tumbled out into the sweet, spice-scented, breeze-
fanned air. They rushed towards the boats, a pale-coloured
frail line, like a wisp of foam which the tide had flung inland
and was now drawing out again. The nutmeg tide of Banda.

"Some women and some children in each prahau, please,"
said Annabet, running amongst them like an anxious sheep
dog amongst a distracted flock. "Mevrouw Graef, this way.
If you travel with Corrie there will be only two adults to ten
children. We must even the loads."

They were so meek, so anxious to be told what to do.

"Julendi, tell the men that it is Shal Ahmi's order that the
boats are to go, with their best speed, straight to Matu. Tell
each one that and then tell them to start, one by one."

Out of the orderly confusion a voice cried here and there,
"What about you, Annabet? Come with us. See, there is a
place here." But she pretended that she had a place in
another boat, always in another boat. As the last one shot
out into the moon-silvered water she stepped backwards
behind Julendi and the three men who had helped him to
provision the prahaus so quickly. The men talked together
for a moment in Malay and she listened to the tone of their
conversation. It was difficult to assess, but she was curiously
sure that there was no anger and no criticism in it. Shal Ahmi
had commanded and the thing was done. Julendi turned
back to her. "And now, Mevrouw, I will take you back to the
Fort."

"In exactly one hour from now," she said, and went and
sat on the steps of the deserted warehouse. She watched the
prahaus grow smaller until they were mere dots in the moon-
lit water. Then, dot by dot, they were lost over the shining
horizon.

Shal Ahmi was awake and waiting when they returned to the Fort. The rice bowl had been removed and the brazier sprinkled with a fresh handful of herbs, but the bottle of wine and the glass and the little dish of cakes, still stood on one corner of the table.

"We have wasted almost two hours, Mevrouw," he said in an unhurried manner. "Head the letter as I suggested before, 'From the Justice Room in the Fort of Banda.' And today's date by your Dutch reckoning. So. Now we will make no claim to titles and honours which would cause amusement and lead to disputation. On the next line write, 'From Shal Ahmi, who has this day won back what his fathers lost.' And then, 'Your Excellencies. . . .'"

He leaned over her and studied the clear Italianate handwriting which the governess from Brussels had taught to little four-year-old Annabet in the schoolroom of the great house at Janshaven.

"That is beautifully done, Mevrouw. Now I will tell you what I want said and you will put it into good Dutch in that beautiful writing."

His arguments and his suggestions fell smoothly, following one another like the beads of a rosary.

As she set down sentence after sentence, giving great care to punctuation, which had always been her weak point, Annabet could feel no doubt as to the letter's reception. "At the first sign of hostility from you," she wrote, "the sixty-three hostages will be killed, and axe and fire will be loosed in the groves. The first white man to visit Banda uninvited will find no single tree in flower." That threat alone showed the unassailability of his position. By their own act the Company had concentrated the trade within the limit of these few tiny islands; the loss of the Banda groves would strike the Company a deathblow. For the sake of the nutmeg groves alone the islands must be left to Shal Ahmi for as long as his power lasted.

And she had seen enough of the quiet, deadly orderliness of his revolution to know that his power would last as long as he did. After that?

She rested her pen and looked up. "I'm curious about one thing, Shal Ahmi. Who will rule Banda when you are dead?"

"It is queer you should ask that question," he replied amiably, without any sign of that superstitious shrinking

from the thought of his own demise which would have
shown itself in almost any normal man at such a moment.
"In my quiet times today I have thought about that too. I
could not get a son, Mevrouw, until the land was mine again.
Could I condemn my own flesh and blood to walk humbly,
like a slave, to be eaten up alive by the hunger for power
which I have known? But now I shall look about me and find
some healthy young woman of the purest Bandanese blood
remaining. And she will bear me a son." His supreme
confidence pervaded the room. "I am not yet an old man,
Mevrouw. I was but a boy when Coen came. I shall live to
see my son reach manhood; I shall rear him like a prince of
Banda; but I shall teach him, too, the lessons of patience and
industry and cunning which I myself learned so hard. If that
answers your question, Mevrouw," he said pleasantly, "let us
proceed. We have almost done."

She set the quill in motion again, obediently putting each
sentence into the clearest form, the plainest writing. But part
of her mind moved independently. Without leadership the
natives were useless, she thought. If Evert had been at
Coenpark this afternoon Shal Ahmi's men would have been
routed. In his absence the faithful ones had been overcome
with hardly a struggle. Even the revolutionaries were meek,
schooled in obedience, looking to Shal Ahmi for guidance in
everything. If he could be removed . . .

Faced with that thought, she felt weak and futile and
wished fervently that she had been other than she was. One
brave, clever woman, or even a stupid one, sufficiently
resolute, might turn the tide of fate even now. He trusted her
implicitly, saw in her nothing but the useful tool the gods
had prepared and tempered for him long ago.

We're like Sisera and Jael in the Old Testament story, she
thought. But Jael drove the tent peg through Sisera's temples. If I were Jael this letter would never reach Batavia. The
Greta and other ships would sail back, and the island might
be retaken.

But she had never, in all her life, entertained a really
violent impulse, and as she looked at Shal Ahmi's hairless
head shining in the candlelight the idea of inflicting a
physical injury upon him made her feel sick.

Yet the man had killed harmless, kind little Jean Vehk,
treacherously; treacherously he had dealt with Evert and all
the other white men in the islands; even Kaerko, who had

risked unpopularity by his support of him, had been killed.
And he had tricked her into an act which had caused her
such remorse that it had killed her self-esteem and her will to
live and her will to love. He was ruthless and pitiless. And if
one had an obscure feeling that his single-mindedness and
confidence were somehow admirable, that was only because
squeamish, weak-nerved, muddling people were bound to
admire qualities they lacked themselves.

His blood, shed now, would save much bloodshed later
on. But he had only one real enemy in the island, Annabet
Haan, who had never killed anything bigger than a fly, and
avoided that as often as not.

"My name, at least, I can write clearly," said Shal Ahmi,
taking the papers from her and plunging a second quill into
the inkpot. "Write now your letter from the sixty-three
hostages. You may add, in all truth, Mevrouw, that your
husband died like a hero in the defence of the town. It may
add weight to your appeal and is no more than his due. Had
there been ten like him——Yes, Julendi?"

The door at the far end of the room had opened, and the
native came in, soft-footed.

"Wan Tau has collected the bodies," he said, addressing
Shal Ahmi without preamble, but in a tone of such complete
respect that no title known to man could have enhanced it.
"There are fourscore and six of the white men and their
slaves. He asks what shall be done with them."

"Burn the heap as it lies," said Shal Ahmi shortly.

"And Pua asks if the six wounded may be taken elsewhere.
The well in the square is hidden under wreckage, and it is far
for Pua to fetch the water. All the time they demand water."

"Tell Pua to cut their throats and throw them onto the pile
with the others."

Annabet heard her own little whimpering sound of horror.
Shal Ahmi looked at her. "Mevrouw, they cannot recover.
Dr. van de Lijn is dead, and they suffer." He turned back to
Julendi.

"The prahau I ordered is ready?"

"It waits."

"Carry the order to Wan Tau and Pua, and then come
back for the papers."

He watched while Annabet, with a hand growing less and
less steady, wrote the last sentences of her false appeal.

Shal Ahmi studied it carefully. "It is very well written,

Mevrouw. So long as you remain in Banda, playing the part of sixty-three hostages, you shall write all my letters."

He opened a drawer of the table and took out a stick of sealing wax and the governor's official seal. Very carefully he folded his own letter and hers and enclosed them in a sheet of stout paper, folding over the ends and pressing them flat.

She watched him while a process too swift, too urgent, too incoherent to be called thinking took place in her brain. Those three words, "cut their throats," had been like a flash of lightning, making clear in half a second what had been vague and misty. They showed the whole mind of the man. His plans were reasonable, his arguments plausible, but they all led to one end: complete and absolute power of a kind which no man, even a good one, could possess without danger. Nobody could pretend that the white people were perfect—there were bad men, cruel men, false men amongst them—but their powers for evil and cruelty and falsity were curbed by something which would not exist in Shal Ahmi's Banda: the force of public opinion, the tenets, however lightly held, of Christianity, the vague, faltering, faulty, but vital concept of justice. Coen and Gomarus had been cruel, but they had been open to censure, and there were many Dutchmen who refused even to recognise the brilliance of their leadership on account of their faults of character. That didn't wipe out the cruelties, but it would lay a foundation for merciful dealings in the future. There had been cruel perkaniers; but in Holland there were men who, drawing their incomes from the dividends which the Company paid, had been just enough and disinterested enough to register their protests against practices which it would have paid them to ignore. There were Dutchmen who might conceivably have said of six helpless wounded men, "Cut their throats"; but there would always be near at hand some other Dutchman who would raise a voice in protest. There was always amongst free white people a will to good, though it might be too feeble or too late to avert evil. It came plodding along, and one day it would win. But the thing Shal Ahmi stood for left no room for that. One could see very easily what Banda would be like, left to him and to the son he intended to rear and train. A slave community. And if anybody were a nuisance or useless, "Cut their throats." . . . He stood, for all his suavity and plausibility, for the old, dark, evil things.

He had risen and was holding the wax to the flame of one of the candles when the door opened again very abruptly, and Julendi, not waiting for a word of recognition, padded rapidly across the floor. Shal Ahmi looked at him with displeasure.

"Close the door, Julendi."

The man halted, opened his mouth to speak, thought better of it, and turned and closed the door quietly. Then, halfway back to the table where Shal Ahmi was pressing the seal to the warm wax, the urgency of his news overcame his awe and he said breathlessly, "There is a Dutch ship coming. A fishing boat brought news."

Annabet's heart gave a leap, but Shal Ahmi only turned the paper about and calmly sealed the other end.

"What ship?"

"One lately here. The *Eastern Venture*. Why should she return?"

"No need to worry about that. Is she visible from the quay?"

"Her topsails only. But the wind and the tide are with her."

"They must come in suspecting nothing. Then I will deal with them. Hassim has the Dutch flags. Tell him to hoist them along the harbour. I myself will bring out my letters and make further arrangements in a few minutes. Hoist the flags and say nothing of the ship until I come."

His calmness was contagious. Julendi, who had rushed into the room in a state of nervous excitement, left it at his ordinary pace and as quietly as usual.

Nor was Shal Ahmi posing. Alone with Annabet, whom he had now no reason to deceive or impress, he gave no sign of agitation or anxiety. He laid his sealed packet on the corner of the table and seated himself in his chair with movements as smooth and deliberate as ever. It was easy to see that his confidence in himself and in his destiny was so rooted that in the arrival of Piet's ship and a stout Dutch crew he could see only the promise of another tricky victory. And his confidence would be justified. The sailors would see the flags in the moonlight and imagine that they were flying to celebrate a victory. They would come ashore unsuspectingly. Then Shal Ahmi would organise a surprise attack on them. Piet Odshoorn, so kind and honest, would be added to Shal Ahmi's long list of victims. Unless she— unless—unless . . .

A violent fit of trembling seized her; even her head was palsied. Even if I could think what to do, she thought wildly, I couldn't do it.

Shal Ahmi, with unfaltering hands, pushed aside the writing materials and moved the wine bottle and the glass to the extreme edge of her side of the table. She could reach it now without rising from her chair and putting her shaking legs to the test. She put out her hand and poured some of the wine into the glass. The clatter of glass on glass was loud in the quiet room, and some of the wine spilled over. But she lifted the glass to her lips. One convulsive jerk of her head made the rim rattle against her teeth, and more wine spilled down upon the front of Isa's jacket. The feel of the cool hard bottle within the clasp of her damp shaking hand remained after she had released it, and it was somehow significant and urgent, but with what meaning she did not know.

Shal Ahmi, having cleared the table before him, fumbled within the bosom of his robe and drew out a little bag of worn greasy leather tied at the neck with string. As his fingers moved to untie it Annabet heard the chink of stones and remembered with a thrill of superstitious terror what he had said earlier in the evening about his tela, the sacred stones which, when they fell, fell from the fingers of the gods. If that were true it might well be that at the first glance he would read warning of her hatred, of her determination to do him harm if only she could think of a way.

But Shal Ahmi, entranced now and absorbed, did not look at the stones, as they rattled out upon the polished top of the table across which the old governor had painstakingly dispensed Dutch justice. Staring straight ahead with empty, unfocussed eyes, he moved his hands blindly over the stones.

The tela had told him that by her hand she would seal his triumph. Her hand, her hand, where the touch of the wine bottle lingered, its meaning—ah, its dreadful meaning—now bursting through the barriers of reluctance and incredulity.

And simultaneously with the flash of inspiration came the memory of Cousin Jean Marie, Father Vincent, whose teaching had been at once the ruin and consolation of her life. It was the spirit that mattered. And God knew—O God, You must know and pity me and strengthen my heart and nerve my hand—that the evil she was about to do was to be done in the right spirit, in the interests of mercy and justice. She had seen for herself how Shal Ahmi had calmed

Julendi's panic; he had so versed himself with all power and all control that without him the rebels would be powerless. His death could end the rebellion if Piet and his crew acted firmly.

Shal Ahmi gathered the stones into his hands and flung them out onto the table. He leaned forward then, resting his hands along the edge of the table as he studied the cryptic message. There crept over his face an expression of baffled perplexity. Annabet, with a suspension of all conscious thought, took the wine bottle in her hand again, as though to refill her glass. Shal Ahmi never raised his eyes. He gathered his stones. He cast them again and again and leaned forward. Annabet, softly and swiftly as a cat, rose to her feet and rounded the end of the table, altering the grasp of her hand on the bottle neck as she moved. Her very loathing of what she was doing made the blow one of unimaginable violence. Chance, or something less blind, guided it truly. It struck the bowed bald skull at its base, just where it joined the neck.

Shal Ahmi fell forward like a broken puppet. Blood and wine ran out over the stones of the tela which had spoken so truly. For with her hand she had established his triumph. Established that he should never know reverse or slow decay.

Still moving as though obeying some other will than her own, she lifted the sealed packet of letters and held one corner to the flame of a candle. The last evidence of Shal Ahmi's plans and dreams flared, shrivelled, and blackened between her fingers.

The door opened, and Julendi, nervous and anxious, again entered hastily. The *Eastern Venture*—whose appearance so immediately following Shal Ahmi's death was to demoralise the rebels and make the reconquest of Banda practically bloodless, and whose captain was to receive praise and adulation and a generous pension for his disobedience—was making phenomenal speed. With the tide and the wind with her, and Piet Odshoorn at her helm, she was already nearing the harbour, and Julendi thought his master should be told.

He had actually uttered a word or two of this message before he saw what had happened during his short absence. He whipped out his short curved knife. Annabet, with a wild memory of Shal Ahmi's words about the gods and their overlapping plans, knew in her last moment why she had come to Banda.

CLASSIC BESTSELLERS
from FAWCETT BOOKS

GREAT ADVENTURES IN READING

Let COVENTRY Give You
A Little Old-Fashioned Romance

☐ LADY BRANDY   50165 $1.75
by Claudette Williams

☐ THE SWANS OF BRHYADR   50166 $1.75
by Vivienne Couldrey

☐ HONORA CLARE   50167 $1.75
by Sheila Bishop

☐ TWIST OF CHANCE   50169 $1.75
by Elisabeth Carey

☐ THE RELUCTANT RIVALS   50170 $1.75
by Georgina Grey

☐ THE MERCHANT'S
   DAUGHTER   50172 $1.75
by Rachelle Edwards

CURRENT CREST BESTSELLERS

☐ THE NINJA
  Eric Van Lustbader   24367 $3.50

☐ SHOCKTRAUMA
  Jon Franklin & Alan Doelp   24387 $2.95

☐ KANE & ABEL
  Jeffrey Archer   24376 $3.75

☐ PRIVATE SECTOR
  Jeff Millar   24368 $2.95

☐ DONAHUE *Phil Donahue & Co.*   24358 $2.95

☐ DOMINO *Phyllis A. Whitney*   24350 $2.75

☐ TO CATCH A KING
  Harry Patterson   24323 $2.95

☐ AUNT ERMA'S COPE BOOK
  Erma Bombeck   24334 $2.75

☐ THE GLOW *Brooks Stanwood*   24333 $2.75

☐ RESTORING THE AMERICAN DREAM
  Robert J. Ringer   24314 $2.95

☐ THE LAST ENCHANTMENT
  Mary Stewart   24207 $2.95

☐ CENTENNIAL *James A. Michener*   23494 $2.95

☐ THE COUP *John Updike*   24259 $2.95

☐ THURSDAY THE RABBI WALKED OUT
  Harry Kemelman   24070 $2.25

☐ IN MY FATHER'S COURT
  Isaac Bashevis Singer   24074 $2.50

☐ A WALK ACROSS AMERICA
  Peter Jenkins   24277 $2.75

☐ WANDERINGS *Chaim Potok*   24270 $3.95

Buy them at your local bookstore or use this handy coupon for ordering.

COLUMBIA BOOK SERVICE, CBS Publications
32275 Mally Road, P.O. Box FB, Madison Heights, MI 48071

Please send me the books I have checked above. Orders for less than 5

books must include 75¢ for the first book and 25¢ for each additional
book to cover postage and handling. Orders for 5 books or more postage
is FREE. Send check or money order only.

Cost $_____   Name _____

Sales tax*_____   Address _____

Postage_____   City _____

Total $_____   State _____ Zip _____

* *The government requires us to collect sales tax in all states except AK,
DE, MT, NH and OR.*

This offer expires 1 March 82   8177

CURRENT BESTSELLERS
from POPULAR LIBRARY